From The Women's Press Ltd
124 Shoreditch High Street, London E1

Marge Piercy   Photo by Robert Shapiro

Marge Piercy is a writer concerned with social change, a poet and a novelist. She is the author of seven novels, of which *The High Cost of Living* and *Woman on the Edge of Time* are also published by The Women's Press; five volumes of poetry, and a play. She has been politically active since the 1960s, and since the late 1960s primarily in the women's movement. She has travelled widely, but now lives mostly in Wellfleet on Cape Cod.

'I write to change consciousness, to reach those people who don't agree already. Cultural work is one of the most effective ways of reaching people. If you don't support alternate ways of imagining things, people aren't going to be able to imagine a better world'   Marge Piercy

MARGE PIERCY
VIDA

The Women's Press

First published in Great Britain by
The Women's Press Limited 1980
A member of the Namara Group
124 Shoreditch High Street, London E1 6JE

Reprinted 1982

British Library Cataloguing in Publication Data

Piercy, Marge
Vida.
I. Title
813'.54(F)   PS3566.I4

ISBN 0-7043-3851-3

Printed in Great Britain by
King's English Bookprinters Limited, Leeds

for the street and alley soldiers

PART I

The Present,
September

1

"**N**o, thanks." Vida placed her hand over the top of the tulip-shaped wineglass. "No more for me. Thank you."

"This is a good Vouvray. Louis in the wine store recommended it." Hank tried to nudge her hand aside with the cold dripping base of the bottle.

"It's lovely. I've just had enough." She made herself smile. It felt like a date, a bad date. She had to keep smiling across the debris of the dinner for two. "The chicken was wonderful!"

"Recipe from one of my books. *Skinny-Dipping, or How to Eat Yourself Slender*."

"You wrote a cookbook?" Keep him talking. She nibbled another olive, although she felt bloated with the best and certainly largest meal she had eaten in weeks.

"I produced it. For *Family Day*. Supermarket package." Catching her as soon as she lifted her hand from the glass, he poured more wine. "Of course, what I'm really doing is the oral history of the '60s."

Annoyed she pushed the glass away. "How's that going?"

"Come on, Vida, you used to love wine. Remember when I got Hill at Random House to take us out to lunch, and you startled the shit out of him by ordering the wine. A Montrachet."

"A Puligny-Montrachet. Even I wouldn't have had that much nerve. . . . I wonder if you could remember to call me Cynthia?" It was not the name on her current I.D., but the name she used when she didn't quite trust enough to expose her present cover. "I don't drink much now,

Hank. Really, the wine's lovely." She felt a headache starting behind her eyes.

"That's when I was producing that tome on Students Against the War. You SAW stinkers tried to hold me up." He grinned, fingering his goatee. He had had a full beard then. Every time she saw Hank, every couple of years when she needed shelter in New York, he had a different arrangement of facial hair: moustache, goatee, sideburns, muttonchops. He was very fair and the ornamental borders never produced an abundant crop —a pale brown darker than his straw-colored scalp hair but, like it, skimpy.

"Bit of a cut-and-paste job, I recall," she said, and wanted to bite her tongue. Don't anger him. He can take his revenge all too easily.

"Had to get it together in six weeks. Catch the public mood on the wing. . . . SAW didn't last much longer."

"Till '71. Four years, actually. . . . I'm not feeling up tonight. My period started, and I'm having cramps." She was not, but the wine, the tête-à-tête supper made her wary enough to start building an excuse. Hank had wanted her in the old days. She'd forgotten. In the Area Coordinating Office of Students Against the War, everybody had joked that Vida could always handle the straight media johns. She rose with the wineglass and walked to the window, away from the little table between his kitchenette and his white-wooded Venetian living room. "May I open the draperies?" She dribbled the wine covertly onto the soil of a spiny purplish plant on a plinth.

"I don't imagine anyone can see you unless they're in a helicopter over the river." Hank rose and strode after her, looming at her elbow. He was wearing one of those leathery male perfumes and Ivy League clothing: soft-shouldered tweed jacket, faintly striped shirt. His clothes had come full circle in the eleven years she had known him, from Brooks Brothers through suede into leather and studs into denim and back to Brooks Brothers. Welcome home, Hank Ralston! She waited while he pulled the cord on the traverse rod. "God!" She let her breath out painfully. After a while she roused herself to say, "It's so beautiful. I forget. Manhattan! . . . You must have the finest view in the world."

"The apartment's still a bargain. Don't come back to New York much, do you?"

Near and unreachable. Might as well be looking at constellations; might as well be gawking at Betelgeuse in Orion as across a river at the lit buildings. Towers of a forbidden world. Leigh in one of them. The WBAD studios were in Midtown, actually, and he could be taping there; he could be home on the Upper West Side in their old apartment on 103rd Street; he might even be on the air right now. She did not know his current working schedule. She would have liked to ask Hank to turn on the FM tuner to WBAD, but she did not want to mention Leigh. She did not want to prompt Hank to ask questions about whether she ever saw Leigh. She would lie, of course, but lying about her husband was especially distasteful.

"Not often," she said, moving up to the glass. Light seemed to form clouds over the buildings. The sky was no longer clear.

"Er . . . what're you in town for?"

"Just some business to take care of."

Now he stood away from her, rubbing the back of his neck. "It isn't some . . . bombing, is it? It isn't that?"

"Come on, Hank, I don't do that kind of thing anymore. I've given it up for miniature golf and origami." She wanted to stand and stare at the towers studded with brightness; she wanted to feed her eyes on them. She had fallen for New York the first time she had seen it. When she had escaped from her first marriage, she had come straight to New York where her sister, Natalie, was living, and there she had stayed. "I never go into Manhattan," she said softly. "Never."

"Why not? They don't guard the bridges."

"Too much heat. Too many people've been caught there. Angela Davis. Joan Little. Linda Evans. At 110th and Broadway an FBI man sits all the time in a car reading a newspaper. He's got our pictures on the seat beside him, and he waits."

"After all these years?" Hank laughed skeptically, bringing up the wine bottle and pouring more.

"After all these years." She sipped her wine pro forma and put it down on an antiqued white table. Except the rare times she felt safe, she never permitted herself to blur at all, not even to get a little high. "How beautiful it is. Cliffs like galaxies." She could see herself striding up a canyon of skyscrapers to meet Leigh, strolling arm and arm with Natalie along Broadway to buy delicatessen. "Look, a freighter's docking."

"Do you wish you were on it?"

"What for? I've had chances to leave the country. I don't want to go into exile. Exiles are so . . . ineffectual."

"Are you getting a lot done?"

"I keep busy," she said drily. She almost asked him if he had heard of their pirate TV broadcasts in L.A., but 'the Network' had not claimed that action publicly. "I keep them busy, too." As she slipped past him, he held out his arm.

"Where are you going?"

"The bathroom."

She put in a fresh tampon, last in her purse. Have to go to the drugstore. Not too smart. Her cheap Timex said ten thirty-five. She had never been able to replace the good watch Leigh had given her for her twenty-seventh birthday. It had broken when she was scaling a tall wire fence, the time the Network pipe-bombed the department of correction. She saw it plucked from her wrist by a protruding coil of wire, watched it smash on the concrete below. That had been 1973, and she still mourned it. The watch had been a gold wrist alarm with large clear numbers and old-fashioned curly black hands. In her head Kevin snarled, "I'm glad it's busted! Toy from your bourgeois past." She had not bothered to argue with Kevin that her past was no more bourgeois than his, a fact he had used often enough when they were on the same side. That was already rare by '73. Where was he now? Thinking of him brought a wave of corrosive anger through her, an acid aftertaste.

She washed her hands, staring deliberately in the mirror. She had not examined herself for a few days of hard traveling, and she looked with a defensive wince. Surprise, she looked good. She smiled then. Yes, she was looking good—a little thin, but she was making that up here. Hank didn't mind treating her, though he might be expecting something he wasn't getting. Lowering her chin, she flirted with herself and then abruptly moved closer to the mirror.

Damn. That was why she was looking good. Her hair was growing in. It was suddenly livelier in color. Her own red-gold hair was showing at the part, and the brown was losing. She counted on her fingers. Let's see, she calculated: she had dyed her hair last in L.A., where she had been living, and she'd been five weeks on the road. She had been visiting the little clusters of fugitives that made up the Network, politicking, taking political readings and holding workshops in the pirate TV technology the L.A. cell had developed. She had been working her way east to see her own people, somehow, and to get ready for the big annual meeting of the Network Board that set the year's priorities, that would be held—clandestinely, of course—sometime in the fall and somewhere in the East.

Wistfully she touched the inch of her own hair at the part, spreading like brushfire. Sunrise-colored, Leigh had called it in a romantic moment. She could hear his voice: Butterscotch. Cognac. Tomorrow with luck she would see him. Tears stung her eyes from the inside. In the mirror she saw she was hugging herself. Whatever stickiness, she would not sleep with Hank the very night before she saw her husband. Hank had ripped off Students Against the War for a long run of money with his instant bookmaking; he had given interviews on them, casting himself as a bearded expert. He could put her up for a night now and then without exacting payment in flesh.

She wanted to spend the night on the lumpy plush couch where she had collapsed when she arrived at dawn, before Hank left for work. She wanted the insomniac pleasure of allowing herself to feel how much she missed Leigh, to be full and empty at once with wanting and to know it would be lessened briefly by a meeting. Always she was forbidding herself to think of her family, always controlling her pain. Only at times did she let down her longing as she used to let down her hair, the huge burnished coil of it unwinding. . . .

She came into the living room with her face twisted in a smile of entreaty. "Hank, I'm going to have to ask you to do me a little favor. . . . I need a couple of things from a drugstore."

"Best thing to do is walk down to Montague. Then turn left."

"I was asking if you'd go out for me."

"I'm tired. Go on, Vida, you can't be scared to walk a couple of blocks!"

"Why can't I be? What do you want me to do with a rapist, show him my Wanted poster?"

"If you can't take care of yourself, who can?" He raised his eyebrows, shrugging with an exaggerated heaviness, Wasp imitating Jewish mannerism. Sitting in the plush armchair, he raised his feet onto a matching hassock to demonstrate his rootedness.

She made herself smile again, a smile like a large plaster ornament on her face, a cupidon, a wreath of grapes decorating the old cornice of this room. "Violence against women is a fact I have to take into account, just like any other woman. I don't carry a gun, Hank."

"Why not? Armed and dangerous. What would you do if you saw a pig?"

"What would I do with a gun?" She controlled her voice, talking to a spoiled child. All a televised drama to him, the blood wiped off and the body good as new. "Actually, I carry a bomb at all times in my purse. Plastique. Set to detonate if I scream. Like this." She opened her mouth.

"Shhh! Don't scream in here. The neighbors will call the police. There's been a lot of break-ins. . . . Really, I think it's a riot. You playing the helpless female. Who'd ever believe Vida Asch is scared to walk to the corner drugstore by herself, scared of the dark?"

She flinched at her name, never spoken now. "Every other woman fugitive I've ever known. Hank, if I'm raped, I can't even go in the hospital."

"What do you think the odds are you'll be ravished between here and the corner?"

"Pretty good, I'd bet. . . . Are you going to help me?"

"If you're so scared, wait till morning."

"I need tampons and I need hair coloring. My period won't shut down for convenience, and I can't put off dyeing my hair. I have business to conduct tomorrow, and I need my hair a nice dull brown."

"You imagine I'm going to sashay into the drugstore and buy tampons and hair dye? I live in this neighborhood. I've lived on Columbia Heights for ten years. You imagine I'm walking into the drugstore where I buy the fucking *Times* every Sunday and my razor blades and tell them, Well, I want to dye my hair and stick a tampon up my ass?"

"It's after eleven. Come on, Hank. You have to help me. I need the damn stuff."

"You sound like a creeping junkie!"

"Look, please." Crawl a little; he wants you to crawl. "I'm dependent on you for help. For survival. I have nobody else I can turn to. I'm alone here. Please help me."

"Why do you want to turn your hair that dead color anyhow? You must be trying to make yourself ugly. Like that crazy dyke sister of yours."

The sweet crisp pleasure of breaking a lamp on his head. "Are you meaning Natalie? I don't think you know her."

"We were on Channel 13 together one time. . . . You were really a beautiful girl, Vida, you know that? Sure you know it." He snapped his fingers. "Thought you were Queen of the May."

Were beautiful. Tomorrow she had to see Leigh, and she could not afford to be someone who had been beautiful ten years ago. Hank was out to cut her, but she could not take offense. Ignore all references to Natalie, who at least could not hear them. "Look," she said gently. "I need the dye for security reasons. Walk with me. Please. I'll go in. You can wait outside."

"Suppose somebody recognizes you? Suppose they call the cops?"

"I'd be happy to wait outside while you go in."

"But I don't want to go in!" He writhed in his chair, petulant. "I worked all day while you were lying around here eating up my food. I'm tired. I cooked dinner."

"I'll wash dishes the moment I finish my hair. . . . What would you do if you were living with a woman?" Once he'd been married, she remembered. He had married an editor, an arrangement lasting six weeks. Maybe his wife had asked him to buy her a box of tampons.

"Any woman I'd have around would do her own fetching and carrying." But he got up, making a sour face. "All right, all right, I'll walk with you. But I'll stay outside. And if anything happens, you don't know me. I'm splitting."

"Fine."

The night was cloudy and cool, a touch of rain in the wind. She wanted the next day to be sunny. She had not seen Leigh since early April when they had celebrated their birthdays together, meeting at the end of the subway in the Bronx. Leigh had given her two hundred dollars and a blue challis dress that fitted perfectly. She weighed only a few pounds less than she used to when she lived with Leigh on 103rd Street: 132 pounds, now maybe 127. She had the blue dress in her pack to wear tomorrow. She had not seen him since, the longest time they had gone without meeting after the first desperate months underground.

As they walked, Hank would not talk to her. He strode very fast, making her hasten to keep up, but he got out of breath before she did. The hole in her boot was getting bigger. The cold pavement nosed her as she stepped. She would have liked to walk on the promenade and stare at the lights of Manhattan, where she longed to be, to watch the freighters on the East River, to take in the Brooklyn Bridge, but she was always wary in New York and must stay inside as much as she could. This walk had sharp edges enough, that sense of danger in things. With brown hair and glasses she did not need, any friend, any old acquaintance could still recognize her. It had happened. It must not happen tonight.

"That's the drugstore." He stepped into a doorway, actually turning from the street to conceal his face. "I'll stay here. If you aren't out in five minutes, I'm leaving."

"Do give me ten, Hank. They might be waiting on somebody else." She went in. What had she been using? Warm chestnut it was called. If only she dared auburn. Anything but mouse brown. Ruby dyed her hair auburn and looked wonderful. Ruby's hair hadn't begun to turn gray till Vida and Natalie were in college, but when Ruby started coloring it, she didn't stick with her own rich brown. Ruby said, My daughter has red hair, why not me? Oh, Mama. She was staring at the Clairol boxes, with the same woman's face repeated forty times on the shelves and they all swam. Ruby was much harder to meet than Leigh or Natalie, for she was no political activist and it was next door to impossible for Ruby to learn to follow instructions exactly and evade surveillance. Vida breathed haltingly, controlling tears as the packages swam. Missing never diminished, not a bit.

She bought only one package. She had no spare money, and she hated carrying dye among her clothes, where the bottle might break. Further, she did not want anyone who didn't know who she was asking her why she dyed her hair. This evening had gone so badly she wasn't going to be able to put the bite on Hank for money. Too bad. His liberal guilt was wearing thin. Waiting at the register, she remembered the first time she had made contact with him the year after becoming a fugitive. Then he had felt flattered. He had wanted to have a party for her, and only with difficulty had she persuaded him that showing her off to people he wanted to impress was not worth twenty years in stir to her or a lot of legal trouble to him.

When she came out, looking around for Hank, she noticed the sign in the window. "ALL TRANSACTIONS IN THIS PHARMACY ARE VIDEOTAPED." A jolt to the brain like an electric prod. Sweat broke out on her palms, under her arms, along her back. Come on, probably a lie. Probably they just said that to scare would-be burglars. Probably nobody scanned the tape. Probably. She made herself continue to walk slowly toward the doorway where Hank was skulking. "Hi, there," she said brightly. "Thanks ever so much. . . . Say, do you have a hair dryer?"

2

Putting her pack on her back and her glasses on her nose, Vida set out for the BMT, keeping to the blocks of the trim row houses and away from Montague itself. An unclean filmy rain flattened her new brown curls. She wore the blue challis dress, her last pantyhose and her boots, with a Peruvian poncho over it all. Warily she walked the neat tree-lined streets, wishing she had an umbrella, to keep her dry and partially conceal her face. From 1965 to 1971 she had lived in New York and lived publicly. A dozen lovers, two hundred friends, thousands who had heard Vida Asch speak at rallies, millions who had seen her photograph in the newspapers or on television were spread in an invisible web. She felt the tingle of casual danger brushing her elbows and finger ends as she walked.

Saturday-morning shoppers. Her foot was soaked, and as she climbed down the subway stairs, her boot squished. She had a fifteen-minute wait for a train. When it arrived, she walked back several cars to the end, sat down, watched. Was anyone coming after her? Leigh had told her he need not be back until Monday morning, for he had invented a cover story about an interview in Chicago. Whenever she was going to meet somebody from the old life, one of her own people, she felt helpless. She was utterly dependent on their caution, their honed paranoia, their will to be vigilant, but with Leigh it was heresy to suspect he would not be on guard. After all, in 1974 when she had been living in Philadelphia, he had commuted back and forth sharing her life until she had been recognized and had to run.

At Fulton she changed to the Flatbush line and once again walked through the cars, on guard. Then she sat in the second-to-last car in the last seat and finally permitted herself to space out for the long journey to Sheepshead Bay. How much time she wasted traveling to and from meetings, trekking the long way around, taking buses to the ends of lines, standing on random corners in the cold wind. If there was anything her life demanded, it was endless patience. She could never rush but must ooze circumspectly toward the rendezvous, as Leigh was tediously maneuvering toward her.

She imagined his face, the nose sharp as an urgent question, the brows bristling like shaggy exclamation points, turned toward her. Yawning, showing his purple tongue, he was waking in the queen-size bed in their apartment. Did he still have the featherbed from his grandmother? She had dragged it on the subway down to Orchard Street to have it repaired and covered with new ticking. Over the bed she saw the Cretan wall hanging embroidered on coarse red wool that was one of the few mementos from her first, her Greek marriage. Leigh had never minded its origins: the embroidery was beautiful work and never had hung in the house of Vasos' family.

The Kalakopouloses disdained peasant work. They had a Degas ballet dancer from an Athens furniture store in their living room across from the icon of Agios Giorgos. She shook her head angrily: why was she drifting off to Vasos? Little pleasure in remembering that mess. Her romantic marriage: she had married Greece; she had married the dark stranger; she had married classical studies, the famous Mediterranean light, three thousand years of culture. Unfortunately for everybody, she had also married Vasos Kalakopoulos, civil engineer whose parents ran a Honda dealership on the edge of Heraclion, on the road toward Agios Nicolaos.

Okay, she was nervous about seeing Leigh after much too long. Why hadn't he managed to come west since she had been here in April? During their scheduled phone calls the first Tuesday of every month, pay phone to pay phone, always he had said "Soon. Soon." Her busy husband. When she had escaped from the dead end with Vasos, she had told her sister Natalie she would never marry again, never! Then Natalie had married Daniel Brooks, and six months later Vida married Leigh Pfeiffer. . . . Leigh had worn an embroidered white shirt open at the throat, a deep V down to his curly chest. Around his head he had bound a red scarf. His pants, loose and flowing, tied at the waist. Purple, she thought. Many things were purple that year: purple tights, purple dresses, purple lights, purple walls, even purple boots. Had she worn one of her crotch-length minis? No, she had been married in a leaf-green Mexican wedding dress, tiers of floating puckered cotton separated by bands of open lace. Nothing under it but a green bikini. She stared at herself across the years, amazed. Of course, she no longer dressed with that flash and dazzle—she could not afford on any level to call attention to herself—but she would not have walked a block in a minidress now. What such clothing proclaimed was availability. Yet she had not felt that then. She had loved the glory and speed of miniskirts; she had felt like an emissary from a saner, jollier future, one of the crew from *Star Trek* beamed down to a primitive troubled world for a brief bumpy mission.

Natalie had found the green dress for her in the Village at Fred Leighton's. "If you're going through with this, why not wear something special?" Natalie didn't like minis as much as Vida did. "You look smashing in them. I look dumpy. I'm bowlegged." Only a little. Natalie had worn a red Mexican dress cut low, with her breasts swelling out of it like rising bread. What had Daniel worn? Natalie's husband was missing from the wedding pictures in her head. Vida could not remember her brother-in-law.

Leigh and Vida had a June wedding on a farm some antiwar activists had rented in New Jersey, a ramshackle white house inundated by ivy on the north and a rambling rose on the south. The mole-tunneled lawn sloped down to a stream lined with weeping willows. Torches were planted in the lawn. The Holy Rollers, a band who played all the Movement bashes that year, made raucous sound. And food! Anything Leigh was connected with featured splendid food. A whole roast suckling pig. Had Lohania cooked that? No, they had not met her until the year after. It was an old Puerto Rican girlfriend of Leigh's who had married a friend. Mrs. Pfeiffer, Leigh's mother, whom Vida had never been able to call Stella or "Mama" without translating that from an originally thought "Mrs. Pfeiffer," had cooked stuffed cabbage, a spicy pot roast, stuffed derma. Natalie had come through with a pâté en croute and a two-foot-high chocolate cake with a red flag and a black flag on top.

On the riverbank, the hippest rabbi in New York, Meyer who went to jail for ten days in '69, married them in a double-ring ceremony by the splashing waters. She remembered his severe face and her own twinge of guilt, for he had made a fuss that he married only people he knew, and they had persuaded him. She had never told him she was only half Jewish; that her real father was Tom Whippletree and she had taken the name of her mother Ruby's second husband, Sanford Asch, because—because—it sounded better and she hated her own name, Davida Whippletree, because—because—she was unfaithful, just like her mother, and she preferred Sandy to her own dad. Her mother had married Sandy, and she had taken Natalie to be her own flesh-and-blood sister out of daydream. Now Natalie walked ahead of her, married herself and already pregnant, her belly not yet overreaching her breasts, but growing, growing with Sam.

This time it's got to work, she had thought, gripping the roses cut from the rambler and then Leigh's hand. I want him so bad! He was perfect for her, her own sweet-and-sour. How he had danced that afternoon, leaping and prancing. "I picked you out of that first meeting for spring mobilization," Leigh said. "You were the best of the crop."

"Like cabbages? What crop?"

"Girls new in the Movement that spring. You were the best-looking, and when you opened your mouth, real words came out. You spoke up loud and clear."

With her hands shaking so hard she had to clasp them behind her. She had felt a failure at twenty-three: a botched marriage, not even a degree, a false start, older than the college students around her. She had set out to succeed in the Movement in New York, and she was going to succeed with Leigh. "We won't box each other," Leigh said. "I don't expect to own you." And don't you expect to own me! She didn't. It was right: they would give each other room to grow, to change, and they would grow wiser and more wonderful together.

Yet the night of their wedding Leigh had angered her. They sat at a big table inside with the friends still left who had not yet gone back to the city after a full day of eating, drinking, getting stoned, dancing and more eating. Mrs. Pfeiffer was presiding. Leigh's father had died of a heart attack the year before, down in the garment district where he was a cutter. One of the things Vida trusted in Leigh was that unlike many of their friends, he loved and respected his mother. He didn't see a lot of her, but they talked to each other as friends, the way she and Ruby did. Vida put faith in that. That his parents were both Communists, although they had left the party years before, fascinated her too. It seemed glamorous, clandestine. Vida asked Mrs. Pfeiffer how the wedding party differed from the Communist festivities of her youth, and Mrs. Pfeiffer answered that nowadays the kids didn't listen to as many speeches and there was a lot more rock-and-roll.

Leigh shouted down the table, "We'll do this again next month, when Vida and I get divorced!"

Although Leigh was four years older than Vida, he had never before married, and he'd been surprised how angry his joke made her. Mrs. Pfeiffer pursed her lips. "Is that why you're keeping your name, Davida? Because you're getting divorced next month?"

"I'm keeping my name because it's my name. Leigh can have it if he wants." She wasn't changing her name any more times.

Coming back to the train clattering above Brooklyn, she snorted. Never change her name, huh? She'd had six identities since she'd become a fugitive, beyond her political nom de guerre, Peregrine. Her current I.D. was in the name Vinnie Rappaport, a dead baby from 1946, four years younger than Vida; but she knew objectively, as she had to, that she looked in her twenties still and could have passed for younger than Vinnie's age of 32. Eyes. She felt eyes. A man staring. He was holding up a newspaper and staring from it to her. Why? Her spine gave her an electrical shock. The train stood in the Kings Highway station. At once she rose and bolted from the car, jamming the doors open enough to hop out. She ran along the platform, then swung back. No one else had got out of her car. The train pulled away. She stood trembling, embarrassed. Should she run for it? But she had acted on blind impulse. After all, men frequently stared at women on the subway. Why would he look at the newspaper and than stare at her? She sat down nervously to wait for the next train. She'd be a little late.

At last she reached the stop. Paused to see who else got off, then slowly descended the steps. Green here, leafy. Gradually she circled around past small shops and apartment houses to Emmons and the block-sized tan stucco mass of Lundy's. Its red-striped awnings spanked smartly as sails in the brisk wind off the narrow bay, where sportfishing boats were huddled.

The rain still insinuated from the air, a fine clinging drizzle with a salt tang. None of the cars suggested a stakeout to her. She did not sense anything amiss. Slowly she walked into the dim interior, letting her eyes accustom to the bluish light from the diamond-paned windows with their red escutcheons before she proceeded. At a few minutes past twelve, the huge room was only half full. Wandering the forest of tables, she spotted Leigh sitting against a wall. Sometimes she could wish he were less striking in appearance. Tall and stoop-shouldered, he was holding his reading glasses out to scan the menu, but not putting them on because he was farsighted and wanted to watch the entrance. Still he did not see her until she was upon him. His hair was a curly tan stippled with occasional silver, silver glinting in his thick rabbinical beard, in his bushy brows. He had something elegant about him, a care in his dressing, an awareness of posture even in khakis or jeans; he sat as someone sits who is used to being watched, talked about, admired.

She took a chair across from him, her heart annoyingly thudding. She took off the silly glasses and set them on the table next to his real ones. He put out his hands, and they touched over the table. Her hands felt cold and clammy in his warm dry palms. "Leigh, so long this time, so long! You won't believe how I've missed you!"

"Hey, honey . . . ah?"

She had to strain to hear him over the room acoustics, which magnified noise—the roar of diners chatting, the clash of dinnerware meeting plate, unidentifiable music which played as if underwater. She did not want to shout. "Vinnie Rappaport."

"Good Jewish name. I have some rotten news for you. Talked to the station this morning—I think it's in the later papers?"

"What?" She felt bloated with shyness. Feelings stormed though her, while she must sit politely and merely stare at him. His light hazel eyes watched her through their long, long lashes. He had beautiful eyes. A touch of purple in the full lids. He wasn't the best-looking man in New York, yet women always pursued him. Hearing him on the radio, women fell in love with his butterscotch voice. Then he looked into their eyes and he had them. She touched his hands, hairy on the backs. Hair grew even on the first joints of his fingers. He was a lean bear with studious shoulders. "What news?"

He was watching her carefully, but not entirely with sympathy. A steely curiosity probed her. "They got Kevin."

"Kevin? When?" Immediately she saw the man on the subway and felt faint.

"Picked him up last night on West 4th."

"Manhattan. Nobody should ever go into the city," she said automatically, seeing Kevin fall, crumpling to the pavement, Jimmy's face forming in death grimace. "Did they shoot?"

The waiter was over them. "Two plates of cherrystones. Then we'll have lobster. Boiled for me." Leigh turned to her. "Want yours boiled or baked and stuffed?"

"Boiled."

"And two draft beers."

He was being his old dominating self, his manner before feminists had filed down his edges, when he would never hesitate to order for anybody. The Movement's resident gourmet and wine expert. He was watching her with care that had a trace of annoyance. As the waiter moved off she asked quietly, "Is he okay? Any shooting?"

"No force involved. They just up and tapped him on the shoulder. 'Hi, there, Kevin Droney, why don't you just come along with us?' And he went, meek as a sacrificial lamb."

"I'm glad of that. I'd *hate* to watch it on the news tonight."

"Like Jimmy?"

"Like Jimmy and Belinda." She fumbled at her water glass. They had known Jimmy better, but Belinda was just as dead.

"I hate to be the one to break bad tidings over your head. . . . Were you in touch with Kevin?"

"I haven't seen him since the big split in the Network in '74. I heard he was in Canada procuring automatic weapons for the IRA."

"The IRA? What next? Was he on his way to Belfast?" Questioning her like the newsman he was.

"It has nothing to do with me. I just hear gossip, the same as you."

Kevin was a sore between them. Trust Kevin to get himself busted that morning, just to interfere with their reunion. If he'd known, he'd have chosen the time himself. Tentatively she caressed the back of Leigh's hand. No ring, of course. They'd left off wearing their rings in '68. "Kevin doesn't know I'm around. We've been enemies since the split. He never forgave."

"Then you're not worried that he's been busted?"

"I'm scared when they catch anybody, Leigh. How could I not care? It's one less of us surviving. A victory for their side."

"I don't know if Kevin and I are on the same side," Leigh said with a thin grin taut in his beard.

"Do I know any more? But I do know we were on the same side of the law, Kevin and I," she said bitterly. "The outside. Here come the clams." She felt buffeted by a hard cold force in Leigh. Was this going to be one of their bad times, after so long? Did he blame her for the months' passing since they'd seen each other? Times had been hard in L.A., hard for the fugitives. She felt a moment of fierce longing for Eva, to talk to her. Eva would feel exactly as she did about Kevin: Eva would be able to hate Kevin and still mourn his being taken. In L.A. they did not even have a phone in their little house. What would they say on it? Alice and Eva perhaps did not even know the news yet.

With the first taste of the clams, his temper seemed to lighten. "Sweet little darlings. Good this time. Couldn't be better."

"I haven't had these since . . . a year? At least."

"An honest pleasure. Eating a clam that can't fight back. That tastes like an angel's come. Pure protein. You could eat these till you couldn't stand up, and you wouldn't gain an ounce."

Leigh had put on a little weight. Nicely cut casual jacket and pants tailored like a bush outfit in black corduroy. Who picked that out? She'd used to dress him. Leigh did not like to shop for clothes, associating it with childhood excursions to places where relatives could get it for you cheap, and "it" was always too big and never what the other guys were wearing. He liked to be given clothes, but they had to be chosen carefully, because his taste was precise. "Not that shade of orange. Want me to look like a walking Orange Julius?" The shirt was a muted plaid in soft wool, predominantly blue and gray with a touch of yellow. "You're looking sensational," she said.

"Getting older. Know I'm going to turn forty in March? Forty!" He shook his head. "And they used to say never trust anybody over thirty. 'Course, I never said that. I was twenty-nine when the foolish kids started saying that, and I was damned if I was going to be retired by superstition. Forty, though, that's a tombstone. That's a real clunker."

Who'd bought the suit and shirt for him? What was the name of the woman he'd been seeing in April? Leigh always had women in his life—old lovers, new lovers, and her, the old wife. With a prick of resentment, she realized she was going to have to charm him. He wasn't paying enough attention to her. He wasn't gazing hard enough. She took off the poncho and sat up across the table. No more hand holding, piteous for reassurance among the battered stainless steel flatware. Finishing her last clam she set her head at a becoming tilt, the face a little turned, the chin up, and gave him that old slow smile. "Well, you may be turning forty, old dear, but I'm just thirty-two on my I.D. I grow younger now each year—I find it superior for the figure and the disposition."

He grinned, then looked as if finally seeing her. "You do look younger. On the thin side, though. We can fix that. Feed you up. Here comes the lobster. Ta dah! Let's pray devoutly they haven't overcooked it."

"To whom do you pray? Con Edison?"

"Neptune—isn't he the fishy one? So you're not broken up about Kevin?"

"I don't like them chalking up any wins. But it's nothing personal."

"How do I know? You used to be crazy about that loudmouthed bulvon. Thought he was Che come again."

"We all make our mistakes. I've had to live with that one." She smiled wanly. Leigh's jealousy was not sexual but political. He could not forgive her for having believed with Kevin in the need for armed struggle, for having disagreed with him, and for having acted on that disagreement; whereas she felt guilty not for that ideological difference, since she still did not think Leigh had been correct, but for the fact that she had been crazy in love with Kevin.

"When you admit you're wrong, you're irresistible." This time Leigh took her hand and squeezed it hard. For the first time that day electricity began crackling between them. "How's your lobster?"

"Great!" She began eating with relish, feeling him looking at her, feeling his desire. "Ha, I got a female. Want some roe?"

"Absolutely. They're gay in this place. Gave me a male and you a female to eat out. Ah, my love, your lips are red as a lobster's roe. Your eyes are green as a lobster's sweet liver. How's that for poetry?"

"Fine, if you're a lobster. If not, not. How would you like it? Your eyes are hazel as a stream polluted with algae."

"I've got a cat now. I call her Babes. You know, she has eyes just as green as yours, and sometimes they look as big. Sometimes I talk to her as if she was you."

"Don't try sex with a cat. If she goes down on you, it'll hurt like hell with that sandpaper tongue." She was flirting, and yet she felt mildly hurt. A cat. He had not had a pet since Mopsy their spaniel had died—of missing her, it was said, and she had cried. Poor Mopsy. Leigh was being unfaithful to her and to Mopsy with his new cat.

"They overcooked this. Rubbery. God damn." Leigh looked as if he might make a scene, and she caught her breath.

"Please, love, forget it. Don't call attention, please!"

"All right, all right. But why be meek about bad food?"

"The clams were good. My lobster's fine. Have some of mine."

He smiled sardonically. "You know, my dear, ever since you've been . . . uh, under . . . your disposition has been far more conventional. Don't run that red light. Please, it's turning amber! That's a No Parking sign. Please don't litter. Please, no phony credit-card calls! And don't put the stamps on the letters upside down."

"I have to obey the small laws, Leigh, the better to go on breaking the big ones."

He tasted her lobster. "It's almost as overdone as mine."

"But Leigh, to me it's wonderful. I haven't had lobster in years and years." She wanted to beg him not to spoil her treat, her treasure, by telling her exactly how wonderful it wasn't against some absolute standard. It tasted fine to her. She could have eaten it all day, and indeed, she was eating slower and slower the way she had as a child when she was licking an ice cream cone and didn't want it to end. Then it would melt and drip on her shoe, and now the lobster was getting cold. She must finish it. She must enjoy it and let it be done, like this precious time already sneaking past them and away. She wished she could give a bite to Eva, who sometimes ate fish and shellfish. It would be such a treat for her too. The last months had been especially hard for them in L.A.

When they were leaving, he put his arm around her shoulders. "I rented a car. . . . Don't worry, I did it right." A dark blue Chevelle.

"You drove here without any tickets?"

"I drove like an angel."

"Sure. Flying all the way." She slid into the driver's seat. Leigh was a New Yorker born and bred, one of probably the only collection of men in the country who don't view the automobile as their birthright. He had his driver's license, although she had never been able to understand how. It seemed wantonly permissive of the State of New York to certify him, when he was obviously incompetent and actively dangerous behind the wheel of the car. Any traveling they had done by car she had managed. Leigh didn't care. He preferred to be chauffeured while he talked, pointed, gesticulated. Of course, he did the same thing when he was driving, which was part of the problem.

Leigh was spreading out a map on his lap. "Let's see. You want the Belt Parkway."

"Leigh, if you'd tell me where we're going?"

"Montauk. Thought we'd run right out there. This time of the fall, it shouldn't be mobbed."

"But somebody out there might remember us." They'd rented a small house in August. "Was that . . . '67? '68?"

"That was eons ago. We'll put up in a motel. Don't worry, baby, we wouldn't look like the same people. I'll check us in. No problem."

No problem but us, she thought, to get back in touch. Heading out on the island, she drove five miles under the speed limit with extreme caution, keeping strictly to the right, always signaling intentions, never tailgating, precautions second nature by now as she concentrated on drawing Leigh out. "How're things at the station?"

"We had a flap when it looked as if we might be sold to a conglomerate, but it fell through. I'm doing the interview show Friday nights and the morning news weekdays. I have to get up at six, which is a royal drag. I want the evening news, but as long as Roy hangs in there, I'm blocked. They think I'm too radical for the evening news. Red sky in the morning? I don't know why I'm the right shade of red for 8 A.M. but too red for 6 P.M. The corporate mind at work is a wonder to behold." His long legs cocked up on the dashboard, he lay back in the seat not bothering to watch the scenery. He wasn't big on scenery, Leigh: he called trees future toilet paper of America, and mountains he found bumpy and wasteful. He could not understand why people lived all those outlandish places beyond the suburbs of New York City. The West was Jersey City and the Far West was the Poconos. The proof of his love for her was that for most of '74, before he had landed the job at WBAD, he had taken the train down to Philadelphia to spend half of every week with her, Stanley braving the alien jungle. He had to travel in his work, but always did so with a sense of undying shock: My God, all those people living in the Great American Desert! Once she had felt the same way, having grown up in Cleveland and then in Chicago. New York represented glorious civilization. Everyplace else was the second city, second best. People lived in New York City; they only settled for Charlevoix or Portland. She had had that nonsense knocked out of her.

"Are you still enjoying the interview program? Do they give you enough freedom to use it politically?"

"I maintain a pretty free hand. They get flack, but they dig that if it's the right kind. Once I month I do a special for Sunday night. Last month I did cuts in day care—how's that for strokes with the women's army, hey? And this month I'm focusing on unemployment among kids. Like what happens to all the kids who don't go on to college and don't find jobs? What the hell do they do all day, every day? What happens to them? Do they fall apart like their old man would? Do they start boozing? Shooting up? Do they join gangs? Do they take to a life of crime? Just sponge off the folks? Just hang around? . . . Lord, do they think I'm a weird old man!''

She realized what struck her: how relaxed he was. He lay back on his spine with the words flowing out in his deep smooth voice with the honey and fog in it and he never watched. He did not keep track of the cars behind them, ahead of them; he did not watch every person in every car; he did not foresee possible confrontations; he did not experience that metal skullcap tightening on her when a cop car idled on the side of the highway, behind some shrubbery. "Are they willing to open up with you?''

"Listen, everybody wants to be interviewed. Everybody wants to be a star even for five minutes anonymously. The point is to provoke them into saying something useful and then shut them up. They get pissed if you don't want to record them for hours. Every punk has a philosophy of life.''

The rain had not let up, and the traffic was light for a Saturday in late September. "And you really get up at six every morning?''

"Damn straight. Six A. in the M. Susannah won't even get up with me. I grind the coffee, I put the water up, then I get dressed. By the time I get my clothes on straight, the kettle's boiling. So I have coffee, I eat a container of yogurt standing—''

She listened to him, amused. A man proud of discovering he could actually get up in the morning by himself, make his own breakfast. She could not imagine a woman living who would think such a thing worth reporting.

". . . just make it. Fortunately, I've straightened out the coffee situation at the studio. A Mr. Coffee with Zabar's blend in it is workable by the most imbecilic of the staff. And at home Susannah's finally learned how to make espresso without explosions.''

Susannah. Was that the woman he'd been involved with in April? A couple had been sharing the apartment with him for a while. The Dorfmanns. But why would he expect Mrs. Dorfmann to get up with him? She decided to assume knowledge. "Susannah's living there?''

"Sure. You knew that. . . . Hadn't she moved in the last time I saw you? I thought . . . Let me remember.''

"I didn't know she was really living there.''

"Aw, come on, Vida—''

"Could you remember to call me Vinnie, please?''

"In the fucking car?''

"How do you know the car's not bugged? You were talking about Susannah.''

"She's not news by this time. I've been living with her for a year.''

"The Dorfmanns aren't living with you any longer?''

"They moved out when Susannah moved in. Did I forget to tell you in April? Maybe I wasn't sure how it'd all work out. . . . Let's see, I guess the Dorfmanns moved out in March. Susannah was staying over all the time anyhow, and she had that damned remote pad in farthest Brooklyn."

He had got very involved with Susannah since April, that was evident. She was positive now she had heard Susannah's name, but along with a Lois and a Maggie, all through the last winter. He certainly had not been living with anyone but the Dorfmanns, and now this Susannah was occupying her apartment. Where she couldn't go.

"Come on, baby . . . don't sulk. You knew about Susannah. Anyhow, what difference does it make to you? We can't live together."

Part time, we could, just as we did in Philadelphia, she thought, which was one thing she wanted to arrange this trip; but she was already seeing that wasn't the way his plans were running.

He said plaintively, "Here I am cheating on her to spend this weekend with you, and do I complain? It means a lot to me to see you. It's worth any risk, any expense, any amount of finagling and covering up."

"Cheating, to see your wife? That's a new one." Make me feel guilty, why don't you? She sighed, grimacing into the rain. Say something bland quick. "Have you any ideas about motels?" She had let too much time go by without seeing him. She had to stay East now. Eva would just have to understand. L.A. would never be Vida's home. She was losing him finally, losing him utterly. Another woman in the bed she had picked out. Would it have been a worse sign if Susannah got up with him Monday through Friday at 6 A.M. just to see him off into the early smog? Also, it was typical of Leigh in their whole marriage to keep a disturbing piece of information from her—an overdraft, a bill, a problem—and then to announce it all at once when it had reached postcritical explosiveness as if she had really known all along, just as he did. Control. Retaining information gave him control. She found herself angry, and again she sighed at the rain.

". . . so I made a reservation," he was saying. He sat up as they approached Montauk. "Take the shore road, next right. Let's see if we can find it. Sounds nice."

He had chosen a colony of duplexes scattered over a hillside on sand paths that twisted among stunted pines overlooking the ocean, just across the blacktop road. Vida felt a little nervous. It looked expensive. But it would be Leigh's treat. She wondered if she looked shabby, but the blue dress was still in good shape. She had not worn it much in L.A. She had a picture of herself in the dress sitting there, and she thought she looked good as he went in to register. Then she realized that in her mental image of herself she had red-gold hair halfway down to her waist. Somehow she saw herself as still looking that way, just as she saw herself as really married to Leigh and active in Natalie's life and an aunt to her nephews and niece and a friend to her best friends.

"I'll show you the way, Mrs. Biggs," the woman said, pointing up the pathway but giving Vida a quick scornful glance.

She followed Leigh uphill. He had a suitcase and a briefcase; she had only her pack. "Biggs?" she asked.

"E. P. Biggs. E. Power. Get it?"

E. Power Biggs played Bach on the organ: some level of sexual pun, she supposed, and was annoyed he trifled with unlikely pseudonyms. The pines dripped, the sea faded into a fogbank, but the air smelled freshly laundered. No one was in the other side of the duplex, through the knotty-pine wall. They had a big room with a double bed, a couple of pleasant chairs at the table, a modern bathroom with tub and shower, and an outside counter lit up like a theatrical makeup table, with bulbs all around the mirror.

Leigh bounced on the bed. "Not bad at all."

Shyly she sat beside him, against the headboard. He opened his briefcase, took out a bottle of dry sherry—Amontillado—and opened it, pouring some into two tumblers from the bathroom. "Here's looking at you, kid. Hey, didn't I pick out that dress?"

"For my last birthday."

"That's right. It's too pretty for anybody else to have chosen. Right classy."

"Who would?" she asked. "Do you like it as much as you expected?"

"Absolutely." He put his arm around her forcefully, if a little awkwardly, and grinned through his curly beard. "Now, enough of the dress already."

As they made love, she was preternaturally conscious. It meant too much. She wanted to take his face between her hands and stare at him for hours. Every caress of his dry warm palms on her, every inch of his body brought back memories. The experience was too strong emotionally to move her sensually. When he entered her and she felt his weight, the pressure of his known body on hers, his dense hairiness, the pelt of him, the bones jutting, the outsized joints, the full hammering of his penis in her, she wanted to beg him to stop, to wait, to slow down, to lie still on her and let her endure the onslaught of wanting that could not be used up in sex. She felt as if she would weep with happiness, but she soon realized she would not come. She had not made love in a month and a half, she had not been with a man since the last time she had been with him, and her vagina had tightened. She could not jam the circuits of her mind, could not find the easy sensuality she had repressed on the road. Nor was she acclimated to him yet. Yet his thrusting pleased her, moved her intensely. Her pleasure was of emotions more than sensations, but she did not care.

However, after a while she realized that he would mind if she did not seem to reach orgasm. With so few times to make love in the course of a year, fierce pressure fell on each of them to be perfect, or acclaimed so. She did not want to get things off badly, and she knew she had no way to make him understand she felt totally satisfied to make love with him even without a climax. She was too conscious of him, too moved by his presence, to sink into her muscles. Finally she moaned several times and clenched him hard; then from the way he began to move she knew he assumed she had come and was getting ready to come himself.

"You came okay, babes?" he asked her afterward, lying propped on his elbow. His loins were pale, but his chest and arms were still tanned from the summer. By midwinter all his skin would be pale, with blue veins strongly showing raised in his sinewy arms.

"Wonderful, Leigh. It's beautiful to be with you!" Because it was. She did not like to lie to him, ever, but he would not understand her pleasure. She had a dressing gown she loved, a chinoiserie kimono that took up little space in the pack and looked just as good wrinkled as not. Putting it on now she faced him, sitting cross-legged on the bed. He wore a navy velour bathrobe, the sort of thing his mother got him on his birthday every other year. "How's Natalie?" she asked.

"Two weeks ago I had dinner out there. Daniel's getting to be a first-class bastard. We got into a fight about municipal unions. Then he and Natalie tussled over picketing dirty movies. It was a great evening. Natalie's for wiping out porn these days—sounds like the Legion of Decency."

"What's she doing lately? Are things still the same with her and Daniel?"

"They seem to jog along from year to year, regardless. Oh, Peezie's taken up running. She's a jock—every morning at six thirty she's out doing three miles. And Sam's got a Puerto Rican girlfriend they are determinedly accepting."

"Well, why not? Is she pretty?"

"If you like giggling twelve-year-old jailbait. They talk Spanish together, which drives Daniel secretly crazy. He can't stand not knowing what they're saying, and he can't admit, the big Cuban expert on the basis of a ten-day trip, that he can't speak Spanish well enough to follow them. Listen, Sam's going to be a real linguist. That kid's okay, you know that? I been taking him along on my Bronx excursions. The Ricans dig the way he talks the lingo now. He's my interpreter. Peezie's in her ugh-ugh phase. All she does is grunt, act macho and stumble around like a ten-year old dyke. Never mind! Don't jump me. Natalie gets mad enough for two.''

''And how's Fanon?''

''He's called Franky now. He's too young to tell yet. All, I want it, I want it, I saw it on the TV. Overweight whining brat.''

Fanon was the least real of Natalie's children to Vida. She had waited in the hospital during Sam's birth to see him first in the vivid rainbow colors of the newborn. She had toted Peezie around in a pack on her back in Central Park. Both of them she had fed with a spoon, screamed at, kissed and cuddled. Fanon had been born after she had gone underground, and she had seen him only once when he was too young to understand what was going on. Only Sam as the oldest was able to keep up his connection with her.

''Picnic time,'' Leigh said, bringing out black bread that they used to get Saturdays in the bakery at 101st. The loaf was huge and round, and he had bought a wedge of it. Along with the bread he unpacked a can of good French pâté, a wedge of Port-Salut, and a Camembert. ''Your favorite—and, I trust, ripe enough.''

''It seems great. Oh, when did I have Camembert?''

''We can have some more sherry tomorrow. I have a nice wine here. A Sutter Home zinfandel, a '74, Amador County. Give me your glass and I'll rinse it out.''

Her tongue was going crazy. Her tongue was fattening on sensations. She had a sense of slippage with Leigh, that now she and her husband belonged to different social classes. He had become more affluent in recent years. He was doing well with the station, he wrote regularly for left and liberal periodicals, and once in a while he did an article for a slick at a good fee. He did some paid television as an expert on one social problem or another—panel shows, talk shows. She was not sure exactly what he was making, but it circled around twenty thousand, she guessed. She lived so marginally, she was not sure whether she spent four thousand in a year. What money she had was in her wallet—less than fifteen dollars. Her possessions were mostly in her pack. She had a West Coast stash (no identification in it) and an East Coast stash up at Agnes' in Vermont with winter clothes, but basically what she carried was what she had, and it would hardly have filled an airport locker.

''Tell me a little more about Natalie. How does she look?''

''Aren't you going to see her?''

She did not like his asking. He had no need to know. Furthermore, that was not a question she could ever answer with a sense of accuracy —whether a clandestine meeting would prove safe. She hesitated long enough to make him aware. ''Could be. Who knows?''

''Flying turds, Vid—Vinnie, do you think I'm going to tip the Feds?

Come on, you wouldn't bob into New York without seeing your sister."

"You aren't getting along too well with each other, huh?"

"We always get along, except when she's crazy with her women's chauvinism. She's a good egg, under it all. Too bad she married that jerk-off Daniel, though, he's settled into the academic rut. That's a pun: he's making his way through the coeds as usual. She's into battered women lately, but I'll say this for her, she's always got it in the kitchen. She made a Mexican seafood soup that was from heaven, with little bowls of chopped hot peppers and avocados on the side. And for dessert, a caramel mousse light enough to fly."

A sharp pang of loneliness for Natalie hit home, vexing her with herself. Here she was finally with Leigh and missing yet another loved one. They picnicked on the bed. "Remember Sunday mornings?" She touched his beard. "We'd fight for half an hour about who'd go out for the *Times* and the deli?"

"The loser would get it, and we'd have café au lait with the good dark French roast."

"Then we'd get back in bed and take the phone off the hook and read the paper and make out."

He reached for the wine bottle. "And haggle over the book review and the entertainment and The Week in Review. Then we'd fuck. Then we'd put the phone back on the hook, and before my hand got loose, the thing would start ringing every two minutes for the rest of the day."

She kissed his sharp curving nose. "Doesn't it still?"

"I got a machine now. *It* answers the phone." He fiddled with the room radio trying to pick up his station, but he couldn't tune it in. "Weather's rotten for reception. Let's hope it clears tomorrow. Get the last of the beach days in."

"Did you get out of the city this summer?"

"We rented a house in Setauket for August. July I was covering the Cahoon trial for *Seven Days* and the station. Got an exclusive interview with him. Did you see it?"

Who was Cahoon? It must be a local case. "Maybe you could show it to me?" Was *we* Susannah too? "A big house you rented?"

"Nah, a shack. In back of another house two blocks from the bay. Paper walls and hot and cold running ants."

She heard herself laugh, realizing she was a little drunk. The zinfandel was good, and she had had three glasses without considering, on top of the sherry. Her head was floating. She never drank now, and the wine had gone straight to her brain and then suffused through her body. What presents he had bought her!—wine and cheese and a fancy meal at Lundy's and a night in a beautiful clean motel by the real ocean, the

Atlantic, and his body and his voice and his presence and his love. She felt cherished, coddled, enveloped in caring. Rain pattered on the roof, gurgled in the eaves, but she was out of the storm for once and snug. . . .

The first time, the very first time he had brought her to his apartment, she had expected the usual bachelor grubbiness. He had one room and it was untidy, but he had sat her down on the couch, given her an aperitif —something she had never heard of at the time, and in memory it remained something absolutely exotic staining her tongue with fruit and fragrances and hidden herbs—and gone to prepare a fettuccine Alfredo with a salad whose dressing he made in his blender and garlic bread he slathered with something he told her was pesto di basilico. She was more than impressed. He was politically correct; he was Leigh Pfeiffer of the spring mobilization; he was smart and witty and brave and a marshal at peace parades. And the first man who had ever cooked for her. He knew how to live very, very well on fifty a week.

She had not quite decided that evening whether she was going to let herself succumb to him or not. She was waiting for the pass. But after they had eaten and eaten, he said, "We're much too full to enjoy making love. Let's go take a walk by the river. It's gorgeous outside, and we can have an espresso in a while. After all, we have the whole night. We even have the morning."

She had been finessed. That neatly. She appreciated the ease of the maneuver even as she resigned herself to it. But wickedly she said, "If you never ask, nobody ever says no. Right?"

How he had grinned at her, swinging around in the doorway, lithe and skinny with his satyr beard pointing at her and those marvelous light eyes glinting into hers. "You want to say no? Go ahead. Supper's on the house."

She didn't want to say no. Then or now. They were still mated; they were still married. The Network was in a slack period, a phase that scared her, threatened her, but might nonetheless give her the freedom to choose to live within commuting distance of Leigh once again. She was beginning to think about programs to propose at the annual Board meeting, more important this year than it was usually because of the widespread sense she had picked up on her way from L.A. that the Network was drifting perilously.

In Cincinnati people had been excited by the pirate-TV technology, but in Omaha the fugitives were doing nothing more progressive than study groups and infighting. It had taken her a week to get the two factions to speak to each other again. Back in Denver the fugitives had had a V.D. scare, and nobody was sleeping with anybody and depression was being passed along like a flu bug. She had put them on paramilitary discipline with hikes and target practice, but it was only a holding action.

Perhaps she could propose some kind of action centered on pirate media and get Leigh involved. It would be good for him politically. Then they would share work and begin anew to share a life. Eva would like such a project. Vida was always trying to come up with some new way that Eva's music could be used and thus given some place of importance in their world. Eva had been cut off from an audience for years. Involve Eva's music, involve Leigh's knowledge of radio and print media (she had a quick image of counterfeit editions of newspapers, the editorial page-through clandestinely replaced). Involve the Network in a lively new project that would jolt everyone out of depression and lethargy and infighting! Cheek pressed against Leigh's arm and lips to his warm skin, whose fur tickled her, she lay plotting changes.

3

Vida was always a little nervous in public with Leigh, for he had the habit of commanding and the willingness to confront when service was not up to his specifications. On the other hand, he could be charming, and that sometimes ended up worse, making him the center of local attention. He was chatting with the woman at the desk about what was open for breakfast.

"Oh, if you and your"—the woman glanced at her hand—" 'wife' want a nice breakfast, the Surf Clam's open early." As Vida walked after Leigh, the woman looked her over: Vida could feel the hostile gaze like a crab scuttling across her back. Mrs. Pine-Acres wanted to run a family business. No whores, no fugitives, no clandestine rendezvous. She had to remember to dig out that worn gold band she had in her pack—not her own wedding ring, symbolically thrown into the sea at the Battery that day in '68, but Ruby's old wedding ring from her first marriage to Tom, Vida's father. With her husband, she had forgotten to wear it.

The Surf Clam at seven thirty was almost deserted. A group of fishermen warming up from the raw wind, a family on their way to or from church, a couple having a quiet spat in a booth, their eyes glaring over pursed lips and stiffly held menus.

"Mrs. Pine-Acres thought we were pitching illicit woo in her nice big bed," Vida said, playing with envelopes of sugar on the beige Formica tabletop. Pictures of famous women on the packets. Clara Barton. Julia Ward Howe.

"Should I be boldly wicked and order waffles? Probably frozen. Pancakes? I'd face the calories if the taste was right. . . . Reminds me, talked to your lawyer lately?''

"No." She did not have any reason to be in touch with the law firm and hadn't yet checked the drop she used.

"Oh. . . . So they didn't tell you the divorce is finally coming through?" Leigh high-signed the waitress, who was elbows on the counter deep in conversation with a young man in a slicker.

"It is?" Now she remembered that they had vaguely discussed the possibility of eventual divorce in April. Once or twice before he had begun proceedings, but dropped them. "You had a lot of heat on you lately?"

"Almost none. I assume the phone's tapped—we've always lived that way. But not bad. Here she comes: at long last, service."

They ordered. The waitress poured coffee and left. A Jeep stopped outside and a man came to order coffee to go.

Leigh continued, "The Feds check me once in a while, fill out their routine forms. Julio tells me when they been by."

"He's still there!" Julio, one of the janitors in their building, had always kept them cued to surveillance. "How is he?"

"Julio's got bleeding ulcers. He's on some medication that makes him feel lousy, but without it he could die. . . . Every so often there's a flurry. I don't mean to imply I'm a forgotten man. Last May when I was doing a piece on the longshoremen, I was tailed for a couple of weeks. Thought it was the Red Squad or the Feds, but my God, it was the Mafia! I was flattered."

"Be careful when you go back. With Kevin busted, it may heat up. I guess disavowing me legally might help, but they'll likely continue to watch you when they get active in wanting me."

He glared. The waitress brought his pancakes and her eggs, keeping him quiet until she had gone again. Then he said in a low grating voice, "They'd watch me if you'd never done anything more exciting than knit argyles, *Vinnie*. I'm one of the most prominent media voices on the left. They watch me for *me*."

Oh, my, she thought, what provoked that? "Of course, sweetheart. Everybody knows your broadcast journalism. But sometimes you get extra heat from me when you least expect it. . . . How come you suddenly decided to go ahead with the . . . ?"

"The what?" he asked stubbornly when she trailed off. "The piece on the longshoremen?"

"The legal proceedings."

"Ah, babes, we talked about that so many times. I can't explain to Susannah why I stay married to you. Listen, we have to clear this up. I want to be able to tell her about you."

"No," she said levelly, sitting upright and methodically eating her eggs.

"She doesn't know where in hell I am this weekend. She thinks I'm in bloody Chicago, and she's going to be wondering why I haven't called her. I lied to her all week. I'm going to have to lie to her when I go home again."

"Lying now and then is something we all have to get used to," she said, chopping her eggs fine.

"Why lie to *her*? She'd understand."

"I never met the lady. Why take chances?" Vida tore a piece from her English muffin and mopped at the yolk. The muffin felt like bits of furniture stuffing in her mouth.

"Damn it, Vida, do you want to meet her?"

"Could you remember my name?" Vida sipped her coffee, carefully placed the cup on the Formica. The liquid was lukewarm and acid in her throat. "I have no need to meet her. In no way would her knowledge that you see me help me survive or accomplish any political purpose. Or am I missing something?"

"You're jealous of her!" He sat back grinning.

"I'm jealous of her. Of course. But whether or not I am, I must act rationally or I won't continue to survive. Jealousy would lead me to insist you tell her I'm still your . . . lover, that we see each other, that I'm still in your life, that I want to be with you. That the only reason I'm not with you is because they won't let me be. But caution and the desire to survive and the accumulated political wisdom of the Network lead me to tell you that she cannot know."

"She's not about to talk to anybody else. I think making her suspicious of me is far more dangerous."

"I don't. Surely you can handle that. You've always been skilled at keeping space for yourself. . . . Did I ever demand you account to me in any way? Surely she trusts you."

"Sure she trusts me, and here I am letting her down."

"Leigh, it seems important to you right now to tell this lover, but you've had many women over the years. Suppose you'd told every one of them about me? Suppose you'd told just half of them?"

"I never wanted to. I wasn't living with them."

"You lived with some on and off. Remember Fran? And you have wanted to tell before, Leigh. You wanted to tell Lohania."

"That was different."

"Right. Lohania had more real interest. But not enough for me to let you do it. . . . Leigh, all relationships feel permanent when they're good. But usually they end. We've been close for thirteen years, and that counts for something in how I trust you." She was aware that under the obvious argument she was debating him about the sudden importance of Susannah, of a relationship which had been one of three diversions in March and which now represented a surrogate wife, a hearth goddess. "You can't tell how long your affair with Susannah may last."

"It's pretty real." His voice was low and surly. He squished his remaining pancake around the plate. "We've been involved for a year already. I can tell what I want, Vinnie. I've never had any trouble telling what I want and what I don't want."

"Right, and the hot lover you want in October is frequently the nagging bitch you're bored with by January." She heard her voice rapping out and drew a deep breath. This was Leigh, not an enemy. "I don't want you to be lonely. God knows how long our separation is going to last. But you can't gamble politically that this new affair will be there in two years. You can't gamble with others' lives and freedom that you won't do something to infuriate her, that you won't walk out in a huff. That one of you won't fall madly in love with somebody else. . . . You're a wonderful man. A woman may do and be anything for a while to please you. But small incompatibilities swell into large ones over time—"

"Sometimes people get closer. She's not pleasing me. She's a strong woman too in her own way."

"How old is she?"

"Twenty-six. She's mature. She's not a kid, if that's what you're getting at." He was absolutely furious.

She was glad Natalie couldn't overhear the conversation, because she felt guilty enough about trying to undermine Susannah; but Susannah was young and free. What could Leigh mean to her? "Leigh, I can't let you tell her. Next year we can review the situation. But I don't even know what she's into politically. Have you ever really checked her out?"

"V— . . . Vinnie! I've been living with the woman!"

"We all felt close to Randy, and he was more than a informer, he was an agent! Leigh, I don't want to upset you. A security check is a nasty business. Only you can't make what's a purely political judgment on a purely sexual basis."

"It isn't purely sexual!" But he was looking a little shaken. He would think for a while that it might be.

"I can tell you care about her, and I'm sure she's crazy about you." She made herself smile. "How many women have wanted to marry you over my dead body these thirteen years? That's not a basis for bringing her into the Network!"

As they walked out of the restaurant, the sky was a blurred watery blue. They could hear foghorns moaning; a wall of cotton batting stood out to sea, but the sun was burning off the overcast. The day felt washed and hung out to dry. Leigh took her hand as they scrambled down to the beach. Now she understood what had been going on between them in Lundy's. He had felt guilty. He had been living as a couple with Susannah. When Vida and Leigh had lived together, he had always needed to be open with her about his sexual encounters; he had wanted to carry back experiences and observations and problems to her. Thus even the other friends and lovers they had became part of their common experience.

She would block him from discussing her with Susannah, mostly because it was dangerous to her, but also because she would not permit him that additional measure of intimacy with Susannah that would come from turning herself, Vida, into matter for their communication. She felt better, as if an enemy had come into the open where she could fight. He too was in a more affectionate mood. Being honest about Susannah had made him more relaxed after the initial sparring at the table. I will survive her, I will, she thought. She can keep him warm and feed him and enjoy him, but she can't take him away from me. I won't let her.

She drew in the sharp smell of the sea edge, the damp tossed-up seaweed, the crushed shells of small salmon-colored crabs, the salt, until her body rang with energy. Snakes of surf coiled in, slithering white up to her feet. *Thalassa, thalassa,* the surf said, as it did in calm weather, singing its name. *Ta thalassa.* Leigh's arm was sharp and bony against her rib like an umbrella.

Brown-and-buff birds at the water's edge pattered after the waves' retreat, danced back from each advance. Eva would know what they were. She was always pointing to a bird on a wire and telling Vida its name, so that Vida felt as if she should bow and acknowledge the introduction. As soon as Eva told her the name of a bird, Vida started seeing it all over the place, as if naming made it appear. Suddenly Say's phoebe or the house wren was sailing for insects everywhere. She opened her mouth to tell Leigh and shut it. Enough other names circled them like sea gulls crying. She realized he did not know Eva, who had not been part of their New York scene before becoming a fugitive. She remembered the first time Eva had pointed out a roadrunner to her; she had thought roadrunners cartoon figures, not live birds, and they had enchanted her. In the desert the fugitives were training for an action. She felt displaced with Leigh, remembering Eva, remembering herself preparing for the pipe bombing of the offices of a landlord notorious for rent gouging and burning out his own tenants—arson at a profit, with a little incidental death of three Chicano children the week before. Her group was taking reprisal on property valued over children.

They walked a couple of miles, picking up shells to admire and dropping them again. "Remember that place we had in Montauk?"

"That was a great summer," he said. "You baked that bluefish whole stuffed with a caper dressing. And when the crew from the *Roach* was out, you made bouillabaisse. . . . Let's turn around.''

By the time they hiked back to the motel, Leigh was talking about lunch. He got out his briefcase and sent her for ice from the machine to chill a Hanns Kornell champagne. Riesling. She commented, ''You've got into California wines.''

''Maybe you can drink French wines at current prices, but I've had to look around. Besides, it's fun to explore. There's a lot of good California wines from small producers these days.'' He tapped the bottle cooling in the ice bucket. ''I visited that winery.''

With Susannah? And when? And why had he come and gone in California without seeing her?

He added at once, second-guessing her, ''I was just out there for a broadcast-journalism conference at Stanford. Rented a car and made a couple of excursions.''

''Does Susannah drive?''

''Sure. Like you, she thinks I'm a menace on wheels.''

He loved to learn something new, enter a field of expertise, and obviously Susannah had shared that exploration with him. She was determined not to give way to jealousy again. He was with her and she was going to repair their intimacy. While the champagne was chilling they showered together. Afterward she slipped into her kimono and knelt on the bed smiling at him. He slid his hand under her robe and began to caress her breast. How strange his body felt to her still, covered with a pelt of curly hair. It was like being in bed with a lean and sinewy racoon. ''You have such a neat body.'' He was staring at her in a way that made her feel clumsy. ''You're a gorgeous woman. Neat, that's the right word. Not an ounce of flab and yet all the furniture's in place.''

He was not comparing her with somebody, he was not; he was just being appreciative. She wriggled out of her kimono and pulled him down on her, remembering where and how he liked to be stroked. Strange and familiar at once, his weight and bones and curly hair, the chugging of his buttocks that were long and pale half-moons, the jungle of his thighs, the savanna of his back, his beard tickling her ear. She squirmed and settled into his rhythm and began to float backward, to move out on that long arc where words faded, where the mind dipped into the flesh and happily drowned, where she strained and hauled on him and pressed upward, where she ballooned out more urgent and she had to have, had to and then finally pleasure quickened, held, teased and then broke inside and fanned outward, flushing hot in her arms and breasts, and at last ebbed.

When he came too and slackened inside her, she tried to go on holding him. After a while he slipped out and then turned with a deep sigh onto his back. She curled sideways facing him, fitted into the curve of his arm.

The scent of sweat like fine erotic perfume. The smells of after-sex, salt marsh, salt sweat, rank and soothing. She couldn't remain still but crouched over him, kissing gently his flat cheeks, his drooping eyelids, his pointed beard, his nipples, his wet slippery shriveled cock, his bony square kneecaps. She adored him. "Leigh! Leigh, I missed you. I missed you so much. I love you!"

His lids fluttered. "Love you too, babes. . . . Good together."

After sex they'd used to share a cigarette, passing it back and forth. In '67 Leigh had given up smoking because he realized it was coarsening his voice. One morning as he coughed and spat, he announced he was done with it. He never smoked another cigarette. She admired his will-power, crouching over him. He indulged himself but he also drove him-self; in some ways she thought of him as the essence of what she loved most in New York.

In midafternoon he unpacked the dark bread, smoked oysters and another good pâté from his briefcase. "Let's catch some sun."

"Aren't you going to play some of your programs for me?" She wanted to hear what he had been doing politically.

He hefted the champagne bottle. "Let's picnic now. I'll take the pro-grams along. How about the lighthouse?"

"Leigh, the fishermen will be shoulder to shoulder for the stripers. What's that other park, where we used to swim?"

Hither Hills, it was called. Leigh said it was next to Thither Holes, where the locals sank the tourists in quicksand when they got out of hand. The campsites looked full and they kept away from that part of the beach, following a trail into the dunes and piny woods. The sun was strong by now, and the beach was settling with families and couples.

On the blanket filched from the motel she sat eating slowly and trying to memorize each moment. She felt distended with happiness. Leigh took off his shirt and lay propped on an elbow, savoring the champagne drunk out of a paper cup. That was Leigh, all right: the best for his palate and he'd eat it out of an old shoe. A champagne picnic on a scuzzy blanket. That was so typical and so reminiscent of good times together in the past that she had to clutch herself to keep from crawling all over him with affection the way he detested. Instead, she finally got him to play two of his specials on his little cassette player, one about longshoremen and the other about an old folks' commune. He gave her a couple to carry away to hear when she could. Then she would burn them; her life at times reeked of burning tapes, tapes the Network sometimes used to commu-nicate internally and with the outside world. She wished he had played the programs in the motel room. She had trouble concentrating under the mild blue sky and the warm soporific sun.

A couple ran over the dune. Immediately she shut off the player. The

43

man and woman were photographing each other, mugging, posing, shooting from a crouch, lying back languorously. She would have liked a picture of Leigh to carry with her. She would have liked to give him a photo of her, not to forget her, to carry her with him, but that was a pleasure as forbidden as strolling into her own building, greeting Julio and gossiping a few minutes as she picked up her mail, riding up in the elevator and walking into her own apartment. Among the furniture they had bought together so long ago she would sit down with one of her own books. In the wonderful old tub long enough to lie down in, she would run the water very hot and pour in her pomander bath oil. Then she would dry and come into her own bedroom with the red velvet draperies or into Leigh's with the venetian blinds and the blue burlap curtains.

They had always had separate rooms. Leigh's overflowed with clippings, tapes he was editing, splicing equipment, files, a dandruff of loose papers she could not endure. Leigh suffered from occasional fierce insomnia, stands of nights when he could not bear anyone in the bed with him, when he would get up and read at 3 A.M., work on an article, record his ideas or projects. Her room had been consciously sensual, a place to make love, to sleep, to talk hour after hour curled among heaped cushions on the big bed under the Cretan hanging, a room with two mirrors and a hanging light with a stained-glass shade, a modern imitation of Tiffany but lovely, lavender, cobalt, maroon. . . .

"Do you and Susannah have separate bedrooms?" she asked.

"What?" He was shielding his eyes from the sun, stripped down to his swim trunks now. "I had to move the bed out of my office a while ago. I've got too many files. I put in a couch. It's big enough for fucking." He grinned. "Black Naugahyde, looks like a doctor's office. I can do decent recording there. I had it soundproofed. Not studio quality, but decent."

Time was spinning faster and faster. When the couple wandered off, she turned on the cassette player again, listening as Leigh dozed. She bent over him. He had gained some weight. He had a visible soft stomach, but he was in remarkable shape considering he almost never did any physical exercise beyond making love and climbing steps out of the subway. He did walk a lot, blocks, miles around New York, often preferring to walk from 69th to 42nd or from their apartment up to Columbia, rather than take public transportation or a taxi. Somehow he burned up the good eating.

As he dozed, stirring in his sleep, grimacing slightly, she sat over him while his rich voice came tiny from the cassette interviewing a multitude of other New York voices. He was aging some, nicely. White hair flecked his beard, glinting in his brows. Lines were etched under his eyes; a deep furrow stood between. How good it would be to grow into middle age with him, talking, incessantly talking, chewing over their life together, tasting and trying and learning, always learning, coming home again to talk it all over. She loved him. He was a permanent part of her. They had helped to shape each other. He had the key to her body. They had much in common and could have so much more if permitted. Yet in the early morning they would separate, and she must depend on luck and the inefficiency of the government to let them come together again.

The cassette was over. She liked the programs, but it seemed to her he was growing perceptibly less political. The push of the times was away from social content. A couple of years before, he would have made economic points about the old folks and why they couldn't manage; now his emphasis was on human interest. She did not think he was aware of the drift. He needed her too, to keep him honest.

4

Monday morning over 5 A.M. breakfast on the highway, Vida had to hit Leigh for money. After failing to get any from Hank, she had all of thirteen dollars and thirty-eight cents. She wished that Leigh would mention money himself. Over breakfast he was abstracted, moving already into the day's, the week's business. With the road dark outside the plate-glass window, she felt as if they had been wrenched from sleep and dumped into a cold river of traffic. "I'll have to park the damned car somewhere and then return it on my lunch hour," he was grumbling. "Otherwise I'll never make it to work on time."

"Leigh . . . I'm completely broke. Do you have something to share with me?" So awkward. At first she'd used simply to tell him what she wanted. After all, he had their bank accounts, the furniture, books, stereo, audio equipment, all their joint property and assets. But as time passed and passed and passed, she had begun to feel like a poor relation begging.

"How can you travel around broke? That's dangerous in itself. Suppose something happens?"

"I'm always in the situation of having to make nothing happen, unless I'm making it happen." She waited.

Finally he yawned, reaching for his wallet. "Good thing I remembered to stop at the bank. Actually, Susannah reminded me—I was supposed to be going to Chicago." He counted out a hundred in twenties, paused, met her gaze, slowly counted out a second hundred.

She was disappointed. After all, he usually gave her eighty or a

46

hundred every month whenever he saw her. Since they'd missed so many months, she expected him to be a little more generous, but she did not want to fight about it their last hour together. Next time she would take up the issue of money with him.

"Next Tuesday at 10 A.M. I'll call your pay phone. Then back to the first Tuesday in the month at 10 A.M. If the first call fails, a follow-up Wednesday, same time, same phones. Okay?"

He sighed. "Sure." He roused himself to pat her hand. "It's been beautiful to see you. You're looking good, kid. I hope you're making it okay."

It occurred to her he had asked her almost nothing about her life. That might be tact, but it might mean that her life had become unreal to him. She decided to risk a slight breach of Network security. Everyone had some discretion about discussing actions; and members of the Board had considerable freedom, used mostly for fund raising. "Did you hear about a pirate TV station that appeared in L.A. for a whole Monday night, on one of the vacant channels?"

"Yeah?" He looked more alert. "Sounded clever. People in masks reading all kinds of far-out news and gag interviews and alternating it with a showing of *Salt of the Earth*." A film about a strike among Chicanos and the women's role.

"That was us."

"No kidding? I didn't think you had that kind of capability."

"It doesn't take much," she said.

"Will you do it again?"

"Not in L.A. They're waiting for us."

He chuckled. "You could do some real interesting things that way."

"We did. We even wrote comedy routines on local politicians."

He dropped her on South Street in Oyster Bay. Over the years she had hung around every town within a radius of twenty miles of East Norwich, where Natalie lived, except, of course, East Norwich itself. Thus at seven thirty she was wandering around with time to kill until 10 A.M., when the call with Natalie was set up. Early morning was an awkward time. She marched along the streets of old clapboard houses behind front-yard fences overrun with the last roses of fall. Big cavernous trees whose leaves were streaked red and yellow loomed over her. This was how the landscape was supposed to be, bare to the bone in winter and brimming lush in summer, not the reclaimed desert of L.A. with its dry rivers. Finally she headed into the business district and settled in a laundromat. She could do wash from her pack and read a paper looking for the latest on Kevin.

She found it: a recap of his capture and a big feature on all of them, with that old picture of her taken in 1970 with a smirk and her eyes wide at the camera that embarrassed her, as if she were coming on forever to all and sundry. Ugh. Photos of Kevin, Jimmy and her. No photo of Lohania. No picture of Randy, whose name was not even mentioned.

No, *there* Randy was, not as a member of the Little Red Wagon, not as the agent who had entrapped them, but as an expert on fugitives: Randolph Gibney, on the staff of the Kings County D.A. She had heard he had finished law school. Did it make life hard for Lohania when something on them suddenly blew up in the media? Lohania Fernández y Isnaga, whom the paper called simply Lohania Fernandez, might have changed her name, might even be married. She had forgotten to ask Leigh for news of her, if he had any. Lohania had been the only one of the five members of the Little Red Wagon who had ended up serving time—so far. The usual paragraph about Jimmy's death, the shoot-out and explosion. But nothing on what was happening to Kevin, nothing at all. It made her nervous. He could go up for thirty years, she thought, clenching her hands in her lap, fighting the bite of nausea. Whenever she had to think of prison, she told herself she could do it if she had to. People did. Her people did. But always she felt as if she were suffocating and gasped for breath.

Oh, she knew Kevin well, very well, as you know a man you were with for years. Even after they had stopped loving each other or whatever it was, even after they had begun fighting incessantly, they had had to deal with each other intimately. She was not even sure when they had really stopped sleeping together. Like pulling a burr out of a dog's coat, cutting a shiny burr from Mopsy's silky fur when Leigh and Vida had taken her to the country for a day: except that her disentangling from Kevin had been deeper, more painful. Cutting a barbed arrow from the thigh muscles. Something that ate deep and could not be uprooted from the flesh without ripping open a deep bloody wound.

They had certainly been close. At the height of their political unity they had been a single person. They had spoken the same words, screamed the same slogans; on tapes she had heard they even sounded strangely alike, speaking the harsh rhetoric of those times with the same jagged passion, the same desperate anger. Yet she did not know him intimately as she knew Leigh. They had never had a domestic life. They had faced death together, but they could not live side by side; they were not suited.

She knew what Leigh was capable of, she thought, putting down the paper and surveying the laundromat: what generosity or meanness, what he would do and what he could not do; she could have small surprises but not large ones. She had not the same conviction of having mapped Kevin. His bottomless anger made him unknowable. She could not be intimate with a volcano, or finally, with Kevin. Kevin did not always know what

Kevin would do, although after he had done it he would slap together a set of reasons. Because of his charisma, because of his temper, because of his brute strength, few people challenged his reasons; she had been one of the few to do so, wrenching herself slowly free of him, a Siamese twin slowly sawing through the bridge of bone and gristle night after night. Let me live my life, she thought, and never see him again, never face him across a room, a courtroom, a field, a ditch. We would kill each other.

Yet she shuddered when she thought of him still after so many years, and the mud of shame filled her throat. Wrong, somehow all wrong. A compulsion gone rotten. She was able to make doing the wash last until nine thirty, when the laundromat began to fill up. Then she loaded her pack again; discarded the newspaper, tearing up the relevant page, and set out at a brisk walk. She wanted to locate a good phone: one in a real booth, not likely to be tapped, not too conspicuous and in working order. She called the operator with a question about collect calls just to be sure the phone worked.

At five to ten she moved into the booth to make sure she had it at ten. Pretending to be talking to someone, she located the numbers for Natalie, translating the letter code in her head into digits. She never dared carry anything resembling an address book, but used scraps of paper with apparent notes on them. At ten on her watch she dialed the first of the numbers. It rang and rang. Six, seven times. She had to hang up. It was dangerous to let pay phones ring too long, because somebody would pick them up out of curiosity or annoyance, and it did not do to call attention that a particular pay phone would ring at certain intervals. She dialed the second number. Natalie had to be there. Again it rang, rang. On the sixth ring she hung up.

Checked her watch. Could she be fast? She would wait five minutes and try again. Natalie could be late. With kids anything could happen. Natalie's car wouldn't start. She got caught in every red light. Again Vida mimicked making a call until it was five after and she could try the numbers again. This time for a change of luck she dialed them in the reverse order: first the second, which again rang and rang. Then the first. She let it continue this time. Ah, an answer.

"Hey, who're you trying to call?" a male voice asked.

"Jimmy, is that Jimmy? Is Mom home?" Vida said quickly.

"You got the wrong number. This here's a drugstore, lady." He hung up.

So much for that today. Damn it, she was half tempted, but only half, to call Natalie's house. Where was she? Was something wrong? Had Natalie forgotten? No, not possible. Now Vida had to kill a day until tomorrow. She thought about taking the Long Island Rail Road into the city and descending on Hank, but she didn't want to. She felt nervous about him, a tingle of apprehension. That videotape in the drugstore; Kevin caught. No, she didn't want to go into the city to wait, but she had to see Natalie. She was missing Natalie all through. She wasn't scheduled to call into the Network until tomorrow, so they'd be of no help sheltering her overnight.

She wandered the pleasant old streets disconsolately, her fatigue sloshing in her limbs. Up since four thirty after maybe three hours' sleep, she was hungry, she was tired, she didn't relish hanging around all day with a pack on her back. She also didn't want to go sit in a restaurant and start pissing away the money Leigh had given her. A hairdresser's, a boutique, a thrift shop, a news dealer's, a health-food store. She paused. Health-food stores were useful for getting off the streets. She could usually chat with people working there, who wanted her to try their favorite diet or supplement. At least, she could lay her pack down and stand for a while reading a book on nutrition or a good herbal.

Alice and Eva and she had studied herbs and passed on what they learned to the other fugitives. In their yard in L.A. they grew thyme, rosemary, sage, comfrey, basil, horehound, fennel, lovage, sweet cicely, various mints. Herbs were cheaper than medicine and didn't require prescriptions. Mostly fugitives had to doctor each other. The Network had a couple of doctors they could trust—one in New York whom Vida had seen when her leg was infected, and another in Portland—but they could not overuse them. Mostly they learned what they could and practiced on one another.

In Los Angeles the three women roommates had lived on a child-care job Eva had and what Vida picked up from an off-the-books job with a local food co-op. All through the summer Alice had been too sick to work. She had caught the flu in the spring, she was anemic and she could not shake a cough. They ate a lot of brown rice, backyard vegetables and co-op surplus for the week—fifteen pounds of potatoes one week, fifteen pounds of carrots the next. Vida found it frightening to watch Alice grow weaker without being able to help. When Bill, Alice's boyfriend, came back from several months in Mexico, he had been shaken by her condition. The next day Bill and Vida broke a fugitive rule and shoplifted eight kinds of vitamin pills. After that Alice seemed to pick up and began spending part of the day sitting in the garden and sometimes felt well enough to weed or water.

This was a cozy store. Some health-food stores tried to look like pharmacies; they wanted to be scientific and respectable. Others wanted to be country stores with bins, big old-fashioned glass jars and long wooden counters. That was the style of this one, packed into a narrow slot between a pizzeria, not yet open for the day, and a news dealer's, where her picture was hidden in the piles of newspapers. A woman with a baby in a stroller was picking over the meager selection of organic vegetables, but once she had paid and left, Vida was alone in the store with the husky blond woman behind the counter.

She wandered around looking at the grains in their bins, the oils and syrups, the vitamin pills and natural cosmetics. As she passed the cash register she set down her pack casually, partly so the shopkeeper would not think she meant to boost anything but mostly to get it off her shoulders. That felt better. She was dizzy with hunger. The fragrance of the breads and nuts filled her mouth with saliva. She glanced at the counter but did not see a newspaper anyplace. She hoped the shopkeeper did not bother to read the papers daily.

The woman behind the counter dialed a number. Vida froze. Then she drifted closer, picking up a can of yeast as if to read the nutritional information.

"Hi, yeah, it's Rena. I thought you were going to come by last night. . . . You did too say that. . . . No, come on, I'm not guilt-tripping you, Sarah, I'm not. I just thought you said— . . . I did make cookies, the ones with the star anise, 'cause I thought you said you were coming by, and I just wanted it to be nice again between us. . . . Oh, never mind! . . . I didn't say that! . . . Goodbye yourself." Rena slammed the phone down.

No hidden messages. A lover lost, by the sound of it. She felt a pang of empathy that frightened her. She had not lost Leigh, just let the strength of the connection weaken a little. That was all. A momentary weakness.

"Are you looking for anything in particular?" Rena asked crossly.

Smiling she came to the counter. Of course I am. She wondered for a moment whether to pretend she had been in the store before, to establish herself as local, to call Rena by name and thus make the storekeeper believe she knew Vida. But another idea impelled her. Rena sounded as if she lived alone. She could admit to being a stranger and try for a place to sleep. "Oh, I was just drawn into the store. I grow a lot of herbs myself. I'm from L.A. . . . . What are these selenium tablets you have on the counter?"

"Wonderful stuff. It's a cancer preventative. . . ."

During the selenium spiel she examined Rena: about Vida's height, but on the heavyset side, with short thick ash blond hair chopped off in a Dutch-boy just beneath her ears. Her large eyes were honey brown behind silver-rimmed glasses tinted pale rose, and she wore overalls and an old blue-and-red ski sweater. Rena blinked and smiled frequently now, quickly, as if asking if she pleased, her voice high and whispery for a big woman. Not much confidence.

Rena was talking about laetrile. Vida briefly debated telling Rena that she had been part of a group running laetrile over the border from Mexico and then immediately dropped the idea. The story was true: Bill had worked out the connection that had supported them in 1978, before the last time she had come East. But high adventure did not seem the right approach. Instead Vida waited for an opening to nudge the conversation toward herbs. She needed to gain a little authority with Rena, but not to scare her. Most of Rena's information came from articles in the magazines put out by the supplement companies, who weren't interested in pushing herbs. Ah, here. . . .

"Yes, but thymol—that's an ingredient in some of the commercial cold remedies—it's oil of thyme. It's a good expectorant—helps you get the phlegm out." Really, flirting over phlegm! But Rena was paying attention now. Vida held forth, watching the shopkeeper carefully. She decided she could trust Rena enough to stay with her if she could manipulate Rena into offering shelter. "I'm East to visit my folks—they live in Philly —and I decided to come up to see an old friend of mine. I haven't been able to find her. I hear she got married and now she's separated, but I don't know her married name."

"What was her real name?"

"Billy Jo Feldman," Vida said on impulse, and into her head popped the image of that young lady, belle of the eighth grade with what was known then as a poodle cut. She had been snotty to Vida, and Vida had slapped her in the face and been sent to the principal's office. There Natalie had chased after her saying that Billy Jo deserved it, so that both of them had been ordered home—their new home together in disgrace that felt like victory.

"I don't think I know her. . . . Maybe . . . I've heard the name, I think."

"I know I can find her, if I can hang around for a day. I know where her cousin works. . . . I'd love to see Billy. We were real close for three years. . . . We had a little fight when she got married, but I never meant to lose track of her."

"It'd be real sad to come all this distance to see her and then go back to California and never find her. Billy Jo Feldman. I sure wish you luck. There's a Maxine Feldman comes in here sometimes to buy vitamins. Would that be her cousin?"

"No, her family's in New Jersey except for her cousin . . . Al. I just don't know what I'll do if I can't find her before night. . . . Is there a women's center or any place maybe there'd be some women who might put me up for a night? I was expecting to stay with Billy. . . . I wonder, if I can't find her . . . Maybe I could help you around the store today some? Clean up or unload or something? Then maybe I could sleep here? Just if I can't find her."

"Oh, you couldn't stay in the store. That'd get me in real trouble. . . ." Rena paused, looking doubtful.

Vida smiled into her honey brown eyes, waiting. Come on, you're lonely, how about a little company just for an evening? And suppose the lover you were fighting with on the phone calls or comes by, won't she be jealous? Do I look dangerous? "Just till I can find my friend . . . I'll give up if I can't find her by tomorrow. I have to get back to work."

"We don't have a women's center I ever heard about," Rena said. "But I'll tell you what. If you can't find Billy Jo, I guess I could put you up for a night."

"Really? That's generous of you! You don't even know me! . . . Can't I help you? I'd enjoy that. It's a real nice homey store you got here."

"Isn't it nice? I fixed it up myself. I have a lot of trouble with the landlord, but it's a mellow place. I like this kind of work. . . . Tell you what you can do. You could help me unpack crates in the back room. Then you could sweep up a bit."

At three Vida went out, presumably to look for Billy's cousin. The day was sunny and reasonably warm. Pulling on her poncho, she hiked to the town park on the bay where the locals without money went. The well heeled in their enclaves had their own beaches and their own police forces to patrol them and keep out the hoi polloi. The town park offered a broken monument to Theodore Roosevelt, for whom everything in Oyster Bay seemed to be named; gray gravel paths, some sad red, white and purple petunias, kids cutting school, old people sitting in the sun, the unemployed gazing at the horizon and local chess and checkers players on the inlaid cement tables.

She found a bench just inside the wall of pinkish stone that bounded the park from the water's edge of silt and grass. To her right a cabin cruiser was maneuvering out of the boat slip. What she meant to do was work on a position paper. She was analyzing the degree to which multinational corporations had become truly multinational, and what this internationalizing of capital meant to the Left, particularly if the U.S. was no longer the center of the empire. What did the flow of European and Arabic capital into this country mean? She had been researching the project in libraries in L.A. It was, of course, to be an internal paper to the Network. What else could she do with it? Unless she tried publishing it under a pseudonym? She played with that fantasy briefly, watching a boat being winched up. *Monthly Review*, say. It would feel so wonderful to have some impact out there. Like Eva's being able to perform her songs.

Reading through her notes, she caught herself yawning. How little sleep she had had last night! Years and years ago, in another life that was hers too, she had imagined herself an academic. She had chosen comparative literature—why? Why on earth? The gorgeous impracticality of it had seemed to her, child of a working-class childhood and middle-class adolescence, to prove that it was real learning. A different and better world. She had wanted to learn all tongues living and dead. "European and Arabic penetration into the capital-investment areas" she wrote "of . . . the United States" (briefly she debated writing Amerika, but she was tired of that end-of-sixties hard rhetoric, part of the attitudes she was arguing against) "represents a judgment that the labor situation here is under better control and is more malleable—"

Shadow on the page. She smoothed out the page, covering it, and let herself glance up. Awfully young to be trying to pick her up, so where was her purse? Out of sight under the poncho. Nothing to rip off he wouldn't have to knock her down to get.

He sat down on the bench, putting his arm along the back. "Hey, you waiting for somebody?"

"Yeah. My friend."

"Yeah?" He slid a little nearer and took something from his pocket. "You like to get high, uh? What do you like?"

"I don't smoke or blow anything. I am an ex–heroin addict," she said, and got up and started walking. That usually did it.

Behind her she heard him mutter, "Fucking cunt. A junkie!"

She walked briskly along the wall, past the flagpole to the end of the park and beyond to the town beach. Every time she saw an old man reading a newspaper, she felt a tremor. Her picture. Kevin in custody. Would he try to bolt for it? Would they give him a chance? Little kids were using the swings and slides behind the beach, but the water was empty. She took a seat at the picnic table nearest the water—rickety ill-used long-suffering tables in a grassless area studded with rusty grills standing on one leg like dying storks under squat oaks. The town was a little microcosm of her country: for those with money, everything, and precious little in the public sector. The waters of Oyster Bay were almost still. The muffled thunk of shrouds against aluminum masts from boats at anchor came to her like deadened bells.

Behind the park, trains were screeching and clanking with the noise of tortured metal. Old people sat in the sun trying to keep warm, staring at the bay. Black teen-agers fooled around with some fishing rods, passing butts and joints. The gulls screamed over the day's washed-in garbage. She fought off a bond of identity. All superfluous categories. The permanently unemployed and the superannuated. Seeing Leigh had not left her feeling strong this time. She felt old huddled on the bench, as if she had outlived her own times, a creature produced by an earlier conglomeration of demands, judgments, necessities, passions, crises. Like a salmon that had forced her way upstream to spawn, she lay dying in the backwaters.

Stop it! You and Leigh are engaged in the same struggle from different foci. That the whole might of the government has not been able to put you away is a victory. Every day you defeat them by continuing. How many years did Ho Chi Minh rot in prison? You are free: relish that. As you sit in the sun pitying yourself because your husband has a new woman nine years younger living in your home, in Brazil and Argentina, in Chile and South Africa women are being tortured to death. Never forget. The same war.

At closing time she strode back to the health-food store to meet Rena, hoping that supper was in the offing. Rena was locking up as she arrived, and she climbed into Rena's old Saab to ride to her house. Don't let it be East Norwich, Vida thought with sudden fear. East Norwich was where Natalie lived; therefore Vida could never go there.

Rena had a small white house nearby squeezed in between two bigger houses, sitting at the back of its lot. A long path led to the front door through the narrow but pretty yard. Marigolds orange and gold were still blooming among scarlet salvia, while tomatoes ripened on vines staked to the fence.

The interior startled her. She was prepared for tacky chaos—a bench leaking stuffing, some yellowing house plants hanging by frayed macrame —but the walls were covered with hangings, part tapestry, part sculpture, and the impression was of a woven nest of a house, a rich cave. "You made these?" Rena had to have made them; she could not have afforded to buy them.

"Do you like them any?" Rena waited for her exclamation of pleasure before she acknowledged her handiwork. "I love weaving. See, I've got three looms. That old one isn't set up now. I have to get it repaired. . . . Oh, I don't know what you'd call them. Just things I make. . . . Show them? You mean to people? . . . Oh, I can't imagine taking them . . . I mean my friends like them, sure, but you know how that is. . . . Well, I did once, but the guy said, Well, what are they?"

Most of the colors were natural browns, beiges, sand colors, rust, wheat, with occasional dull blues and earth reds. The throws that covered a couple of old chairs and a couch were nubbly to the touch, but the hangings were truly three-dimensional, with bits of wood embedded and outbursts of frizziness and pillowlike lumps and masses. . . . "Rena, I like them a lot. I'm no artist. But I travel around, I see things. And I think these are good. Really good. I think many women would like them."

"Really? You don't have to say that."

"But it's true. I can't believe you don't have more faith in them."

"They're so funny. I don't even know what to call them. They aren't rugs, they aren't pictures. When I tried to describe them to Ken—he has that arts-and-crafts shop—he made a face. They don't sound good, I guess."

"Call them sculptures in wool."

"It's not all wool. I use acrylics sometimes, and that's linen there—"

"Never mind the acrylics. Call them Natural Fiber Sculptures."

Rena was silent for a few minutes, mulling over the idea. "Do you really think people would like them better if I knew what to call them? If they had a name?"

"Yes," Vida said firmly. "Bet on it."

Rena had stopped on the way home to buy a bass from the local fish market—maybe caught off Montauk that weekend, Vida thought. Rena baked it, and they had bulgur wheat and a big salad from the kitchen garden. Vida chopped onions, washed greens and set the little table. The kitchen was a corner of the living room, as it had been at Hank's, but she felt more comfortable. They drank good apple juice from the store, and the food was delicious. Vida had been raw with hunger all day. She had eaten nothing since that nighttime breakfast beside the Montauk highway in Bridgehampton except some nuts and raisins and a battered apple. Rena was hungry too and perhaps also shy, so they ate seriously and mostly in silence.

"That was a really nice dinner." Vida cleared the table. "I mean it when I said I appreciate your bringing me back here with you. I'll do the dishes now."

"Ah, do them in a bit. Have some cookies. I made them yesterday."

The star anise cookies for Sarah.

"I'm glad to have the company," Rena went on. "Did you find your friend yet?"

"Not yet. But I have a lead for tomorrow. . . ." Now get *her* to talk. Let's not play out this search for Billy Jo any farther than I have to. "You seem a little sad, Rena. Is something wrong? Is something making you unhappy?"

"Do I seem sad? I guess I was hoping it didn't show. . . . I guess I'm depressed because, well, I had a fight with a real good friend of mine. . . ." It took Rena close to an hour to get around to telling Vida what she had learned from the overheard phone call, that Rena had recently broken up with another woman, Sarah. The house was comfortable and clean, even the bathroom warm and pleasant. Vida realized she had not been in a house that was so thoroughly female territory since she had left Los Angeles and the house with Eva and Alice she did not think she would return to. That decision did not ease her sudden nostalgia. Eva sat on a low wooden stool with one braid forward over her shoulder and one braid back and played and sang to her guitar, her own songs and other people's. They ate a simple supper out in the backyard under their own funny palm tree that Vida could never quite believe was real, shaggy and half brown as it was. A clean tablecloth on a telephone-company spool, flowers in a jam jar. Vida made a mushroom barley soup. . . .

"How do you travel?" Rena was asking. "Hitchhiking?"

"Sometimes. . . . Do *you* like to travel?"

"I always used to hitchhike, before I bought my car. A woman can take care of herself if she travels with another woman. Have you ever studied self-defense?"

"Oh, a little."

"You ought to, Vinnie. It's important for a woman to take care of herself. You have to be able to show somebody you mean business if they get funny."

It was hard for Vida to talk for a whole evening without drinking something, if only tea, but she did not want to ask for anything Rena did not offer. Finally, close to ten, Vida decided it was time to do the dishes and be sleepy.

But when she had cleaned the last pot, Rena was waiting for her. In the narrow confines between refrigerator and stove, Rena put her arms around Vida tentatively and then kissed her. Vida returned her kiss, but then stepped free.

"Have you ever . . . been involved with a woman?" Rena asked her, her hands dropping to her sides.

"I have a woman lover at home," Vida said. "And I used to be involved with Billy."

"I thought so. That's what I thought. You wanted so bad to find her."

Vida hated the storytelling. Rena was nice. Her face was unassumedly pleasant, her manner was gentle, she was a comfortable companion. She debated telling Rena that she was missing Eva, but she could not. It was true and false at once. So fresh from Leigh she could not play the complete lesbian. "But I've had relationships with men a lot too."

"You don't have to be defensive with me." Rena smiled, placing her hand tentatively on Vida's shoulder.

While it was true she missed Eva, she missed her as an old and close friend, as a comrade, a fellow soldier. She was not in love with Eva. Except for Leigh, she had not been sexually besotted, fully engaged with anyone in years, since the stinking end with Kevin.

Rena was saying, "If we're nice to each other, it doesn't take anything away from your love at home."

Vida stepped back a small step. She couldn't make love in a situation like this, for the distance she had to maintain was too great. "Rena, I wouldn't feel right . . . I like you a lot and I like being here with you. But I came to look for Billy. If I get romantically involved with somebody else, I won't find her, and I think maybe she needs me." Violins, please. She was such a fraud. Damn the stories. She started out with a small lie and then she had to build a city of lies. The more involved she got with somebody, the more elaborately she had to build. Then the farther she felt from them, walled in her own creation. It was the opposite of intimacy, and she could not endure it.

"You could work in the store for a while . . . stay here."

She was tempted: near Natalie, catching up on rest, not lonely; and lying day in and day out. "I can't, Rena. I just can't."

Rena looked hurt, blinking as she turned away. "I better see about making up a bed for you."

Vida took the sheets from her and made up the couch, aware she had hurt Rena, turned her generosity back on her. For a moment she despised her life, staying with strangers who had to remain strangers, who never knew how strange she was.

The next morning she helped Rena open the store and hung out until it was nearly time for her call. Then she set out to find a good phone booth. Ten on the dot. She dialed the first number. It was picked up on the second ring. "Hello?" a funny voice said, not Natalie's. Vida started to hang up. "Hello, Vinnie?"

She started with fear, looking quickly around. "Who is this?"

"This is the son of Emma, calling for Emma to Vinnie."

It was Sam, Natalie's son. Emma Goldman was one of Natalie's old pseudonyms. She remembered them signing in and out of university buildings, where she would sign Rosa Luxemburg and Nattie would sign Emma Goldman. "Is this the oldest son of Emma?"

Sam giggled. His voice was cracking. "Yeah. Now let me say this straight. She had me memorize it. It's too hot to meet her but I'm clean. Do you need money?"

"Sam, is anybody near you? Anybody listening? Do you know if you were followed?"

"Nobody. I was supercareful."

"Okay. Then talk normally. Just remember to call me Vinnie. Now what kind of heat? What's going on around here?"

"Mom thinks it's the Irish problem. Anyhow, we've been visited, and Mom was followed yesterday morning. So she didn't go to the booth."

"Tell her I'm not surprised that it stirred things up."

"Do you want to meet me? I'm supposed to ask, do you want any money?"

"I have enough for a while. Should we try next week?"

"She says, Yes, keep trying. She has a task for you."

"Good! Listen, Sam, tell her Mondays and then Tuesdays at the numbers next week, then on to the next week if she can't make it. Thanks for coming to talk to me. You know not to mention me to anybody except Natalie. Nobody!"

"I understand, Vinnie, don't worry! I grew up with all of this, I know how to take care." Sam sounded funny, reassuring her in his changing voice that broke deep and then high. "Peezie and Frankie are too little, and we don't tell Dad."

"Sam, I want to see you real bad. Maybe you can come with Natalie when we finally make it. I'm just a wee bit scared. I may have to keep away from here for a while. Kiss your mother for me."

He cleared his throat. "You be careful."

"You too, Sam. You're wonderful. I wish I could be a real aunt to you."

"Aw, come on, everybody has aunts. Mostly all they do is pat you and give you sweaters that don't fit and say, 'My, how you've grown,' " he mimicked in falsetto.

"See you soon." She hung up. She hated ending phone conversations with people she loved. Sam was an amazing kid. She walked toward the station, shifting the pack for comfort. At half past ten she had a call arranged to the "Studio," important because of Kevin's arrest and Sam's news. It was dangerous to hang around Natalie's part of Long Island with surveillance active, and she went straight to the train station to find out the schedule. It wasn't a very long wait. If the train ran late, she would have time to make the call; if not, she would have to skip it. At ten thirty she was waiting on the platform for the train to finish backing and filling and got onto the phone there. It was not in a closed booth, but nobody was near enough to listen.

"Peregrine here," she said. Her political pseudonym.

"This is Birdman broadcasting. Where're you?" A familiar male voice spread warmth through her. A slight flat drawl to it, Midwestern. Familiar, dear.

It was Larkin. What was he doing in Minneapolis? "I'm in Long Island, old dear, but I'm getting out any second, when I can. A lot of heat here. Some suspicion it has to do with events around"—for a moment she blanked out Kevin's old pseudonym—"around Jesse."

"Hmmm. More trouble than he ever was worth," Larkin said sourly. He too had not forgiven Kevin. "Maybe you better go to ground for a spell."

"I'd like that."

"Go to Lady Doc in Bulltown. You know Lady Doc?"

"Mmmm. Is she in the phone book?"

"How else would she practice, Perry? She'll tuck you in for a spell. Now, if she fails somehow—"

The train was loading. "Bye, Birdman. I'll ground myself if she can't." She hung up and ran for the car, feeling as if she were dragging an umbilical cord from the phone. On her own now. She gripped her ticket and found a seat alone at a window. She was off to Boston, where she hoped Laura Kearney would shelter her for a week or two.

Larkin. If she came East permanently, she would have to make up her mind about him—something she had been avoiding for four years, since she had parted finally with Kevin. She felt Lark's frail wiriness and spun-steel will and experienced that mixture of compassion, attraction and uneasiness he always stirred up in her. He had been in Cincinnati just before her, but they had missed each other by a day. She would see him soon enough, since there was work to do before the Board met. She sighed. Could she get Leigh to come up to Boston? It was only slightly farther than Philadelphia. Except for the weekend with Leigh she had been emotionally alone since the summer, and she was tired, with a deep and pervasive hunger of the senses and the heart that must stay unfed. Two people down the coach were reading newspapers: touch of danger. She retired her face behind her own.

So Natalie had a task for her: excellent. An immediate political task would lighten her mood, till she could connect with the Network again, and do her much more good than hanging around libraries doing research on capital flow. Not that she did not enjoy libraries: they soothed and stimulated her at once, like one of Natalie's good tisanes. But she could have become a scholar by staying in the university instead of running off to marry Vasos, and a fugitive scholar was a bizarre notion. She needed a job to do, not set by herself, to feel part of the world of working people.

5

Laura Kearney, a divorced pediatrician whose son had died of leukemia she blamed on radiation, sheltered fugitives for a set period of up to two weeks per visit, as long as they were political. Vida had once lived for a week in her basement in Newton, in a former coal bin fixed up as a sub rosa guest room. She expected to be put up, or down, there again.

Instead Laura drove her out to Cape Cod. "I'm taking you to my summer home."

"I'm nervous about off-season places. Berrigan got caught on Block Island."

"He was living pretty openly, wasn't he? You're safe at my house. Just don't hang around town. It's a couple of miles. I've stocked the place with food, and I'm leaving more with you. Oh, you'll have a housemate."

"Who?" She felt a rush of anxiety, huddling against her side of the car staring at the headlights eating into the dark highway.

"A very nice young man. I didn't ask his name any more than I ask yours."

It could be anyone she knew or anyone she didn't, a plant, an agent. Did the Network know he was here? She balked at the idea of being dumped in the woods with some strange man and left to manage as best she could. "Why can't I just stay in the city?"

"Really, the accommodations here are much pleasanter than in my cellar. Don't worry about that young man. He seems quite well mannered. I'm sure he won't bother you. The house is big enough so that you needn't get in each other's way."

At a little after nine, Laura turned off the highway and began driving on a pair of sand ruts through pine and oak woods. The road was dark and bumpy. The Datsun slithered into dips and thunked its muffler on exposed roots. The sky had clouded over, and the woods pushed in on the narrow road, black and uninviting. They passed an occasional cabin, dark too. To their right she saw faint sky shine reflecting off the waters of a pond. The Datsun labored up a steep hill and over a bump. Then she saw another pond to their left. They drove along it high on a wooded bluff. One house showed its lights at each end of the oval pond. Laura gestured at the far lights. "That's my house."

"Doesn't it seem conspicuous?"

"A burglar wouldn't turn the lights on. I told the local police I'd be using my house all fall, so they won't be excited at someone being there."

"Who's at this end?"

"She teaches the second grade. He's a carpenter. They have three kids, name of Kensington. They live here year round. They won't bother you." Laura turned sharply left and they bumped along a road in even worse shape, the bottom of the car scraping on the overgrown middle as the wheels struggled in the deeply eroded ruts. "We're almost there."

"Do you ever get stuck?"

"Oh, in the winter. I've ruined a muffler or two." Laura sounded cheerful. Vida could see the lights again through the trees. Suddenly they went out. Laura pulled into a driveway to park. "We need to walk down to the house—it's on the water. Could you take a bag of groceries?"

Laura strode ahead whistling and swinging her keys by a finger. Vida, carrying two sacks and her pack on her back, clambered awkwardly down the rough stairs of railway ties and sand after her. The house was a log cabin with a wide deck around it, the pond glimmering dully like pewter just beyond.

"Hello, hello!" Laura was calling. The man must be hiding. "It's me, Laura," she shouted, sounding amused. How our precautions amuse them; Leigh was the same way. Forgetting to call me Vinnie, as if it were an arbitrary demand without foundation, yet they'd be furious if we endangered them. He, whoever he is, must be frightened in the dark watching us.

Laura went into the house turning on lights, switching on the outdoor floodlights, calling in the tone of voice she might use to a child, a patient, "It's all right. Hello there, wherever you are. It's me, Laura, and a friend who's come here to stay. Hello?"

Vida felt wary about walking into the light but the bags were heavy, and finally she lurched forward to rest them on the kitchen counter. A man came out of the woods and shambled toward them. He was not tall, perhaps exactly her height with dark hair. He was wearing a black T-shirt underneath a denim jacket and jeans with his hands shoved in the pockets. Slowly he came toward them, climbed the deck and pushed open the sliding glass door.

"Hi," he said with a small gritted smile. He stared at Vida. "I wasn't expecting company."

"Sorry to surprise you, but with the phone disconnected, there's no way to get in touch. She's in the same boat you are. She'll be staying here." Laura turned, not bothering to take off her coat or gloves. "You should both come out to the car with me to carry the groceries. I want you to have enough food. Then I must be off."

They stumbled up the log steps from the squares of light thrown by the house, into the darkness beyond where the car waited. Then Laura gave Vida a key to the house, instructions for returning it if she left in a hurry. At once Laura drove back along the road. In a few minutes they could see the headlights touching the trees across the lake as they stood side by side, the groceries at their feet, before he led the way back to the house.

First they put away the food. "Aw, coffee, that's good. Didn't have none," he said appreciatively. He had a pleasant voice—not butterscotch like Leigh's, but warm. Not Eastern. Not Midwestern either. What? She wasn't sure yet. "Sardines, canned chicken, ham. She ain't exactly the warmest woman I ever met, but she does right by you. There's still veggies out in the garden, too." He turned and looked her in the eyes.

"You have green eyes too!" she said in surprise, and then was angry at herself because it sounded flirtatious. "It's cold in here," she added irritably. "I don't suppose you're cold?"

"Would you like a fire? Matter of fact, that's all we got to heat this cabin—the fireplace and a wood stove."

"I'm cold and tired. I had to hang around Boston for hours till she could meet me. . . . I could use a bath. Is there hot water, or is that disconnected?"

"I turned it on. Look around, it's a pretty cabin. We're smack on the lake. A sandy beach at our door. I even went swimming this morning."

"Swimming?" she shuddered. "Did you cut a hole in the ice?"

"Water was warmer than the air. I like to get exercise."

"Where's the john?" At last she would be alone, relax.

He pointed the way. "Want some fresh coffee when you hop out?"

She didn't. She wanted to sleep; but she had better wake up, battle her fatigue and figure out who this kid was before she rested. It was indulgence to bathe first, but she could not find the strength to deal with him until she had somewhat collected herself. With real satisfaction she locked herself in the bathroom, stripped and ran the water good and hot.

She took a long soak, washing herself slowly, trying to blot anxiety from her mind for this interval. She needed sleep, she needed rest, she needed quiet and safety. Her back ached from too many nights on couches. The last time she had stayed someplace was a week with Saul and Dee Dee in Cincinnati, where she and Bill (who was on his way back to L.A.) had run a workshop on how to do pirate TV actions for the five fugitives in the area. That was the last time she had unpacked, relaxed and done some political work. She felt crazed with traveling, bumping warily against strangers, weaving a veil of lies and dancing within, moving, constantly moving.

Green eyes—that clear hard green. Suddenly she knew him. She sighed profoundly and slid into the water with a shiver of relief. Joel his name was, Joel White. He was a kid who hadn't made C.O. and had deserted when he was nineteen and been a fugitive since. He'd hung around with Jimmy. Joel wasn't really in the Network but one of that much larger group who loosely related to it. Jimmy and he had traveled together before Jimmy settled at Hardscrabble Hill with Kevin and her. Joel was okay, then; he had been under a long time, and he was safe. Only what connection might he have with Kevin? She had to feel that out.

When the water had lost its warmth, she got out of the tub reluctantly and cleaned it, dried herself. She did not want to put on the same dirty clothes. No, a clean pair of cords and her funky moss green velour top. A squirt of Laura's Femme cologne from the medicine cabinet pricked up her spirits.

Coming out, she scanned the house, a log cabin but hardly Lincoln-esque. The floor was pine in the bedrooms and slate of various subdued colors in the kitchen and huge living room, while heavier slabs of the same stone faced the fireplace. Two walls of the living room were glass, the third wood paneling, and the fourth was open to the sizable kitchen. The furniture was rattan. A settee heaped with plush cushions faced the fire he had built. At one end of the settee he was waiting, one leg crossed over the other. On the coffee table he had placed a tray with the hot coffee in a heavy blue ceramic pitcher, cream in a jug, a sugar bowl and two mugs and spoons. Beside that apparatus stood a bottle of Johnnie Walker red and a couple of glasses with ice in them. "Dug that up too. I figured you might go for it. I sure do."

Wavering, she wanted to take the chair, well away from him to inspect him better, but that would represent obvious avoidance after the way he had set things up. She settled for curling at the other end of the none-too-wide settee with her legs brought up between them. "I'll have a little, Joel."

"Didn't think you knew me!" He grinned. "I recognized you immediately. Vida Asch."

VIDA

He seemed to enjoy saying her name, while she experienced an automatic spurt of cold along her arteries. In contrast, he had been flattered when she called him by name—not frightened or at least startled as she had expected. That had not given her the commanding edge she had anticipated, but rather had eliminated some small advantage she had not been aware of. "I'm not sure we should be finishing her Scotch."

"I don't think she's a heavy drinker. The bottles had cobwebs running between them."

"We scared you when we drove up."

He ignored that probe. "I'm not a big Scotch drinker. Like sour mash better."

"So do I."

"Yeah? I always think of New Yorkers drinking Scotch."

"I was born in Cleveland, and I finished growing up in Chicago. Where're you from?" She wanted to place that voice.

"Born in New Jersey. Family moved to North Carolina. Then at fifteen, to Sacramento."

"Such a cosmopolitan upbringing!"

"We both know there's nothing cosmopolitan about Passaic, Roanoke Falls and Sacramento." He raised his eyebrows at her, over his glass. His hair was black and thickly wavy and his complexion ruddy through the remains of what had been a dark tan. He looked contagiously healthy. He was not slight, as he had seemed at first in his boyish faltering approach, but solidly built, muscular, although his features were delicately made: a small slightly puckered arrogant mouth, beautiful ivory teeth, a well-modeled flaring nose, arched brows, a perfect lightly cleft chin. His manner of speaking was emphatic, almost flirtatious. Oh, he's gay, she realized, of course. That was the nice tea tray with the coffee, the cups, the Scotch, the air of elegance as he sat there in worn denims with a soiled bandage on his left hand. Probably he had been lovers with Jimmy. She should have guessed that earlier. She relaxed against the back of the settee, letting her spine sag. Nothing to worry about, then.

"So we're both from the provinces," he said.

"Exactly." She nodded. "I remember seeing New York for the first time and wanting it, wanting it the way you want somebody gorgeous you see at a party, some guy you see dancing."

He smiled very slightly and knelt to put another log on the fire. "We danced together at Wichita."

"You and I?"

"Oh. You don't remember. Why should you?" He was pouting, drawn up aloof on the couch again. He rattled the ice cubes in his glass and poured in more Scotch.

What vanity! What a perfectly self-centered kittenish puffball! Ugh—

and she would have to get along with him for however long she stayed here. Then she remembered he was a fugitive too. He was not sheltering her. She was not forced to get on with him any more desperately than he must get on with her. It was equal! How delightful: she was free to dislike him if she wanted to. They could divide up the house and ignore one another. They were of no use to each other whatsoever. How marvelous and unusual it was. She didn't have to please him, she didn't have to take care not to step on his prejudices, she didn't need to extract help or money or transportation or information or message delivery or mail drop or anything at all out of him. They could fight. They could scream. They could take out their ill temper on each other because neither had any power. The only people with whom she ever let out feelings were her real family when she saw them, and sometimes, as with Leigh, she had to be cautious even there. The Network was artificial family. You could let out feelings, yes, but you were stuck with each other till death or disaster parted you. When a divorce occurred, as it had with Kevin, the result was possibly lethal.

He was glancing at her with that pout. She asked, "There are no houses near this one?"

"She's got neighbors to both sides—you'll see when you walk around —but they're boarded up for the winter."

"How long have you been here?"

"I thought we weren't supposed to ask each other questions like that? Never mind. What day is this?"

"Tuesday night."

"Since last Friday. . . . I think she has a boyfriend at her house in Newton and that's why she toted us out here. We had to turn on the water and open up the house, and all the time she was in an awful hurry to rush back."

She finished her drink and let the coffee stand. "I'm going to bed. . . . Where have you been sleeping?" She added quickly, "I don't care which bedroom I take."

"I've been sleeping in my bag in front of the stove." He pointed to the wood-burning stove between the living room and the kitchen. "It gets pretty damn cold."

"I'll put on a lot of covers."

The bed was double and covered with an Appalachian quilt. She checked that the window opened and that she could pry herself out through it if she had to. Undressing swiftly, she launched herself into the iron-cold sheets. Immediately her teeth began to chatter as she curled into a ball. He was right: the room was appallingly cold. Her body felt as if the warmth were seeping from it. Weary as she was the cold kept her awake, but she would not go in there with him. She did not want his company. She stayed in the double bed on the Great Greenland Ice Shelf and froze.

As sun warmed the house in the morning, she slept late. She was exhausted through and through, and what was there to get up for? She recognized that she was close to an emotional bottom and must coddle herself. It happened from time to time; it happened. She did not want to get up and face the day, him, her life, anything. Leigh with his new all-too-serious affair. Surveillance on Natalie. What the hell was the Network doing with itself? Marking time. Generating rhetoric like an antiquated wind machine in the desert. She had been in the forefront of a movement that had blown away. Her days were spent in simple survival. It was fine for Larkin; he lived on victories in Angola and Afghanistan. It was fine for Kiley; she lived on abstractions. How did Eva manage? Gently, Eva and Alice and she had kept one another intact, but survival was not enough. Their little actions felt paltry to her. She could not live on distant struggles.

Finally she realized she was smelling coffee and eggs, and she promised herself another hot bath. In L.A. Eva and Alice and she had a tiny gas heater. In a day it was possible to generate enough hot water morning and night for one bath or one shower or one dishwashing or one clothes washing in the sink. Therefore, at most she could bathe every two days. Traveling, she had often had to go longer. Her skin crawled. Leigh had once told her she kept her pussy so clean a crab couldn't find it on a dark night; certainly she was used to being called fastidious. Hot water was her favorite luxury.

In the kitchen, the wood stove was stoked up. Joel had made coffee and juice. He was sitting at the table mending his spare pants, where a seam had opened in the crotch. A real domestic type.

"Would you like me to scramble you some eggs?" he offered.

"Oh, I can do it." Better than he, she suspected, for from the evidence of the pan he cooked eggs on too high a flame.

Breakfast was a nice quiet meal, but he seemed disturbed by the silence and finally began to make conversation as she sipped her coffee. "Worst thing for me is no TV. No radio, even. No papers. You can't find out what's happening."

Her first impulse was to mock him: poor child, baby-sat by television. But then she realized that she was deprived of any news about Kevin. "That's not good," she said more agreeable than she had intended. "It makes me nervous too."

"Not that there'd be a thing about me," he added defensively. "But I mind feeling cut off. That's an occupational hazard anyhow, feeling out of it." He got up to feed the stove. "We need more wood. It's been keeping itself chilly."

"You can say that again."

"Oh, you were cold last night." He grinned.

"Where do we get the wood?"

"In the woods. It grows there." He was enjoying himself now, playing man of nature. "I'll take care of it. I'll get to work chopping."

"Look, I know how to use an ax. If you don't, you can leave it to me," she said firmly. Don't tell me even this one is going to try to play macho! "I lived on a farm where we had nothing to keep us from freezing to death but three wood stoves."

"Then we'll both chop," he said very gently, reproving her for her vehemence. "The tools are in the shed. That was Hardscrabble Hill, wasn't it?"

She stared at him with the fear back.

"Look, I used to live not far from there. I worked on their cars. Couple of winters ago I stayed there for a while. Tequila and Marti talked about you."

Enough branches in the woods had broken, enough trees had toppled in the storms of the summer and the winter and probably the winter before and the winter before that, so that they could chop downed timber. They worked for two hours and then hauled the wood back. How long had it been since she'd done that much labor? He was a good worker, and in the woods she liked him better, although she guessed he was no more bred to such labor than she was. Probably he'd picked it up the way she had, holing up some winter on an isolated farm. . . . "Do you know Kevin?" she asked suddenly.

His face closed a little. "I know him. . . . Not well. Your old man, wasn't he?"

"Not in a long, long time. He got busted, you know?"

"No! When?"

Of course. He'd been here since Friday night. "I heard it Saturday."

"You must be real upset?" He looked over his shoulder at her as he carried his pile of logs.

The small of her back hurt dully and then sharply. She could feel another pulled muscle in her left shoulder. She could hardly walk upright. For too long she had not used her muscles, not since she had dug the garden in Los Angeles. He was still waiting for an answer, the logs on the pile and his arms hanging loose at his sides.

She dumped her logs. "Not in a personal way. Look, Kevin and I hate each other. But I don't want him busted."

"I don't want to hate anybody I've been close to. Even somebody who left me. I mean, I guess I want her to suffer some the way she made me suffer, but that's not hating. Just a little desire for revenge." Tipping back his head on its short neck, he laughed. "Would you like to kill him? Is that what you mean by hating?"

Turning away, she scowled at the bright blue water. Sun struck the small brisk waves, firing them. "I suppose I mean the opposite of love. What love that turns bad turns into."

"Isn't that just pain?"

"No. Though there's pain in it. Kevin has to control a woman."

"He likes to control men too," Joel said lightly. "He likes that a lot."

"Did you love Jimmy?"

Now it was his turn to look away from her to the pond. "I guess so. He was hard to love. He hated himself so much."

"Didn't he!" She was touched by the justice of what he said.

"We had a kind of sexual relationship, but Jimmy didn't like sex all that much, and I'm basically heterosexual. It's hard for me to make it with a man, and if he's having trouble with it too, it's a lost cause. . . . He wouldn't let himself be tender. But when they got him . . ."

"Did you watch?" she asked compulsively.

"Yeah."

They looked at each other. He said, "I was in a redneck bar in Detroit —I can say that because in a way that's who I am, a misfit Jewish redneck. They shot him right on TV, and I went in the john and threw up. I just kept puking, though I hadn't drunk but two beers."

"I was in Philadelphia. I was living with a . . . friend part time, but he wasn't there that night." Suddenly she felt as if she could admit her fatigue. "My back's killing me. After all, I'm a lot older than you. I think I'll take yet another hot bath."

"Sure. Then I'll give you a massage. I give great massages. Kiley taught me."

"Oh, she did." She tried to remember exactly what she had heard about Joel. Had he been with Kiley in Wichita?

"But you didn't say what you meant by hating Kevin."

"Let's talk about it later." He was pushing her, she realized. She drew back, not so much repulsed as startled. Yet dragging her sore body away, she realized she was enjoying herself. It was a relief to be with another fugitive. She observed cautions, such as not mentioning Leigh's name, but such censorship was so slight, compared with the reticence with others, that their talk felt yeasty and spontaneous.

When she came back, he had built fires in the wood stove and in the fireplace. "Actually, if the fire wasn't so pretty, it'd make sense to block up the fireplace," he said. "We lose more heat up the chimney than we get from the fire. . . . That's a pretty dress. You look beautiful."

"Sure," she said sardonically. It was the blue dress. "I used to, anyhow."

"How come you don't believe me?"

"The way my back feels, I'm an arthritic old woman."

"Let me give you the massage I promised. Really, I'm good."

" 'Cause Kiley taught you?" She was teasing, curious.

"She gives a mean back rub."

Kiley had been a fugitive almost as long as Vida had, and along with Kevin and Vida and Larkin and Jimmy, she had been involved in founding the Network. She was a tight-bodied small blond Wasp from a family that owned a department store in Waukegan; she had gone to Radcliffe; she was very bright, articulate, five years younger than Vida and never more in love than she could easily handle. She was tough and charismatic, and Vida had had good times and bad times with her. Always, though, Vida had been a little, a little jealous of Kiley, to whom so much seemed to come easily. An underground anecdote told about a bombing Kiley had taken part in that had had just about everything go wrong with it that could, with final success—an anecdote about a bunch of fugitives trapped in a basement under their own bomb. It had as a punch line "And then Kiley began to sweat. Two drops." "Were you involved with her?"

He grimaced. "Yeah. But was she involved with me? You want a massage?"

She felt absurdly hesitant. "Why not?" Actually, she could think of several reasons, but they made her feel silly. She lay on her belly on the braided rug before the fireplace and he straddled her, applying his weight carefully to one segment and then another of her spine. "Where does it hurt?"

"Ow. There. There too. Yes! . . . I guess all over."

"I'd do a better job if you took that dress off."

The wool rubbing on her skin irritated, but she was sorry she had agreed to the massage, fast becoming too intimate. At the same time, she would feel stupid if she demurred over taking off her dress. What did he care? Matter-of-factly, trying to look bored, she rose to her knees, pulled the dress over her head and folded it gently on the settee.

Again he straddled her and began to work. He did give her a good massage. Relaxing under the strength and knowledge of his hands, she began to enjoy it, but also to become conscious of the body set on hers. So damned quasi-sexual, massage was one of those counterculture gray areas. A back rub wasn't supposed to be sexual: it was supposed to be sensual; but who drew those lines? They weren't drawn on her body. His thighs pressing her flanks excited her. Carefully she controlled her breathing. Her nipples itched, pressing into the rag rug. She suffered a ridiculous fear that he could guess she was excited. Say no to all back rubs. That was how she had happened to make love with Eva the first time. The better the back rub, the less likely she was to stop with having her back rubbed.

Did he have an erection? But why would he? Getting your back massaged was exciting, but massaging somebody was hard work. When he paused, she said, "Thanks enormously. That really helped!" She flexed her muscles as if to rise, so that he released her and backed off.

Dress in hand, she hastened to her room. A little shaken, she wondered at her volatility. That had belonged to a previous life. She had thought herself grown cold and rational and slow in the senses. No more back rubs! She stayed in her room reading an old *Natural History* magazine about parasites in western Africa and then about the life of the tree frog. She forgot her own life completely, let go of her worries and her obsessions and her political concerns and floated in fascinating and irrelevant knowledge, a back rub of the mind with no erotic side effects.

When she ventured out, he was in the kitchen. "I'll make supper," he offered. "I took out this chicken to defrost, and now I'm cutting it up."

"Fine," she said. "I'll make supper tomorrow."

He smiled into her eyes as if she had said something marvelous. "Great!"

Let's see, suppose he was nineteen in 1972. He'd be twenty-six now. Susannah's age! Leigh was involved with someone the same age as Joel? She was subtly shocked. Kiley was thirty-one, so he must not be incapable of being interested in an older woman. After all, she had no competition here in the piny woods. He could even be twenty-seven, but no way could she stretch his age farther. "I'm going to take a walk, then. Which way is the ocean?"

He pointed. "Be back around six."

Walking helped her back. The oaks had begun to brown spottily but the beeches and maples had turned to towering torches, and the first fallen leaves brightened the ground. As she approached the ocean, the trees, tall near the ponds, dwarfed till only small scrub oaks stood up, and then nothing but grass blew on the dunes. The wind smote her, but she found a sheltered alcove of sand. The shadows were lengthening blue toward the water, the air felt chilly, but crouching with her eyes on the horizon, she felt better. The ocean calmed her, quieted the silly buzz of desire, dispersed that dangerous gathering energy. She must sit tight here till she could talk to Natalie or until the Network told her to break cover.

Natalie had a new task for her. To be useful would build her spirits. Once it had been a matter of recovering some seized documents on the battered women's shelter. Years before it had been helping a runaway. Another time it had been a matter of dealing with a rapist known to women along the North Shore as the Stocking Man, for the nylon stocking he wore over his face. Women had tracked him down and identified him as an Olds dealer, but the police could not or would not prosecute. He specialized in baby-sitters.

That was the only time Kevin had been involved, which placed it in time neatly: 1973. With nylon stockings pulled over their faces they had let themselves into his office, catching him as he was leaving work. Kevin had raped him, an act she had thought rather fitting, although the dealer did not. That had been the end of the Stocking Rapes. Kevin had perhaps enjoyed it a little too much, but she, to whom Natalie had described the bleeding and battered young women, knew that she would have found it in herself to kill him, if that had been asked. She saw that in herself as a fact, observed it. Were they beating Kevin now? His having worked with the IRA lately might do him some good in New York; there were still Irish cops. It might save his butt from savaging.

She came back to the house calm and hungry. What could Joel give or take from her? Nothing much. As she came in from the fresh piny cold, the house smelled of chicken basted with lemon and broiled, of home fries, of wood smoke. "You want to toss the salad?" He winked at her. "You just got back in time. It's after six, and this dinner is hopping ready."

As they sat at the round glass-topped table on rattan chairs looking onto the darkening pond, the lights of a house at the far end, the mauve tint of the last vibrations of a quiet cloudless sunset, she tasted melancholy like a steely dry wine on her palate. A mock couple, they sat down to eat. How much easier it would be if she were alone here, and how beautiful if she were alone with Leigh. Would she ever have that again— Leigh with her as an ordinary couple sharing quarters, meals, at least part of a life? How awkward to be dumped into a false intimacy with someone so ill suited to her, puppy and alley cat keeping house. She noticed he had put candles on the table, their almond flames wavering in the twilight. "Candles! You like that sort of thing, don't you?"

"Don't you?" He made a defensive grimace. "Anyhow, they're here. How much work is it to light a match?"

She was being cruel. He could not help that he wasn't Leigh. "The way you set out the coffee last night. And supper tonight. It just strikes me. I'm not attacking—it's nice."

"You think so? Really? I like to make things nice, if I can. How much comfort do we ever get?"

He was not Leigh, who wanted the very best wine, the best sturgeon, but would not care if he ate them on the floor. He preferred plastic dishes, because they didn't break and were easy to wash and moreover, he thought them a proletarian taste. He liked to combine high-bourgeois tastes with proletarian preferences. Thinking of him, she felt a little desolate, a little abandoned. But contact had been reestablished, and she must push to see him soon. In the meantime here she was in a cozier oasis than she had seen in long traveling. Much better chicken over-cooked a bit and drunk with water in the company of a fellow wayfaring stranger and harried exile than perfect poulet aux herbes de Provence and Pouilly-Fuissé with Hank the Bank. Leigh had a rhyme about him in the old fundraising days:

> Hank the Bank
> He's long and lank.
> Turn his crank
> Till the money comes out.
> But it doesn't.

Always been tight. She had more in common with this young stranger.

After supper, they sat by the fire sipping coffee and some bourbon from a dusty bottle of Jim Beam. "If tomorrow's nice, we should take a walk," he said. "Get some exercise."

She reflected that from her point of view they'd got plenty today, but amiably she agreed. The evening wore on. Together they looked at a picture book of photographs of American Indians taken in the nineteenth century. The heavy book was spread across both laps while their thighs touched. It was not boredom that made the evening interminable, but wondering if anything was going to happen between them. She didn't want to spend another cold night alone. If they slept together, if that proved nice, this might be an even more pleasant interlude. Probably they would meet again in another three or four years. She planned to stay put in the house until she called Natalie from some pay phone she could hike to on Monday morning. Warm against her, his thigh did not move away. He seemed very animated leaning over the book. Perhaps he was nervous fearing she would want him to sleep with her; perhaps he was nervous fearing she wouldn't. He could also be nervous for ordinary fugitive reasons, as this house on a sand road offered no easy exit. They could hardly escape across the pond in a canoe.

They took turns piling wood on the fire and poking it and feeding the wood stove, which gave out ten times as much heat as the fireplace. Then they pored over a local Geodesic Survey map and planned a tentative walk. After they had finished looking at the picture book and then the map, there seemed no excuse for continuing to sit thigh to thigh. When she got up to feed the stove, she positioned herself at a more discreet distance. Nothing was moving forward. He must not be interested; or perhaps he was gay in spite of Kiley.

He sewed a button on his jeans jacket. She fetched pants Eva had given her from a thrift shop, good khaki pants about two inches too long. Her own legs were long enough; the pants must have belonged to a grasshopper. After a while he frowned at her ragged stitching. "You must hate to sew," he said.

"Right. It drives me crazy. It's so . . . deentsy. I'm always stabbing myself."

"That's what thimbles are for." He took the pants from her. "It'll show through. Want me to do it for you?"

"Absolutely!" she said. "My sister can sew. I used to start projects I wanted done, like trying to re-cover cushions on a bench—this is when I had a gorgeous apartment in New York—knowing that Natalie would take them away from me. I'd be doing such a rotten job she couldn't stand it, just like you. Whereas if I'd asked her, she'd have said she was too busy to do it, but she'd teach me. You see?"

"I thought you came from Chicago."

"Natalie moved to New York before I did. After my first marriage broke up, I came there partly because she was there already."

"You've been married?"

"Twice. You've never been married?"

"I lived with a girl for almost two years, before I had to skip. Out in Sacramento. She politicized me. And Kiley and I, well, we had some kind of thing for nearly two years. . . . Two years must be my sticking point —or unsticking point, when everything comes unstuck."

Small items of data were cautiously given and greedily considered. Probably neither of them was lying, which was without doubt unusual. But they were talking less. "No more," she said when he lifted the bourbon. He did not take more either. The fire was dying to coals. How long could they sit yawning? How long could she wait up for nothing to happen? She stifled a yawn, maneuvering a glance at her watch. Midnight.

"Why don't we turn out the lights and just have the fire?"

"Fine." Then she'd doze off waiting. Just fine. She must not appear to pressure him, because they had to survive this week and any awkwardness could loom immense.

He turned off the lamp, stood over the fire looking into it for a long time. She stuck out her tongue at his turned back. Finally he cleared his throat. She waited. He did not say anything. Instead, he sat down on the settee at the same distance with a small sigh—of contentment? Anguish? Fatigue? "What are you thinking?" she ventured.

"Nothing much."

This was getting sillier. The hell with it. "I guess we, I, should go to bed. It's past twelve. . . ." She did not move.

"Yeah . . . Well, would you like company? It's stone cold."

"Yes, it's cold. Yes, I mean I'd like company."

Tentatively he put his arm around her shoulders. Then he laughed. "We're both so stiff. Feels like those awful parties in seventh grade when you begin necking, and all you can think is, are you doing it all wrong?"

She laughed too, gratefully. "How is either of us supposed to mind-read? When nobody's being piggy or pushing, it's hard to read through the politeness."

"I do want to go to bed with you. . . . I wanted to when we danced together two years ago, that time you don't even remember."

"That isn't true, Joel. It came back to me today from watching you." She did have a vague memory now, too generalized to be reliable. She would not have been open to anybody then; besides, looking at his face in the firelight, she suspected that he was a man becoming more attractive as the softness of adolescence wore through. Confidence had to replace diffidence before he could carry his finely modeled face boldly.

His hand was surer on her shoulder as they turned to kiss. His mouth was soft but knowledgeable on hers, his tongue touching hers in small darts as if beginning to taste her. She felt relaxed, committed, curious. No more decisions. When they got up, she would put in her diaphragm. It was in her pack, in the inner pocket with a new tube of jelly she had bought for Leigh. Who, after all, was with Susannah.

The bathroom felt cold as she put in the diaphragm, and the bed was too cold. They both undressed like a speeded-up old movie, tearing off clothes, flinging them, not from passion but from chill. On the slab of glacial sheets, their bodies met seeking comfort. Sleek, his skin, fine-grained and sleek. After Leigh's body she noticed his lack of hair. As her hands moved over him, she kept wanting to see him, but that would have to wait. He felt good, his body compact, muscular, beautifully propor-tioned, no more than five feet seven but built to last. Strong thighs, strong shoulders, strong arms, all with a satiny surface resilient as the flanks of a horse. Against her he was erect, making her breath catch.

Shyly he nuzzled her breasts. "Do you like that?"

She laughed breathily. "Of course."

"Some women don't." He tongued her nipple.

"This woman does. My breasts are very sensitive."

"Am I doing it too hard?"

"Not sensitive *bad*." When she got excited, she liked having her breasts squeezed, but she was hardly about to set out presenting him with a set of instructions as if she were a mechanical squirrel-resistant bird feeder to be assembled. "Sensitive for pleasure."

Then he slid his hand between her thighs; he touched her well. He was paying attention. She was struck by that. It was more like Eva touch-ing her, a man who had been trained to pay attention to exactly what excited a particular woman, who was aware of the differences, the nuances, who listened for them as he touched. He made her feel almost clumsy taking his prick in her hand, because she felt less sure what he liked. She was beginning to feel an excitement that verged on aching. "Come in," she said huskily into his throat. "Come in, now."

"You want me to come inside you?" He sounded almost surprised.

"Please, now." She guided him in.

Again, the way he moved was good. No mindless thumping. He was trying out various strokes and angles and carefully monitoring her responses. The trouble with him is going to be getting him to relax, she thought, to flow. A little too much the careful handyman. Very complete training but wants passion. She tried working on his back in various high and low ways, across the neck muscles, kneading the buttocks, circling in the small of his back, but he seemed to think her pressures were hand signals to go faster, which she actually did not want.

"Gently," she said.

Suddenly he reached between them and began to touch her clitoris as they were fucking, and she came in several moderate waves of electric pleasure.

"I've come," she said. "Now your turn."

"Did you really?" He sounded suspicious. "Take your time."

"I came. Really and fully. Now you come."

Suddenly he was soft in her. Yet she knew he had not climaxed. "What's wrong, Joel?" She cradled him against her.

"Nothing. I don't think I can come."

A man not going to come? This was a new one. "Why not? Let me excite you."

"No," he said. "Really, it's all right. Coming doesn't mean that much to me."

Where have I heard that one? she thought. Me being polite.

His relaxed penis slid from her, and they curled side by side. "You didn't really come, did you?" he said sulkily.

"Sure I did."

"But it was so fast."

"Fast?" They must have been fucking for five or six minutes by then. "I didn't think I was fast. I wouldn't have come right then if you hadn't touched me that way, but that did it."

"Oh, you liked that? I wasn't sure. . . . But you really came, just from that?"

"Why not? . . . What are you used to?"

"I didn't think women came from fucking."

"If it lasts long enough and if I'm excited first. A lot of women come more easily from being touched or eaten—but you're not in bed with most women, just with me. . . . Don't you give me a hard time about that too. There have been times when other women have made me feel like a fink, like a completely male-identified counterrevolutionary sellout, because I have orgasms from fucking."

He laughed. "Kiley told me fucking was oppressive to women."

"Well, it has been a lot. Men call the shots. Their shots. A lot of times you get into bed with a man and it's like he's fitting you into how he wants it. He wants to fuck in position A-4 or B-12 and you're to put your legs up around him whether you like it or not and he wants you to do X and not Y, and say certain words. Then he'll go on for as long as he needs to come, which may be about ten seconds. That is oppressive. Also dull."

"Did I do that?"

"Oh, Joel, not even slightly. My problem with you is that I came and you didn't. That's no more satisfying for me than it would be for you. I want you to have pleasure too." It all sounded so exotic she felt like laughing and hugged him closer. Sex role reversal, all right, and she found it delightful. "What do you need to come?"

"Nothing special. Just to be less nervous with you." He grasped her tightly. In a short while his breathing began to open into sleep. She lay tangled with his strange pleasing body and smiled at the invisible ceiling. She felt as if she had come upon a truly new breed of human being, a man untouched by old macho roles, vulnerable and open, gentle and emotional as a woman. How dear he was, she thought, and stretched out relaxed under the weight of his thigh dropped across her, thick and substantial as a log.

6

Waking, they got up, padded to the kitchen. She laid a fire in the wood stove as he made coffee and juice. Then they retreated to bed with mugs, to lie there until the kitchen defrosted. "I love breakfast in bed," he mused. "Always had to drag myself out at home soon as my old man did. He sure did hate people being in bed when he was up. It had to do with him resenting having to support us all."

"What did your father do?"

"He failed." Joel's teeth glinted over the mug. "In textiles. A little shit executive. First in New Jersey. Then in Roanoke. Now he runs a carpet store in Fair Oaks—outside Sacramento. There's one man who's sure he's been screwed, but he never looked up for the cause. His wife nags. His kids are ungrateful bums. The Blacks are greedy. The white trash whine and cause trouble. The unions are breaking business. The cheats on welfare raise taxes. All that talk about brown lung is ruining the textile industry."

Perhaps she had not realized how beautiful he was because she had not stared at him. Suddenly she realized his eyes were no longer that hard green, but a rich dark brown. "Your eyes!"

He dropped his gaze. "Forgot to put my lenses back in. Guess I hoped you wouldn't notice."

"You wear tinted contact lenses?"

He nodded, rubbing his chin. "Got them when I was with Jimmy and things were hot and heavy. . . . I like the way I look with green eyes. But you fell for that because your eyes really are the color of grass and you don't even need those social-worker glasses you left in the bathroom yesterday.''

"Oh! I forgot them. Where are they?''

"I stuck them in a drawer. So you wouldn't wear them again till we leave. They're stupid.''

"But . . . you act as if I should care what color your eyes are. You look fine with brown eyes.''

"Really? You don't feel taken advantage of?''

She laughed. "I only wish my brown hair was a wig and I could pull it off and underneath would be my own red hair.''

He shrugged. "Eh. I'm not crazy about red hair.''

"You'd be about mine.''

He grimaced mockingly at her. "I'm no hair freak. What I'm attracted to is your face and your body, but much more to you. Who you are. How you talk and laugh, what you say. You can't fuck hair.''

They walked the road behind the last dune, sand tracks with bleached grasses and maroon leaves of poison ivy growing in the shaggy middle. The tracks dipped into hollows that cupped the warmth of the sun, rose onto the dunes and into the wind, now and then giving them a dazzling cobalt ocean that soared way up the paler sky. A crisp breeze slapped them as they stood gazing on the empty beach far below where the long serpentine lines of breakers slithered in.

How depressed she had been in Oyster Bay, and now she felt marvelously restored. A little lovemaking, a good night's sleep and a few days to play house. Her toes wiggled in her tennis shoes, her spine was fluid as the waves, her long legs pranced. A pretty boy, nothing more, nothing to roar about—but nice.

"But if you hate Kevin, you're still tied to him. Hating's as passionate as loving,'' he was saying, head down, glaring at the sand.

"You make me feel I've got used to living in shorthand. As if I don't have relationships any longer where people really call me out personally. The friends I've been living with the last couple of years, they're nice women, but not articulate that way. With Leigh, with Natalie, I always have to . . . had to explain myself. They don't either of them let you off the hook. But nobody else listens that carefully.''

"Why would they?'' he asked scornfully.

"Why would you?''

"What weapons do I have but knowing how to listen and psych people out?''

"Don't I do the same thing?''

He shook his head. "You're brighter than I am. Yes, you are—don't pretend at me. You're an intellectual. I never read a book even. You figure out what to do from facts or theories. But I pay sharp attention to people. . . . Likely nobody's been as interested in you as me. . . . Leigh is your ex-husband. Who's Natalie?"

"My sister. Also my best friend."

"Still? I'm not asking any questions. I might as well be dead to my family. A nice tombstone you can visit on Memorial Day. Our son. Run over by the government. Or a box shipped back from Nam. That would've been dandy."

"You don't feel connected to them?"

"That glue came unstuck years ago. Glue? Sure. Airplane glue is thicker than blood, and a lot more fun to sniff in the ninth grade, no lie." He flung himself down in the sand moodily. They were on a shelf hollowed from the dune face. The cliffs dropped off so abruptly the beach below was invisible under the shadow of the dune.

Stretching out on the hot sand beside him, she sighed with pleasure. Her head filled with sky. The moment shimmered like a glass of full-bodied wine. Red. A Rhône. Purple Hermitage.

"It's real clever how you didn't answer me about Kevin," he said, rising on an elbow. "How instead you flattered me to change the subject."

"I wasn't flattering you. . . . I suppose I don't want to think about Kevin because that makes me worry about heat and trouble, precautions. I want to escape from that a little."

"I'm not some aspirin you can take to get rid of a headache. This is real too."

"Is it?" She opened her eyes to smile at him. "Are you sure?"

"Kevin counts because he's a heavy. He was cadre. I'm just a little shit draft dodger."

"Oooooh. Come, Joel. None of us are leading armies. You and I are in the same boat, as Laura put it."

"So why aren't I real too?"

"You are! But you're ten years younger than me and hung up on Kiley. This is a vacation for both of us."

"I'm no fucking vacation. I don't want to sleep with you anymore if you feel like that."

"I assumed you felt like that too." She sat up. "I do want to sleep with you."

"Just for the sex." Head bowed, he was sulking. He sulked beautifully, but she felt a premonition of trouble.

"What are you sleeping with me for? The exercise? I like you."

"Do you really?" He looked at her. His eyes were green again from the lenses. His own dark brown hid behind.

"Was your hair really that color?" He had his cheek against her mons.

"All of it."

"Too gaudy," he said. "You'd clash with everything." He ran his hands over her belly. "You compare things too much. What would it matter if we were both bald? We could still do this."

He lay half over her, kissing her and kissing her until she melted and put her hand on his cock to guide him in. But he refused to enter her yet. He teased her until she moaned and reached for him again, and then finally he entered. "I like it when you make noises like that," he said. "Do noises bother you?"

"No. I used to make more noises. I got in the habit of keeping quiet when a lot of us were living in a big house in Vermont—Hardscrabble," she said realizing he knew already.

"I like seeing you. It's scary making love in the dark with someone you don't know yet."

"What would you be scared of, Joel?"

"Does that feel good?"

"Everything feels good."

"You don't have to say that."

"I could lie to you. But I'd rather lie with you. Oh, that does feel good, that does." A twisting motion he had, as if he were actually screwing her. At a confluence of energies, a gathering of tensions and pulses, she knew she would come from that certain swollen urgency in the muscles around her vagina. After that gathering, unless the ceiling fell, the police burst in or he lost his erection, her orgasm was inevitable. Cautiously she brought her hand under him and cupped his balls, exploratorily, gently. "I'm going to come very soon. Very soon."

"Is like this good?"

She only moaned, letting herself go in sound. If he liked noises, noises he would get. All that was incidental. If a partner wanted moaning, whistling, singing opera, so long as the act itself went along nicely, what did she care? The waves of orgasm radiated up to her breasts, more intense, more long-lasting than before, good, unendurably good. Then slowly dwindling, a sunset of the vagina. "Come now," she said. "Come."

"Inside you?"

"That's what the diaphragm's for." Gently she began to squeeze his balls again. Please, let's bring it off this time, right.

He began driving harder, pushing high into her, and on impulse she raised her legs to let him enter more deeply. She could not climax with her legs up—her clitoris did not get enough impact—but after she had come she would just as soon endure less direct stimulation that became almost painful. She took her hand off his balls and wriggled it around to his ass, With a loud screaming moan, a sound such as an animal, charging, might make in pain or rut, he came. She could feel the contractions and the rush of the warm semen. With a great sigh she relaxed. He was truly functional. That was better. There.

The night was clear and vibrant up to the Milky Way arched over the pond. They huddled on a small dock. Minute ripples tickled the sand, but the air was still, stiff as a cardboard. The lights in the far house twinkled yellow. "About the only thing I ever read for kicks was science fiction," Joel was saying. With his arm around her and the same coat over their backs, she could feel his deep voice in her ribs. "I wanted to go to some other world. Any other world."

"I never could get into it. Fancy gadgets, and all they could imagine were kings and queens and empires. Forward into the feudal past."

"I love gadgets. . . . Imagine you're a two-bit Jewish businessman trying to claw up a ways and what do you get? A son with reading problems who wants to work on cars. Bad karma."

"You're not like anyone I was ever with," she mused. "Most of my lovers were intellectuals." She felt his body tighten. "I don't mean that in a positive way. Intellectuals are people to whom ideas are more real than people."

"Intellectuals read a lot, right? And there's nothing to read at Laura's except antinuke pamphlets and some *Time*s from August. . . . I see you pick up the pamphlets and toss them down again like you couldn't care less."

"Well, I'm not awfully interested. . . ."

"Before you came I had nothing else to do, so I read some of them . . . and if it's all for real, how can you not be interested?"

"Nuclear power is basically a bourgeois issue," she said, squinting up at the stars.

"Oh." He was silent awhile. " 'Cause that's who cares?"

"Right. Quality of life."

"Oh. . . . Who got upset about the Vietnam War first?"

"Touché." She turned to look at him. She was a bit surprised, a bit startled. "Do you want me to read the pamphlets?"

"Yeah. . . . It bothers me. I never thought about it before, but it gets to me. . . . Like if there's no future, what's the point of what we did? You see? We might as well have got off on drugs and stayed high. I'd like to talk about that stuff, if you'll read it. If you don't mind talking about politics with me."

"I'll read it," she said more humbly. What he had said still stuck like a dart in her brain. She had to think about that, off in secret.

VIDA

When they woke, the windows were covered with frost tracery.

"I can't believe that just happens by itself. No wonder people believed in fairies," he said.

"Marvelous flowers. Aubrey Beardsley arabesques. Like Art Nouveau designs."

"What's all that shit?"

"Oh." She could be startled yet, not just by him. The political children, how little they knew. They arrived at college knowing nothing but television. They never finished school. While in college they seemed to be taught none of the grounding in culture she had received almost automatically. "The pattern on the glass made me think of a style of decorating where everything curved and the ornaments were built on natural forms—like flowers, leaves. I'll show you sometime and then you'll know what I mean."

The marigolds outside were brown. "Oh, of course," she said, "It really was a frost." She made their bed, tidied, both housewife and soldier's neatness.

"Is everything dead in the garden?"

"Only the tender stuff. After breakfast, we better pick what we can save. The lettuce, the kale will grow all right for a while."

"How come? How come the flowers die and the lettuce goes on?"

He always asked questions. He wanted to please, he asked questions, he needed approval in enormous heaping spoonfuls all day. She thought of him as innocent, but his eye was exacting.

After a breakfast of the last of their eggs, he was shaving, with her perched on the toilet seat watching him, when they heard a car. Quickly he snapped off the light, wiped the lather from his face. She edged past him into the hall. The car had stopped outside. "It's not Laura," she hissed.

"Let's get out of here!" He thrust into his shirt.

"Too late. They'd see us." Two people were getting out of the car, a man and a woman, while a child stayed in the back seat. They were walking down the steps toward the house, both carrying baskets.

"We'll have to hide," he barked. "Come on."

They crammed into the closet of the bedroom where they had been sleeping. She was glad she had compulsively made the bed, that she tended to make beds as soon as she got up. Darting out of the closet, she grabbed her pack and his, dragged them in, shut the door but for a crack for her ear.

"Laura! Laura! It's Mike and Wendy," a woman was calling. "Laura, are you home?"

"She's got to be here. We saw the lights. There's dishes in the sink."

"Her car isn't here," the woman said. "Maybe she went into town."

"We left the fucking door unlocked," Joel whispered at her ear. She shook her head fiercely at him to shut up.

"She wouldn't go back to Boston and leave her door open," the man said.

"What should we do, honey?" the woman asked. Her footsteps came nearer. "Laura? Are you asleep?" She sounded in the room. Vida eased the door shut. "Nobody's here either. She must have gone shopping."

"Let's just leave the stuff for her," the man said. "Come on, I got to get back to the job."

Vida took Joel's hand. In the dark of the closet she scarcely breathed, standing pressed among Laura's musty sundresses, beach wraps, the webs of spiders whose present whereabouts she preferred not to consider. Her hand was cold and Joel's hot. His hand inched up to close on her breast. Standing crushed together, she felt his erection. Unbelievable. How could he get excited under these conditions? With Kevin in tight situations she had always had to pay as much attention to him as to the outside danger, because he might suddenly go berserk and decide to fight. With Eva she could draw comfort and worry about the real dangers. But Joel seemed to take danger too lightly. She realized he had never lived as a normal adult. Would the woman ever leave? Vida could have sworn she was poking around Laura's dresser, handling things. Would she decide to go through the closet too?

"Come on, Wendy. Don't be so nosy. Suppose she walks in?"

The steps pittered away. For an interminable period the couple muddled around in the kitchen. Once again, Vida made a crack for her ear. Wendy said, "She's not here by herself, Mike. Look. Two of everything for breakfast."

"She got herself a boyfriend, finally. Remember that guy we saw paddling her canoe on Labor Day?"

"I'd love to meet him. I wonder who he is."

"What do you care. Some doctor. Let's get out of here."

"Wait. I'm writing a note. Mike, should I ask them over?"

"Forget it. I want to watch the World Series. Who wants to spend the evening with some doctor? Her going on about radiation and nukes."

Finally the door shut. After a while they heard the car start up and drive off. Joel pushed the closet door open and drew deep breaths. "Thought I was going to suffocate."

"We had plenty of air, dear one," Vida said. "This closet is roughly slapped together."

I get claustrophobia. You don't, huh?"

"If I did, I guess I'd be dead. Once I had to spend fourteen hours locked in the trunk of a car."

"What did you do about going to the bathroom?"

She laughed. "That would be the first thing you'd think of. I pissed in a jar."

"Who the hell were those people?" Cautiously he moved out of the bedroom, walking on the balls of his feet. "I thought she was going to start searching the bedroom."

The kitchen counter was covered with green tomatoes, undersized bell peppers, eggplants the size of a thumb, fingerling zucchini. "The frost last night. They had to harvest everything. They had so much they decided to give some to their neighbors—I bet they're the lights we see at the end of the pond."

"They could make themselves a nuisance." Joel glared at the produce.

"Which reminds me, we better go out and salvage what we can. Then we have to think how to shut off their curiosity." Walking, Vida felt weak through the legs. She picked up the note.

Dear Laura, Here are some extra vegetables from our garden. Hope you enjoy them. Let's get together if you're going to be around. Your neighbors, the Kensingtons.

"Green-tomato soup," she explained, chopping. "I remember it from my childhood. Ruby always had a garden. She doesn't cook a lot of different things, but what she does she cooks well. Sort of Cleveland Jewish peasant plus what you learn to please a goyishe husband who was a meat-and-potatoes man."

"Who's Ruby?"

"My mama. I always called her Ruby. My father—my own father, I mean—didn't like it, but 'After all, that's my name,' she'd say. Ruby Rose Lyubkov Whippletree, and then Asch. She should have stopped with the Ruby Rose."

"Was your old man Jewish or not?"

She sliced the tomatoes in silence, deciding whether she wanted to open that up or not. The trading of intimacy, was it worth the bother? Traveling, she tried not to invent excessively. Her own stories had sunk deeper and deeper into her.

"You don't want to talk about it?"

She shrugged. "For a long time I haven't. . . . It seems fruitless."

"Think I'm too young to understand? Try me."

"I guess I'm not sure what's happening," she said baldly.

"Who do you love?"

"Who?" She felt almost afraid to answer. "Natalie, Ruby, Leigh. Paul—that's my brother. My friend Eva."

"You're loving people in the past. But we're stuck here. We're not even real to them. All you really want to do is crawl back into your own past. That's why you think I don't count. 'Cause I wasn't around then, back when you think it was all really real."

They lay in bed. He kept his back to her. Putting her arms around him, she tried to thaw him into forgiveness. "Joel, you're right. I agree. I'm trying to hold on to the past, because the present isn't feeding me and I'm scared."

"I'm small potatoes compared to Leigh and Natalie and Kevin. All the big guns."

"That's not true." She cuddled her face into his neck, pressed her breasts into his back curving away from her. "I'm scared, is all."

"What are *you* scared of?"

"You."

"How come me? A little shit like me."

"Joel, why do you hate yourself so? I know I could love you." Why had she said that, why?

For a long time he did not answer, until long after she had let go of him and lay on her back staring at the ceiling. Finally he said, "But you don't want to?"

"Do you want me to?"

"You couldn't."

"How can we argue about whether or not I could love you? Joel! I like being with you."

He flipped to face her, the atmosphere at once lightening. She had the feeling he was smiling in the dark. As if idly, he began to play with her breasts. "You like to fuck, don't you?"

"Don't say it as if you were observing I like to kick old ladies down the stairs."

"Is it the same with any guy?"

"Don't be ridiculous. Some women get off on strangers, let go best with somebody they don't feel intimate with—"

"That's what you're like?"

"No! I have the most response with somebody I feel close to."

"But you came with me."

"Maybe because we're both fugitives. And you were very gentle."

He was moving his finger around and around her clitoris. Then he slid two fingers deep into her. "You're juicy already. Want to?"

"I don't even know if you're excited."

He laid his prick against her. "I'm excited."

When they were resting entwined and sloppy with semen and sweat and cozy with pleasure, she realized that the sex had been marvelous. Suddenly they had moved to another level. She had not been conscious of his experimenting on her, and he did not remain rigidly in control. She had come and come for what felt like minutes.

"Maybe because it's all getting better and better it scares me. It's moving fast," she whispered.

"Who knows how much time we got?"

"Before you have to go someplace else?"

"There's no place I have to go. Depends on you. And on how much time before they make a special out of us and burn us on the evening news like Jimmy and Belinda."

"It's better for you too, now?"

He laughed. "Terrific. Coming back to life. It's like my body's been numb."

"From what?" She was dying to ask him about Kiley.

"You won't even tell me about your mother."

"Yes, I will."

He chuckled. "After a good fuck, you'd tell me anything."

"Don't say that! It alarms me."

"Kiley didn't like sex. She liked being wanted, because that's power. At first I thought she enjoyed it with me. I'd swear she came. But after a few months, she wouldn't even let me eat her. It was like maybe once a month I could make her come with my hand and I could rub myself against her ass. That was our sex life."

"Didn't you mind?"

"I went crazy. Maybe she did love me at first, but I think she didn't for a long time. I wouldn't give up and let go."

"If she didn't love you, why didn't she break it off?"

"I guess it was convenient," He grimaced. "Kiley's a lonely person. Maybe she even got off some on making me suffer."

I can't latch on to him because he's a good lover, she thought; we can't live in bed. But that was her forebrain issuing memoranda from the dean's office that all the workers—the feelings, the muscles, the gut— were about to throw in the garbage.

"Laura told me the wife taught school and he's a carpenter. So eleven ought to be safe," Vida said as they walked around the pond. They passed boarded-up houses, houses empty for the winter; but when they came to the edge of the woods near the Kensington house, a white colonial of two stories with an attached garage, the pleasure fled and they huddled behind a high blueberry bush. The Kensington house was built directly on the road that led out to Route 6, but they had approached on the path that went round the pond for privacy. Now they had reached the far border of security. "I'll go alone," she said. "She'll be less alarmed if she's there."

"Suppose he's goofing off work? I'll go."

"The car's gone." They could look through the garage window and see the doors open. A small motorboat was up on sawhorses. A kid's bike lay on its side in the grass. They strained for sounds from the house. Vida felt like a child. Sometimes she felt as if becoming a fugitive had reduced her to permanent childhood, to playing continuous hide-and-seek. When she and Natalie were thirteen, this was the sort of game they had played: pretending the adults were cops, the enemy, Them; sneaking around pretending danger. Even after so many years of pursuit she had trouble believing in this game: that now a slip would cost her her freedom and perhaps her life. They could not skulk all day staring at the blank windows of the white house. "I'll go. A woman is less scary."

She marched resolutely out of the orange-and-brown woods across the damp lawn to the door. A red ball covered with blue stars lay in the path. Then she saw movement at a window, and it was all she could do to force a smile and keep marching. Somebody at the curtains.

No, a white cat was rubbing against the window as she came up. Pet me. A long-haired white cat with blue eyes rubbed its forehead against the glass. "Hello, pretty," Vida whispered. She opened the screen door and stuck a note where it would be obvious: a note thanking the Kensingtons for the food and saying they were Laura's tenants. They were leaving soon and did not know when she planned to come out. Joel had invented the tenants story, saying if they claimed to be Laura's relatives, Wendy might still be interested, but nobody would care about somebody renting a place for two weeks. They'd only be sorry they'd wasted their vegetables.

She hastened to him across the lawn, and impatiently he stepped out to meet her. "Nobody there but a pussycat."

"That ought to hold them." He took her hand and they strolled back. "Tonight the summer people who still come out weekends start arriving. We better keep close to home and lay low till Monday."

"Let's leave our lights out and just have a fire. We don't want anybody else dropping in."

Dragging the mattress from the bedroom, they slept near the wood stove. That night two more houses showed lights. In the morning they chopped wood. Then she tried to work on her paper, gave it up and read the pamphlets Joel had been underlining. Then they took a cautious walk, made supper. Every day they made love twice. Vida, who had not had much sex in years, felt overwhelmed. More and more she had lived in her head and her nerves and less and less down in the rich body with its bird and frog songs, its yammering complaints and its overweening thunderous urges. The descent into the flesh startled her. She had thought of herself as grown past the violent onslaughts of desire. Now she felt as if she was in heat, as if wanting him was a constant whether she was momentarily aware of the response or not, that wanting him was a condition lurking in her that need only be triggered to surface. In fact she studied the pamphlets, making notes to prove to herself she was still politically motivated; if she could concentrate on an argument, she was not altogether lost.

Finally the city people left and Monday came. "When Jimmy was resenting me, he said I'm always in a relationship with a woman." Joel walked the woods road toward town, kicking a small rock before him, chin jabbed into his chest. "That I run from one to another like a rabbit streaking for a hole. If not one hole, then another."

Now he's issuing warnings. Have we moved too fast? She kept her back very straight, pacing along. "I haven't fallen in love with somebody in years."

"But you're still in love with this Leigh?"

"But I've loved him for fourteen years. . . . For a year and a half after Kevin, I didn't sleep with anybody."

"How come? That's a long time to sleep alone. . . . I've never gone that long, even when I was really on the run. I mean, I'd pick up *somebody* . . . then I'd get involved."

"I felt like Natalie was right, there was something cuckoo in how I acted with men. I had to live without a core relationship with a man. I had to be alone in my . . . my innards, my soul."

"You seem like a real strong woman. I can't see why you had to cut yourself off like that, just to prove something to your sister. She's married, right? Who's she to tell you that you got to hang by yourself?"

"It wasn't proving it to her. It's just when she talked about women's issues in New York, I was a pure Marxist-Leninist and I shut her up. Then when I started knowing things wrong in my own life, I felt she'd seen a lot I'd missed."

He shrugged heavily. His bones seemed to enlarge in his face and forehead. "Maybe she's right. That's what I ought to do—be a hermit. Maybe Jimmy was right."

Three pay phones stood in a row outside the pharmacy. Joel loitered, pretending to skim notices on a weathered board. Cake sale for the volunteer fire department. Yoga lessons. A '73 VW station wagon with snow tires. At five to ten she set herself up, coins arranged in rows, phone code turned back to digits, cold hands grasping the phone. The street was mostly empty, cars clustered around the open coffee shop. People walked with their collars turned up against the drizzle. The measure of how far she had come with Joel was that she no longer knew whether she wanted Natalie to tell her to come to Long Island or to caution her to hold for a week. She wanted to see Natalie, but she also wanted more time with Joel. The intimacy they were weaving could be cut off. She felt guilty at how intensely she wanted another week alone with him. By next Tuesday at the latest they must leave anyhow, as Laura permitted no one to stay longer than two weeks.

Ten. Time to dial. It rang. "Hello?"

"Natalie!" She should not have burst out, but she knew she hadn't mistaken that wry throaty voice.

"Hi, love. How are ya?"

"It's cool for you now? To talk?"

"For the moment. Now listen quick. Are you nearby?"

"No. North."

"All the way north?"

"No. I can get there by tonight."

"Hmmm. Got a better idea. This weekend there's a conference in Boston—women's health. I wasn't going. These days I'm working exclusively on battered women. But we got an invite, why not? So I'll take the shuttle up Friday night, drop by the conference next morning—it's at B.U.—and then clear out. Where can we meet?"

"I don't know Boston well. *Not* Cambridge."

Natalie pondered. "I don't know Boston awfully well myself. . . . Listen, there's a department store there. Filene's, downtown. Let's pick something. Like lingerie. There can't be more than one lingerie department in Filene's. I'll meet you there twelve on Saturday. How's that?"

"Okay." Downtown areas jammed with people were not her favorite stomping grounds. Saturday noon in shoppers' paradise sounded like a mob scene, and she had no idea how she would get to Boston. All that was minor compared with the lack of any other place to suggest.

Joel and she decided they might as well shop in town. Then she splurged on a bottle of zinfandel. By the time they had hiked all the way back to the house, it was afternoon and they were exhausted. He opened a can of sardines, she fried some of the green tomatoes lined up on every sill and they ate greedily. Then they stumbled into the other bedroom. In the middle of the day they did not dare lie down in the living room, in plain sight through the expanse of glass to any visitor.

The rain crept over the house, streaking the windows. In the center of the bed they huddled. She slept curled against him. He always seemed beautiful to her: beautiful as he nuzzled into sleep; beautiful as he slept snoring softly; beautiful as he woke and opened his eyes, dark as the wet bark of the pines.

VIDA

. . . . The way Hank looked at her made her uneasy. She rode up beside him in the ornate creaking old elevator of the huge apartment building that made a hollow square around a courtyard. The Seventh Heaven, it was called. The lobby was Moorish. The gates of the swaying elevator were of wrought iron. In the grimy courtyard an object like a bomb crater had once been a fountain. Sconces with stubs of bulbs, long broken, lined the hall.

She was wearing a mechanic's coverall daubed with grease. That embarrassed her, following his tweedy tailored back into an apartment. The apartment was Moorish too: overstuffed divans, harem cushions, brass tables. I need clothes, she thought. Where can I get clothes?

"Hank, I need something to change into."

"Such a bother. You're always making demands. I assure you, you'd look absurd in any of mine." He was annoyed. She saw then that he did not desire her any longer. The only threads that had coerced him were spun of unsatisfied lust, and now that had unraveled. Partly it was the awful mechanic's uniform. She did not want him; she was repelled by him. But she needed him to desire her sufficiently to hide her, to help her. Now she heard him using the telephone in the next room, and sweat broke out on her body under the filthy jump suit.

"I have to get out of New York," she heard herself saying. Hank was sitting cross-legged on a big blue cushion smoking dope in a brass hookah. She peeled off the jump suit and stood naked before him.

"You haven't anyplace left to go. Except round in circles." He was giggling the way some people did when they smoked too much dope. "Round and round."

The police were coming up the fire escape. They were outside in the hall. Now she was naked and there was no time to dress. She was naked and running, out through the service door into the back hall and up the steps onto the roof.

The tar was hot to her bare feet as she ran. She had a gun now, a .38 Police Special. She was kneeling there naked, embarrassed and scared with the rough hot sticky tar of the roof chafing the skin of her knees, shooting back. Then she realized that men were swarming over the roof and behind her, men in boots running. Through her bare knees she felt the roof quiver. Then the bullets tore her flesh like bolts of fire. She saw her blood wet on the tar, thickening in the heat as it poured from her, faster. The gun fell. Slowly she slumped onto the roof. A shadow fell over her. She could not raise her head, although she tried, tried again. A booted foot kicked her in the ribs to flip her over. . . .

"A bad dream," she said to Joel, clinging to him. "Just a bad dream."

"What about?" He stroked her hair, her cheek.

"Being hunted . . . shot."

91

"Welcome to reality. How awful to have a dream about being hunted and how wonderful to wake up to being hunted for real." He gestured. He was sitting up in bed reading the Boston *Globe* he had bought in town. Outside, the rain continued and the day loomed prematurely dark. "I've been looking for something about Kevin."

"Isn't there anything at all?"

"Sure there is." He passed her the paper.

She skimmed. Kevin Fogarty arraigned today in . . . bail set at $50,000 . . . released in the custody of his attorney, Ben Bassett. . . . "Who the hell is this Bassett?" she asked, more to herself than to Joel. "He's not a Movement lawyer. Is there a magnifying glass around here?" She bounded out of bed to look under stronger light at the accompanying photo of Kevin just leaving the courthouse. He looked seven feet tall and jaunty, a leather cap over one eye. It was not Kevin's lean nonchalant face she was peering at. Beside him stood a beefy lawyer in a double-breasted suit, but just behind and between them a woman was following. "Lohania," Vida burst out. "Lohania's come to him. Double shit. Mother of all shit!"

"Who's Lohania?"

"An old friend. She was Kevin's lover. She and Leigh were lovers too."

"Oh?" he said sarcastically. "And were you and her lovers too?"

"Briefly. Abortively, but—"

"And Kevin and Leigh?"

"Don't be silly. They detested each other. . . . Lohania and Leigh and I were a family. And Lohania and me, Kevin, Jimmy and Randy Superpig were the Little Red Wagon collective."

"And were you lovers with Randy too?"

"No! We never got along."

"First man I ever heard you mention you neglected to go to bed with. . . . Okay, so Lohania's busted now too?"

"Lohania got busted in '70 and eventually did two years. She wasn't with Kevin and Jimmy and me the day of the bombing. They didn't go after a thirty-year sentence on her. Randy was into her, or wanted to be. She copped a plea." Lohania and Kevin come together after all those years; why should that make her nervous? Because Lohania had been injured by drugs and prison and could not quite be trusted. Leigh and Lohania, stranded aboveground, deserted in the glare of sudden publicity, had tried to make it as a couple but had failed.

"Do you trust me?" He raised himself on his elbow, glaring.

She stared, her pattern of thought broken. "Sure." She sat down on the bed.

"I don't think you do. Or you forgot how to talk to another human being you're connected to. You give me these glib answers. All these names. I'm supposed to be a newspaper morgue of old radical history. Either tell me the whole thing or tell me to shut up, but I can't have a relationship with somebody who won't talk to me. I mean talk. Not wave some kind of signs at me and expect me to pretend I know."

She felt chilly with fear. Clutching herself, she knelt on the bed, wanting to flee him. Get out, clear out. To what? "It's work. To communicate. I'm out of the habit. Mostly I try to persuade people subtly not to ask me questions."

"I don't know how to be lovers with someone and remain strangers. Either open up to me or we just give up and go our separate ways. But you got to show me more respect."

"I do respect you! You haven't told me much either."

"Have you asked me?"

"I'm out of the habit of trying to penetrate other people too." Something caught in her chest, words like a switchblade sprung open. "The phone call this morning. I'm meeting my sister Saturday."

"Is that safe?"

"Of course not. But I have to see her. We always manage."

"Can I meet her?"

"Maybe. Let's see. I think so." She felt as if she had jumped off a bridge and not yet landed. "I'll tell you my life, you tell me yours. We have till Friday morning, depending on the bus schedule."

When he was convinced she meant it, he got the bottle of wine and they camped in the bed, hidden, the house locked up, no lights on but a candle on the bedside table. From across the pond came sounds of a small party at the Kensingtons'. A cricket had got in the house and creaked from the living room. Side by side they sat against the wall, pillows heaped up behind them. "What were you doing when you were my age?" he demanded. "What were you like? Tell me."

PART II

October 1967

7

"**L**isten to him lie! Listen to him! In that corn-pone voice. Like it's just a real homey little truth that we have to murder all those people, it's really good for them." Vida paced.

"Shhh." Leigh shut off the machine. "You get too excited, Vida. Go work on the collage with Lohania. You're driving me crazy." He squeezed her around the waist and then gave her a push toward the dining-room table, where Lohania was cutting and pasting.

"I just hate him so much. The peace candidate!"

Leigh was playing Johnson's speeches from the campaign of '64, putting together a tape to play in the War Pavilion at the Smash-the-State Fair the next day.

"How come you hate him so much?" Lohania asked, hand on her hip. "Just one more lying politician like all the rest."

Vida looked at their dining-room table covered with a mural in progress. Lohania was putting together ads, political advertisements, news stories, photographs, Revlon lipsticks and Corvettes and maimed babies and bombed villages. Lohania's black curls had bits of rubber cement and ends of paper caught in them. "If I cut, you can concentrate on the arty part," she offered to Lohania. She could not explain to Leigh or Lohania why she hated Johnson personally; during the campaign of '64 she had been married and living in Crete with Vasos and his family and America had been legendary and unreal, what the village people always said to her when her country was mentioned: "Poly lefta, poly aftokíneto." "Much money, many cars": their automatic response. She hated Johnson because she felt she and Natalie had been taken in completely by Kennedy. They had campaigned for him. They had listened to his speeches in hushed silence. They had believed that Jack and Bobby would do wonders for civil rights. . . . She had resented Johnson as the gross successor, but she had come to hate him as the one who showed the corporate inside of Camelot, the imperialistic dreams behind the clean-cut Harvard rhetoric. Johnson pursued openly what Kennedy had secretly set in motion—the invasion, the war. He had made her see how duped and silly she had been weeping at the cortege in black and white on the television set in the dormitory lounge.

That was why she understood the kids, the SAW troops, better than Leigh or Lohania did, she thought: because they were angry as she was angry, because they had believed in the dream of American justice, President Shane in the white suit. It was the liberals who had made her responsible for the deaths of peasants in their paddy fields and ordinary guys, men she'd gone out with, who didn't want to have their bellies torn open in somebody else's backyard. Lohania's family had hated Kennedy for calling off the Bay of Pigs: they were right-wing Cuban exiles. That Lohania had changed her politics completely around did not give her that sense of having been seduced and then betrayed that Vida had.

Leigh was whistling as he worked, his shirt open, listening to the tapes and then splicing bits and pieces. He hopped around like a cat playing with a mouse: relax, listen, then pounce, dash, grab. He was doing a good job, and she loved watching him. "Some blood of the bull!" he roared. "What a thirst I have."

She opened a bottle of the Sangre de Toro they bought by the case—good cheap red Spanish wine—and poured out a tumbler for each of them. For once the phonograph was off, because of their not wanting to interfere with Leigh's tapes, but he whistled and sang snatches of current rock songs, and Lohania and Vida joined in. "Earlier movements sang political songs," Vida said thoughtfully. "We don't do that. Maybe we're being co-opted."

"The Beatles and the Rolling Stones and the Jefferson Airplane, they're political," Leigh said vehemently. "That's our music, and all the kids are boogeying to it. Who wants to stand in some attic singing 'Solidarity Forever' when you can take over the airwaves and reach everybody?"

It felt so good, home with her own tight family and doing their work together, she felt a pang of annoyance when she looked up and saw Kevin saunter in. He was Lohania's new boyfriend, an ex-con who had served a couple of years for robbery and who was working on the docks in Hoboken. Since when had he had a key? He gave her a cold hard stare as he ambled past, looking around warily as always, as if he might be walking into an ambush or a fight. A great shock of yellow hair fell over his forehead, and he was growing a wild beard, fuller and shaggier than Leigh's. He was a head taller than Vida, taller than Leigh, and Lohania looked as if she ought to stand on a ladder to kiss him. Immediately as he walked in Lohania's expression changed to one more kittenish, her eyelids fluttering, her full mouth pursed, standing in a way that emphasized the full bow of her hip toward him. "Hey there, the Big K," she said. "What blows you in?"

"It's Saturday night," he said. "Must be a party someplace. What is this, hippie kindergarten, cut and paste?"

"It's for the Smash-the-State Fair tomorrow," Lohania said. "I'll be done in a wink."

"Jesus, Smash the State, huh? You ain't doing that with rubber cement, Lulu."

That was his awful nickname for Lohania. "I'll finish up," Vida offered. She'd just as soon get him out. He made her edgy.

His eyes lingered on her, wearing only a T-shirt with THE BREAD IS RISING on it from the last spring mobilization and her cutoffs, as the night was warm for late October. She turned away, going to stand by Leigh, who was splicing and mumbling, oblivious, snapping his fingers to a tune played in his head and editing Johnson into Johnson in blatant contradiction. Lohania was wearing a pretty paisley minidress, because, as Vida realized, she had been expecting Kevin to appear.

After they had left, for of course there always was a Movement party to go to—Oscar and his new girlfriend Jan were throwing a Halloween bash in their loft—she finished up the mural and then helped Leigh till they both were done. Then, hearing in the hall the couple from Chapel Hill who had been sleeping on the living-room floor, they retired with the remains of the bottle of wine to her room, to chew over the week together, political, sociological, psychological profiles, and then to plot the week to come.

"Lohania must have given that guy a key," she said sullenly, her head resting on Leigh's furry chest.

He was playing with her breasts, idly. "Her new Irish rover? Why not?"

"Well, he did go to prison for robbery." She rolled over on her stomach, feeling that Leigh was merely pretending not to understand.

" 'When the gates of the prison are opened, the real dragon will fly out,' " Leigh quoted Ho Chi Minh. "Aren't you being a mite bourgeois?"

"Why does Lohania like them so mean?"

"She likes me, and I'm sweet as a chocolate éclair—or so my ladies tell me." He tugged at her hair. "My strawberry blond. What makes you think he's mean?"

"He looks mean," she said stubbornly. "He marches into the kitchen like he owns it and pulls out half the refrigerator. Then he helps himself and leaves it for me to clean up."

"Kevin's a real radical, down to his toes," Leigh said, taking the male side at once. "Good instinctive hatred of capitalism. He knows where and how he's been oppressed."

"And he plans to oppress Lohania and me as much as he can."

"You don't like real workingclass men, you know that? Only intellectuals like me. You think every real workingclass man is your father. Tom What's-his-face. Takes an intellectual to make your juices run."

"You never met Tom," she said defensively. She knew better. The reason she felt attracted to Kevin in spite of disliking him was that he did remind her of her father. Her father Tom. Not her father Sandy. Kevin's anger had a similar trim to it. "My old man had a pretty good line on class. Didn't prevent him from being a pig at home. He wasn't even particularly racist. He liked Japanese women from when he was in the Occupation. Said they knew how to please a man. He said that to Ruby a lot. . . ."

Blue filled the morning windows. Their apartment was on the fifteenth floor of an old rent-controlled building that ran half a block along West End and around the corner on 103rd Street. For a Manhattan apartment it danced in light, the high-rise across the street not being tall enough to cut off the sun, while east along the block they overlooked a row of brownstones.

Naked as she slept, she got up, reflecting what to put on to go to the kitchen. Lohania lived with them part time—she commuted from New Jersey, where she had a room in a big Movement house—and she had probably come back here from the party last night. A couple from North Carolina, members of the SAW chapter at Chapel Hill, had been sleeping on their living-room floor all week. Therefore, she put on her slinky tangerine Empire-waisted slit-to-the-thigh nightgown, but put over it her plain-Jane green corduroy duster.

In the living room, the North Carolina couple were fucking in a sleeping bag as she pretended not to notice, going by in the hall on her way to the dark central kitchen, least pleasant room, to light the gas and then pour the milk to measure in the ceramic mugs an earlier potter girlfriend of Leigh's had made. His lovers always gave him presents, she reflected, gazing at the closed door of Lohania's room. Lohania had the room off the kitchen that had been a maid's room, the subject of endless not amusing jokes from other people about their domestic arrangements.

She listened carefully, hoping Lohania was there but that Kevin had gone back to Hoboken. She wanted Lohania to herself today. They had to sit down with Natalie and plan a strategy together for the meeting of the Steering Committee. Carefully she spooned sugar, a dash of cinnamon, a bit of cream into each mug, ground the French Roast from Zabar's, brought water to the boil while keeping an eye on the milk heating. Then she cut off the stale edge from the dark Russian bread and set the slices on a blue dish on a wooden tray they had found in a Maryland junk shop on the way back from a civil rights demo—decorated with blue-and-yellow flowers that looked like eyes. After she had added a hunk of sweet butter, she ladled out bitter orange marmalade. Apricot nectar this morning. Lohania always bought flowers. In the room beyond, the sunny dining room, with light glittering on the parquet floors they had refinished, Lohania had put bronze chrysanthemums in a vase on the mahogany table Leigh had inherited from his Aunt Fanny. Vida slipped in quietly not to disturb the couple in the living room, separated by glass doors they had shut for privacy, and stole one chrysanthemum for her tray. There. Ready for Leigh.

As she set the tray down on the stool beside the bed and flung off the wrapper, she gloated over the Cretan embroidery that formed the headboard of her fine big bed and the embroidered hairy chest of her own sweet lover with his pointed curly beard of glossy bay brown pointing straight up as he yawned. She did not mind getting up and waiting on him, for she tended to think of men as frail. They could only do it sometimes. Once a day was pretty good to get out of one of them. She wanted Leigh as she sidled into bed beside him, plumping pillows, and handed him his mug.

He had switched on the bedside radio to a rock station, The Grateful Dead singing over their café au lait. "You know what I really want to do, babes? The hell with this commentator crap. I want to be a New Left disc jockey. Leaping Leigh, the first of the Red Hot Papas. That's how to reach the kids. Play the beat, and in between you can chatter and comment and really lay out some hot licks on where the country's at. That's my true fantasy."

She smiled at him. "And adored by seventy-two thousand teenyboppers, sure."

"Nah, I just want all the freebies on the new releases. And to interview all those guys . . . But I always wanted to be a disc jockey. I was the jockey for the dances in high school, you know that? Except for the big ones where we had five jerks in to play."

Breakfast over, she removed the tray and leaned to kiss his mouth, tasting of coffee and marmalade. The sun fired all the hair tangled on his arms and chest. "My bear," she lilted. "My brown bear, my cinnamon bear." His prick was already standing, making a funny tent of the sheet. She slid under.

"Leave the gown on this time," he said. "It's exciting. Slithery."

Leigh never liked to dally long in caressing. He claimed to be insensitive except for his prick. Sometimes she wondered if so much hair dulled the nerves. Mopsy, lying in the blue easy chair beating her tail in hope she would soon be taken out, was more sensitive to touch than Leigh was. He would go down on her to get her ready. Then she would have to decide whether he was up for a long one or a short one. If it was going to be quick, she fantasized to come; if he was going to take his time, she just enjoyed it and stayed with him. The only problem was trying to guess early enough to gauge herself. Once he was inside her, he liked making love. He was vigorous and responsive.

"Where did you get that nightie?" He dangled it off his hand as he sat watching her dress.

"Natalie got it for me."

"Your sister. Ha. I thought it was some hot young lover."

"You're the one gets presents. Ever noticed, in our neck of the woods it's the women who give the men presents?"

" 'Cause we're all so wonderful."

"Especially you. Right?"

"Right. . . . Besides, you have more time to shop."

"Wow! Are you living in an illusion. We have time? Natalie? Me? Sure, from two to four in the mornings on alternate Mondays. Well, for that you can just walk Mopsy this morning."

He strolled back to his own room whistling a Beatles song, and Mopsy followed him, wagging her tail harder, as if she had understood. Vida sat at her vanity, brushing the snarls from her silky red hair. Time, huh? If anyone in New York had a busier schedule, she had yet to meet them: perhaps Mayor Lindsay, but she doubted it.

Dressed, she ran out the service door, down three flights and into the wing of the building on West End. She rapped on Natalie's door, gave the back buzzer a Dah dah dah DAH, waited impatiently. Natalie answered the door in her old red bathrobe. It had been a good cashmere bathrobe when they had gone away to college together. She rumpled Natalie's curly brown hair, kissed her rosy mouth and hugged her, plump cuddly zaftig Natalie. "Get rid of that damn old bathrobe, Nattikins. Off with it. It's practically dragging on the ground, and it looks like somebody's mother ought to be wearing it."

Natalie wrinkled her snub nose at Vida. "Fuck you. I am somebody's mother. And that ain't all. Come in."

"Daniel still in bed?"

"No, he went out to get the *Times* and he's not back. But he took Sam in his stroller, so blessed be. Let's sit in peace. Want some coffee?"

"Sure. Black."

"Me too."

"How come, Natty?"

Natalie patted her belly. "I'm on a diet."

"I like you the way you are. You don't look fat to me."

"Gee, thanks. But I'm going to be a lot bigger soon."

"Oh, no." Vida could not pretend to be delighted quickly enough. "Not again."

"Yeah." Natalie shrugged, rubbing her belly. At different times Natalie looked to her like a Buddha, like an implacable peasant, like a beaming child. "Another one."

"Don't you use the diaphragm?"

"Yeah, I use it. . . . But Daniel gets pissed sometimes, when I get up to put it in. He liked the pill. Only it made me swell up like a dyspeptic whale. Belching, farting, all the time fireworks. . . . He says if I don't put it in first, if I have to get up, he doesn't feel in the mood by the time I get back."

"You going to have it? You don't have to."

"What's the use being married if you still get abortions? I ask you." Natalie blew on her coffee. "Everybody says that only kids are neurotic. The folks will be glad."

"So when is it due?"

"Don't call a baby *it*. Like you're expecting a monster. Let's see, middle of May. At least I won't stagger through the summer like a one-woman slum the way I did last time, remember? . . . Had your breakfast?"

"With Leigh. Nice this morning. Lohania's home, but I don't know if that new dude of hers is squatting on her today."

"Surly, isn't he? We need to confer." Natalie sat up straighter, spooning plain yogurt into her bowl. "I want the leaflets to offer some political content this time. Not just, Wow, let's all go dance in the streets and stop traffic."

"Well, it's got to be today. Tomorrow Lohania will be back in Newark and I'll be at work. . . . Which reminds me, you and I have to knock out the monthly budget. We ran over on food again."

"Why don't you ask Kyriaki for a raise?"

"Not a chance, Natty. . . . I wish that couple camping on our floor would kick in something for food."

"They figure we're too bourgeois to care. Between our two households we probably hold more real jobs than the rest of the New York Movement put together."

Natalie spoke cheerfully, although Vida knew her sister had disliked quitting her job at Brooklyn College, where she had been intensely interested in her students and had served as faculty sponsor for the SAW chapter. Natalie had been enthusiastic about having a baby, but would have liked to go on teaching too. Sam would soon be old enough for day care, and she had been looking forward to teaching at least part time. "Maybe you could get a job at the free school," Vida said, knowing her sister would have followed her thoughts.

"I like to work in mainstream institutions—that's my bias. Counter-institutions aren't for me. I don't like the prima donna men who hang out down there. . . . I want to reach students who have to get the degrees, not the ones who can play around."

She squeezed Natalie's hand, feeling the unyielding wedding ring. It said, I belong to Daniel, who has just stuck another baby in me. Sam was nice and cute, almost as cute as Mopsy, although a lot more work, and now that he was talking, amazingly bright, but who needed another? She wanted more of Natalie's time, not less. "Did you tell Ruby and Sandy yet?"

"I'll call tonight. You want to make it a group call? Get on the extension?"

"Sure. It's easier that way. Excuses us for not writing, and the confusion speeds it along." She loved her parents, but they were upset by their daughters' political activities. A photograph of Vida in *Life* after the last SAW national convention had frightened them. She was making a speech outdoors, holding up her fist in front of an NLF flag, looking fierce. Actually, she had been making a report from the first women's caucus in SAW about the lack of day-care facilities. She had been angry, all right, because the men had been chatting and ignoring her report. Not that Vida cared much about day-care facilities except as the lack of them impacted on Natalie, but she had been chosen to make the report as the loudest of the women, the best speaker, the one with the most charisma on the platform. Yet the moment the men heard "women's caucus" and "kids," they tuned out and started milling around.

"Natty, you got time to do the laundry this week?"

Natalie sighed. "I guess so. . . . I still haven't found anybody from the sitting pool to cover for me Tuesday night."

"You've got to, Natalie. You can't miss another Steering Committee!"

"Maybe I can get Daniel to stay with Sam," Natalie said without much hope. "If he doesn't have a meeting for once."

"Maybe we can actually hire a baby-sitter. Put up a notice in the elevator."

"Some teenybopper I don't know? Don't be ridiculous!" Natalie drew her little self up, sternly maternal.

"Okay, I'll find somebody." One of the kids in SAW who had a crush on her. "Don't worry."

VIDA

"Not some jerk whose idea of fun is feeding babies acid, okay?"

Oscar and Pelican Bob, who were setting up the SAW exhibit in the park, stopped by at noon to pick up the work for the War Pavilion. At two the family set off for the Smash-the-State Fair, Natalie pushing the stroller. Her corduroy jumper came about two inches above her knees. Natalie did not wear her skirts as short as Lohania and Vida did, who were always conspiratorily shortening together, another inch, another, egging each other on. Daniel and Leigh walked in advance, with Mopsy trotting between them proudly, tail high. Leigh paced with hands shoved in the pockets of his flight jacket, Nagra recorder slung over his shoulder. Daniel swung his arms, leather patches flashing on the elbows of his sport jacket. Daniel was a big man, barrel-chested. When they stopped to wait for a light and Leigh turned back to face Daniel, she could no longer see Leigh at all through Daniel's solid wall of back.

Just in the middle of the group Lohania and Kevin walked, holding hands and talking intently in low voices. Lohania had to take two steps to his every one. Kevin was the tallest and most athletic-looking of the men. Without flab and tightly muscled, he had an alert springy walk, looking from side to side in automatic wariness, his chin leading. Lohania was the darkest of them all, her hair black while Natalie's was dark brown. Her Cuban exile family had made her suffer for her dark skin. Lohania was always in rapid motion, bright, nervous as a butterfly. Lohania and Vida wore the same dress, scoop-necked velour shifts that ended halfway up the thigh. They had bought them at Alexander's on the way back from the last Steering Committee meeting. Vida's was moss green; Lohania's, plum.

They had loved buying the same dress. Lohania was pear-shaped, her waist curving in sensuously and then her ass slinging out a baroque balcony over her short, slightly bowed legs. They were both wearing flats and fishnet stockings, while Lohania had pinned chrysanthemums to her dress and into her wild curly hair. Lohania and Vida both loved the air of scandal that attended them, that they shared Leigh, that they were such tight friends. They were given to dropping hints about being lovers, which wasn't true but almost true, for they did love each other and besides it was fun to tease people. Wearing the same dress amplified that air of scandal. Vida decided they had to get Natalie the very same dress. Alexander's had had the dress in a beautiful dark gold velour that would look gorgeous on Natalie. Vida giggled aloud, but she would not yet tell Natalie why. Épating the bourgeois was fun, but shocking their own movement more to the point in daily life. It was so fine to walk attended by that buzz of naughtiness, such a powerful aphrodisiac that sometimes Vida thought she had only to smile in the right way and she could try on just about any man she wanted in New York.

"All these people!" she gloated as they approached the Sheep Meadow.

"Looks like a frigging Be-In," Daniel said shortly. "I thought this was supposed to be a political-education project."

So much dope was in the air she felt high just breathing. A person covered with body paint was playing the flute, sitting cross-legged surrounded by a circle of stoned music lovers nodding and swaying. Nearby, a Russian wolfhound was mating vigorously with a malamute. Mopsy slunk close behind Vida, tail low, cowering. People with shaven heads wearing orange caftans surrounded them chanting Hare Krishna, to which Leigh replied as always, "And a Harry Kirschner to you too! Have a fine three-piece suit," Harry Kirschner being an uncle on his mother's side who had been a skilled tailor as well as a good communist.

"We aren't near our people yet," Vida said shortly. "You ought to be pleased the hippies are around. Don't we want to reach them?"

"Reach?" Daniel snorted. "They sit in my classes glassy-eyed and all they say if you poke them hard is *Wow*."

This year the earnest idealists and organizers of SAW had cross-fertilized with the gypsy hoards, and no one knew yet what the hybrid armies in the parks would turn out to mean. The organizers were smoking dope and growing their hair, and the flower children, weary of being beaten by the police, were beginning to talk about the war, but mistrust between the tribes remained. The Fair had been a proposal of Vida and Oscar's, to attract the crowds that milled around the continual Be-In that was the Sheep Meadow. Daniel was too staid to see that a great thick fog had lifted from the American landscape and people in the new sunlight were mixing colors and sounds and cultures and life styles, always perhaps with an eye cocked to the mirror, but the mirror was singing like Crow Dog its own authentic magic chants.

"There's our people," Vida said. One of their street-theater groups was performing Search and Destroy in a crowd. Several actors mimed cooking in their huts, sewing, rocking babies; the army came through, dragged them out to be shot and set their huts on fire. Oscar, his dark hair bunched under a red sweat rag, was drumming for them. Oscar was not a good drummer, but he was a happy one. Oscar, the ideologue who had not gone to the beach all summer ("We're making a revolution, Vida, let's be serious!"), was sitting cross-legged in the October sun smiling beatifically as he pounded away in the midst of the crude agonies of the playlet. If Oscar had realized, he would have been ashamed to be seen.

Vida walked arm in arm with Lohania, Kevin having gone off to argue with some guy in a turban. Lohania smelled of sandalwood, the only scent she ever used. Even the silk scarves she wore around her wild hair to keep it back were stored in a sandalwood box that Vida had given her. Leigh was off into the crowd bird-dogging with his Nagra recorder out, Mopsy close to his heels, sniffing, shy at the crowd, the firecrackers, the circle dancing. Natalie pushed the stroller over to the benches where the mothers who weren't stoned were collected, watching the action near the booths SAW had set up and overseeing the kiddies and talking together. Vida felt a pang of dismay for Natalie's being stuck there on the fringes as she plunged in with Lohania.

The ball-throwing booth with the faces of McNamara, Johnson, Westmoreland, Rusk was popular, and so was the game called Draft that the Steering Committee had enjoyed working out. But the rock band was outdrawing the political exhibits, and even their own people were mostly off dancing. Daniel strolled with a colleague, puffing on a water pipe they handed back and forth much as he usually puffed on his meerschaum. Obviously they got their pleasure from commenting on the lurid but curiously placid scene. A rainbow had spilled over the people, luminous, garish, whimsical, silly, starkly religious. She passed kids looking as if they were dressed in everything they had found in the attic of a Victorian transvestite. Balloons floated and popped. The day was almost hot. Musicians, beggars, vendors, dope dealers plied their trade. The Chamber of Horrors wasn't working. Nobody would look at photographs from Vietnam. The booth with political pamphlets reported only modest sales. "We should sell pamphlets and popsicles at the same booth," the kid behind the counter said. How could they educate the dancing children? She watched, she flirted, she talked to acquaintances and strangers, she wandered about. Every so often she looked for her family.

As Lohania and Kevin were dancing, no one watching them would doubt they were lovers. But Kevin speedily got bored and backed away. She could feel his boredom like an actual presence, like a big German shepherd that must be fed and restrained. It could not be locked up indefinitely or ignored. His physical presence was tiring to her, almost noisy. How did he manage to center scenes around himself just by standing there glaring?

"Hey there, it's Ida Red!"

She turned. "Oh. . . ." In Washington, at the Pentagon, one of the marshals had called her that. A folksinger, in the SAW chapter in Louisville. "What on earth are you doing here?"

"Picking and politicking and pursuing sweet pussy."

Oh, yes, she thought, he had been one of those. He had his banjo on his back. From under his fringed leather vest he took his stash and offered her a joint. It was a social thing, like a secret handshake. "You need a place to stay?" She asked because she felt obligated. What was one more on the floor? All the people she knew had the sense they could travel from city to city and always they would find Movement offices and people to put them up and feed them. She could go anyplace and be recognized by clothing, by catchwords, by hair and dress. Hospitality was a sacred obligation, like sharing your dope with anyone present.

"Yeah, I'm staying with a great chick in SoHo, but I wouldn't mind . . ."

Leigh was at her elbow, Nagra on the ready. "Hey, I heard you blowing that banjo. . . . Introduce me."

Fortunately, she made out the words embossed on his much-decorated guitar and realized that was the name he went by. "Yellow Brick Road, this is Leigh Pfeiffer. Yellow writes some great songs."

She got them going together and then faded back. Lohania was dancing alone, absorbed. Every bit of her body shimmered and shivered and wriggled in its separate but conjoined ecstasy. Her eyes were half shut. Some kids were playing with long paper streamers, weaving patterns in and out. It was a scene of fantasy from the back of her head, a subversive musical comedy poured out of the closets of America, people dancing in the streets, bumping in huge good-natured crowds, peaceful as soap bubbles jostling. Never would the authorities be able to cram the genie back in the bottle: this was a permanent change of the American psyche. Daniel didn't grasp how powerful beauty and energy were. When the music changes, the walls of the city tremble, she quoted to herself with a smile.

Back at the bench, Natalie was getting to her feet. "Sam's cranky. I think it's time to go."

"I'll see who I can round up."

She took Lohania gently by the arm, bringing her back to the dusty afternoon. Kevin was lost, but Lohania did not seem worried. "He's supposed to eat supper at his ma's house in Newark, so he can make his own way." Lohania spoke fast, as always. She had no accent but a standard New York one. "He's gone off drinking with some old alkie he knows from the docks. You'd be surprised where he finds them. . . . He's standing in some dim Irish bar on Amsterdam getting them to tell him stories about the black-and-tans and the IRA. . . . My feet hurt. Hey, Sammy, come to your tanta. Whoopsa, you giving your mama a hard time? . . . So, who's he gonna look like this time?"

"Don't call my baby *he*. I don't want a boy, and I wish people wouldn't assume I do." Natalie sounded cross.

"Want a girl? Or something else?" Lohania stuck out her tongue. "Mama, we're going to take you right home and fix you up. A nice meal. A back rub right where it gets you in the small of your back. Tonight I cook!"

Vida found Daniel deep in conversation. Proprietorily he put his arm around her and gave her waist a squeeze, without interrupting the flow of his argument: ". . . and force heavier and heavier demands on welfare until the whole system buckles."

How dare he act so patronizing? "Natalie's tired. She'd like to leave."

"Fine," Daniel said. They were both always saying that when nothing was fine; it was a habit of their coupledom. You could say to them, I have pneumonia, and they'd say, Fine, I'll call a doctor. "I'll see her later. You girls run along."

Really, she thought as she dodged through the crowd, he acted superior just because he had a university job. *Girls!* Leigh was the only man she knew who did not diminish the woman he was with, who did not think because they fucked that he owned her or she was his little garbage bag. Daniel treated Natalie just like . . . a wife. She was fiercely grateful to Leigh, dodging a circle dancing around a couple of conga drummers, for their way of being open, trusting and above all respectful. She could love other men briefly, affectionately, as friends, as lovers, but only Leigh could be trusted in the center of her life. No other man could ever love her and let her survive intact, her appetites, her abilities, her will, her intellect not diminished or pruned but encouraged. She peered into openings in the throng as she slid through, hoping to see him.

Lohania pushed the stroller and sweet-talked Sammy, as Natalie and Vida strolled home arm in arm up Broadway. Broadway was a paler continuation of the park, with Sunday-afternoon crowds milling from shop to shop and old people sitting on benches between the uptown and downtown streams of traffic, a puddle of strutting pigeons at their feet. "Sorry I got crabby," Natalie said. "I just want to go home and get our strategy together for the staff meeting."

Cool shadows crept across Broadway, the sun slanting down over New Jersey. Vida caught sight of herself in a mirror in a shop window and grinned. Her minidresses sometimes looked like a little girl's frock, sometimes like uniforms from *Star Trek,* the costumes of a future where the dull grim problems of racism, poverty, starvation had all been worked out. "Natalie, Lohania, do you ever, ever feel like this is just the center of the universe?"

"A real New Yorker talking." Natalie patted Vida's behind. "Who'd ever know she came from the Midwest?"

"I mean here and now. When I was in high school, remember, Natty, I had this idea of history concentrating in moments of decision. Like 1890 was the time to be in Paris and 1917 in St. Petersburg. It feels that way now—as if things are happening faster than we can understand. As if we're pushing on some corner about to turn the whole thing over! We're *making* history—"

"You're a romantic," Lohania snapped. "History is a science."

"I don't believe that." Interest lit up Natalie's face, making her look all of eighteen, digging her hand into her brown curls, wrinkling her nose. Natalie loved to argue about ideas, now as when they had first met, when Natalie was twelve and a half and Vida twelve. "History's a myth. A million things happen in every moment. Each historian selects certain to stress. The stock market. A cholera epidemic. Wars. The changing status of women. The baby boom. The inflation rate. The rise of soybean production. The thawing of the Antarctic ice cap. The extinction of species. A strain of bacillus resistant to penicillin . . . The War in Vietnam obsesses us, and for good reason, but a historian in the superpower of Togoland in 2067 might ignore the affairs of the backwaters of North America altogether."

"Pluralist nonsense," Lohania said. When she talked Marxism, she looked different. Her mouth drew thinner, her eyes narrowed and shone, she stood with her small shoulders thrown back. Lohania nursed a raw sore anger toward her parents because they had taken the family from Cuba, because they had punished her for being dark, because they doted on her brothers and scorned her. "When you comprehend the economic base, when you master the dialectical process, when you analyze the stage of imperialism we're entering upon, then you know what moves history and how best to throw your forces into the struggle."

Vida tuned out the theoretical argument. What they had to decide was what to do at the meeting; once they got upstairs, that was their agenda. Every person in SAW had their own politics—anarchist, liberal, communist, democratic-socialist, syndicalist, Catholic-worker, Maoist, Schactmanite, Spartacist—but what mattered was the politics of the act. Decisions rose from solving problems in struggle. Everyone was accommodated in the vast lumbering movement. Vida was content to be of the New Left, without a fancier label. All that hairsplitting—that was what the poor Old Lefties had sat around doing in dreary meetings in the fifties nobody else attended while the resident FBI agent took notes. Now they knew that everything must be done and they must speak to everyone, through the poetry of the act, through the theater of the streets, through the media, the music, irrationally and rationally and subliminally. History was a sense of urgency, a rush in the blood and a passion to make things better, to push with her whole life on what was. SAW was a fiercely, totally democratic organization, open to anyone with or without the low dues, with an elected leadership usually galloping in one direction while the members marched in another. Chapters did as they pleased and projects happened because enough people did them. Program was hotly debated and then often coldly ignored, unless it really was up from the grass roots. SAW was uncontrollable and lush as a vacant-lot jungle.

When they walked into Vida's apartment, the living room was filled with twenty people sitting on everything available and the floor. Leigh looked annoyed. "Closed meeting. Only *Roach* staff." Mopsy wriggled to be petted.

She'd forgotten that Leigh had warned her the newspaper staff would be meeting there. "Sorry." Lohania and she trotted downstairs after Natalie. The phone, which had taken its Sunday-morning break, was ringing, as usual, every ten minutes. After Natalie had begun feeding Sammy canned goo in his high chair, Vida or Lohania continued whenever she was called to the phone. Lohania began supper, a process continued by whoever was not at the moment dealing with problems. Vida took calls about a women's-caucus meeting (Wednesday night. I'll try to make it. I have to meet with some chapter delegates from Queens College. Of course I think it's important, but . . . I'll put her on. Natalie!) The feed is broken on the Multilith press; who knows how to fix it? (Victor does. Call him at Betty's after eight); Do you have a copy of Gorz's *A Strategy for Labor?* I'm writing an article. And when are we going to see each other again? (Leigh has a copy. I'll bring it to the Steering Committee. I love you too, Pelican, of course.) Nan got busted spray-painting at Whitehall Induction Center (Call Martin Abrahmson at his home number on Central Park West. The number is . . .).

Natalie's apartment was not as sunny as Vida's, down three floors and facing West End, but the atmospheric difference was in the style of messiness. Not as often were random Movement extras from Tucson or Seattle camped on the living-room floor or taking unaccountably long baths reeking of dope and bubble bath or tying up the phone in long-distance calls to Alaska on fake credit cards that would be traced here in two months. Instead, more toys lay scattered underfoot, more small garments were abandoned on chairs and odd plastic nipples of the pacifiers Sammy insisted on sucking were stuck like flattened mushrooms to the sink drainboard and the windowsills. Both apartments had the air of being part-time offices, with mimeographed piles from mailings and political-education pamphlets stacked in every closet and covering varying amounts of the floors.

Daniel burst in, his face florid. "The kids were sitting in to protest ROTC and the administration bastards called the police. Lots of casualties. One with a broken back. They threw him down a flight of steps. I've got to get on the phone."

After Lohania cut short a call to Newark about starting a community radio station, Daniel took over for a series of staccato queries. Then he stormed into the kitchen, shoving his arms into his "respectable" overcoat. . . . "Who's got the emergency kitty?"

"Upstairs, my room. I'll go with you." As Vida ran beside him up the service stairs, feeling the anger and concern radiating from him like heat from a burner, she was sorry she had felt negative about him all day. It was she, Vida, who was saying at meetings that they must attract more ordinary people into war protest, and then she became impatient because Daniel and Natalie were a real couple and had babies all the time.

"I know the kid whose back they broke," Daniel muttered. "His brother was killed in Nam. Big gangly overgrown mutt just turned nineteen. And the papers will go on about student violence tonight."

She found the money for Daniel without disturbing the *Roach* staff. As they were leaving, she encountered the Chapel Hill couple carrying their sleeping bags. "That meetings seems like it might go on for hours," the guy said. "We're going to stay up by Columbia."

"Sure. Take care," Vida said, wishing she could remember their names.

After Daniel rushed out, a pork chop in his hand, Natalie, Lohania and Vida sat down to eat, while Sammy kept up a steady babble. He was playing baby. When he felt his mother was failing to pay all of her attention to him all of the time, he deployed a battery of devices. One of the ploys Vida found the most irritating was when he pretended to be a baby again and drooled and cried and made nonsense sounds at the top decibel level his baby-bird throat could gape. GAH GAH GAH GAH, he bellowed, banging a spoon, and then he giggled and waited to see if Natalie would not pick him up.

"Turn it down, Sammy. I have to talk to your Aunt Vida and your Aunt Lohania. You can it, now; I mean it," Natalie said—her voice, however, wheedling.

"Goo goo goo goo goo goo goo goo goo," Sammy shouted.

"The basic problem," Natalie bellowed grimly, pretending she could not hear Sammy, "is to ensure that this coming demonstration has political content. That the kids learn about the nature of the power structure and imperialism and not just get some exercise. We're moving people, yes, but we're not changing the way they think."

"What did you think of the Fair?" Lohania leaned back in her chair, touching up her nails with Mauve Magic. She had the longest nails Vida had ever seen in real life. They were a particular vanity and passion, a hobby, an artwork. Lohania liked them to be slightly grotesque.

"Eh . . ." Natalie sighed, letting Sam crawl into her lap and sit there grinning, victorious. "That's not my favorite constituency, strung-out kids. How can you talk to somebody who's stoned all the time?"

"We're reaching them," Vida insisted. "Sure, you can't get into long rational arguments with them like you can straighter people, but they have a feeling for who lies to them and who tells the truth. We have to reach everybody, my darlings, *everybody*—and we're doing it. We'll mo-

bilize every sector and we'll stop the war by
by the spring.''

"If we don't get out some troops for '
Thursday, they'll think we're losing mo
always saying we've peaked—as if we were
.Lohania snapped.

She had a vision sometimes of a movement lik
parades—not the kind of more militant demonstratio.
mounting, but the big spring mobilizations with old peopl
pushing strollers and men in suits and kids in body paint and .
priests and shamans and marching bands. Everybody would be
everybody but the ruling class. More and more people were against
war; more and more people were for change. The climate of the age was
warming. She felt bursting with strength when she thought of how far
they had come, from a tiny minority, timid and isolated, to a force that
felt as if it was becoming the mainstream. Now there were social workers
for peace, sanitation workers for peace, secretaries for peace, grandmoth-
ers for peace, zoo keepers for peace. They would take the country and
make it fulfill its promises, its good dreams.

When Leigh's meeting finished, he came downstairs. Sammy was
tucked into bed, still audible, while Vida made notes on points to present
at the meeting of the Steering Committee. Lohania was giving Natalie a
neck rub. When Leigh came in, she halted and winked at him. "So, the
Roach got its priorities straight for another issue?"

"Only a mere four hours to reach four decisions. . . . What did you
do with the men? Eat them like black widow spiders?"

Natalie's eyes shone with anger. "Men project their own violence
onto women!"

Lohania fluttered her lashes. "Since when do you mind being eaten?"

Vida said nothing, for she interpreted Leigh's question as meaning Is
Kevin gone? He had come down not after her but after Lohania. The two
of them had not made love all week. Vida had no desire to interfere, but
she wished she had second-guessed them earlier. She saw herself stretching out in her big bed for a nice night's sleep. Good to have an occasional
night by herself. The propaganda wasn't working. She felt too overwound
to remain alone.

She excused herself and called Pelican Bob back. "I found the Gorz.
If you want it, I can bring it by." Nine thirty on a balmy October night;
there were lots of people on Broadway. Pelican lived on Claremont by
Tiemann, right off 125th, so she would have two short blocks to trot from
the bus. Further, she experienced the pressure put on all Movement
women never to admit being afraid in the streets, afraid of any neighbor-

ally Black. Pelican Bob was nicknamed because he had
. Florida and once, while stoned, he had broken his usual
o speak for perhaps half an hour on the virtues of that bird.
re many Bobs in the New York Movement, so the title helped.
not want to sleep with Pelican, but dropping by his apartment
oe pleasant. She could relax and incidentally lobby Pelican and his
.mates to support her in Tuesday's meeting. She might need his vote.
had slept on their couch before.

Into her Greek carpetbag she packed her working clothes for tomor-
ow. The only disadvantage of sleeping at Pelican's was everybody's
ribbing when they saw her dressed for her secretarial job; but probably
none of them would be awake when she left.

8

The next morning, nobody at Pelican's was awake. Her dress for work was demure, the skirt not as short, the colors not as throbbing, no long dangling tinkly earrings. She daubed on her off-white lipstick and combed her hair back, put on her paisley hat and a flowered shift and she was ready for Kyriaki. Perhaps she spent an occasional impulsive night out to appreciate her household. Sour milk in Pelican's kitchen, Wonder Bread, potato chips. In her apartment Leigh rose with her and breakfast was a social occasion, sometimes the only quiet time to talk until night brought them to bed together. The tub at Pelican's was stained with the dirt of the ages, and the toilet smelled of men who pissed in the dark and sometimes missed. She hated to begin the day without a good hot scrub and soak.

On the subway she put her mind into shape for her job, doing English-to-Greek and Greek-to-English translating and typing. At Kyriaki they assumed that she was Greek—she had applied for the job under I.D. still in her old husband's name—and that she had then married outside. Her name was Mrs. Pfeiffer there. Never had she been Davida Asch on the job. She enjoyed being half invisible, as if under an alias.

Knowing she was married, they thought they knew all about her. The older women asked her when she was going to have a baby; the younger women consulted her about their boyfriends; the men told her their troubles with their stomachs, their wives, their in-laws. The duller her routine at work was, the more it soothed her. She felt like Clark Kent: glamorous, dangerous Vida Asch disguised as Mrs. Secretary. She was well paid and did not feel exploited. Using her Greek was delightful, and sometimes even her French or Spanish was called upon. She only wished she had an excuse to study Russian or Chinese. Every language was a new code, and cracking it a zesty pleasure. Further, the objects the company imported were pretty. Sometimes the girls in the office got samples of a new blouse. In Vida's living room the rugs were Greek knotted carpets of bright peasant designs, bought at wholesale. Occasionally one of the men put his hand on her ass and she removed it. Such attempts were not serious. She had worked there since 1965.

Why did she feel as if she were pretending, sitting at her typewriter? Teachers, social workers, taxi drivers, city planners belonged to antiwar groups and marched and organized; but most of the full-time SAW organizers did not work at outside jobs. Gobbets of money floated around, fat in the economy. Anybody could find a part-time job. It was easy to get unemployment, easy to get on welfare. Cooperative shrinks or doctors wrote letters. Some full-time staff people came from families who sent money. But she did not. Ruby and Sandy were more comfortable than Ruby and Tom had been when she was a child, but with two kids still at home, Sharon and Michael Morris—the baby, who was now in junior high—they had nothing to spare. She'd always worked. She made more money than Leigh did or anybody else except Daniel. Why did she feel she was playacting? She sometimes suspected if she were a truer revolutionary she would immediately quit her job and live off the cuff the way Pelican and company did. Voluntary poverty had no appeal, for her whole childhood had been spent in the working poor, and she liked her comforts. Wonder bread and cockroaches, ugh. She herself ran a clean tight kitchen.

Tuesday night she bought Chinese takeout on the way to the SAW office from work. Though the meeting was not until seven thirty, she had a lot to get done. Heaped on her desk were requests for antiwar literature, requests for speakers, letters from chapters with problems who wanted a regional representative to visit, donations, clippings, a threat from Minute Man marked with the cross hairs of a rifle sight, a love note from Pelican, an obscene hate letter addressed to Vida Ass and a notice to vacate their loft from the landlord. Have to call their lawyers on that one. The hate mail she shredded by hand and discarded. She tried not to read it when she opened it, but could not ever quite keep her eye from traveling over it. She never spoke of how sick it made her feel; not even to Leigh; not even to Lohania, with whom she shared most of her personal wishes and fears.

She was not romantically interested in Pelican, but she did not like to let a man understand that. She wanted him to feel good, to think at any time they might get together. That kept things pleasant. She hated to hurt people's feelings, and always she was convinced she could juggle events to satisfy. Therefore, when Pelican came in, she gave him a special long smile but was careful to keep away from him for the rest of the evening.

The SAW office was in an old SoHo loft, a building occupied by artists and light industry. Above them, a metal press ran all day stamping out forms. They had one long room, with the desks clustered near the windows that gave on the street, the meeting space of random old chairs in a circle toward the middle, where racks of literature on every aspect of the war, radical history, labor struggles, student unions and bibliographies for study groups lined the walls. The back of the room filled up with junk —old posters, broken furniture, signs from demonstrations, clothes left over from a rummage sale. When almost all of the circle of chairs had filled by ten to eight, she jumped up from the still towering pile of requests on her desk and slipped into the chair next to Lohania, who held up her hands to show off shiny black polish.

"Isn't it wicked? I'm the Dragon Lady herself," Lohania said. She was flirting with Bob Rossi, but stopped when his girlfriend Brenda started glowering. Lohania didn't like Bob Rossi particularly, but she liked to flirt. If the other women criticized her, Lohania told them they didn't understand cultural differences, that it was very Latino to flirt. She didn't say that to Vida. To Vida she said, "Eh, it's fun. I like to make those guys wag their tails!"

Vida smiled at Lohania, who wasn't watching. Sometimes she could feel in her friend the child poking through, the skinny dark unloved urchin with all-A grades, trying desperately to get rid of her accent and chewing her nails down to the quick and into the quick, always with a sore or infected finger from all that wanting and rage turned inward. They were bluntly honest with each other, much more open and talkative about sex than she had ever been able to be with her sister Natalie. Lohania needed to prove her attractiveness on men time and again; yet she also needed to give herself over to loving violently, as if she were throwing herself down a flight of stairs. And all of the time she was dead serious politically, their Marxist-Leninist whose room was lined with all those dull-looking books and pamphlets Vida could force herself through only when they were in some study group. The unwanted scabby urchin, the revolutionary scholar who read Marx in German, the compulsive vamp all coexisted in her friend.

The three dominant males on the staff were Oscar Loeb, Bob Rossi and Larkin Tolliver. Oscar was dark, stocky, erudite, intense, the best theoretician. Like Leigh, he came from an Old Left family. His father had been killed in Salerno while he was a toddler; his mother was a Party functionary who worked in a box factory. He had been the first man she had got involved with after settling in with Leigh, but the affair had not survived their being often on different sides politically. Oscar cared more for words and ideas than for people, she judged, and would sacrifice the real gain for the paper victory. Still, she felt close to him. When his best friend had gone to prison for draft refusal three months before, she had sat up with Oscar, holding him all night as he wept.

Bob Rossi was heavy and big like Daniel, but chestnut-colored in hair and eyes and handlebar moustache. He was a Maoist and craved action. Again Vida sometimes found herself on his side and sometimes not, because she found him prone to be where the action was, whatever it was. Larkin Tolliver was an unknown factor. He came from Kansas with some of the Midwestern SAW mannerisms, the address Brothers and Sisters, the air at times of a Baptist revival preacher and the reputation of burning commitment and a tremendous ability to organize. Basically, he had come to New York to look over their press setup and to take part in organizing the demonstration next week against the Foreign Policy Association meeting. He was a small tightly built sandy man with freckles and dark blue eyes, out of which he was looking now with unconcealed curiosity at her. The curiosity was mutual.

Besides Lohania, Natalie and herself, two other women sat on the Steering Committee: Jan, who was Oscar's girlfriend, and Brenda, who was Bob Rossi's. Both were juniors in college, both were blond, both were small and cute. Lohania, who claimed she could not tell them apart and who resented the fact that they always voted with their boyfriends, called them the Bubble Gum Twins. Pelican was an anarchist who insisted on challenging any show of authority. He was a member of the IWW, mostly for sentimental reasons. The other three men, Bill, Marv and Big Al, were all sidekicks, loyal to Rossi or Oscar. Larkin, known as Lark, would have to carve his own following if he stuck around instead of returning to Kansas.

"Lark and Pelican." Oscar rubbed his head. "We're turning into an aviary. Where the hell is Natalie? Again."

"Some kid from N.Y.U. was supposed to baby-sit Sammy. But he hadn't shown up yet when I talked to her ten minutes ago," Vida said.

"Damn it, she can't sit on the Steering Committee if she can't come to meetings," Oscar said sternly. "This isn't an optional activity if you happen to take time off from waxing your floor."

"You won't let her bring Sammy," Lohania said loftily. "Me, I think we should start them young."

"I'd sooner let her bring a dog. Ten dogs," Bob Rossi said.

"Well, what do you expect her to do?" Vida became aware she was being isolated by her defense of her sister.

"I don't know," Rossi drawled. "Maybe she could give it away."

"You're the one always saying we should organize the working class. Going to tell them to give their babies away too?"

"Natalie's supposed to be cadre," Oscar said. "We expect sacrifice from cadre."

"Good," Larkin said mischievously. "Then cadre can baby-sit. Why don't you volunteer? It would be a great sacrifice."

A short silence stood among them, bristling with armaments. Then Rossi said, "I move we ask Natalie to resign from the Steering Committee if she misses another meeting." His sidekick Marv immediately seconded the motion.

Lohania and Vida exchanged looks. They did vote as a block on certain issues, but she had not realized how much Oscar and Bob Rossi had come to resent that. Then why didn't they attack Lohania or her? She guessed the answer. Natalie was the only married woman on the committee, the only mother. She realized she was not counting herself as married, but nobody else did either. The rest of them were all, at least theoretically, available to each other as sex objects, but Natalie wasn't; somehow that meant they could take things out on her. It was unfair, but not something Vida could even say out loud without everybody's telling her she was crazy; everyone but Natalie, who always understood those subvocal interplays in groups. She and Lohania looked at each other again, urging caution. She flashed Larkin a grateful look.

"Yeah, Natalie ought to join Another Mother for Peace," Jan said sarcastically, looking at Oscar to see if he would approve.

Maybe Larkin had better politics toward women than Oscar or Rossi; she would see. Only Vida, Lohania, Larkin and Pelican voted against the censure of Natalie. Rossi was always talking about China. Vida had said she was all in favor of fund raising to send Rossi on a tour of the States to find some genuine peasants to ally with, to build the peasant–student alliance. Her big mouth got her in trouble.

But why was Oscar angry? She sensed that he felt she was growing too uppity. Her photograph in *Life*, not his. She had loved Oz, her pet name for him, partially out of gratitude because he did not view her as defined by her marriage. The year before, there was Leigh casually picking up day-glo girls at parties, in the Sheep Meadow, wandering through the bazaar of sexual possibilities plucking now an apricot, now a fresh green fig, now a pineapple; and there she was, Leigh's wife, expected to listen to everybody's love troubles, sympathize, bandage the wounded, mourn the missing, be prodded and pinched but harbor no sexual feeling toward anyone around her. Oz treated her exactly as he treated everyone else working with him on the teach-ins they had been organizing at every college around New York, the big spring demonstration they were joining in, the exams on the war they were handing out to students to show how popular assumptions about the war were erroneous. He treated everyone in a friendly and just manner, she thought. Inside, she glimpsed a lonely man. When she kissed him, he melted like a lump of milk chocolate. Now he was punishing her for her success, and she felt betrayed. Lohania was cautiously presenting snippets of their proposal: "Political education leading to action, that's how we grow. It's not like asking them to do study groups. We're going into the streets next week."

Was Larkin trying to make her part of his power base? That would remain to be seen, but he was surely backing her for a reason. She felt fiercely loyal to Leigh. His love for her was her real base, her strength, her support, her rallying point, her refuge, but he did not charge for his love what other men did. He let her be herself. He let her survive intact. She would live with him forever and ever until she died—she hoped, before he did. Other men were just decoration. Nibbles. Dalliances. A way to paint in a few colors on a friendship. Explorations. Fantasies.

Lohania and she got about half what they wanted. She was assigned with Lark to write the propaganda for the demonstration, which had to go out to all chapters by the week's end. Time was short for the job. The demonstration was scheduled for Thursday night of the next week, when the Foreign Policy Association was meeting at the Hilton and Dean Rusk was addressing it. The easy task was to pull the kids out against Dean Rusk, the glib corporate liberal vulture. The harder task was to pull them out against the Foreign Policy Association, to explain how the ruling class controlled political options and discussion: a subtler education in how power worked in peacetime as well as in war, in setting perimeters to inquiry, establishing the terms of argument, defining the questions and issues. She did not think Larkin understood the battle. He was supporting her because he wanted to take on Oscar and Rossi. Tomorrow night she must write the pamphlet with him. Natalie could tell her what had been discussed at the women's caucus. First things first. The demonstration was pressing; the women's caucus would be around in two weeks. She never had trouble with men, anyhow. Some of the SAW women had been meeting since the spring to discuss their problems in and out of the organization and give one another support.

"How about a little inside action?" Bob Rossi said. "Can't we manage some stink bombs?"

"You people aren't going to discuss that kind of thing in your office, are you?" Larkin stared.

"What's wrong with a pie in the face or a bit of stink in the ventilating system? You scared?" Rossi sneered.

"What's wrong with you that you can't figure out you might as well send your Red Squad notes on what you're planning? Surely this room is bugged," Larkin sneered back. "Get your volunteers and go for a walk to make any plans you mean to keep secret."

Everyone looked startled. "You really think it's bugged?" Vida asked.

"Don't you take yourselves seriously enough to assume that?" Larkin asked with apparent innocence.

Rossi said, "Okay. I'm volunteering to go for a walk to decide what I'm volunteering for."

"Me too!" Lohania flung up her black-tipped hands. "I love pigs in pokes." Rising, she held out her arm to Rossi. "Shall we stroll in the cool of the evening?"

Jan rose, her round face pinched with desperation. All meeting, Oscar had been ignoring her. "I'm not afraid. I'll go inside too. I'm not scared of being busted."

After the three had left, Vida remained a little shaken. They joked about the FBI and the CIA and the Red Squad, but this was the first time anyone had suggested altering plans on the assumption of routine surveillance. The rhetoric and the reality of the Movement were wide open. Anyone could come to meetings and propose anything at all and take their chances. A strange chill remained in the air.

The first time she sat down to work with anyone was awkward. How much would Larkin give and take? Where would the inevitable battles be joined? Automatically she sat at the typewriter, the way she worked with Oscar, who paced behind dictating ideas she turned into conversational English or argued with. Larkin pulled up a chair, facing her over the old machine. Slight, frail, with hair and lashes the color of wet coarse sand, he sat hunched and tense. She imagined him waiting for an opening, but to say what? "I want to use the demonstration for political education," she said bluntly, showing him the outline she had produced with Lohania and Natalie: a rundown of corporate connections of the personages who would be dining at the Hilton, an analysis of the Foreign Policy Association's means of manipulating public opinion. "I want the kids to learn how the power structure functions."

He looked at the list. "What's all this about South Africa and the Dominican Republic and CIA conduits? Sugar, oil, banks, foundations— this isn't a war of banks or words. What has this got to do with the shooting war we're trying to stop?"

"What this group does is form public opinion. Big American corporations make most of their profits abroad. They want to influence what ordinary people think they know about what's going on in other countries and what they see as options for the U.S. to do. You have to start manipulating public opinion before you invade," she argued.

"This isn't a school, it's a demonstration. To show our strength."

"Every time we act, the kids learn or give up." She paced around the battered old desk. A metal lamp hung down above them on a long grimy cord.

"Your pieces of paper won't make them care."

"Everything we know is pieces of paper. Including the war."

He grimaced. "I wish *I* knew about the war from pieces of paper. Maybe if I'd been born luckier."

She was startled. "Are you a vet?"

"Sure. That's why I can talk to guys. I got my damn medals. I did my damn time."

He was perched on the desk's edge, birdlike, a heron. As she passed him, she noticed he was wearing socks of different colors. A sign of indifference. The war service disconcerted her. Veterans were just beginning to come into the antiwar movement in numbers. On one hand, she was delighted to have someone with experience in Vietnam. On the other hand, what had he really done over there? It seemed pat: served his time, got his medals and decided it was all a mistake. "When did you start opposing the war?"

He snorted. "Too late to do me any good."

"What good do you think it does resisters?" She was thinking of Oscar's friend in prison, of her friend who had burned his brain on amphetamines marking time through appeal after appeal.

He looked as if he would answer sharply, but controlled himself. "All I care about is ending the war."

"*I* care about ending the war. I also care about building a movement for social change that will survive the end of the war. Do you think stopping the war will stop racism here? Or poverty? Do you think Vietnam will be the last place we invade?"

"That's theory. What I want to stop is real. Real people really dying in real mud right now."

"My war is right here. For this country."

"Oh, sure. Hard to get shot up in this one."

"Don't bet it won't come to that," she said. "If we're serious."

"Are you serious?" He raised his thin eyebrows at her.

"Serious enough to sit down and knock out this pamphlet. Time is short."

She ended up writing most of the pamphlet, simply because he was no phrasemaker.

"In school you learn to discuss 'issues,' " she wrote, "to interpret 'objectively,' to avoid dirty economic interpretation and asking who owns things and what makes them richer. You learn to 'discuss the text' and raise no extraneous issues. You make one Great Decision after another, fill out your multiple-choice questionnaire and depart, having sharpened your decision-making skills—presumably to make a wiser choice between toothpastes and candidates and whether you will buy your facts from *Time* or *Newsweek*. . . ."

While he vetoed suggestions, he could seldom block them with concrete ideas in concrete language. He was driven by a simple pure fanatical hatred of the war, and what she sensed of him besides was rather sweet, she thought. A steady type, not at all pushy. If he hung around, she had to think who might want him; he should not be wasted. Would Lohania like him? He might not be tough enough for her. Kevin played streettough, as did some of the men in SAW, but underlying the assumed persona was a real and tried capacity for action. Leigh was tough in another way, the New Yorker through and through who could talk his way in and out of almost anything—more than the survivor, the successful competitor. Lark felt vague by comparison. Still, she would talk to Lohania about Lark. She rose to her conclusion: ". . . sure are 'responsible leaders.' They are responsible for the plastic bread you eat and the filthy air you breathe; they own the buildings that line your streets and the means of production and the means of distribution; they rot your mind with wanting what they have to sell. They own your bodies to fight their wars. They sell you their brand of *Playboy* sex and their religion of greed and their science in the service of power and their sterile and alienated art. They are responsible, and you should be articulate. Come to the Hilton. . . ."

By four they were exhausted. The pamphlet had to be at the printer's at nine. That left too few hours to make it worthwhile to take the subway uptown to sleep and come back with the copy. They made a bed of old clothes left from a rummage sale. Unpurchased clothes stayed in the loft because she had not yet got around to calling a rag dealer. Oscar had said he'd take care of it and hadn't. After the demonstration, she must make some calls. In the meantime, stained summer shirts, faded cotton dresses, out-of-style trousers and suit jackets formed a nest for them. An athlete he wasn't, moving stiffly, awkwardly among the heaps of clothes.

Lying in the almost dark of the loft—light from the street coming in through the tall windows at the far end, the red light of the exit sign—she had trouble relaxing. Some animals—mice, she hoped, as opposed to rats —were scuttling in the old leaflets piled near the freight elevator. She did not feel comfortable lying beside him. He had not got undressed, and she had imitated him, lying stiffly in her clothes, annoyed at how wrinkled they would be the next day at work.

Lark was not sleeping either; she could feel him stirring. He fumbled at his shirt and lit a cigarette, the flame huge in the darkness. She was irked. She did not like smoking in bed, even if the bed was a pile of old clothes from a rummage sale. Finally she said, "Would you mind not smoking in what's doing us for a bed?"

"What? Oh. Do you really mind?"

"I do. I'm afraid to sleep for fear of waking up on fire."

"Oh." He put out the cigarette on the floor. "Would you hold me, then?"

If there was logic in that, it escaped her. She was stupefied, half sick with exhaustion, a light shaky feeling in her limbs. More than anything else she longed to be unconscious. Obediently and without enthusiasm she moved over and put her arms numbly around him, light, small as a child. Unsubstantial next to Leigh, or any of the stocky, firm-feeling men she had loved—Vasos, Oscar. When you held them you knew you had hold of someone real, whereas he felt like a scaffolding of a man. Stiffly he lay in her arms, and she had begun drifting down to sleep when he spoke again, startling her.

"Are you squeamish?"

"Wha?"

"Are you squeamish about people? If something's wrong?"

Half asleep, she saw herself holding Natalie's head as she had morning sickness, sponging her face. Every morning for two months. "I have a strong stomach. I get it from my mother."

"What do you think about amputees?"

Now she woke up. "What do you mean, what do I think?" she asked cautiously.

"Are you upset? Does it turn you off? . . . It's my right leg."

She forgot to breathe for a while. "I didn't know," she said, and then got angry at herself. She had to do better. "From the war?"

"My war. Not yours."

"Don't you think we're on the same side now?"

"Well, does it bother you or not?"

"Of course it bothers me. It bothers me for anybody to be hurt that way. How could I pretend I don't wish you had your leg? But it doesn't make me think you're less of a person."

"Or less of a man?"

"Of course not," she said loudly. How do I get into these things? She knew she had been mildly curious about Larkin, the way she was always curious sexually about any new man who came into the SAW inner circle. She knew too she had been flirting with him automatically, the way she flirted with every man a little unless she disliked him too strongly to carry it off. Just her way of greasing the wheels. She would sometimes in the middle of a serious conversation catch herself looking at a man in a certain way she had learned over the years as apology to men for being smart, aggressive, political, for being a competitor in the real things. Putting out a certain sexual buzz was a way of apologizing for being herself. She had not considered having sex with Larkin, but if she did not now he would think it was because he lacked a leg instead of because she was fatigued and not particularly attracted. How far up was the leg off? she wondered, and suppressed her curiosity as if squashing a cockroach. What did it matter? Legs were not sex organs. She reached for her purse with the diaphragm inside.

Then she moved up against him and brought her mouth down on his and coolly, feeling like a professional working on a client, began to caress and kiss him. She excited him, covertly touching herself to make sure she was damp enough to get him in, then slid over him, inserted his prick and brought him to climax in her. Gently she disengaged and rolled off. For a moment he lay relaxed, and she considered the episode finished, until he rose on his elbow and then gradually, moving with the stiffness and care she was beginning to understand, let himself down between her legs, pushing her thighs wide apart. The flesh leg, the plastic leg stretched out behind him. "I don't like favors," he said. "Unless I can return them. See if I don't know how to eat you out. If I can't make you come." He went down on her with his lips and tongue, after a while using his fingers inside her. He was skillful, persistent, patient, and yet she felt something savage in him. He lived with a lot of successfully swallowed anger—a lot. If Lohania could feel that, she thought—and then stopped thinking for a few minutes.

"You could come again," he offered.

"I'm tired," she said. "That's enough for me."

Beside her he said dreamily, "I never was a good fuck before. I always came too soon . . . but afterwards a nurse taught me how to do that. She made it with men and women. Now I understand women better. Most women don't like fucking, really, but if you know how to eat a woman, you can get her to come."

Vida actually preferred intercourse, but she knew that Natalie didn't. "It was wonderful," she said soothingly.

"I don't have the energy to do this a lot. It takes my strength to get through each day. Not to let people know I'm disabled. A fucking cripple. You know it now. I can't lie down with a woman without her finding it out."

"You can trust me. But why keep it a secret?"

"I hate pity. I hate it!" He was silent a while. Then he said gruffly, "You can't organize people if they know you're a cripple."

"It seems to me you do everything anybody else does."

"I can't run. At demonstrations it's hard. I volunteer to man the phones or something. But I'm always scared some two-legged bastard is going to call me a coward. . . . You'll tell your boyfriend. The guy on the radio.''

"A lot of things I know he doesn't. We aren't into all the same things politically. . . . But why keep it a secret? You ought to be proud how much you get done.''

"Never. I don't want their pity. . . . I don't sleep with a lot of women. But you liked it?''

"Of course. Couldn't you tell?'' In a way, she had. She felt caught in him emotionally.

"I can't do it often . . . I'm cut off from my body. I numb it out. That's not all that's wrong with me, understand. I stepped on a mine. I numb out the pain a lot, and that means numbing out everything physical.''

"You do that with your mind? Or drugs?''

"Hate drugs! I'm on medication . . . but not for pain. My mind's all I got. . . . But I like you. You're serious. I like smart women. Women who know how to take care of themselves. . . .'' He was silent so long she thought he had fallen asleep, and indeed, his voice came groggily, patchily. "When I'm sizing up people . . . I think how they'd act . . . places I been. I think, What would they do up to their waists in mud and under crossfire? . . . Would they drag me out? Would they run like hell? . . .'' His voice faded into mumbling and breathing, emerged again farther down the line as if from a tunnel. . . . "The sarge said, Go on, stick your bayonet up her. . . . They cut off her nipples, her back was broken . . . my pistol and shot her in the head. The kindest thing I could think of. . . . So I look at these dudes and I try to figure them out. . . . You're okay. You'd drag me out. You'd hold up a long time. What I figure . . . Women are tougher than men when you come down to it. . . .'' He had talked himself to sleep, and soon he snored softly. She did not sleep that night.

She took off her earrings, pinned up her hair, put on boots, jeans and Leigh's buffalo plaid jacket over a man's shirt. A helmet or not? Helmets protected your head against the clubs that could bash your brains to jelly, but sometimes they seemed to attract police wrath, if not enough others were wearing them; and they made it hard to hear. She put the blue football helmet back in the hall closet.

Leigh was checking his Nagra, whistling, dressed no differently than on any other day except for his bright press pass pinned on. She felt distant from him before a demonstration. He went, sure, but not as a participant. His role was useful to all of them, the voice telling people not present what was going on; yet he faced little danger. His belly would not feel stiff as the old washboard her grandma used to wash clothes on with kosher soap; his colon did not jerk spastically, keeping him on the toilet for half an hour expelling everything, everything inside him till his anus burned.

Finally she emerged with a great stiff plaster of Paris grin stuck on her face and met Lohania dressed in a Hilton maid's uniform. "How's this for typecasting?" Lohania said sourly.

Her apartment had never felt cozier, warmer, more homey. All the books she had no time to read cooed like pigeons from their shelves. Together they clattered down the service stairs to Natalie's.

"You goddamn well can't!" Daniel was bellowing, trussed into his demonstration khakis, looking like the football end he had once been. "If you want to lose this baby, pay a good abortionist. But don't lose it from stupidity in the streets!"

"Daniel, I don't plan to brawl. It's as much my duty to demonstrate as it is yours!"

"Your duty is to your unborn child! You're staying."

"They don't ask Vietnamese women if they're pregnant before they drop napalm on them!" Natalie yelled. "What kind of fink do you suppose I am to sit home while everybody's putting their bodies on the line? Do you think I have some kind of pass out of having to take chances, just because I'm a mother?"

"Natalie, I came down to ask you if you can man the telephones with Larkin. It's awfully important tonight," Vida said, trying to make peace in her family. Besides, Lark deserved to meet Natalie for voting on her side. Maybe Natalie would for once fall in love with somebody else, just once! Lark was much nicer than Daniel; maybe he'd like a ready-made family. She had already passed on a few titillating details to Lohania on the scene between them. Lohania had been intrigued, for Lark's maiming did not put her off. "Could you get to the SAW office fast? Just take Sam along. We need people to handle the media and arrange bail."

"You're just trying to make me feel as if I'm still a political person," Natalie said, close to tears. "When I'm eight months gone I'll sit in the stupid office. But at this stage my baby's protected against earthquake and even a couple of casual pokes in the belly!"

Natalie was sent off to the SAW office. Lohania was annoyed. "Why didn't you back her up? She has a right to be with us." Lohania marched out alone, to try to penetrate the Hilton.

Daniel, Pelican and his roommates and Vida set off together. "She's so little," Vida said to herself about Natalie. Her sister seemed to her less able to run through the streets. For once she sympathized with patriarchal Daniel. As they emerged from the subway among the many passersby on the evening midtown pavement, they recognized knots of their own kind. The placards were being hoisted; the chants were beginning. Suddenly more and more of them began to come together. A group from Teachers for Peace was singing "We Shall Overcome." Her chest burned with excitement. Yes, look! Yes. Everywhere her people came together, marching arm in arm linked and shouting. The demonstration was starting. It was truly happening. Some words on a page she had written and people responded.

The legal segment of the demonstration, where protesters walked with signs to and fro in a corridor between police lines, was two blocks away. Here demonstrators were stopping the cars of dignitaries, the limousines, the chauffeur-driven Cadillacs and Chryslers. Into the path of the cars they darted screaming. Bland faces peered at them through thick glass as if they were the menace, they who had never ordered a death; who controlled no bombs, no death rays, no machines of mass terror, no chemicals that brought starvation and changed the genes forever; they who wore no diamonds mined by black captive labor in the bowels of South Africa and invested in no Afrikaans enterprises burbling stolen profits. A kid was dragged half a block on a car that would not slow down and was helped off by a medic, leg crooked, nose bleeding.

"No, guys! Not the regular cars!" she was yelling. "The limousines. Stick to the limousines!" You had to keep reminding the troops what they were supposed to be attacking. Too much Halloween. They could get intoxicated by the crazy raggedy feeling of running in the streets whooping. "Only the richies! Let the regular cars through." Had they even bothered to read the pamphlet? How could you do political education when people can't read any longer? Maybe that was the purpose of the slow destruction in the schools. The media were under tight control, while anybody with a printing press in their garage could produce the written word. The new illiteracy imposed by the schools. She wrote a leaflet in her head, running at full tilt to keep track of the action. "Only the richies! Only the limousines!" Corporate lawyers who specialized in military contractors, the folks who had founded the CIA and invented the missile gap, sugar magnates fresh from engineering an invasion of the Dominican Republic, officers from the Export-Import Bank, the Foreign Bond Holders Protector Council, Mobil Oil, Con Edison, IBM, the Dallas Citizens Council, Chase Manhattan Bank, ALCOA, IT&T, Pan American, *The New York Times*, *Time-Life*—they were in those cars. She knew their dossiers, compiled painstakingly in libraries by Movement researchers, but she could not tell one face from another.

Barbarians, a professor at Columbia had called the Movement in the *Times* that morning. Maybe the barbarians, the savages were always those who had less lethal weapons. Bows and arrows versus tanks and artillery. Their own lithe bodies dancing in front of tons of metal. That made them savages: lacking the metal. Lacking armor, lacking armies, lacking the underlings to do it for you.

Although the night was crisp, Vida felt hot under the wool shirt, running. The pavement pounded up into her bones. She strained, leaping over occasional stoops, knocked-down garbage cans, running hard because a mounted cop was galloping after her trying to ride her down. She stayed out from under the horse's hooves by keeping close to the building, but then he leaned out of the saddle swinging his nightstick and caught her a glancing blow on the shoulder that almost brought her down. Police sirens whooped hysterically in the next street to the left as she twisted and dodged away from the blows of his club, plunging into a group of people in evening clothes emerging from a bar. A woman screamed at the rearing horse. Was her arm broken? She tried to move it as she ran. She jumped across the open stairway that led down and then plunged between two buildings, into a narrow passageway where the horse could not follow. The cop galloped on after other prey. She fell panting against a building. Her arm throbbed. Was it broken? She felt cautiously, then moved it. Ow—her muscle felt torn; but the bone was intact.

Chanting in the next street. "Hey, hey, L.B.J., how many kids did you kill today?" As her breath slowed, she stumbled to her feet and turned toward the troops. Time to regroup, time to storm the hotel again. Turn them back from random charging down random streets. Back t. square one. She had not liked being chased by a cop on horseback. Why were they always the ones running? Why were they always the ones getting beaten?

Glass breaking. Screaming. She scrambled up a chain-link fence and dropped into a parking lot, crouching after the jolt of her landing on the pavement below. Then she trotted out into the street, broken-field running among cars. She caught a glimpse of Kevin slugging it out with a counterdemonstrator. No reason to do that. It accomplished nothing politically, although she recognized a certain satisfaction in the sight. The movement had begun in pacifism, and she had twice been beaten by counterdemonstrators when they had caught her alone. They liked to trap Movement women and try to disfigure them, shouting *Whore!* Kevin was less easy prey, but fighting with thugs was not their purpose. They were out in the open to demonstrate, to show the government—and tonight especially the invisible government, the decision makers—how much anger existed against their war.

She ran down the street hoarsely bellowing, "Back to the Hilton! Back to the Hilton! Come on, let's get them!" She had a moment of ice-water disassociation as she turned to lead a pack toward the center of the action. All this did not come naturally, not naturally at all. It felt weird. It felt, at the oddest moments, sharply improper. Her inner barricades were as well manned as the police lines she could see ahead. Between those barricades the mass of demonstrators marched chanting, waving placards. Things were orderly here. The crowd shuffled in the narrow corridor permitted them, a block from the hotel where the Association was meeting, while the cops lined up taunting them, swinging their clubs, thwack, thwack, in their hands. They passed comments on the women, laughing.

We brought all these people here, she thought, but felt afraid, of them, for them, with them. The press mostly stood across the street and looked at them as if visiting a zoo. Photographers from the papers snapped pictures, as did those who worked for the Red Squad. There was the video truck they called WFBI. This was the legal demonstration site. Of course, most of the action was happening on the far side of the hotel where she had been stopping cars with groups of SAW irregulars and where occasional cat's-paws of troops tried guerrilla assaults on the hotel, aimed at any disruption they could produce. They did not really expect to get inside, but they hoped to frighten the powerful, to ruffle their security. The guilty shudder sometimes even before children jumping up and down with paint on their faces and scrawled placards in their hands; that is, the ones who aren't too bored. It was necessary, the pressure they put on, to keep the escalations to a certain size. They had not yet stopped the war, but they had contained it.

Where was Lohania now? Had she penetrated the hotel? Vida had a moment of pure terror while the pain from her shoulder threatened to engulf her. Her side ached. Her feet hurt from so much running on pavement. Somewhere she had cut her hand, probably scaling the fence. It had stopped bleeding, but it too hurt. Against a building a medic was tending a girl whose scalp was freely bleeding down into her eyes over her smashed glasses. He was picking bits of glass out of her face. Oscar, carrying coffee for the marshals, stopped to comfort her. Then he saw Vida and made his way to her.

"Want some coffee?" Oscar asked her, passing a paper cup. He had a rough bandage over his forehead, making him look rakish, a pirate: scholarly Oscar. "They busted Rossi and Marv."

What did he feel? Did he feel responsibility bearing down on him? Was he scared? You called them and they came and that made you responsible for every injury, every accident, every maiming. No, they had choices. They were angry. They needed to fight back. She did not know what she felt except that to stop and reflect made her buckle with fatigue. "They're busting a lot tonight," she said. "Do we know what precinct,

Oz?'' She used the name she had called him when they were lovers, but he did not notice.

"All over, to make it harder." He stepped closer. "Good idea to send Natalie down to cover the phones. It released Lark."

Oh, dear, that couldn't be good for him. "I thought we could use two people down there."

"Know where he is?" Oscar stepped close enough to speak in her ear. "Inside."

"With Lohania?" She looked at the hotel, asking with her eyes.

"She went in first. Rossi got busted trying. Then Lark volunteered."

"It's dangerous," she said helplessly.

"Jan was going to go in, but she chickened out," he said bluntly about his lover.

"I'm heading back out. Diversion, anyhow."

"This gives us practice in mobile street tactics," Oscar said with deadly seriousness as a flying wedge of police came at the line of demonstrators from across the street. "Here they come. Hold that line! Hold that line!"

She dropped the coffee, battered against the wall before she could budge. Then she began struggling out of the melee. Stooping to gather a fallen placard—NO MORE BOMBING/CALL THE TROOPS HOME—she dodged out of the trap and, shouting hoarsely, led a countercharge across the street blocked with police lines. They could shoot, she thought, charging the line. Someday they will. But the police had not been prepared for their sudden attack, and they rammed through on surprise into the street in front of the hotel. She felt like laughing; she was grinning as she ran with her comrades. Charged right through, how do you like that? She wished she could see herself on film. She loved herself; she loved all of them. She saw Kevin running just to her right, fending off assaults by sheer force. He was a good man in street action, she had to admit. She wondered if he knew Lohania was trying to plant a stink bomb inside; would she have told him? She leaped another barricade, astonishing herself. Her best moments were when she did not stop to think in a demonstration but seized an opening. The mass of demonstrators, attacked on the right flank of the police, surged after the first batch. Soon there was fighting in the whole block.

A motion on her right. She turned to see the truncheon coming down on her, saw it suspended in a moment of terror as her arm started to rise to protect her head and the arm could not rise—she could not use that arm with the shoulder injury—and then Kevin launched himself between. He hit the cop full force in the elbow and the truncheon went flying. Then they were beyond.

"Thank you," she said as they ran on side by side. She turned her head to smile at him apologetically.

"Don't mention it." He was grinning out of his shaggy blond beard. "What's with your arm?"

"It took the brunt earlier. Cop on horseback."

"They can't get horses in here." He surveyed the street almost leisurely. "Good brawl."

She realized he was enjoying himself, and she did not know whether she was impressed or appalled. Then she saw Daniel go down under three police swinging clubs and disappear from sight. As she struggled toward him, she saw him finally dragged free and thrown into a paddy wagon. He did not land with a thump because they threw him on top of the pile of people already loaded; and then they locked the doors.

A while later she looked at her watch and realized that it was ten and the crowds were beginning to thin out. Arrests, casualties, fatigue. "Break it up," she began passing the word. "Time to move out." Those lingering would be busted for sure. She could find only Pelican and his roommate Fred. They stripped the obvious signs of battle from themselves so they wouldn't be picked off as they entered the subway, and then wearily, without conversation, rode home. Automatically Pelican and Fred followed her into her apartment, one of the nerve centers. Leigh was waiting, a bottle of Sangre de Toro open on the table.

"Did you get good coverage?" she asked him.

"Pretty good. Cop chased me at one point trying to get the recorder, but I got away. Natalie's still on the phones downtown."

She began running the water for a bath. "God, I'm tired." She carried a tumbler of wine into the tub with her and set it in the soap dish. Her shoulder was livid, too sore to touch. The phone was ringing all of the time. Let the others deal with it.

Leigh burst in. "Lohania's busted. Caught inside with a stink bomb. She'll have heavier charges than the others. We have to zip down to night court."

Still moist and swollen, she shoved herself into respectable clothes, dressing as she would for work. Leigh took the emergency kitty and their bankbook. They rode downstairs in the elevator, leaving Fred and Pelican getting stoned on the living-room floor, happy as a couple of linebackers after winning a high school game. They could answer the damned phone.

"Daniel got busted too," Vida suddenly remembered as they stepped onto Broadway. The air felt cold, abrasive. She tasted her exhaustion like bile in her throat. "They beat him."

"I don't think Natalie knows. We have to find out where they took him." Leigh stepped off a curb and hailed a cab. She was startled but glad, stumbling in after him. He put his arm around her and she nestled close. "Did they say anything about Larkin?"

"Larkin? Who's he? Don't think so. . . . Oh, yeah, Natalie mentioned that somebody'd come back down to help her out and maybe she could get off by midnight. Lark, I think she said."

"That's him." So he got out of the Hilton safely. Had he reached the air ducts with his stink bomb? She'd know soon enough. She was not sure quite what they might have done to him in jail, but she had a few vivid ideas. Closing her eyes, she saw Daniel go down under the three policemen, and she wondered how to tell Natalie so that she would not be terrified. Maybe she would simply say she had seen him arrested.

"Tired, baby? Just lean on me. . . . Let's see, Natalie said Sammy was sleeping just fine. . . . I'll wake you up when we get there."

By and by, by and by they would be home again together, at rest under the Cretan embroidery. In the meantime, Lohania and Daniel must be located and if possible bailed out. From somewhere she must squeeze the energy to function. But not now. In the cab she collapsed against Leigh and shut her eyes. His flannel shirt was soft to her cheek. He put his leather jacket over them. Close she curled, smelling him—sweat, the funky lingering smell of dope, a trace of Lohania's sandalwood, the spicy bath oil, all blending with a faint smell of leather and perhaps wood smoke from their last camping trip on Mount Marcy. His chest was firm and warm; his arm, with its curly thick fur, encircled her. She moaned as he touched the bruises, but was too tired to explain. She only moved his hand to her waist and snuggled closer. Soon enough she would be in the dingy environs of night court among the prostitutes being shunted off, the plea-bargaining lawyers, the drunks thrust into the tank. Then she must wake up and manage, talk coherently, argue, plead, save her people. Now she could doze against Leigh. How wonderful to be connected widely and richly to people all over the world, she thought—people trying to change things, move them forward—to a web of the caring in every city and college town. How wonderful to have family and friends and lovers, community and meaning. How wonderful to have him.

PART III

The Present, October

9

Filene's was a big department store in downtown Boston, jammed with shoppers on a Saturday in mid-October. No downtown abandonment here. She located Lingerie on the chart, then parked Joel in Men's Wear. "So try things on."

"Men don't do that," he said sullenly. "They expect you to buy something."

"I'll pick you up right in front of the Levi's at two. If something goes wrong, we'll meet at six on the north side of Faneuil Hall"—another landmark she had found on the map.

"I don't care if I meet her or not."

"Baby, that has to depend on how things are. How she feels."

"She'll feel hostile. Why shouldn't she?"

"Ah, Natalie'll be tickled pink I'm with somebody for a change. Now I have to rush."

"Sure. You have to. I don't drag you off to Sacramento to meet my parents and park you in a shopping plaza somewheres. I think it's dangerous for you to see your sister. I didn't expect you to be so sentimental."

"I have to go! I'm going to be late." Like pulling off sticky flypaper, she had to tear loose from him, not finish the conversation but rip loose of it and flee. As she rode down the escalator, she felt peeved. Really, what did she want to drag around with him for? Sulking, sullen. As soon as he was out of her sight for the first time in days, she felt a swell of panic. She wanted to run back upstairs. Fear of losing. Fear of never seeing him again—him too, one more lost. From moment to moment, what could she take for granted except the need for vigilance?

She went all the way down, walked a slow circle and then rode up. On edge, on guard, watching now, her skin all eyes. That woman, wearing a drab green raincoat. The coat was unnecessary. Shoplifter, probably. For a minute they eyed each other; then both turned away. Slowly she cruised past the flimsy pastel nightgowns toward corsets. A woman near the bikini panties was going through the sale bins without looking at anything. Although she remained standing there, the salesgirl did not come to her. Pig, yes, but what kind? Watching the other women. Now sauntering off in the wake of the woman in the raincoat, whom she had at once noticed as Vida had. Store dick, okay. Keep away from her, don't finger the merchandise.

Past the bras Vida ambled, turning in slow arcs of reconnaisance. At the far wall, Natalie was zinging dressing gowns along a rod. She was actually looking at them, pulling out a filmy bronze wrapper to peer at it, then shaking her head and passing it along. She knew suddenly that Natalie was thinking of her, her love of sleazy dressing gowns that slithered in the boudoir, that invited touch. When her hair had been red, she would have looked superb in that shade, and Natalie had suddenly realized that and therefore rejected the wrapper. Now she was fingering a soft mauve. Better, Natalie, better, she thought; maybe I've finally taught you some feeling for clothes. Small cute pinchable Natalie with her round ass sticking out of the dressing gowns peered at the buttons on the mauve satin. Her curly hair was cropped close to her head, the Afro of several years shorn. She wore a dark blue bulky sweater with tan cords, boots, suede jacket some years old and her oat-bag purse both slung over her shoulder.

Softly, softly she stepped up behind Natalie. "It won't do, Natty. Daniel would have a heart attack if you sailed out of the bathroom in that."

"He wouldn't notice." Natalie covered her surprise with a matter-of-fact tone. "Besides, he's not around in the mornings nowadays. . . . Can't I even kiss you?"

Briefly, fiercely they hugged. Natalie's hot soft dear body bumped her; her fuzzy curls tickled Vida's nose. Natalie's eyes teared, and she ran her finger hard under her nose, scowling, and pinched the dressing gown. "Wouldn't you look great in this?"

"Sensational. But if you really want to get me something, I desperately need boots."

Natalie fingered the material. "We'll go right to the shoe department . . . but you'd look fine in this."

She disentangled the price tag. "Natty, it's sixty-five dollars. I know you don't buy yourself sixty-five-dollar bathrobes. Let's go get me some winter covering for my soon-to-be-bare tootsies." Yet she felt contrarily tugged as she marched arm and arm with Natalie away from the rack. She wanted the mauve; she wanted it to entice Joel, her lover; she wanted to parade in it to and fro looking sumptuous. All the pleasures she had taken for granted with Leigh, never to be shared with Joel.

The shoe department was crowded. They sat side by side waiting for a salesman, with a list of numbers and styles to try, while all around them women and girls were shoving feet into bright clunky high-heeled shoes. "I hate to see high heels coming back," Natalie said, looking where Vida was looking. "Remember those killer spikes? Always getting caught, always snapping off."

"Remember when you were in love with that supercilious Trot? You walked five miles with him in your heels and you were crippled for a week?"

"I was a jerk," Natalie said. "A masochistic jerk. Now they're trying to bring back all that foot-binding torture from the '50s."

"They want to abolish the '60s. Take back everything we gained. Concessions they made under threat. Close the system tight again."

Natalie leaned close, pointing at her overblouse. "Hey, wasn't that a dress?"

She looked down: her moss green velour pullover. "Hard to believe now. We all had this dress, you and me and Lohania, in different colors. . . . Do you still have yours?"

"I'm sure it went to the Goodwill years ago. . . . We won't let them take all our hard-won gains back. We push, they push back, we push, they push back. We never expected it to be easy."

"Oh, sure we did." Vida grinned. "Don't worry, I'm less depressed than I was. Guess what?"

"You met somebody?"

"How did you guess?" She felt transparent.

"When you grin like that? You haven't made that face in years. Years and years." Natalie poked her. "So *who?*"

"A man. A *young* man."

"Somebody who's sheltering you?"

"No. . . . He's . . . like me."

"Do I know him?" Natalie's eyebrows came together; she was thinking, no doubt, of all the macho hardheaded hardhearted know-it-alls she had detested in SAW in its last foaming loudmouth stage.

"He didn't move in our circles. Natty, he really is *young*."

"You keep saying that with tongs. Fifteen?"

"Twenty-seven. I'm serious about him. I'm crazy about him. . . . Are you shocked? Speak to me. Am I completely nuts?"

"No, love, no. It's very young men or women, that's the only choice we all get now. The men our age won't change with us, won't let go of the old privileges. They're scared of our changes . . . so, it's younger men with less stakes in the old roles, or women.''

Vida giggled. "You make it rational. You always say, There, there, falling out the window with your nightie on fire is a frequent occurrence in elevator buildings with this kind of population density.''

"Okay, what can I do for you ladies today?'' The salesman smiled without looking at them. He glanced at his watch. Natalie had the numbers ready to read to him. Vida felt oddly excited, a child getting new shoes. She could not remember the last time she had been in a department store. Did they have department stores in L.A.? When she thought of shopping, she remembered May's in Cleveland when she and Ruby had gone downtown to get her a few things for school, September jaunts clutching hands and every penny figured. Then she thought of Natalie teaching her to use the first charge card she had ever seen and certainly the first one for Ruby also. Natalie and she stood in Marshall Field's picking out sweaters together and feeling so haughty with adulthood they giggled all the way home on the El.

Mainly when she thought of department stores . . . "Too wide. I need it in narrow. Do you have these in narrow?'' . . . she thought of the different pleasures of Bloomingdale's and Alexander's, cheek by jowl and different worlds; of Altman's, of Macy's, of forays into Lord and Taylor's, Bonwit's, Bendel's. The days of casual shoplifting, a scarf, even a minidress carried off. Her own purse full of charge cards and the pleasant rustle of packages filled with little treats for Leigh, for Lohania, for baby Sammy, for Natalie.

"Do they fit now?'' Natalie peered at them suspiciously. "Be sure they're comfortable.''

Back and forth in the new boots she marched. "Natty, I trust him. I am trusting him. What do you say?''

"You want me to meet him?''

She flexed her foot. "How does that feel to you?''

"I have some business with you. If you're going to travel with him, I guess it'd involve him. Think he'd be into exporting a woman for us?''

"If not, then I should find it out now.'' The salesman was tapping his foot impatiently. "Yeah, hi, we'll take this pair. All right, Natty? You satisfied?''

"You're the one got to be satisfied.''

"They're not too expensive?''

"Vinnie! When do I get to buy you a present anymore?'' Natalie fumbled for her wallet. "I wonder do they take Master Charge?''

"Cash. Pay cash.''

"Okay." Natalie did. When the salesman went to ring up the charge, she said, "I just wanted to save as much cash as I can to give you."

"Charging leaves a record. Not a good idea." She looked at her watch. "We've got an hour. Let's wait to eat with him; he'll be hungry. Where can we sit and talk?"

"Outside the beauty salon on the mezzanine. As if we're waiting for someone."

Side by side they sat down, facing each other. She pushed the cropped curls from Natalie's face, tweaked her turned-up nose that had been the envy of their high school class, squeezed the plump hand on which the ring was suddenly missing. "Did you lose your wedding ring?"

"You might say I'm in the process." Natalie pulled her lips down in a wide arc. "At long last, I suppose."

"You're splitting?"

"You said it. The atom didn't take any longer to split, did it? I'm a persistent woman. Should have left him years ago, I know it. But I loved him!"

"But you could have loved somebody else too."

"Kids ought to have fathers, if they have to live in this society run by old men. Might as well get used to it. . . . Not that Daniel thinks he's old. His new girlfriend is twenty-three."

"Gee. At least Leigh's is twenty-six. . . . Have you met this Susannah?"

"She's nice, Vinnie, I think you'd like her."

"Do *you?*"

Natalie swallowed. "Oh, you know, she's okay."

"You do like her!" She wanted to weep with betrayal. "She must be wonderful if even you like her so much!"

"Aw, come on, she's nice, that's all. She's crazy in love with Leigh, she has some politics. She's good with the kids—Peezie adores her."

Stealing the love of her niece. "What does she look like? Describe her. Exactly."

"She's not beautiful, but she's pretty. A little shorter than you, a little heavier. Her hair is reddish brown. She has beautiful skin—peachy. It glows."

"How much heavier?"

"You know something funny, love? She kind of looks like you. I mean like you looked, you know, when Leigh married you. But she isn't anything like you. She's a softie."

"Hmp. What does she do? Besides love Leigh like crazy and live in my apartment."

"She teaches handicapped kids. What they call special needs. When

Leigh met her she was working out on the Island and they only saw each other weekends. Then she got a job in the city and they started living together."

"How serious is this thing? For real. Tell me."

"Vinnie, he really did wait for you. But it's not about to pan out for you two. . . . He meets lots of women. He's a minor celebrity, he's available. Susannah's the best one yet. You should have met the actress he was running around with in the winter—no politics, a monstrous sore running ego, and manipulative?"

"*Why* is he serious about her? Why *her?*" She experienced a moment of guilt in front of Natalie, plotting to expel this unknown young woman from her husband's life. Not exactly female solidarity. Natalie could make Vida feel her deficiencies.

"She's the physical type that knocks him dead, and probably he thinks he can, you know, hold on to this one. She won't join the guerrillas in the mountains or even me in the battered women's shelter."

"He'll get bored." She rubbed her eyes, feeling the skin for lines. "It wasn't so good with Leigh this time. He never came West and I couldn't get East, so a lot of time went by. . . . Sam sounded great on the phone. I'd like to see him."

"I thought about bringing him along, but taking him to a women's health conference seemed a little much. He's five feet nine already, and his voice is changing. I'm scared he's going to be seven feet tall. And he eats and eats. One of the reasons I've been slow to leave Daniel is 'cause I can't afford to feed Sam on my own. He eats so much I get hostile sometimes. I feel like I'm shoveling it into a furnace."

"But he sounded *together*, such a person already."

"He is. So's Peezie. My gazelle, my antelope. Fanon's a little slower coming along."

"Well, he's younger."

"Not just. Slower. Whinier. More dependent. Got spoiled, maybe. He could shape up." Natalie sighed, picking sand out of the corner of her eye, one of her nervous quirks when she was upset, along with turning her ring round and round, the ring that had finally disappeared. "Peezie and Sam, they were Movement babies. Frankie grew up out on the Island. It's supposed to be better for kids, but I don't know. . . ."

"What's happening with Daniel? Why are you finally breaking up? Why *now?*"

"There's nothing left, kid. I realized that. Listen, Daniel called from the city to say he wasn't coming home on a Friday night, and I felt so much relief I was startled. The next day, this storm hit us. The basement was flooded, the power was off, trees were down in the street. I called him at his girlfriend's—Katy—and told him not to try to drive. Somehow, going through the whole weekend without him was a treat. I realized I don't like living with him. Slowly it's come to that. I just don't like it.''

"But you've lived together so many years," Vida said doubtfully. "Won't you have trouble getting used to being alone?"

"I'm not scared. It isn't as if I don't work and don't have my own friends. . . . It's been getting worse. Less and less talking. Less sex. More political differences. . . . It's like a noise that starts off so soft you can't hardly hear it. Real slow it gets louder until you realize it's driving you mad. Then it stops. And you know you just don't want to live with that noise anymore." Natalie shrugged, palms up. "Daniel's that to me. Awful to say it. Finally there's no love and just this big growing annoyance."

"What are you going to do?"

"I don't know, sweetie. Sometimes I think I'll move into the city, into Park Slope in Brooklyn maybe. I got a lot of friends there. But I'm real involved in our shelter. . . ."

"Natty, how's Ruby? Is she mad at me because I haven't been able to see her in so long?"

Natalie touched Vida's cheek. "She never really understands. She wants to see you, a lot. She counts the months. . . . But she never really learns how it is with you. When the birthday present came from Cincinnati, she says, Oh, Vida's in Cincinnati, when I know you'd never have something mailed from where you are—"

"Did the sweater fit? A friend knitted it." Alice had, in the latter stages of her recuperation.

"That shade of blue is gorgeous on her. It's a little tight, but she said it's stretching."

"I wanted to stop by Chicago, but I couldn't. I had to go through the Southwest and up through Arkansas. I had work to do. How's Paul?" Even though Paul and Natalie were not blood relatives, since Paul was Vida's older brother, they were close enough so that Vida knew Natalie always saw him when she visited Chicago.

"Always a mess!" Natalie shook her head. "This new wife, she's got the mind of a pencil sharpener. Why did he leave Joy? Our niece Marsha is having a baby. And his own baby boy is darling."

Dutifully Vida asked about Sharon and Michael Morris, but she hardly listened to the answers as they went to meet Joel. Vida clutched her sister's arm, holding the package of boots on her far side. She had never been able to care for Daniel and had not seen him since 1970; yet an impending divorce scared her. Things were changing with her unable to influence the course of events, unable to bear witness, give counsel, help, hold, comfort. "Natalie, you've been married to that oaf since 1964. What'll you *do* on your own?"

"Now, now, after you busted up with your *oaf* Kevin, you went years with nobody. This here is the first time since you went . . . traveling you're serious about some guy. I won't be alone. Far from it, with three kids."

"There isn't anybody else?"

Natalie shook her head no. "Vinnie, I don't have time to tie my shoe tight. You think I got time for *romance?*"

"What about Suki? Are you sorry you didn't leave Daniel when she wanted you to?"

Natalie scratched her curls. "I don't know if I could live with Suki even as long as I stuck it out with Daniel. It was so romantic, sweetie. I needed a romance after all those years, I guess. But she wanted me to give up the world entirely and cleave only unto her."

"But . . . if she really loved you?"

"I like the idea of being alone with my kids. I can't seem to explain it. I know we'll have money troubles, believe it. But . . . when Daniel and I first set up housekeeping, it was like playing house. It was such fun. I feel that way about living with my kids—I can't wait for us to play house. You know?"

"How do the kids feel? What do they know?"

"Everything. I've never been good at lying to them. . . . Sam doesn't get on with his father. He's too hardheaded. He takes my part. Peezie gets more caught in the middle. It'll be toughest on Fanon—he's his father's favorite. He's more malleable than the rest of us. Daniel takes him along to Katy. He's young enough so it doesn't look as odd. With Sam or Peezie, everybody thinks Katy must be Daniel's daughter too. It's embarrassing. So he's been withdrawing from them."

Vida blurted out, "There he is."

"Let me guess. . . . Tall guy with the beard?"

"No! Slouching over by the corduroy pants, looking ticked off."

"He's handsome. Really."

"Natalie, he can't help that. That wasn't why I picked him out. You can call him Terry."

She did not bother with introductions but sailed up to him. "My sister says we'll go eat upstairs. The restaurant even has booze. We can have a drink for a treat."

"I'm hungry," he said. "I thought you maybe ate."

"Without you? Never."

Stiffly, looking straight ahead, the three rode up in the elevator. Not until they were all seated at a minute table did Natalie start. "Do you know where you're going next? Don't tell me, just say if you have some-place you have to get to."

"I'm staying East," Vida said. "My scene in L.A. is done."

Joel only made a noise in his throat, looking at his hands.

"Sometimes Vinnie does tasks for me," Natalie said cautiously, looking hard at him, trying to get him to look back. "For women who need help."

He looked at her then with his vivid hard green stare.

"If you ever get to have babies, they'll be gorgeous," Natalie said in one of those spontaneous blundering comments she was famous for. "I just mean, you're both so good-looking," she added limply.

For the first time Joel smiled. The waitress appeared.

"Eat as much as you want," Natalie said. "It's on me."

"Really?" He took her at her word and ordered two sandwiches, a soup and a gin-and-tonic. "If she says to trust you, I'll trust you. What do you want us to do?"

"I have a battered woman married to a cop. He's pistol-whipped her and thrown his son across the room. He's dangerous, he's armed and he uses the police force to track her. So it's dangerous."

"Quite." Vida smiled. "An interesting problem." She was showing off a little to Joel, but excitement did course through her. Something useful to do after all. "What does she want?"

"To cross the border from New York to Vermont. Right now she's well hidden, but she can't hole up in a dinky apartment with two kids forever. The sooner she's out, the better."

"Is she serious?"

"Vinnie, by the time they get to a battered women's shelter, they're all serious. It's a big step. For her it was declaring war."

"How do you know he hasn't tailed her?" Joel leaned forward.

The drinks came. Vida put hers aside to wait for the food. Again, she could not afford to be drunk. Joel sipped his. She must discuss that with him later. Natalie continued when she could: "When he found her in the shelter, he came in with a drawn gun. The next day the city started harassing us. We're quasi-legal. A building inspector appeared and they shut us down. We're still fighting it, but we got everybody into storage in private homes. . . . We got her in Long Beach, in a house that a woman who's given us a fair amount of money rents out. If he knew where she was, he'd barge in. What would he be waiting for? The longer he waits, the more chance she has to get away."

After the food came they worked out strategy, with Natalie drawing them maps on scraps of paper. Where the borrowed car would be waiting. Where to take the woman and her children. What she could be told. Route. "Soon as possible," Natalie insisted.

Joel propped his head on one hand. "Tomorrow?"

Natalie laughed. "Too soon. I'll fly back tomorrow. I can get her ready by Wednesday. . . . She'll give you two hundred—one hundred when you pick her up, one hundred when you deliver her in Vermont."

"Two hundred?" Joel drawled. "Dandy." Vida, attuned to him, felt the temperature soar. Of course, he did not have a sister and husband to supplement what he could scrounge, beg, borrow, steal, work off the books for. Fake Social Security cards were possible but risky. When she had been Joan Wagner in Philadelphia, she had had one and had taken a straight secretarial job, during the period when Leigh had been spending half time with her and their marriage had been real again. Then the Feds had closed in and she had to drop that identity and run. She still resented the paycheck she had never received, the week before and three days of the last week she had worked, a total of $180 the government had stolen from her. When was the last time Joel had had two hundred in his pocket? She still had $124 and change from what Leigh had given her.

She remembered the early fugitive days when half the police in the country seemed to have nothing to do but search for them, when a massive posse of FBI agents pursued them. No time for false I.D., no time for laying down new lives, no time for anything but running, never sleeping in the same place two nights straight. People had hidden them; people had run them through the night from hidey-hole to hidey-hole—the kids, the middle-aged factory workers and teachers, the Old Lefties and pacifists and Quakers: many she had never seen again; some, like Laura, still there to help.

The worst had been times they had lost their contacts and been cast on their own wispy resources, with no shelters, no I.D., no money. That was when Jimmy had tried selling his body on the streets of Chicago, with only modest success. That was when Kevin and she had robbed a liquor store at gunpoint. She had not told Joel, never told Natalie, because she considered the action politically dubious. She understood Rap Brown and the shoot-out on the roof of the bar, if that was what had really happened. Years of reading her exploits in the papers had made her aware the newspapers were slightly less reliable than Marvel Comix. But at a certain point with no money and no legal status, you did what you had to. You gave up or you survived. She had been there briefly. Life for white political fugitives was seldom that rugged. But she had been there and she knew it. Her terror standing in the store had been that something would go wrong and they would kill someone who was not their enemy.

"What's wrong?" Joel asked, and Natalie stopped talking as they both stared at her.

"I shouldn't drink at lunch. I'm not used to booze anymore." The gin-and-tonic, cushioned by food, had not affected her. Only the memory. The middle-aged clerk had a bald freckled head that got very red and then paled, the anger in the blue eyes behind bifocals, the fear in the sweating palms sliding on the counter. She had remembered Sandy and his fear of being robbed at night in the drugstore and Ruby's fears for him, and she felt wrong. It was one thing to bomb Whitehall Induction Center or Mobil Oil and quite another to scare a man working behind a counter late on a Tuesday night. "Lohania's photo was in the *Times*, Natty. Standing just behind Kevin on the courthouse steps."

"Oh?" Natalie glanced at Joel, rubbing her snub nose till it shone. "Some people never learn."

"Maybe she made him into a myth," she said, forcing herself back to the table, the present. "You can go on loving the idea of a man, like a religion. A saint's picture in your bedroom. Something you can talk at when you're low. . . . The reality can be less encouraging." She tossed off the last gin-flavored ice water in the bottom of her glass. "Let's get some coffee."

"Don't you do that with your ex-husband?" Joel asked conversationally, leaning back smiling broadly, invitingly.

"We're all getting divorced." Natalie waggled her fingers at the busy waitress. Her brown eyes sought Vida's. "How upset are you about it?"

Joel sat up. "You mean you're still married to that shmuck? You're still *married* to him?"

"Probably not by now." She brazened it out with a shrug. "His lawyer must do something for his money."

"Three coffees. . . ." Natalie turned to Joel. "The etiquette of the situation holds me back from asking all the questions I'd love to."

"What, do I love your sister? Can I support her in the style to which she is accustomed? Are my intentions honorable? Are my prospects good?"

Natalie's fat, happy giggle resounded. "This one has a sense of humor, for a change. . . . No, I'm curious about you yourself. Where do you come from, originally?"

"Born in New Jersey. When I was in the fourth grade, my old man's company moved him to North Carolina. I suffered down there till they fired him and we moved West."

"Suffered how?" Natalie asked. "You're Jewish, aren't you?"

"You *are* a sister," he grinned. "The way I remember it is, I had trouble understanding how the teachers talked. Everybody made fun of me. It was wrong if I tried to talk the way they talked and wrong if I didn't. Jewboy Yankee, sure. I began to have what they called learning problems."

"What about the rest of your family? Did they hate it too?"

"My younger brother grew up talking like them. I tried to make up for everything by eating. He never had weight problems, he always fitted right in. . . . Today he's probably minting money. . . . I don't know, maybe he's pumping gas, who knows?"

"You don't have a Southern accent," Natalie said. "Maybe just a trace. Where west?"

"Sacramento. . . . I liked it. I'd learned to work on cars. When we moved to Sacramento—my uncle was there—my brother moped but I was happy. I didn't say a word to my parents. I didn't let on, but I knew. That was my chance."

"To get out of the South?" Natalie asked.

"To get out of myself. The fat stupid blubbering creep. . . . I started running and swimming. I ran in circles in the backyard at first. So my mother, who'd been carrying on for years I was too fat, kept trying to push food at me."

"I remember the dieting," Natalie said. "I'm always plump, I just accept myself that way."

"I like you plump, Natty," Vida said. "Everybody doesn't have to look like a boy." Were they getting on? She thought so; she hoped so. Joel was certainly opening up. Were they liking each other? She wanted to kneel on the floor and beg them.

"So, did your life change in Sacramento?" Natalie asked.

"Being into cars was mainstream there. I got into dope, I got into the Movement. I came in there doing my con job and I discovered I could even get laid. . . . But I never believed in it. I knew I was putting it over on them. Inside, I was still back in Roanoke Rapids, the fat turd who got picked last for every team."

He was bonding with Natalie around the weight, she thought. Telling her that in his mind he was still fat. She smiled.

Natalie was confiding now. ". . . so you got to understand my father and her mother fell clandestinely in love. Unlikely as it seems. Oh, Ruby has style, even flamboyance—"

"For years that was all she had," Vida said. "Grit, persistence. And a conviction just from daydreams that things could be different for us."

"You like your parents," Joel said wonderingly.

"Oh, within limits." Natalie laughed. "My own mother died when I was eight, and I didn't resent Ruby. I was glad to be done trying to run the household with occasional cleaning women. It was like I could go back to being a kid again and stop being so damn responsible. . . . A stepmother, you're supposed to hate her. But Ruby was warm. I felt a little patronizing, I imagine: she'd been poor; my own mother had gone to college."

"But suddenly we had each other. Given, perfect. The sister you fantasize."

"So you aren't real sisters," Joel said, picking the last crumbs from all their plates.

"Yes, we are!" she said. "Nothing's more real than that." Eyes. The prickly feeling of eyes. As if casually, she turned, playing with the ends of her hair, and found the gaze. A man at a table of men, wearing a business suit, not expensive. She let her gaze drift past him, smiling. In a softer voice she went on, "Someone's looking at me. I'm going to get up to go to the john. You sit on awhile and then pay the check. Bring my coat. Watch that he doesn't follow. I'll meet you back at Lingerie in twenty minutes. . . . If he does follow, Terry, shake him and we meet as previously set up . . . okay?"

Casually she rose, stood over the table talking for a moment, then sauntered toward the bathroom. She went in and then came out a moment later and strolled out of the restaurant. An elevator was just loading, and she hurried to squeeze in.

Natalie had arranged housing for them from the list available for the conference in a house in Dorchester. They shared watery zucchini soup and heavy wheat bread, a salad too generously filled with inadequately washed, sour sprouts. The food was free and they ate it. She tried to be grateful, cursing her food snobbery that after seven years of exile and often hunger had never deserted her. Finally the many children were put to bed and the adults vanished, leaving Vida and Joel the dining-room floor to spread their sleeping bags on.

She asked, "What did you think of Natalie?"

"She didn't like me."

"How can you say that?" She was astonished. She could see Natalie at the table eagerly swapping childhoods. "She hardly ever opens up with men that way. She told me she liked you a lot."

"Really? What did she say?"

"What I said. That she liked you a lot."

He scowled. "You made that up."

"I did not! She told me that when she was saying goodbye."

"How much did she slip you?"

"Two hundred." She tasted guilt. Natalie had little extra. She had a part-time teaching job and a minor stipend from the battered women's shelter where she worked for over forty hours a week.

"Wow, with the dough for running that woman to safety, we'll have it made. Think she could give us these jobs pretty often?"

"Mostly the shelter works fine and they don't move women. But Natalie knows everything going on. She does liaison a lot with other political groups. She's an incredible organizer, Terry—"

"Why do you got to call me that? Nobody's listening."

"We're in somebody's house. We have to use the legal names."

"We're alone in the fucking sleeping bag. You think they got the sleeping bag bugged?"

"It's a habit. All we need to do is slip once in public and not say Terry or Vinnie—"

"I hate it! I hate for you to call me that name."

"Love, keep your voice down. I understand—"

"Call me by my name!" He lay rigid, his fists clenched.

"It's dangerous."

"We didn't get here by playing it safe. Call me by my name!"

"Why are you coming down so hard on me about this?"

He turned onto his belly, pushing his head into the sleeping bag. "I'm lost! Who am I, anyhow? Where are we going? Just running. From who? Do they give a fuck anymore? Just running in sand. I want to remember who I am. Call me by my name when we're alone. Call me by my name!"

She sat up beside him, hands twisting in her lap. She could not do it. Years of security habits; years of taking care; years of never knowing when she was bugged, watched, photographed, filmed; years of having to break dear old habits seized her tongue. It's so hard for us, she thought, staring around at the dingy but cheerful room with its hanging plants and combination of political and travel posters on the walls. Why was she with this creature? How had she ever thought life with him was going to be a bowl of nonchauvinist cherries? She could be in a hundred rooms in a hundred houses kneeling on more comfortable beds with saner and stronger men—or better yet, alone! Why didn't she just bolt and run?

He raised his head and looked at her with accusing brown eyes that reminded her for a moment of Natalie's. "You'll get bored struggling with me. You want to leave me for some guy who's got it all together."

"I never met a guy who had it all together." She could not leave him for anybody. He was a lot of trouble, but he was in touch with her, and she had been lonely for a long, long time. She knelt to put her arms around him and into his ear she whispered, "Joel. Joel. My love."

10

She had expected to call Leigh from a roadside booth Wednesday morning, long after Joel and she had picked up the battered woman, Tara, and started north, but Tuesday night the pickup was put off until Thursday morning. She and Joel ended up in the cheapest motel they could find in Hempstead, waiting. She had to call Leigh Wednesday from a pay phone three blocks from the motel.

"Are you coming out of New York soon?" she asked him. "I'm nervous about going there right now." She was too close for comfort.

"Reasonable enough." Even over the phone Leigh's voice was caramel. "Not clear if old Kevin's going to be tried for gunrunning or old stuff or all of it."

"You haven't talked to him?"

"He gave a press conference with his Mafia lawyer last week—a surprise in itself—sounding blustery and martyred. I went and he looked right through me. Wouldn't recognize me when I tried to ask a question."

"Not good." Jealousy? Contempt? Kevin had always detested Leigh, but arrested politicos usually wanted his attention. "A *Mafia* lawyer?"

"A good one. Pricey."

She speculated glumly, but she could not protract the phone call. "What's your travel schedule?"

"Let's see. Got my calendar handy. . . . At Thanksgiving I'm going down to Miami to see my mother."

"How would I get to Florida? Besides, it's dangerous. Too many Cuban exiles, too many Feds."

"Well, this coming weekend we're visiting friends of Susannah's who have a ski lodge near Twin Mountain—that's up in New Hampshire."

"You're a skier now? I don't believe it."

"Nah, I just watch the idiots risk their bones while I toast at the fire."

"This weekend . . . Leigh, I can make it. I can meet you nearby. . . . Are they political?"

"They're musicians. Classical. You know, resonance up where brains ought to be. Fine mahogany heads. . . . But good-hearted. Both first-class cooks. He cooks Roman and she cooks Indian and Mexican. He is Italian, she's a Wasp. So it goes. You could call in on their phone. Pretend you're my fucking station. They always hector me." He cleared his throat. "But we won't have much time. I can't disappear on them for hours. Brief meet—if you think it's worth the bother."

"Of course it's worth it," she said hotly. "To me, anyhow." She had been gone from him altogether too much already. Should she break her own rules and meet Susannah? Their involvement seemed to have thickened to the point where it would be more useful if she made the woman take her into account; yet Leigh had gone through fifteen women in the last few years.

Time to check in. She dialed. "Hi. Peregrine reporting. Who's this?"

"It is I," said Kiley's crisp high voice, assuming quite correctly but, Vida felt, a little arrogantly that she would be recognized. "We need to talk. Preliminary to the full BOD."

The Board of Directors—what had at first been slang for the central committee of the Network had taken over, so that the joke had become the real name—were due to meet, but now Kiley was pushing for something less formal. "How about Goat Heaven?" Agnes' farm, up in Vermont. "Or Hardscrabble Hill?" Eva's name for the farm they had all lived on, a name from an old song about circumstances not far from what theirs had been that desperate time in '73–74.

"We'll leave word both places. How soon?"

Suppose they got Tara moved tomorrow. Well, give an extra day for problems. "Friday?"

"Friday we'll have word at both places. Meet a day or two later."

"I'm not alone," Vida said. "You know him rather well."

"I do?" Kiley waited her out.

"He has big green glass eyes like a stuffed pussycat," Vida said.

"Oh. . . . Mechanic."

Mechanic? A connection closed in her head, two wires finally touching. Joel was Mechanic: the wizard deserter who fixed old cars that Kiley had discovered. "Should he come? Can he come, rather?"

"I never used to bring him," Kiley said. "But if you want. It's not official, after all." She hung up for punctuation.

Maybe she shouldn't, she thought wryly. It would certainly be a test of his true interest. She hurried back to the motel. What was on Kiley's huge and pointed mind? Lucky that Joel was a mechanic, given the condition of the car they were to use.

The car belonged to the son of the woman who was sheltering Tara, and it was home because it had needed a new clutch. After they delivered Tara and her children, they were to bring the car up to Goddard, near Plainfield, Vermont, where the son was studying social ecology. The car was a bronze Subaru several years old that had been driven through fire and mud and storm, but Natalie insisted that the garage had checked it out thoroughly and put on snow tires.

Joel wore dark glasses and a ski cap pulled low on his forehead, concealing his hair. She had a frosted ash blond acrylic wig over her dyed brown hair and different dime-store glasses than she usually wore. It was just getting light when they pulled into the driveway, right on the dot, but the woman was not waiting. Vida had to go and rap on the door of the little apartment tacked on the back of the long, low brick house. She hoped that it was the right door and she was not waking the other families who lived in this house—three apartments in all. She could see her breath. The sky looked as if it might rain or even snow—low ranks of clouds scrambling by, tumbling over themselves in the strength of the wind blowing off the cold gunmetal sea just three blocks to the east. In the early-morning stillness she could hear the surf. No lights were on in either of the neighbors' houses, but a cat crossed from yard to yard, ducking under a boat trailer. Where the hell was the goddamned woman named Tara? Her stomach tightened.

Lightly she rapped on the door. She did not want the neighbors, the occupants of the other apartments, to wake, to observe. Joel looked absurd standing in the driveway beating his hands together to keep warm, with the ski cap pulled down and sunglasses on at dawn of a cloudy day. She rapped again, restraining the impulse to shout.

Finally the door opened. Tara, a plump blond woman in her late twenties wearing a print pantsuit and a neck brace, peered out at Vida, a baby crying behind her. A boy bundled up so he was shaped like a beet in his maroon wool coat sat on a kitchen chair with his legs stuck straight out. A glass of milk was sitting on the table in front of him, and something pinkish had spilled on the floor.

"I'm Cynthia. We're here to transport you. We expected you to be ready."

"We'll be ready in a second. Tommy! Drink it down. We have to go soon."

"Don't want it. It's cold."

"All right! But don't tell me you're hungry in a little while!"

Tara, juggling the crying baby on her right arm, took the glass in her left hand and emptied it into the sink. "We just have to clean up breakfast dishes—"

"Leave them."

"We can't go and leave the breakfast dishes. It'll just take five minutes."

She hardened herself. No delaying tactics. "We're leaving now. If you want our help, put on your coat and come. . . . Your shelterer will clean up. It's just one more favor. The biggest favor you can do her now is to clear out before your husband arrives and shoots up the place."

"We're not catching a plane. I just have to clean up the kitchen."

"Tara, this car leaves now. Get in it or stay. We have other deadlines to meet. You aren't the only woman in trouble."

"Oh. You help other women." Tara paused in her dashing to and fro. "Just a minute." She put the baby under her arm, still squalling, and rushed to get a suitcase. "You can take this out. And the baby's things." She pointed to a plastic carryall.

I'm a genius, she thought. That was the right thing to say to get her moving. Stooping, she picked up the suitcase—Jesus! full of gold bricks, no doubt—and the carryall and staggered out to the car.

"What's happening in there?" Joel hissed, his shades shoved back on his striped ski cap like aviator goggles.

"Just stow this stuff in the trunk. Put newspapers over ours so she doesn't see what our gear looks like."

"Just get her out of there! We don't want to be seen."

"Honey, I'm trying."

Briefly, nervously they touched dry lips. Over her shoulder, as she trotted back, she said, "Put the food in the car. The Bloomie's bag full of sandwiches and fruit Sam gave us."

"I'm hungry! I'm hungry!" Tommy was shouting. "You took my milk."

"You said it was too cold." Tara was writing a note. "You wouldn't drink it." SORRY FOR THE MESS, it said.

"But you threw it away! I wanted you to warm it on the stove."

"We have food in the car," Vida said. "What goes out next? Where's your coat?"

"Your doggy, Tommy. What did you do with your doggy?" Tara asked frantically, trying to shove her arms into her fur coat while holding the baby.

"Let me take the baby," Vida said.

Reluctantly Tara handed the baby over, and Vida cuddled it. She had not held a baby since Vermont, that winter of '74. She saw a pacifier on the counter, and as the sobs checked she offered it, and the baby sucked. Better. "What's . . . baby's name?" She avoided a pronoun.

"Beverly. She's a real good baby. I don't know what she's upset about this morning."

"Ralph," Tommy said. "Call him Ralph."

"Where's Ralph? Maybe I packed him," Tara said.

"Don't you leave Ralph!" Tommy kicked the chair legs. "I won't go!"

Tara was grabbing objects from here and there and dropping them in another carryall. "Look in the living room," she said to Vida. "It's a Huckleberry Hound dog."

Whatever that was. Toting the baby, she fumbled for a light and looked around the small living room. She found a child's tennis shoe, a plastic fire engine and another pacifier. In the bedroom beyond, she found a heating pad, still plugged in; a cane; a bottle of liquid makeup; a pair of panty hose and in the crib, a lurid doll that had to be Ralph. "Got it!" she called.

Tara had just dropped her purse and was lowering herself to grope for it. Vida saw that Tara could not bend her neck and realized she was partially immobilized from the last beating. Vida felt embarrassed at being judgmental about the lack of organization. "Can I help? I found these things."

"If you can reach my purse. You can give me Beverly back."

Vida recovered the purse, dropped what she had found into the second carryall and bundled Tommy out the door. Tara needed the cane to hobble down the cement steps. Finally Tara was packed into the back seat with Tommy beside her and the baby on her lap, and Vida slid into the driver's seat. She had promised Joel, who was a little intimidated by the network of expressways around New York, to drive the first leg. "This is Dick, Tara."

"Dick . . . Oh, that's my husband's name."

In the rearview mirror she could see Tara peering with sharp anxiety at the back of Joel's head, which must look sinister.

"Why don't you call me . . . Sam, then? That's my middle name."

She smiled, because Sam had been Natalie's courier, meeting them before dawn and his school day with the food and final directions. For a moment she had hugged her too-tall, gawky nephew, and then she had given him an eagle feather she had been carrying for him since a meeting with Native American activists. "They're in more danger just sitting in their kitchens than I am running before the law," she had told Sam. Sam was the next generation, her inheritor, the child she might never have now. "The Feds are an army of occupation on the reservations. The war with cavalry is still going on. Ambushes. Running cars off the back roads. Burning families out.''

''What do you think that kid gets from your one-minute commercials for the revolution?'' Joel asked afterward. ''Handing him some damn feather.''

''He's not some random kid. He's Natalie's son.''

Joel laughed. ''Probably grow up and join the John Birchers.''

''He's half grown. Joel, even in America, not everybody hates their parents. Leigh always loved his. They were old commies. His politics are real different, but there's respect. His old man's dead, but he still goes to see his mother in Miami twice a year.''

''What good old bourgeois virtue. Hot shit. You want to go see mine? We can find her at the local beauty salon getting her hair bleached or lying down with a headache drinking vodka in the afternoon because it's not supposed to leave a smell on the breath. I always could smell it.''

Now they sat in uncomfortable silence till Joel tuned the radio to rock music. He had positioned himself to watch the rearview mirror for a tail.

''Er,'' she said awkwardly as they went over the bridge, ''we were told you'd pay us half on pickup and the other half on delivery.''

''Half?'' Tara sounded vague. In the rearview mirror Vida saw her clutch her purse. ''Oh, is that what they said?''

''They told us that,'' Joel said humbly. ''But if they told you something different . . . ?''

''That's what we were told by the woman in charge,'' Vida said firmly. If something went wrong and they had to ditch, let them at least get that.

''Oh . . . half. That's a hundred now?''

''That's right,'' Joel said. ''I mean, you have it with you anyhow, right?''

In the rearview mirror she saw that Tara was looking scared, her hand at her soft, rather large mouth. ''Suppose you just leave me, then?''

Joel turned around in his seat. ''We're as scared as you are, Tara, but we won't dump you anyplace. We promise!''

Carefully Tara counted out the hundred to Joel. ''Do I get a receipt?''

''You get safety,'' he said grimly. ''Let us hope. Your body is your receipt.'' They were getting off to a rotten start, and it was a damned long way to Brattleboro.

''Mommy. I'm hungry.''

''Oh, Tommy, why didn't you eat your breakfast?''

''You spilled my milk out.''

''You wouldn't drink it! I asked you to, remember?''

''It was cold. I hate it cold. You got to warm it in the pan for me.''

''We didn't have time, Tommy. This lady was in a hurry.''

''There's food in the bag,'' Joel said. ''Why don't you help yourself?

Tommy can have something to eat from the bag back there." His tone was coaxing, conciliatory.

"The kids aren't usually like this," Tara said. "They're upset by it all. They don't know why we keep running. We never even moved before. We always lived in the same house."

She could hear paper rustling, so she assumed Tara was taking a look. "A chicken sandwich. You want a chicken sandwich, Tommy?"

"No. I hate chicken. I want my milk."

"An apple. How about an apple?"

"I don't want a napple!" He started to bawl, and the baby woke and started to cry with him.

"How about a banana?" Tara asked desperately over the din.

Joel turned in his seat. "How about a banana, Tommy? We can both eat bananas, like monkeys!" He scratched his head, grimacing.

Tommy stopped crying, although the baby continued. "How come you got sunglasses on?"

"I like them. I like bananas too. How about you?"

"Yeah, I like bananas—"

"Good. Will you eat one if Mama peels it for you?"

"You peel it! But how come you like sunglasses?"

"How come you like bananas?" Joel still imitated a monkey, taking the banana and peeling it.

"They taste good."

"Dark glasses feel good."

Tommy ate a banana as the baby sniffled back to sleep in Tara's lap. A short silence was broken by Tommy, asking if they were there yet. Then he said, "I got to go, Mommy."

"Oh, Tommy. Already?"

"Mommy, I got to!"

"Number one or number two?"

"Number one."

"Can he do it by the side of the road?" Vida asked.

"On the Cross Island Parkway?"

"All right." Vida took the next exit and pulled into a Shell station, parking off to one side. "Take him in."

"We can't just go and use their bathroom."

"Tara, you got to," Joel said. "They'll be nice about it. If they aren't, we'll just go to the next gas station and try there. They won't shoot you for wanting to piss."

"But why can't you buy some gas or something?"

"Mommy! I got to go!"

"Because the car's filled up already. We haven't used up enough gas to put any in," Vida said.

Looking furious, Tara got stiffly out of the car, poking the way on her cane with Tommy hanging off one arm and the baby waking up on the other.

"Jesus," Joel said. "We aren't doing so good."

"I want to get out of the city."

"We can't let the kids pee in their pants, Vida. Soften up a little. What's wrong?"

"I don't like her. I want to like her, I do! She's a battered woman, we're finally carrying out a political task. We're even getting paid for it. And I don't like her. I want to drop her on her head off the expressway. I swear, if I was her husband, I'd kill her too! Don't ever repeat that. But she's driving me crazy."

"Vida, she's scared. How can you be so hard toward her? She don't know who we are. We look weird." Joel squeezed her hand. "Now, shut off the motor and relax."

She obeyed him. "Is there coffee in that bag? Take a look."

He screwed around to kneel on the seat and poke in it. "Something's in the vacuum."

"Bet it's Natalie's good coffee. I'll have a swig. Keep it in front. We have to drive."

"Baby, you got to soften up toward Tara. She's in pain, she's been through hell. Maybe she's not such a wonderful woman, but she's in trouble."

"What kind of woman marries a cop, anyhow?"

"She didn't marry a cop, she married her boyfriend. Come on, Vida, loosen up. What's bugging you?"

"Somehow she expects to be waited on. She expects it to be comfortable. We're taking risks for her—"

"She don't know what risks we're taking, and she better not guess."

"It's awkward. The only way to get through this gracefully would be to establish personal rapport, but I'd just as soon not have to make up some elaborate story. It seems to me she doesn't try to keep the kids under control."

"She probably feels guilty about leaving him. She's scared. We're used to living out of a suitcase, but I bet she's never done it."

She sulked for a moment, but guilt was welling up. She squeezed his hand back. "I'll be better."

"Just shut up, drive and let me do the talking. I'll fix it." Joel kneaded the tight muscles in the back of her neck. "Here they come." She set the thermos down in front and made herself smile at Tara.

While they were crossing the Throgs Neck Bridge, Joel started a steady patter of gentle questioning. "How old were you? . . . Wow, you got married young. You know we're the same age?"

"You're twenty-five too? I thought you were younger than me."

"I'm two years older," Joel said, and Vida quietly poked him. No facts! "I bet you dated Dick all through high school. . . . Yeah? What was he like then?"

As she remembered, Tara's face in the rearview mirror looked tender, wistful. Absently she stroked Beverly's damp head. "He was *nice* then. He was so nice to me. He used to pick flowers from the neighbors to bring me when I broke my leg. . . . I never really knew any other boy. He was the one I loved from the time I loved anyone. We learned to dance together. We learned to dive off the board. We used to go swimming and ice skating. He was on the basketball team. And I swam for our school. . . . You'd never believe it now!"

"I bet you were crazy about him. What position did he play?"

"Guard. What did you do in high school . . . Sam? Did you play basketball too?"

"I was too short. So what happened when you graduated? Did you get married right off?"

"My parents were real strict. I was scared to do anything with him. Confession every week . . . Are you Catholic?"

"No." He winked at Vida. "A Jehovah's Witness."

"That's Protestant, isn't it?"

By the time she had taken the Hutchinson River Parkway to 287 and that to 22 North, Tommy had dozed off, the baby was sleeping and Tara was blowing her nose over scraps of her marriage. He'll make Tara fall in love with him before we reach Brattleboro, she thought in a mixture of sour amusement and real appreciation.

". . . used to come in his uniform and he'd be excited, hot in the face. Mad-angry and yet up, like he was high on something. Like getting mad used to make him feel good. . . . When I get mad at somebody I love, my stomach hurts. But he used to kind of swell up and almost . . . look happy when he got mad at me."

Her old problem: sympathizing with the oppressed from a distance was often easier than dealing with somebody distorted, damaged by oppression. If suffering truly ennobled, why work to rid society of it? She was glad to be engaged in a real task, and she longed to like Tara, but she could not. Joel could, groping for the common experience, the common feeling. Natalie could. Natalie really could work with all kinds of people from different classes who had little or no conscious politics, without getting bored, irritable, superior, impatient.

". . . then he bought me the new coat. This one. It's from I. Fox, and it's seal. I really wanted it. That old coat, it was nothing—a blue wool with a ratty collar. . . . But he only got me the coat because he beat me so bad I had to go into the emergency room."

Driving cautiously, keeping an eye out for tails, observing every highway sign as they proceeded north on 22 through a morning whose overcast was darkening, she felt penitent. Joel was setting Tara at ease. Tara's presence meant-they could not communicate, and in her necessary silence she was keeping secrets from him. She had not told him about the planned meeting with Kiley—and who else? *We*, she had said, which could mean Kiley and Roger, Kiley and Eva, Kiley and Larkin—or some combination of them. It could even mean that Kiley, like Vida, was traveling with someone not on the Board. Why hadn't she challenged that *we?* She felt she had given away a tiny advantage to Kiley by apologizing for her own company while not examining Kiley's. She hoped it was Eva. Where was Eva? At least, Kiley would have news.

Her own people, in the fullest sense, as Joel was almost but not quite. Should she bring him further into the Network? Should she try to work with him politically? Or was she about to involve Leigh more directly? The full success of her media project required Leigh's involvement, but how realistic was that? She could judge that soon, when she saw him, as she must try to break through the detritus of separation to him. Must. And Joel? She had a sense of having got in deeper than she had intended, but how deep were they in it, really? He could bolt when he saw Kiley. It could all fall apart in a real quarrel. If only she could turn Leigh and Joel inside out and coldly, objectively examine what each felt!

When Tara suddenly realized that they were on Route 22, not the Thruway or the Taconic, and started to complain, Vida did not let herself become defensive.

"I'm not paying you to take me the long way around! This will add hours! My kids can't sit in the car all day."

"It's safer, Tara. No tollbooths. Less state troopers. You don't know for sure your husband isn't looking for you. He may have something out, officially or unofficially. We're better staying off interstates. I'm taking this to New York 55 and then over to U.S. 7. That's in Connecticut. We'll be over the state line in another thirty-five, forty minutes this way."

"Seven's supposed to be pretty," Joel said soothingly. "Once we're on 7, we can stop as often as you want to."

"My neck hurts. It's hard to ride in a car. It's hard on my back."

"That's a neck brace, huh?" Joel said. "I bet that hurts a lot! What happened?"

It wasn't that Vida had never been beaten: she had, most outstandingly by the Tactical Police Force and by the American Nazi Party. Of the two, she remembered that the TPF had concentrated on her head and shoulders and the Nazis on her body. In both cases several men had beaten her together, with obvious pleasure and without her being able to do more than try ineffectually to protect herself. Once or twice Kevin had hit her. Not once or twice. Twice, and twice only. The first time she had not spoken to him for a week, and the second time she had never returned to his bed.

No, the pain went further back. Ruby with a puffy face in the mornings. Tom had been away in her early childhood, off in the Marines fighting Japs. When he came home on furlough it was a rowdy few days with kisses and tears, with Vida and her grandma and her older brother Paul sent off to the movies a lot. Paul and Grandma and she had gotten used to life with Mommy. Mommy worked for the Navy, driving to and from work in a blue Hudson picking up fellow workers. Paul and Grandma and Vida and Mommy made supper and cleaned up together. Vida always helped around the house. Tom had been drafted too late to be discharged right after VJ Day. Therefore, he had served in the army of occupation in Japan, and Vida was five and Paul was ten when Tom came marching home.

The only time Tom hit Vida was when Ruby brought some outrageous act to his attention, which she did less and less because of the consequences, or when Vida was too obstreperous when Tom had a headache or a hangover or was feeling put upon. Only rarely did he hit her. But he hit Paul a lot. Tom seemed infuriated to come home and find a half-grown son. Respect, he shouted; obedience and respect. He loosed a lot of anger on Paul, and Paul withdrew. His ears would get red below his pitiful orange crew cut, and he would clench and unclench his big marvelous hands that were his father's hands too; but Paul never hit her or anybody except other boys at school. "*I* only hit people that're bigger than me!" he screamed once at Tom when he was being punished for fighting in the school yard, and Tom hit him again, in the mouth.

That made Vida feel torn, confused for Paul. But when Ruby walked out of their bedroom in the morning with a bruise on her cheekbone or her arm, when Ruby's face was blown up with that red puffiness, when she painted on too much makeup and still you could see something was wrong, then Vida hated her father and wanted him to go away.

She was his favorite. He took her on his lap and sang to her about "Anchors Aweigh, my boys," "Coming In on a Wing and a Prayer" and "Solidarity Forever" and "From the halls of Montezuma" and "Sons of toil and danger, will you serve a stranger and bow down to Burgundy?" He sang in a loud, rousing baritone that rippled through her as she sat on his lap, bounced by his jogging foot. Sometimes he made the eagle on his biceps wink at her, and sometimes he showed her the other tattoo that said "Tom and Ruby" on a heart inside leaves and flowers as pretty as the handles of Mommy's good silver-plated spoons from the set Grandma had started for her when they got married, but that never got any further than the teaspoons. Vida's first and deepest loyalty was to Ruby, but she felt a muddy complicity. Somehow it was her fault—the bruises, the muffled thuds and whimpers and occasional moans in the middle of the night. When he walked out on them all after a bad long period when he had been out of work, she had felt guilty because she missed him terribly and guilty because they were happy without him.

Then Grandma died suddenly of a heart attack. She was only sixty-two, but she was overweight, and she worked in a bakery. Grandma got out of work late, she was running for the bus and she just fell in the street. By the time somebody called an ambulance, she was dead on arrival. Ruby had cried for weeks. They were a line of women who loved their mothers. She wondered if Peezie carried that on. Physical identification, yes, and solidarity in the face of pain, loss, poverty, hard times, persecution, just plain trouble in the form of man or state or economy or law and the slow or violent destruction of the body. Her hands tightened on the wheel convulsively. She stared at the highway through the day that felt like dusk, with the clouds so low and ominous. She missed Ruby, missed her desperately. Year after year after year . . . Of course, Tom had come back in six months and moved them all to Chicago. . . .

"So how come you felt like it was your fault, Tara? That's what I don't see," Joel was saying.

"Because he made me feel, see, like I provoked him. Like I was asking him to do it to me," Tara said.

"Did you want him to hit you?"

"No! But what I felt like was, I was trying so hard not to get him mad I'd be like shaking, and then I'd put my foot in it. I'd be so scared of getting him mad, I'd get him mad."

"That's like saying he set you up to fail, but it's your fault if you fail. Or somebody saying, Watch you don't fall! Watch you don't fall! Till you're so nervous you fall, and then they say, I told you not to fall. . . ." Joel trailed off.

"You sound like Natalie Brooks. You know her?"

"No," Vida said. "Who's she?"

Tara paused a moment, startled Vida had spoken. "She's a woman who runs the shelter where I was before they put me in that dinky apartment. . . . She's real good to talk to when you're upset. Some of the women there are hiding like me, and some of them are staff . . . and some of *them* used to be battered too. But I liked her the best. . . . She's Jewish, but she's got a family—four kids, I think—and I hear her marriage is in trouble too. The woman said that in the house. . . ."

She was not as useful a political person as Natalie and not as good with people as Joel, she thought, gripping the wheel. It had taken her years to learn Natalie's strengths. She, Vida, had been the more aggressive, more verbal, better known. She had led. Natalie had gone her own

VIDA

way. Years had ground at her arrogance before she had understood the terms of her old arguments with Natalie, before she had learned to value Natalie's virtues. But now they must be careful. Tara could go back to her cop. Let nothing slip, and don't let her get a good look at either of us. The day's so dark, I wonder if I shouldn't put the headlights on. "Afraid I don't know Long Island. I never was there before today."

"Where are you from?"

Here it is, she thought. Worse to refuse to answer. "Erie, Pennsylvania. Ever been there?"

"No. . . . What do you do for a living, Sam?"

He glanced sideways at her, behind the shades. Glint of green contact. "I sell siding. Aluminum siding."

"Oh, I guess people with old houses, like in Queens, put that on because it's practical, isn't that so? You don't have to paint it, do you? We had a brick house. . . . I don't know what's going to happen to us now. I just don't." Tara started to weep again, and the baby woke and joined her.

"Damn it, is that snow?" Joel stared ahead.

"Sure looks like it," Vida said glumly. "Maybe it won't stick."

"I'm hungry!" Tommy was awake. "Mommy? Where's Ralph? Did you leave Ralph?"

"Ralph is in the last thing we carried down," Vida said. "In the trunk."

"I want Ralph! You left Ralph!"

"No, Tommy, the lady says Ralph is in the trunk."

"Are we there yet? Let's stop now."

The baby was bawling desperately. "She's hungry, poor little soul. I have to heat her bottle. You said we could stop on 7 and it says Route 7."

"Okay," Vida said. "But it's starting to snow."

"I have to use the ladies' room, and Beverly's hungry, and I bet Tommy is too. Aren't you, Tommy?"

"I want Ralph. Let's stop now. I want to be there! Mama! Where are we going, anyhow?"

"If they won't warm the bottle, I have a plug-in warmer in my plaid bag. I can do it in the ladies' room."

Joel pointed. "What about that place?"

"It looks like a truck stop. Really!"

"Mama!" Tommy said louder. "Where are we going?"

"Oh, it'll be a nice place," Tara said doubtfully.

"Will there be a color TV? Or black-and-white, like Grandma's?"

"Color," Tara said firmly. "It's only for a little while, Tommy. Then we'll have a place of our own."

"Will there be other kids?"

"Yes." Tara made herself sound cheerful and firm.

"Who?"

"I don't know their names." She was wavering again.

"Will there be swings and slides, like in the playground?"

"We'll see. What kind of road is this, where the restaurants are shut? On the Thruway, they'd be open. That one's closed too."

"Well be in another town soon," Vida said testily. She had to pee too, and finding a restaurant to satisfy Tara and family would do nothing for her problems.

"How about that place?" Joel asked in the next town. "I bet that's where the local people eat. Home cooking."

"I guess so." Tara was dandling the screaming baby. "We'll try it."

Vida pulled up outside. "Do you have a watch?"

"A watch? No. What for?" Tara fumbled for her purse and carryall.

"I'm sure there's a clock inside. In forty-five minutes—at eleven thirty—we'll come back and wait outside for you."

"You're going to leave me here and go someplace? What for?"

"We'll be back in forty-five minutes. Is that enough time?"

"Not to feed Baby and change her and have a little lunch. Poor Tommy didn't even get to eat his breakfast."

"Yeah, you poured my milk down the sink. I want a hamburger. And French fries."

"Okay. We'll pick you up at twelve. Is that enough time?"

"All right, all right. But I need my bottle warmer from the plaid case in the trunk. . . . I don't see why you can't just come inside with me and sit down!"

"I have to call my office and several customers," Joel said. "I can't take off for almost a week without staying in touch. And . . . she has to call our baby-sitter. We'll pick you up."

They drove back to the last wayside picnic area and brought their bag from Natalie to a table. "See how complicated it gets when we have to make up stories?" she said. "I feel like I'm tripping on all this rope strung around."

Joel pissed against a tree, moaning with relief, and she went past him into the bushes. When she came back, he said, "Now we'll both be in better temper."

"Mama, did I have to go! What kind of sandwiches did Natalie pack?"

Lightly the snow fell on the rustic table, on the rocky ground, on the rushing waters of the Housatonic with a faint hissing. The snow touched Joel's ski cap, the glasses he had pushed high on his head, the bag between them. She giggled at the silliness, a picnic in the snow, still melting as it alighted.

"Chicken on whole wheat, roast beef with Russian dressing on dark rye . . ." he said, exploring.

"Oh, give me a roast beef!"

He sulked. "Sure. Take it."

"Baby, there must be another. I know Natalie. Look."

There was. Then they each had a chicken sandwich, and they finished the coffee. "Next time she stops, I'll ask her to get the thermos filled," Joel drawled, patting his belly.

"It's nice to escape them for a little."

"That kid drives me crazy," he mumbled. " I keep wanting to swat him."

"Really, love? I'd never have guessed. You've been an angel."

"Reminds me of my little brother. Spoiled rotten, and nothing's ever good enough. He'll grow up to be just like his old man." Contentedly he picked his teeth with one of his hairs used as dental floss. "I can't get used to thinking of her as younger than me! Why didn't you want to go in the restaurant? Not to have to talk to her or not to spend the money?"

"She can't get a good look at us in the car. She sees the back of my wig and this green scarf and your ski cap. If we sit across the table from her, she has nothing to do for an hour except stare at us. You can't leave those stupid glasses on inside."

"Did you like the aluminum siding?"

"I love it. She makes me nervous. Nice, dull specific answers are the ticket."

"How many kids do we have?" He ate a chocolate-chip cookie.

"A little girl sixteen months old named Amy. Sam and Cynthia and Amy. We came in a Cracker Jack box."

"I'd like to crawl in a Cracker Jack box with you right now. Let's fuck in the car."

"Joel! I can't."

"Oh?" His face darkened instantly, as if five-o'clock shadow of the psyche crept over it. She swore his bones thickened when he sulked.

"It's the facade we have to keep up. I can't put the walls down suddenly for twenty minutes. I can't be vulnerable just for a flash."

"Or you're getting tired of me already. Getting bored."

"I'm not bored with anything except her company. . . . I have friends where we can maybe stay tonight." Agnes' farm. Hardscrabble Hill.

"I have friends up there too, where I used to live. I had an off-the-books job helping make antiques, and on the side I fixed people's cars."

"Making antiques?"

He grinned. "There ain't enough to go around naturally. All the summer people and tourists want them. It was a good job, except for lousy ventilation in the winter. That stuff gets in your lungs. . . . Do you still love me?"

"Of course!" She almost suspected he could read her mind about Leigh, but her better sense told her it was only his usual insecurity. "Are you sorry we took this job?"

"It's good for us to work together. I want that. . . . What do you think?"

"Why not?" She rested her chin on her cupped hand. "Anything in mind?" Recent issues flashed through her mind, riffling through a deck of cards: abortion, gay rights, falling dollar, unemployment, racism in the North, South Africa, tenants' rights, union busting . . . She felt in a closing vise of time. By the weekend she must have at least the scaffolding of a proposal, for she suspected Kiley was looking for a meeting to make a proposal of her own. To come unprepared was to cede too much.

"That nuke stuff gets me." Joel scowled. "It's gross. It's like none of the rest of it will happen if there's no people here, right? I mean, I always believed the propaganda that those things couldn't blow up. But any breeder reactor can blow sky high. One little fucking pinch of plutonium you couldn't hardly see could off a townful of people. There's guys dying right now in England from processing the stuff. It's a poison that don't even exist naturally and they want to make it by the barrel."

"Ummm." She paced around the picnic table. In a way she thought he had a point, and in a way she thought it would cause her a lot of political trouble. Everything had to be done, of course; all issues must be worked on. She could see too that if Joel caught fire on an issue it would be good for him. He needed a purpose beyond survival. If they stayed together, they needed common tasks and shared goals; if they stayed together. Everything was piling up at once: seeing Leigh again, getting plugged back into the Network, Joel seeing Kiley, and preparing her own position for the Board meeting. The organization must act or rot. What did Kiley want? She glanced at her watch. "Time to leave."

Tara was not waiting outside, but she came out with Tommy and the baby within five minutes. Then they had to find Ralph in the trunk. Tara stood to one side jiggling the baby as Vida pawed through the panty hose, toys, baby powder and bubble bath in the carryall. Tara asked, "How come the car has New York plates if you're from Pennsylvania?"

"This isn't our car," Vida said. "Our car could make it too easy to trace you."

Joel took over the driving, sliding his sunglasses up on his head and finally taking them off and putting them on the dash. The thickening snow meant he could not drive over forty-five. Snow was beginning to thatch the bushes and grass, to gust in waves across the pavement. He concentrated on driving as the road got slipperier and the light dimmed and the windshield wipers sloshed in time to the bland sugar rock gushing from the radio. She scanned the map, watching the highway signs and keeping an eye out for a tail.

Driving through the snow in an old car . . . Years ago. She was at the wheel, Eva was with her and they were running two deserters up to Canada from Hardscrabble Hill. It was dangerous, of course, but they were being paid and they had good fake I.D. and they'd done it before. But a storm had closed the road they meant to take, and the old car shimmied and groaned as the trip took hours more than they had expected. To top it all off, Eva and she had got in a furious argument with the two ex-soldiers about the women's movement and abortion. One of the guys had got so angry he had called them whores and murderers, and she knew he would have hit them if they had not been necessary to his safety. When they had finally let off the men, Eva was shaking. "It's all theoretical for me. Women don't make you pregnant," Eva had murmured. "My hand's stiff and sore from gripping the knife in my pocket. I was scared they'd attack us." They had both been scared, but they did not say anything when they got back to Hardscrabble Hill. That was while Kevin still ruled, and neither Eva nor Vida would admit to anyone else being scared of two men. She wanted to tell Joel the story, but in front of Tara she could not.

Tara dozed, except when Tommy poked her. In midafternoon they stopped for gas outside Lenox, and again Tara made a small prickly scene about paying for the gas. She seemed reluctant to let go any money. Vida understood. When was Tara going to get more? How was she going to live? Vida understood, and yet she had no choice but to insist. On they went in the early dark with the snow gusting into the windshield and packing down on the highway. She drove again, lucky when she could get up to forty on a recently plowed stretch. The snowplows were out, and sometimes a long line of late-afternoon traffic was backed up.

They stopped for a four-o'clock snack and a six-o'clock supper and to use a bathroom at seven forty-five. The snow continued to fall. Joel and Vida ate their last sandwiches, walking around the car beating snow from their arms as they waited each time for Tara. The second time that Tara forgot to have the thermos filled with coffee, Vida sent her back into the restaurant. "I'm afraid we can't go on without it," she said firmly. "It would be dangerous."

"Why don't you go in yourself?" Tara folded her arms.

"I didn't eat a meal there. I doubt if they'd fill a thermos for me. If you want this car to move, get the coffee, Tara."

Route 9 was in worse shape. They saw cars in the ditch, a van overturned. Between Woodford and Searsburg they had to wait for twenty minutes at a standstill while a jackknifed truck was cleared from the highway. Their faces were lit by the flashing lights of the police cars. As they stalled there, Joel tapped her arm and took over the driving again. At nine o'clock, traffic began to creep past the wreckage. The car skidded but kept going over the mountains and through the snow drifting in the hollows, piling up in the curves. At a little before eleven, the car crawled into Brattleboro. Pulled over to the side of Main Street, Vida bent over the map Natalie had drawn. "Go two more blocks and then left, up the hill away from the river."

The car labored up the hill, the wheels spinning on ice. To be done, done with all this and in bed! She burned cold with fatigue. Her shoulders, her back, her neck ached from having clutched the wheel hour after hour. She could no longer find a position in which her back did not ache. She and Joel had stopped speaking, because they could no longer spare the energy. Ten inches of snow had fallen and still it came down wetly, thickly. Where the streets had not yet been plowed she could not tell what was roadway and what was not. Cars that had been snowed in looked as if they were parked in the middle of fields. They crept up to the outskirts of town, where the houses were farther apart and the street lights stopped. She had to get out of the car and wade through the snow to read a street sign. "Not yet. I hope we didn't go too far."

"Let me see the map," Tara commanded, wide awake now. "Ask somebody. Look, there's a man shoveling snow."

"I presume the shelter's secret here, but I'll ask him where the street is." She rolled down the window to shout.

"What? . . . That's on up the hill. . . . You got a piece to go yet. . . . But you'll get stuck in the snow."

The wheels spun and they could not get started until they put Tara briefly at the wheel, nervous and bleating, But I can't drive, and Vida and Joel pushed the car free. Then he climbed back into the driver's seat and they inched onward. "Is that a road?" she asked, peering into the dark.

"Get out and look," he said glumly. "How else can you tell?"

She read the sign. "Still not it. I wish they'd given us a better map."

"Oh, she thought it would be fun. Hide-and-seek. Blindman's buff. Find the needle in the haystack. Maybe it's all a joke your—"

She poked him before he got the word out. "You're tired, Sam. Very tired."

"Gee, what else is new?" But he shut up.

"Stop. Maybe that's it." This road at least had been plowed, although not recently. It was the right one. She waded back to the car and climbed into the puddle she had created. Unfortunately, the new road immediately set out to climb a mountain. The car gained some momentum, labored up, labored, spun and then drifted into a four-wheel skid. It all happened quite leisurely. He even had time to say, "God damn," and she to warn, "Hold on!"

The car danced sideways, shimmied and thrust its nose into a snow-bank partway into a ditch. It happened so slowly that no one was more than shaken. But when Vida climbed out to look, the car was stuck good. She experienced a moment of pure terror like a shot of ice in which she imagined the police appearing and questions, questions, questions. Gradually she tuned in to Tara screaming.

"Be quiet," she said sternly. "You're scaring the children." That should fix her—standard guilt trip. "I'll find the house. It has to be near. They can come back for you and help us get the car out of the ditch."

Joel started off with her, but Tara caught his arm pleadingly. "You can't leave us here alone in the middle of nowhere!"

"Stay with her," Vida whispered. "But if there's trouble, run for it. We can meet in the next town south of here where the bus stops."

She plodded off into the dark, hoping that if he had to take off, he'd be able to get their packs out of the trunk first. She felt naked marching off without hers. Her body ached with every step, and her nose was running with the cold. She was exhausted and hungry. She did not know whether to wish a car would drive up the dark road or not, but none did. She slogged on. Finally a mailbox said Crowder, and she turned into an unshoveled walk. The two-story clapboard house was completely dark. Now what? Was it the wrong house, wrong town, wrong place? Or was it just so late that everyone was asleep here in Ultima Thule in a blizzard?

Either way she was not pleased, banging on the door and brushing snow from her shoulders, her wig. The damn acrylic wig smelled funny wet and seemed to be losing its curl much as hair would, exposing some of the plastic netting of the scalp. She tied her soaking-wet scarf firmly over her head. Banged harder. "Hello in there! Hello!"

A light went on upstairs. Impatiently she waited, stamping the snow from her boots on the wooden porch. The porch light went on just after the light in the hall inside, while a face peered at her through a window in the door. Finally the door opened on a chain. "Who are you? It's the middle of the night."

"You know who we are. We're delivering someone to you. From Long Island."

The woman glared, opening the door to let her in and standing aside clutching her plaid wool bathrobe together. "I sat up last night waiting for you. You were supposed to come yesterday."

"The woman wasn't ready. We had to spend two nights in a crummy motel waiting for her. We're exhausted, and the car is in a ditch down the mountain a little ways."

"You're wonderfully efficient, aren't you? Upside down as well?"

"Now, look here, we've been driving since six thirty this morning and its been snowing all day. We were held up on Route 9 by a truck accident and this goddamn map is lousy and we're exhausted. Now help me get her up here and give us a place to sleep. And we need help getting the car out of the ditch. It's not ours. We borrowed it to make the delivery."

"The car will have to stay put till morning," the woman said sourly, stomping off. "I'll get dressed." She was buxom, with a high, shiny forehead under sawed-off light hair, and she was still mad.

"Thanks for your welcome," Vida shouted after her.

"Keep your voice down. You'll wake my lover and our kids."

When the woman came back down in jeans and sweater, shoving her arms into a down jacket, she was just as grumpy. "We have to take her to the shelter."

"This isn't it?"

"You don't think we'd give out a map to the shelter?" The woman frowned, leading the way through the kitchen to an attached garage where a Jeep stood. "Don't you people observe any precautions?"

For an instant in a blur of fatigue Vida was scared, a hot finger on her heart, thinking "you people" meant fugitives. Then she realized the meaning. "I'm not on the staff. My friend and I are just doing a favor." You ill-tempered creep! She climbed into the Jeep and they lurched back into the snow. Finally the snow seemed to be less dense, flakes idling slowly. The woman drove too fast for the conditions, but Vida held on and said nothing. She was too tired to care. It was only a two-minute drive back to the car, still angled in the ditch. Joel had shut off the headlights, and they were all huddled in a knot of misery at the side of the road, Tommy crying, Tara pacing with the baby.

"All right, get in," the woman barked from the driver' seat. "Not him. We can't take a man to the shelter."

Vida leaned over and shut off the ignition. "Let's get this straight. I don't care where we go, but we're exhausted. We have been on this case for three days. Now, you give us a place to sleep and do it soon, or I'll take you on right now. I do not give a shit where you put us, but you put us someplace fast."

The woman stared at her. Then she said slowly, "Okay. Walk back to my house. The door's unlocked. You can sleep in the room off the kitchen. The bed's made up. Now get out. I have to take them to the shelter."

Vida got out. "We'll load your stuff in the Jeep, Tara."

"Don't forget the plaid carryall," Tara said.

As Joel was loading the Jeep, Vida caught Tara's arm. "Sorry about the trouble here. I don't know how we'll get the car out, but you're safe, anyhow. And you owe us another hundred."

"You got your nerve," Tara said. "You're a cold one. Cold as ice!" She fumbled in her purse and counted out the money. The woman in the down jacket watched.

"Some favor," she said.

"Yes, it's been some favor." Vida marched over to Joel. "Let's take our packs. The house isn't far. About ten minutes up the road."

They watched the Jeep disappear. "A charmer," Joel said. "I thought she was going to leave me on the road."

Hand in hand, they stumbled up the mountain to the house. At least, this time the lights were on.

11

"Well, off to Erie?" The woman was wearing the same plaid wool bathrobe as she fried eggs and dough for herself and her older lover, a tall lean grizzled greyhound of a woman who whistled constantly in pure birdsong snatches as she came and went on the morning's chores, till her partner captured her and sat her bodily at the table for breakfast.

"Sure," Vida said curtly. She felt painfully awkward tiptoeing around their unfamiliar kitchen trying to feed breakfast to herself and Joel, who hunched at the far end of the table trying to make himself invisible by drawing his head into his shoulders like a turtle. His refusal to move made her wait on him in front of the two watchful women. "If you could just help us get the car out of the ditch, we'll be on our way." She set down a mug of tea in front of Joel. He bobbed his chin as if even to move would give away some advantage. She felt like screaming at the women, screaming at Joel. They were forcing her to play a straight role out of their preconceptions, and he was sulking and acting helpless.

"Why don't you call a tow truck?" the younger woman asked.

"I don't think the car's damaged, and we'd just as soon get it out and leave. Please help us. We can't afford a tow truck."

"For what you charged her, you could call a fleet."

Vida said, "We've been waiting for her since Monday. So think again. We have to pay a sitter all those days. We have to return this stupid car before we can pick up ours. I don't think the woman who owns it would like it yanked around by a tow truck—she was doing the shelter a favor by loaning it." Self-righteous, judgmental moralist! Probably been working at the shelter a month, probably been gay for a year. Probably throw it all up next year and marry an insurance salesman.

The kids, a boy Tommy's age and a girl a little older, came clattering down the steps, and for twenty minutes Vida and Joel ate their granola as if on the edge of a racecourse. "Who are you?" the little girl asked, but didn't wait for the answer. "Don't put that crap in my lunch! I want peanut butter and apple butter, together!"

When the kids had been bundled off to the school bus—down the path already shoveled that morning to the road—the pepper-and-salt grey-hound came and stood over them. "I'll get it out of the ditch," she offered cheerfully, and slipped off to the Jeep whistling something tiddly and baroque, swarming with rapid notes.

It took all four of them, accompanied by a whistled "Anvil Chorus" from *Il Trovatore*, to get the car out of its snowbank and ditch. The older woman was as strong as Joel and a lot more patient, and she never lost her breath or the thread of her melodies. The younger woman fussed and muttered and complained, but she helped too. "If we can drive it like this, let's clear out," Joel muttered. He was banging out the metal so that it wouldn't scrape the tire. "Get in and turn the wheel when I tell you, so I can see if it's still hitting." He used a crowbar to bang the metal free.

We aren't exactly returning this car in tip-top shape, she thought. I have to report in to Kiley and to Leigh today. If I can just hold on to the car till tomorrow. After all, the kid's been doing without it for a month at least.

When the car could be steered, Joel got in on the passenger's side, nursing a scratched wrist. The Jeep went off at last, the older woman whistling Bach, the younger woman driving too fast, as if to make up for the lost hour. "Fucking creeps! They hated me. What did I do?"

"I didn't think the musician hated anybody." She headed north along the Connecticut River on 5, a road that used to be the big highway before the interstate was built paralleling it. Route 5 wandered through the old towns at water level or rode at the top of the first set of bluffs overlooking the wide water. "As lesbians they resent men who run this society and outlaw them. They resent the privilege heterosexual people have to get married, take good jobs, raise families legally, without fear of the courts or neighbors."

"Legally, ha. We can't get married. I'd love to have that house to live in. . . . How come you say musician?"

She was about to say that she had never heard anyone but a musician whistle the *Goldberg Variations,* when she realized that would lead into one of their mined areas: best to avoid. "She whistled so much, and right on key."

"It didn't sound so hot to me. Damn dykes!"

"Joel! I have been a dyke. I lived with Eva for *three years*."

"Not a real one."

"What's a real one?"

"You like men."

"Not in general. I like you. In fact, I love you."

"Ha!" He gripped her shoulder. "That's the first time you ever said that when we aren't in bed."

She felt a qualm, because she was thinking under the conversation about Leigh, who loved to live in an atmosphere of music. He would be at that cabin in Twin Mountain by afternoon. The sky did not remember snowing. The road had been plowed and sanded. A foot of snow lay mounded over everything in a glitter too cold to melt except for banks at the road's edge that wept and froze again under the onslaught of the sun. "It feels funny to walk around saying it. It's been years since I was in that stage where you keep wanting to say it to somebody. Makes me feel silly."

"A stage, I see. Because you're ashamed?"

"I just can't believe it easily, at my age."

He snickered. "You ain't so old and tough yet."

About an hour north, Joel told her to stop at a garage with a couple of Getty pumps outside where some mechanics were working on a flotilla of partially dismembered cars. "I'm going to take a better look and see what happened. It doesn't feel quite right," he said. "Why don't you take a walk and see if you can find some coffee to bring back?"

When she came back from the bathroom, Joel was already talking intently with the young guy who was filling the tank. He pulled the car off to the side and together they sauntered past her, ignoring her without decision. Grinning wryly, she took Natalie's thermos and marched off in search of an open cafe or diner. She had to walk a mile, from the southern end of town, where the garage stood, to the northern end of town, where the local breakfast place, John's, was open. John, or whoever the guy was behind the counter, refused to pour the coffee into the thermos. He would sell her coffee only in plastic cups to take out, and she had to pour those into the thermos. "But there's a lip on the pot," she argued, realizing as she yanked at her hair in disgust that she still had the stupid acrylic wig on with the green scarf. "It's hard to pour from cups."

"That's your problem, lady. I sell it by the cup."

Therefore she had to pour the cups into the thermos, spilled about a quarter of the coffee on the counter and ordered two more before she had it filled.

"See," the guy said triumphantly. "Four cups' worth."

"But I would have paid for four cups." She had a mile to trudge. She wondered if she dared to take off the horrendous wig before she got back to the gas station, but she was afraid someone would notice her.

When she climbed over the crusted snow by the side of the road and walked into the station, Joel was deep in concentration over the engine of a modified high-slung car the mechanics were looking into. "I got the coffee," she called from the entrance.

They ignored her. Perhaps he had not heard. "Joel, I'm back with the coffee," she called. He looked up, nodded, turned away. She felt like a fool standing there. She got into the car, thinking how sensitive men are to slights *from* women and how insensitive to slights *to* women. That's just the way things are, take it and shut up, they say. Why should she feel qualms about seeing Leigh? After all, Joel knew about Leigh. He must have guessed they still met. She imagined Leigh's presence, so much less prickly, less torturous than Joel's.

She had a growing itch to catch a glimpse of Susannah, to paste a face and body to the name. She imagined trailing Susannah through a supermarket, sitting in the next booth in a restaurant overhearing a conversation between Susannah and her best friend, but even such fantasies were dangerous. She could not risk Susannah's seeing her face.

Opening the thermos, she sipped the coffee. If he didn't care, why should she wait for him? She finished her small cup and poured another. Finally Joel was wiping his hands and strolling toward her, still chatting with one of the mechanics. No, he was stopping again. Laughing at something the guy was showing him from his pocket. Before he got in, coming to the driver's side and motioning her to slide over, which after a moment she did sooner than start a fight in the gas station, she had refolded the map.

"It was a pin in the linkage of the steering column," he said buoyantly. "I hammered it straight. Good as new. Nice guys, real friendly there."

"I didn't notice that."

"Listen, I got friends about an hour north. Let's give them a call. We can hole up there and get fed and rested."

She was scheming, trying to balance Kiley against Leigh against Joel. "What do your friends know about you?"

"That I'm in some kind of trouble. Steve told me once he bet I had a wife and kids somewhere I'd run off on."

Finally she took off the wig, combing out her hair. "Give them a call. Don't say much about me."

He called from a drugstore and strolled back beaming. "It's cool. They say come right over. I know the way."

The antiques store and the gas station and repair shop run by the two brothers stood in the center of town, but their house was on the outskirts where streets faded into country, a towered yellow Victorian with a red barn behind. The huge paunchy patriarch, Steve, ran the antiques business and the family. Cal was as lean as Steve was gross, a younger brother with similar high coloring and hard gray eyes but perhaps half the flesh. The gas station was his. Steve's pregnant wife, Ellen, was a tiny woman who talked constantly as if to herself with the conviction nobody was listening, saying as she smiled wanly, "Oh, Terry, it's wonderful to see you, what a surprise, you could have warned us, and now a meal to fix. It's a pleasure to meet you, Virginia. Now, what will I ever do about supper? I wonder if I can stretch that chicken."

"Ellen and one of the cows are both expecting, ha ha," Steve bellowed. "Took long enough with both of them, right?"

She waited until Joel was neatly inserted into the scene and then she announced with feigned casualness that she had errands to run and friends to visit and would be back at supper. She hoped for a clean escape, but Joel caught her at the car. "What's up?"

She had to sacrifice something. "I'm off to arrange a meeting. I'll be seeing Kiley this weekend. You can if you want. . . ."

"*She's* here? Here?"

She nodded, using his confusion to get into the car and away.

By wayside phone she set up a rendezvous with Leigh for the next morning at eleven in Twin Mountain. Then she headed for Agnes' farm, where she found a message saying that the meeting with Kiley was now set for ten on Tuesday on a hiking trail.

"What is this?" she asked Agnes, a middle-aged Quaker who harbored fugitives regularly. "Isn't Kiley here?"

Agnes shook her head no. "They're gone for two days. They only stayed overnight."

"Who's *they*, Agnes?"

"Herself and Lark, nobody else this time."

She could not keep the car that long. She'd have to try to borrow one of the house cars from Hardscrabble Hill. Why had Kiley delayed the meeting? She wished she knew what was happening, but it was futile to try to pump Agnes. At Hardscrabble Hill she might get some information, but that was too far to go today. She picked up her winter clothes from Agnes and drove back.

She stood in the barn, where Joel had just milked two cows while she watched with queasiness. She wished Natalie were there to discuss her identification with the cows: all flesh and breasts. She felt sorry for the cows and she felt a shameful unity with them, warm milky creatures with melting eyes. Embarrassingly, those huge swollen udders hung pink and sore-looking. Two of the cows had to have their udders sleeked with greasy bag balm. She felt her nipples rubbing against her sweater. Joel was full of schemes.

"Listen, Cal can get us a car. A '66 Chevy, and the engine's sound."

"A car? What for?"

"Four hundred cash. It even has snow tires, put on last year."

"Have you gone crazy? Let's buy a pet dinosaur."

"It wouldn't cost much. Not if I keep it in good tune. Then we could travel easy, we could even sleep in it. It'd be like a base for us."

"Honey, why in hell do you want a car?"

"Why don't *you* want one?" Joel glared. "Don't call me honey in that tone. Think how great it's been having the little Subaru. The insurance is low up here. I could work on it and get it in great shape. When the weather's nice, we can go camping."

"Why not go camping now? It's as practical as using up our money on some great gas-guzzling ogre that'll die in the first mountain pass!" She tugged on her hair in annoyance.

"You don't trust me. You don't believe I'm a good mechanic. Listen, I could take that car apart and put it together in the dark. Blindfolded. With gloves on."

She paced as the cows shuffled. "We have to figure out what we're going to do."

"I can work here awhile. I was talking to Steve. I'm better on the detail work than the couple he has now."

"I can't stay here. They'd drive me crazy." Steve reminded her of a fat and fangless Kevin, lording it over his household.

"Just a few days. I asked Steve for five bucks an hour. No taxes out, no Social Security. If I put in a week, that's two hundred right there."

"Have you made up your mind if you want to go with me Tuesday?"

"Yeah, why not? But what is all this? Are you still for real in the Net—"

She stepped hard on his foot. "What did you think? If we want to work on opposition to nuclear power plants, we have to hammer out some kind of proposal. It needn't be solid till, say, late this month. Probably not till after Thanksgiving. But we need some preliminary flag to wave at Kiley to draw out her reaction." A scheme began to come to her. "Listen, I'll take the car and return it. Then I'll stay at Hardscrabble. You buy the car, get it in shape and I'll wait upstate. You can come up there Monday night for the Tuesday meeting, if you want to, or just come up when you work out the week."

"Ah, stay with me. We could get separated."

"Love, I'm going to push a plate into Steve's face if I have to sit through another meal with him."

" 'Cause he's loud. You like refined types. University men."

"My dad was stone working-class and he never sat at the table like a pig in a high chair. Maybe he didn't know what fork to use, but he knew how to treat people at his table." She stepped closer. "You'd never act like that. He treats Ellen worse than a cow."

"I don't want us to be separated. It scares me."

She found it scared her too. "I'll wait. Come to me."

To drive off in the Subaru for New Hampshire exhilarated her—going to an assignation with her husband in style. Oh, she had certainly traveled enough on buses for nine lifetimes, in other people's cars, handed from car to car; but she had not climbed into a vehicle alone and roared off sedately in too many years for her to locate the last time. By habit, she minimized contact between herself and strangers. She took along cold chicken and filled the thermos with Ellen's perked coffee, boiled to viscosity but hot and full of caffeine. Natalie's gift accompanied her. She wished it were time to talk to her again.

Of all the pleasures of her old life that she had not properly appreciated, the simple ability to pick up a phone and call someone when she wanted to know how they were, what they were doing, when she ached to hear their voice was surely one of the most precious abilities she had lost.

"The first euphoria is over. We rub on each other. Traveling together is hard. Yet the connection holds—isn't that a surprise?" She talked to Natalie as she drove. "Just desperation? Somebody to love after so long? Not that I don't love you and Leigh. There are people who never stop missing the ones they love. I never get used to it: you're there and I'm here, and why? You know, you go underground with a set of people and you're condemned to them. If you can't love one of them, find a mate, you're out of luck. Eva was consolation but not passion. Every woman not you always strikes me they aren't you. Except Lohania. She was herself. Yet even Lohania got jealous of you."

Lohania and she had exhausted evenings in discussions about whether they should be lovers. They agreed it was a terrible inhibition that they could relate only to men, and they were warmly attracted to each other. But they seemed more comfortable talking about their attraction than acting on it. Half the people who knew them thought they were lovers, an assumption they encouraged, but the myth satisfied them for months. They could hold each other, they could cuddle, but below the waist stayed out of bounds. They drank wine, they got stoned, they finally dropped acid together, but they had affection rather than sex. Finally Lohania insisted they had gone too far to back down. It was a politically necessary step.

Lohania thought they ought to go off to a motel, but Vida objected. Instead, they kicked out Kevin and Leigh for the weekend, took the phone off the hook (a preliminary to sex, whose accompaniment was always the mechanical protests of a telephone uncoupled) and marched off to bed to get on with it. Actually she had enjoyed making love with Lohania. At first they were clumsy, but the unease passed. They discovered they could experience multiple orgasms with each other and made love until they were both sore and feeling a little piggish, passing a whole weekend in sensual experimentation while the war burned and all their brothers and sisters rushed about their business.

Brothers and sisters, lord! We did call each other that. She squinted to read the road signs. Please don't snow! Amazing, but we did. From Black religious influence, civil rights days? Whenever it was, it passed in the conflagration, and nobody says it any longer. It would be too sentimental, too warm for the '70s; but I liked it. You just can't say, brothers and sisters, you are a bunch of yellow-dog running lackeys of imperialism, guilty alternatively of right opportunism and left-wing infantilism. It said we wanted to be each other's families. Not that it didn't foster its own flatulent style. The male leader pretending folksiness in a Harvard accent crossed with a drawl borrowed from Bob Dylan records or movies about hoods, "Gee, brothers and sisters, I kind of tink we ought to maybe do this here ting. . . ." But it left more room for paying attention to each other. We did trust each other, amazingly. We were wide open. Anybody could come in, and many did. We coupled off, but we tried to stay open; we did try to care. We were big on Love. A lot of the time it meant nothing but a buzz in the head and an idiot grin, but sometimes it meant trying a bit harder to be close, to listen, to understand.

Lohania and she had not continued as lovers. Why? It took too much effort. It was easier to fit into the men's schedules, easier to focus on the men's demands. To bring them together required disrupting everybody's patterns. Lohania said Vida was really in love with her own sister, Natalie. One day they had a fight about their relationship. Lohania insisted that Vida couldn't put more effort into loving women because she was hung up on Natalie and Natalie was the one she really wanted.

It was that burning cold year. Everybody spun crazy with desperation to stop the war. She had run downstairs to Natalie, who was having a shouting match with Sam because he had knocked baby Peezie on the head with a plastic dump truck.

Peezie had been named Phyllis Ziporah, after Daniel's and Natalie's dead mothers, but after Sam had renamed her she was never called anything but Peezie again. Her name had represented an unsuccessful compromise between Daniel's claims and Natalie's, for Daniel had disliked the name Ziporah as much as Natalie had disliked the name Phyllis.

"Natalie, stop this and listen to me!"

"You stop it!" Natalie sat down thump in a chair. "Take over. Make order from chaos. I quit!"

She could hardly hear her sister over the din. "Shut up, you brats!" she roared at her nephew and niece. "Let's have some discipline. Do you think the children of Chinese cadre stand around screaming and beating each other on the head with toys? You shouldn't get them those department-store toys anyhow, Natty, it trains them into consumption patterns."

"Fine, fine," Natalie brayed. "Go ahead. Take their toys away from them!"

They were screaming louder. Vida climbed on a chair and addressed them sternly. "Stop it. Quiet!" But they did not become quiet. She thought about belting them, but she did not think that Vietnamese hit their kids and she knew that Native Americans didn't; it must be incorrect. But how the hell did you shut them up? "Okay, march," she said. "Into your room." She picked up Peezie, who promptly kicked her in the ribs with her fat little legs, and dumped the kid into her crib. Then she went back and hauled in the flailing Sam and stuffed him into bed too. "Now you stay in here until you're quiet." She slammed the door.

They were screaming but more dimly, through the shut door. She sank into a chair with a big sigh. "Better?"

"If you like misery. How'd you like someone three times your size to pick you up and shut you in a closet? Imagine a cop fifteen feet tall."

"Oh, come on, there has to be discipline. You spoil them."

"I recall you liked being spoiled as a child." Natalie picked sand from the corners of her soft brown eyes.

"Come on, Natty, stop listening to them scream. Listen to me. I have something serious to talk to you about."

"And kids are basically frivolous. Sure." Natalie folded her arms. They were not getting on well lately. They had political differences.

"You know that Lohania and I have become lovers."

"That's supposed to be serious? Davida! Spare me."

"You don't think relationships between women can be serious?"

"I have more serious relationships with the women in my consciousness-raising group than you do with any woman. Including Lohania. You're serious about Leigh and she's serious about Kevin and you're both serious about Kevin and Leigh, but you are not serious about each other. An orgasm or two doesn't mean you put each other first." Natalie turned the ring on her finger round and round, more in annoyance than nervousness.

"Do you deny the importance of orgasm? Do you disagree with Reich? Oh, Natty, Lohania says you and I have a basically incestuous relationship but we're scared to consummate it. We love each other but we shy off from expressing it."

"Sweetie, we express it all the time. We're not doing so hot lately. But you're my best woman friend. You're my sister. We need to talk more. You need to stop trying to feed me the correct line of the week and we need to just talk the way we always did. You need a women's group of your own."

"Do you deny the nature of our relationship? Don't you want to force through the taboo that divides us?"

"Not particularly, Vida. I think we have enough trouble both being involved, if you want to call it that, with Jimmy. And he's just like . . . a dependent, a grown-up child we share."

"It's a bourgeois hang-up. Lohania thinks you're obsessed with minor contradictions, such as the woman question, because of those hang-ups."

Natalie's face drew together in a scowl. "What hang-ups?"

"Look at your life. Husband, babies, toys, dinners. Are you so far beyond Ruby and Sandy? We can't make a new society in the shell of the old if we're living a middle-class existence."

"I'm involved in women's politics because I am a woman. I am a woman with children. I'm not about to throw them in the garbage because Lohania doesn't think it's revolutionary to have kids this year."

"Natalie, are you unwilling to try to get to the bedrock of our relationship?"

"Vida! The bedrock is love. I do have taboos about getting into bed with you. So we make it together. So tomorrow you have to break taboos and make it with the kids. The next week it's the dog. No, we have to draw the line someplace. No dog shit in the kitchen and no fucking the dog. No fucking children. No fucking sisters, sweetie." Natalie sat back, giggling, beaming at her. "You're silly, sometimes, but I love you anyhow."

She was with Leigh on a trail in Crawford Notch, an easy climb on an old carriage road through the snow. They sat on a bare ledge at the top of a small mountain overlooking the notch, with the sheer walls of Frankenstein Cliffs before them. She had taken off her left glove and he had taken off his right so they could hold hands, looking at the V of the valley below. Traffic was light on the twisting highway, and they had met no one else on the trail. "I can almost imagine we're taking one of our normal little vacations—when we'd suddenly steal three days and run off to Assateague in Virginia, Shenandoah, the Berkshires, the Adirondacks. We'd run away together and get marvelously restored. I've never enjoyed traveling with anybody in my life the way I love traveling with you," she said.

"I hardly ever get to do that anymore. This weekend is an exception. I can't take off much."

"But you're reaching people. There isn't another radical has your access to radio time in New York, and you know it." Besides, she did not want him going off on lovely jaunts to all their old oases with Susannah.

"Truer words." Leigh rubbed his beard. "Even Harvey got the ax. I'm the last of the redskins riding the airwaves. The corporate word reigns supreme, except for my two cents plain."

She envied his ability to use his talents doing political work every day and come home with a feeling of accomplishment. He had brought tapes to play, and she had enjoyed a couple but finally persuaded him to let her take the rest away. She did not want to use up their time together, however interesting she found his broadcast journalism. He had made it clear at once that they were not to go off to a motel. He was afraid to be seen, and he was probably, she thought sourly but with resignation, saving himself for Susannah later. Nothing had been said like that. Rather, he'd strongly suggested they take a modest hike together, something they hadn't been able to do in a long time.

"We should start down." She did not want to, but she was getting cold sitting on the rock.

"Yeah." He made as if to get up, but didn't. Something was coming. She waited. Something he didn't want to tell her.

"The divorce?" she said.

"Oh, it's coming along. Listen. I talked to your sister this week."

"Is anything wrong with Natalie?"

"A lot of surveillance. But that's not it. . . . Your mother isn't feeling too well."

"Ruby? But she's tough as a mule." Why, when Vida was a baby, Ruby had received an award from the shipyard for never missing a day. Oh, she got colds and sore throats—she smoked incessantly, a cigarette always in her mouth or dangling from her fingers, often one lit in the ashtray burning down while she had struck her lighter for another, that little snap of the wrist and flick of the chin—but never did she go to bed sick. When Joel talked about his mother lying down with her headaches, her backaches, her muted hangovers, her devastating periods, her ennui, when he spoke of his mother stretched out beneath an ice pack or taking antidepressants, her Elavil, her Tofranil, Vida thought of Ruby, who didn't much believe in aspirin. She had grown up thinking of women as hardier than men. Tom got sick; Ruby, never. Tom went to bed moaning. Sandy wanted to be waited on. Ruby did the waiting. "What could be wrong with mother?"

"I don't know exactly. It's not . . . very serious."

He was holding something back, she could smell it, and she felt a rush of anger. Handling her again. Always he hid problems and attempted to manage her reactions. "Tell me directly. What is it?"

"Now, don't get excited."

"I'm angry because you won't tell me. Give me Natalie's exact words. *Exact.*"

"How the hell would I remember?"

"You have a damned good memory. Journalist!"

He snorted. "Ruby had a mild aneurism."

"Aneurism? What in hell is that?"

"I think it's in the blood vessels. A constriction."

"Aneurism . . . Is that a heart attack?"

"It was a mild one."

"How mild?"

"She's in the hospital, but they expect her to be home in a week or two."

"What hospital?"

He took her hand. "Hold on, now. You can't do a thing about it. She's in Mount Sinai, in the heart unit."

"Sandy must be crazed with worry. . . . A heart attack. Why did she have a heart attack?"

"Apparently she had a mild one before, but she didn't tell anybody."

"Oh, that's just like her! Don't talk about it and it'll go away. That's Ruby. What caused it?"

"She was trying to dig out the car—they had an early snowstorm and she was late to Sharon's. Anyhow, Natalie's flown out to Chicago—"

"Then it's serious."

"Don't exaggerate! Don't get worked up! Natalie expects to be back by Monday—she just went for the weekend. She gave me some new numbers for you to call Tuesday in East Norwich."

"Tuesday. How can I wait that long?"

"Cool it, kid. Ruby had the heart attack Wednesday. You've waited four days to hear about it. You can wait three more days for an update. It isn't that critical. Ruby's going to have to lose some weight and stop smoking and watch her diet and behave herself."

"But she's not fat!" Vida said, rushing to Ruby's defense.

"She's not exactly svelte. You know she and Sandy have been putting it on year after year." He stood now, pulling her up. "Let's go. Vida, don't worry about it. Natalie'll have a full report for you at ten on Tuesday."

"Could you please remember my name is Vinnie?"

He laughed with relief. "When you start lecturing on security, I know you're okay. Think the hibernating chipmunks will turn you in?"

"Habit saves. Or habit betrays." They could not walk arm in arm through the uneven terrain covered with snow. Because of the snow the ground seemed to radiate light under the lowering sky.

"Well, how's your life? Your private life first," she asked.

"Oh. Susannah. She kind of wants to get married."

"Oh, she kind of does?" She made herself laugh. "Kind of married is okay. It was the legal kind we were sorry enough we got into, but probably she has no practice."

"No, she's never been married. I tell her it turns into a nuisance after the first year, but she doesn't understand."

"Remember how hard it was for us to break out of that box? Everybody treating us as a couple. People constantly called you 'a married man' and me 'a married woman' till we felt like we'd turned into our parents."

"That was the first time I ever felt like an older man. A dirty old man. I couldn't go anyplace without people asking me where you were. Accusingly. Complacently."

She slid on a tilted granite block slicked with ice till he caught her by the armpits and eased her down. She went on, "And all the men suddenly feeling they could use me as instant mother. Sympathy, meals, endless support, and if I asked anything back they'd say, But you're a married woman. I was supposed to be a public resource for everybody else, and you were supposed to be the only one responsible for meeting my needs."

"And the first time people found out I was making it with somebody else—"

"Marcie. The tall one with the curly hair she straightened and it looked weird."

"She used to iron it," he said. "Everybody was supposed to have straight hair then."

"Every *woman*. Men could have any kind of hair so long as there was a lot of it."

"When I started fucking Marcie, everybody was going around, all our friends, whispering that we were breaking up."

"So, love, why do it again?" She realized she had called him "love" —a word she used with Joel. Leigh and she did not address each other with endearments, considering it reeking of togetherness, banning "dear" and "honey" and "sweetheart." "Kid," "babes," the tough poke in the ribs—that was Leigh's style.

Leigh did not notice. "I don't want to! Susannah thinks it'd be meaningful. I tell her, Damn right, and the meaning is a first-rate nuisance. It's a bore to involve the government in your private life. They charge you and then proceed to fuck up your records and charge you higher taxes and make everything complicated."

"Hold out. You haven't been a bachelor in thirteen years!"

"She'll forget it. I consider it a passing folly." He grimaced. "I wish my book was as simple."

"What book?"

"I played you those tapes on health stuff—don't you remember? I'm doing an article for *New York* magazine and one for the *Voice* but it's part of a projected book. An analysis of what health care is really like in a city—in this case dear, dirty old Brooklyn."

"You're writing a book? Honestly? I don't mean to sound—"

"My agent talked to a couple of editors and there's interest. Everybody's pissed off at the cost of getting sick. Every contact with a hospital rubs the wrong way. So she figures my book has potential."

She could feel something lurking under his words. "Then why do you have doubts?"

"A mass project like this, don't you always have doubts? Whether I'm compromising my politics . . . I did an exciting program on a women's clinic in Park Slope. Brought in a good response when we aired it. . . . But they're dealing with maybe fifty women a week. They demystify the process, but so what?"

"I suppose it means they lack resources to handle more women."

"Naw, it's just a case of the Movement making sure the Movement community has good health care. It doesn't reach women in Red Hook or Bedford-Stuyvesant, who have shitty care or none." He kicked at a log, hard. "Half the people we used to know are nurses now. Male nurses, yet. God, are they superior! Or gone to medical school—all the ones who didn't go back to school and become lawyers. Must be a lawyer, his own personal lawyer, for every damn radical left active in this country. Anyhow, at one hospital in Brooklyn there's this war going on between the politicos active in the union they fought to get in there and the radicals who are active in the community, who want to take over the board that runs the hospital. At each other's throats. Whatever I say, somebody's going to wring my neck."

"You have to set them into a perspective in which each kind of organizing has a place, Leigh."

"Sure, everybody's right and nobody's wrong in our One Big Union."

They climbed over a tree fallen across the path and continued down, crossing their own footprints climbing. Her gloves were not warm enough, and her fingers grew numb. "Let me lay on you Mother's Patented Blueprint for Struggle."

"I wish somebody would lay a hot toddy on us."

"The women's self-help clinic has the function of providing space beyond the control of the AMA, the drug companies, the medical-insurance companies. You discover things—that lots of what gynecologists learn in school are old husbands' tales. Sometimes an alternative becomes mainstream—midwives might end up delivering most babies again. These alternative institutions are labor-intensive and capital-poor, right? Easily set up, easily wiped out. But you can't ignore the mass institutions—"

"Exactly my point. So what real relevance have they, except as kindergartens?"

"Without them, you can only demand more of the same. More drugging, more hysterectomies. But the attack inside the institutions has to be two-pronged. Any strategy has to encompass the needs of the consumers —kids and parents in the schools, patients in the hospitals—and the workers in that institution—teachers and janitors in the schools, nurses, orderlies, kitchen help in the hospitals. Concentrating on workers alone or consumers alone leads the powerless to fight each other."

"Remember Ocean Hill–Brownsville?" They had come out on the level floor of the valley and were heading back to the highway where her car was parked. He took her arm. "Sometimes it hits me what a loss it is with you out of things politically. You have a kind of common sense that's always in short supply."

Out of things. That hurt somehow. "I see things clearer than I used to." How pleased she used to be when she spoke up in meetings if Leigh or Oscar approved. Always she had been a water bug skating over deep cold water. She mouthed the words that sounded right and she used her anger and her indignation, but she never understood the vast structures of analysis the men erected. Then some years after she had gone underground, she had realized she no longer depended on any man to tell her when she was correct. She could be argued with, she could change her mind, but she judged her own arguments. She knew the criteria by which she made political judgments, and others could influence her only on those agreed terms. She was no longer performing; she was only working.

When Leigh got into the car, he slid automatically into the passenger's side. "Ocean Hill–Brownsville," he repeated. "We've been through so many good fights. Hey, old pussycat?. . . I'm at that point of saturation with my material where bouncing my own ideas off a good brain helps to clarify what I've been thinking. . . . Babes, it'll be a blockbuster. Of course, I'll get a lot of bozos mad at me, but what the hell?"

"I think it'll be tremendous, Leigh. Will you show it to me as you go?"

"Sure. . . . Don't forget to burn those tapes." He leaned back, drumming his fingers on the dash. "Slow down. That motel has a vacancy. How about it?"

She smiled sideways. A little victory. Immediately, she slammed on the brakes, steering into the motel and then neatly bringing them up in front of the office. "Your move."

"I don't really have to be there when they get back. I can say I went for a walk. Wanted some air." Leigh went on talking himself into being late as he climbed out of the car to check in for them. She stayed behind the wheel, hugging herself with delight. Ah, she was getting him back, she was. Their intimacy was rebuilding.

It wasn't until they had made love and he had taken a quick shower and was prowling to and fro drying himself when she realized by a tightness around his eyes, a false note in his voice that something was still wrong. "Did you not tell me the whole truth about Ruby?" she demanded, kneeling on the bed holding herself.

"I told you what I know." He cleared his throat. "The Irishman is talking a lot."

"Leigh! Be careful with saying things like that. That's a serious charge. Why would you think so?"

"They're only running him on an AFT charge—transporting illegal weapons across a state line, possession of weapons, that stuff. They've quietly dropped the old charges. And his bail was reduced. He's out trotting around New York free as a bird."

"I can't imagine him and Randy in the same town. They'll kill each other. Randy has to be scared of him."

"Guess again, kid. I think Lohania brought them together, and I think Randy's making a deal. Our old pal Randy is in the D.A.'s office, and he's up and coming. I think maybe he just bought himself one tough lad formerly of the Hoboken docks."

It was not till she was driving north that the depression hit her—not about Kevin, for nothing was known yet, and she would put that in abeyance until she talked to Kiley, but about Leigh. What was she to him? Did it mean anything? A project that assumed Leigh would work with her at all was a fantasy. Somehow the sexual passage in the motel left her feeling handled rather than loved. Bits of their conversation caught in her like barbed hooks. He had still asked her nothing about herself. Nothing. She wanted to be with Joel. She wanted to run all the way back. But she had so arranged things that she would not see him until Monday night at the earliest. She knew she was stuck with that, regretting it bitterly. From the moment she headed north she began to miss him, and every mile it got worse, a louder, higher-pitched whine of missing.

PART IV

May 1970

12

At noon Vida spoke at a SAW demonstration on the Queens College campus, a thousand students standing in the midday sun. She could feel the anger, the outrage, the frustration simmering from the crowd. "We —*we*, they tell us—have invaded yet another country and are slaughtering ordinary people in their homes in the name of peace—the peace of death and decay, the peace of bodies rotting in the sun. Death turns us all the same color. And they are real people dying there, and you're paying for it every time you make a phone call or work for an hour." Her voice was husky and broken with the aftereffects of gas. "And this school is run to train you to pay more for more Vietnams and more Cambodias and never ask why. If you don't make it in school, you can go and die there. Rich old men with bodyguards have democratically elected you the class of death!" She had to stay for the strike vote and help the chapter plan a strategy for taking over the administration building. Then she had a long subway ride back to the Upper West Side.

On the train she huddled, coming down from the adrenaline rush of her speech. She was late for a meeting of The Little Red Wagon, her own collective. She was always late now—running, running, but never arriving. She never went to bed before three in the morning, and she was seldom allowed to sleep past eight. From the time she crawled out till she collapsed in her clothes, she no longer had time to read a book, bake a cake, listen to music, talk idly—and everything was empty palaver that was not about liberation, not about imperialism or racism or Third World struggles, about the war, the war, the war. If she went to the country, it was for a secret meeting or for target practice. When she ran into an old friend, she could think only what skills or contacts they had that were needed, what kind of speaking or fund raising or organizing or liaison work they could do. Yet she had no feeling of accomplishment, because every morning in the fat *Times*, every evening on television, the war was stronger, and she was closer to exhaustion. They had not done enough, they had not risked enough, they had not tried everything, they had not fought hard enough, they had not, because the proof was before her every morning and every evening the war went on. It was raining blood outside whether she looked out the window or not; the blood was splattering down, and the hot wind that blew across the city smelled of ashes, of burning flesh. Obviously they had not tried hard enough if the war still went on.

As Vida rushed into the tiny dim room Kevin had rented under the name Joseph Blow in a Single Room Occupancy welfare hotel on Amsterdam, the rest of her collective glared at her: Kevin from his seat on the open window, Lohania where she lay on the cot, Randy where he was pacing, Jimmy where he crouched watching Randy. Their anger felt familiar. Lately it seemed as if the closer you were to people, the harder they came down on you.

"And just where have you been?" Kevin spoke from the side of his mouth, tugging at his beard.

"SAW demonstration in Queens. They needed a speaker. They're taking a strike vote to go out in protest of Cambodia."

Lohania lay on the cot, her eyes staring at the falling plaster. "This is an important meeting today."

"We been waiting almost two hours!" Randy bellowed. "Are you with us or not?" The Little Red Wagon never met in their apartments or in Movement offices, being convinced they were all bugged.

"Mass work is important too," Vida said loudly. Neither Kevin nor Randy was involved in SAW. Lohania and Jimmy ought to support her. She wasn't about to drop organizing altogether for the clandestine work of The Little Red Wagon.

Her political statement went right over Randy's head. "No more of this shit." He was a chunky man with wild straw-colored hair. He tied a red bandana around his head to keep the silky strands out of his eyes, blue and bland in a square-jawed face. He had blunt hands, stained with nicotine because he chain-smoked, often drawing so hard he puffed till the filter started to smolder. When for some reason he could not smoke —he smoked in movies, at rock concerts, on the subway—he chewed gum. "We got to work fast."

"Why fast?" She perched on the cot near Lohania. "The war's been going on since I grew up. We ought to take the time to do our action right.''

Kevin, balanced on the sill of the open window as if he might decide to leap out, swung around at that comment. ''Davey, you little punk, we are doing it right. Wait till you see what Dolpho got us.'' Kevin disliked calling people by name and gave them names of his own. Lohania was Lulu, Randy was Dolpho. The first time they slept together, Kevin had asked her, ''How come you got such a weird crummy name like Vida?''

''My father's name was Tom, but his father was David. He named me for his dad. Christians do things like that.''

''Don't Jews?''

''Not for the living.''

''So your real handle is Davida. Okay: Davey it is.''

That first time had been in Washington, under a table where they were sleeping—under the table to keep from being stepped on. Nixon's Counterinaugural. They had both been heavily gassed, and ill from it. Lohania and Jimmy had been separated from them, and Kevin and Vida did not find them until the following day. In the meantime they sought refuge in a house where people knew who they were but did not know them personally. Under a table, sore, bruised from vomiting, worried about their friends, they sought weary consolation, and the sex exploded.

''You're not listening to me!'' Randy accused her.

''I'm listening.''

Randy was one of the newer people coming into the Movement—not the serve-the-people type or a pacifist or a red-diaper baby or a thoughtful anarchocommunist or a Trot or a Catholic leftie, but someone with a huge rage against the war and the government. Randy was a walking bomb, a characteristic Kevin liked, Jimmy worshiped and Vida pondered, sometimes with approval and sometimes with disdain.

Today Randy was proud of himself, strutting past Kevin. Randy's beefy well-muscled arms under his T-shirt pumped at his sides, elbows jabbing the air. ''Did I say I'd get us plans? Did I say that? Don't tell me I bullshit when I say what I'm going to do. I never shoot my face off when I can't deliver—right, guys?''

''Floor plans?'' Lohania sat up, wide awake at once like a cat, raking her hand back through her curly black hair.

''You heard me right.'' Randy ran his hand over her bare shoulder. As the day was unseasonably warm, she was wearing a striped tank top. ''Gather round and feast your eyes.'' From his knapsack he pulled out a pile of Xeroxed architect's plans.

Jimmy—skinny, bony baby of hers and Natalie's, who would not eat if somebody did not remind him—was imbecilically taken with Randy and doted on him like a gawky puppy. Now he ran circles around Randy in excitement. "You got us the plans—you really did! How did you do it?"

"I got a friend works for the Office of Building Inspection. It's a corrupt bunch. I slipped him a twenty and he didn't ask questions. What does he care?"

"I can't believe it's so easy," Vida said, excited herself. "They're wonderful. . . . But does anybody know how to read them?"

"I can." Lohania stretched, slithered over. "I been studying plans all week. I got Belinda to show me. She went to architecture school, you know, but then she could never get a job."

The plans were for the recruitment office in Rockefeller Center and the Whitehall Induction Center. "What happened to Dow Chemical?" she asked.

"Listen, you can't ask for the moon from some guy who doesn't give a shit. He can't spend all day Xeroxing."

"I wanted us to consider Dow," Jimmy said. "For one thing—"

"One or the other. Let's move." Kevin slid from the sill to pace. The room suddenly shrank. Two strides across, two back.

"Won't the guy remember what plans you copied?" she asked.

"What does he care? I paid him. He wouldn't report a murder if he saw it in the hall. I'm telling you, I know him. He hasn't read a newspaper in ten years. All he watches on TV is football and hockey." Randy thumped the plans with his fist. "Time to stop this jawing. We got to get moving, like Kevin says. Let's pick a target. I say Rockefeller Center, the draft board. Too damn much security down at Whitehall."

Kevin visibly wavered between fighting for the sake of not having spoken first and agreeing because he didn't want to spend time arguing. "What difference does it make?" Kevin was out-toughing Randy. "Let's flip a coin. Just so we smash the bastards."

"I don't 'like leaving something important to chance," Vida said. "We ought to decide on political grounds. What we hope to accomplish."

"A big bang," Randy said. "Show them we can hurt them."

Lohania frowned. "They're both good targets," she said slowly. "Destruction at either one will slow down induction, show people there are ways to block them taking kids. We can hit the other later."

Provided we survive this hit, she thought, but did not speak. She despised herself for thinking of failure. Every day Vietnamese were dying in tunnels, in the paddy fields and jungles, in their beds, thrown from helicopters. Nobody asked them if they wouldn't rather survive. Privilege, being a white American, made her able to quibble. "Flip a coin, then," she said despairingly.

"Here's my quarter. Heads it's Rockefeller, tails it's Whitehall."

Randy flipped and clapped the quarter onto the back of his hand. Then slowly he drew his hand away. "Heads it is. We got our target."

"Now we should scout it," Vida said.

"Bullshit," Randy said. "We got the plans. You want to wise them up?"

"What's wrong with scouting?" Lohania said. "I've done a lot of inside work, and it's a good idea to go in first with nothing on you."

"You never did this kind of work, Lulu," Randy said, grinning. "This is heavy stuff. That's what's cooling you off."

"I'm not scared, I just want to do it right." Lohania jerked away from his hand. "How come you're so sure of these plans?"

"You think they tear down Rockefeller Center and build it again every year?" Randy shrugged elaborately. "Go scout it. I could care less. But if you tip them, it's everybody's ass."

Lohania stalked past him to stand by Kevin, relaxed again on the sill. "I won't tip them."

Kevin gave her a finger poke in the belly, proprietary. "Now, we got a connection for the dynamite?"

"Sure, from that construction crew," Randy said.

"What would we do without you?" Vida asked.

Randy narrowed his eyes at her. "Sit on your asses. Take books out of the library on chemistry. The only guns you guys ever laid hands on was staple guns."

"Listen, you never taught me how to handle firearms," Kevin snapped. "My old man taught me, and I was using them when you were in college."

"Sure, man." Randy slapped Kevin's shoulder. "But none of these other kids ever saw a gun before except on TV."

"I saw them." Lohania leaned against the window frame. She was playing gun moll. At times, Vida thought, they all played roles from a B movie. Yet the excitement of sighting through a rifle for the first time, a used Remington Model 788, stayed with her. Lohania was talking about her father: ". . . and a Colt .45 he kept in his dresser drawer."

"Is your dad in the rackets?" Randy asked. Lohania fascinated him. His eyes were usually on her, he listened carefully when she spoke, but Lohania was interested in Randy only as a cell member.

Lohania shrugged. "What does that matter to us? They don't speak to me, I don't speak to them."

Her father ran a laundromat in Queens. Lohania's family was a sore spot Vida was careful to avoid. She never asked questions, but let Lohania talk when her fountain of private bitterness welled over late at night, when something had shaken Lohania's confidence—*that* reminded her of home.

"They really don't speak to you? Ever?" Randy probed.

"No, they really don't speak to me!" Lohania mocked Randy's tone.

Kevin rescued Lohania from Randy by putting an arm around her shoulders. "Now we got a target, we got to get the dynamite, divvy up the tasks and pick a zero hour."

She could not breathe, as if the room had grown suddenly hot and stifling. Were they going to do it? Really? She wondered if each of them secretly did not stare at the others and hope someone would back out. . . . Oscar kept a rifle in his closet. Every so often he would take it out and fondle it, clean it, cart it around his bedroom. Show it to her. Then he would carefully put it back under the loose floorboard in its hiding place—broken down neatly and stored in its own plastic stock. The rifle assured Oscar he was a revolutionary, at war with the government, but she did not think he had ever fired it. Once Oscar had shown it to Lark in her presence and Lark had lashed into him. "You're an asshole! They can bust you for that. It's a toy—for you, it's a toy."

Oscar kept the rifle as a proof of his seriousness, as a talisman against co-optation, a fate they all worried about. Of course, no one had shown a sign in years of wanting to co-opt any of the SAW regulars. People in the other world viewed them as barbarians: professors, journalists, television people, editors, opinion makers who watched the slaughter every night in their living rooms called them beasts when they ran in the streets with NLF flags and broke windows. Nobody tried to buy them any longer.

Over the years, her outside ties had atrophied. She knew by face and name two thousand Movement people, but retained no friends outside. Since the FBI had visited her boss and she had been fired from Kyriaki, she hardly ventured into the straight world. She had not done any neighborhood work or direct organizing among ordinary people since late in '68. Now, except across police barricades, she rarely saw a person who wasn't close to a full-time activist. She worked in the nerve centers of antiwar activity, writing propaganda, making speeches, stuffing envelopes, calling demonstrations, organizing defense committees, but nothing sufficed. Nothing satisfied. Nothing eroded the urgency she felt as she lay in bed at night and images of the war fluttered like filthy bloody rags in her head.

Another damn demonstration. Once more into the streets, dear comrades, unarmed and ready to be mauled. The spring and fall mobilizations, the marches, the rallies, the speeches, the endless slogan-filled speeches went on and on and on and meant nothing. Every day the oily malignant voice of the robot President uttered new lies and ordered more atrocities. Bomb the dikes. Bomb the hospitals. Chemical warfare. Mutations unto the fifteenth generation. A fertile land of rice and mahogany and fishing boats and rubber trees was being bombed moment by moment into the craters of the moon. Every day the cancerous war fattened.

She had inhabited the war since she could remember, and it had cost her years of her life. She had been beaten a score of times; she had had nosebleeds and concussion and bruises and sprains; she had been gassed into permanent damage to her lungs and a huskiness that never seemed to leave her voice. She was lucky. She had her eyesight and her freedom, while friends had lost both.

She turned to Kevin, braced in the window with his elbow resting on Lohania's shoulder, and felt one with them. They had built this group because they could not stand futility. Sensing her mood, Kevin put his other hand lightly on her shoulder. Jimmy, crouched on the floor looking alternately from Kevin to Randy for guidance, was figuring the amount of dynamite they needed to damage a couple of rooms. Bombing was an obvious idea: every day's paper carried news of new targets and new attacks. Bomb scares were even more frequent, and every school and most of the office buildings in the city were regularly emptied by a student or employee seeking some interruption to the dull routine. Half the people she knew fantasized about blowing up one of the obvious monuments to military or corporate power that gleamed like diamonds set in steel around Manhattan.

"It's a lousy time, in the middle of a serious meeting, to fondle your girlfriends," Randy said sourly to Kevin. "Are we working or aren't we? Coupling off is putting strains on this group."

"Garbage," Vida snapped. "We came in with the same relationships we have. They didn't interfere with starting this group and they don't get in the way of our operations. Can it, Randy, you can satisfy your other needs elsewhere."

"Why should I have to?" He grinned at her. "Share and share alike."

"All right, when we get the dynamite, you can insert the blasting caps." A delicate job everybody seemed to think she and Jimmy were best fitted for. A shade too much pressure and the whole charge would blow up in their faces. The two of them had done it on the bit of dynamite they had gotten to experiment with the month before, blowing up rocks in an abandoned quarry.

Waiting behind the shelter of a rise for the explosion had been unendurably tense. They had been trying out a chemical time bomb, using a pipe filled with dynamite, primed with a mixture of potassium chlorate and gunpowder, and then enough sulfuric acid to eat through a cork. The bomb had gone off, all right, but not in three hours. In four hours and twenty minutes it had exploded, deafening them, rocking the earth, terrifying, exhilarating. But that would not do. The bomb had to go off when they expected, to allow enough time after they called in a warning to clear the building, but not enough time for the bomb squad to arrive, search and disarm the bomb. They had driven back to the city subdued, emotionally and physically spent. There had been both release and an access of terror in the explosion that had made it almost enough in itself to persuade them they had acted.

Now they planned to use a bomb with a clock, very traditional and reliable. She asked, "Tomorrow, same time?"

"They sentenced the group that bombed the draft board in Brooklyn," Jimmy said. Faithfully he clipped the *Times* every morning, as when he used to do power-structure research.

"Yeah? So what did they get?" Lohania asked, pretending faint interest.

"Thirty years," he said softly.

"*Thirty years?*" Lohania repeated, staring.

"Wow, that's a long time," Kevin said. "I can tell you, a year is forever. Even with good behavior, they'll be old when they get out."

"Some state rep is asking for the death penalty," Vida said. "Rockefeller just wants to make it mandatory life. . . . Well, till tomorrow?"

"Look, all I'm supposed to do, I need a day to get the stuff arranged, you guys," Randy complained. "We need an extra day to get all our shit together."

She smiled involuntarily. That phrase—one Movement people kept using lately—about getting your shit together always made her see one of those shiny black dung beetles that had been common on the goat paths, rolling their bundles of goat turds uphill end over end among the rocks of the Cretan hillsides.

". . . then we'll close the gap between jawing and doing something," Kevin was saying, rubbing his hands briskly. "Hey, Vida, let's go home and rip one off." He didn't really mean they should run home ahead of Lohania and Jimmy and jump into bed. Rather, he was teasing Randy in his sore spot. Randy really wanted Lohania, but he would have settled for Vida.

As they left singly, timing their going as they carefully arranged their coming, she went first to start supper. Back in her kitchen, she stuck the pot roast in a skillet to brown and then looked for onions to slice. Nothing in the drawer but dry skins. Wasn't anybody doing the shopping? They would be seven to twelve for supper tonight, but nobody shopped. It annoyed her; she blocked her annoyance, as she was learning to do. They weren't starving. Still, onions were vital to pot roast, and she was hungry. She had been up since six, delivering pamphlets to chapters across the city, and had eaten no lunch. The smell of browning beef lapped at her stomach and filled her mouth with saliva. She put the roast on with the dregs of a bottle of red plonk and ran down to Natalie for onions to add. Natalie's house was better organized and she was sure Natalie had done her shopping.

When she rapped on the door, Natalie stood inside and talked through the door. "Daniel, if that's you, you're early. I told you the meeting would run till four. Go get a cup of coffee or see if anybody's home at Vida's."

"Not even I am home at Vida's. You're having a meeting?"

Natalie undid the door. "Hi. We're just finishing. I didn't want to let Daniel in. I swear he likes to walk into the middle of our women's meetings. It bugs him that there's anything in the whole universe he can't control!"

"You don't let him in when you're meeting? Do you throw Sam out in the street too?"

"I would if Sam acted the way Daniel does. Oh, heh, heh, the ladies. You mean I can't stay? I'm not welcome! You mean just because I'm a man . . ."

Why was she pretending she didn't understand? Daniel patronized her too. He assumed nothing she could have to say politically could be as interesting as anything he had to say, and that if they disagreed, it was because she didn't follow his fine reasoning. Yet that circle of women sitting on the old red couch, the rocking chairs and the floor disturbed her. Their eyes went over her and mostly, politely, they looked back to each other, but one or two stared longer.

What did Natalie say about her? Did they sit around discussing how she ought to be working with women instead of The Little Red Wagon? Suddenly she recognized that stocky woman still watching her as Jan, who had served on the New York Steering Committee of SAW as long as she had been Oscar's girlfriend. After Oscar had broken with Jan, she had heard Jan was taking it badly. Since then Vida had seen Jan only at demonstrations. Now here was the girl Lohania had used to call along with Brenda the Bubble Gum Twins sitting cross-legged on the floor weighing fifteen pounds more than she had, with her hair growing out brown from the scalp, dressed in basic Army drab and looking grim enough to curdle milk. Oh, Jan's going to try to talk to me about Oscar, she thought. Her anger at Oscar was strictly political, and she did not want to confuse her precise disgust at his Schactmanism with what must be Jan's woman-scorned dreariness. Oscar had been forced out of the Steering Committee to lick his wounds at C. W. Post, where Daniel, who supported his opposition to the more militant tactics SAW was adopting, had got him a teaching appointment.

"I can come back," Vida offered nervously. "I just dropped by." She didn't want to say in front of the women that she had come to borrow onions. They might think it was regressive that she did the cooking, whereas only Lohania and she knew how, and she hated to eat canned spaghetti.

"It's four," Natalie said. "If we don't keep to a deadline, we go on forever."

Jan stood. "Announcement! I'm running a printing workshop starting tomorrow evening for any woman who wants to learn. We have a press at the center now, just a small Multilith, but look at the rape pamphlet and you'll be surprised what we can do. . . ."

Just what the Movement needed: yet another printing press. SAW had a perfectly good printshop. Then she remembered there had been a fight between a women's group and the printers about something the women wanted run off that the printers, all male, had refused to take.

"While we're learning to print, we'll do some fun things like run off our own stationery, so you can learn layout too. . . ."

Here they were, facing off the cops every day, enduring tear gas and bayonets, and these nuts were designing fancy stationery. As Jan walked out in a knot of women, Vida turned her back and thumbed the pamphlet. It really was about rape. She felt embarrassed. What a weird subject! Next they'd be doing pamphlets on mugging or toothache. "What is this stuff?" she demanded of Natalie as the last visitor straggled out.

"We find in groups that half of us have been raped. You see, when women start to talk to each other, the old assumptions crumble." Natalie gave her a hug. "Glad to see you!"

"Half the women in groups. You get the ones who are mad already."

"Don't you think rape is common?"

"Come on, Natty, what do you mean, common? Is murder common? It sure is in Vietnam."

Natalie rubbed her eyes—a gesture of fatigue. "How about you? You've been raped."

"What are you talking about?" She paced, but carefully. Natalie's was not an apartment where she could pace restlessly or passionately: she'd end up on her ass with a plastic pull toy under her and two kids screaming she'd just broken Jeremy.

Natalie settled at the dining-room table with a deep sigh. "Don't you remember Vasos? He used to force you regularly."

"Oh." She saw herself pinned on the bed under Vasos, unable to cry out because there was nothing but humiliation in screaming when your own lawfully wedded husband exercised his conjugal rights. When he thrust into her, it hurt. She would feel torn. If she was lucky, he would come quickly, but if she was unlucky, he would go on pounding in her, each stroke burning her raw. Afterward when she pissed, it would hurt all night. Vida sat down at the table across from Natalie. "But it isn't rape if you know the guy."

"If you murder somebody you know, it's murder. If you rob somebody you know, it's robbery."

"But . . . he didn't have a gun or a knife."

"Did he need one?"

"I could have fought harder. I used to fight him as long as I could and then I'd give up."

"Why? Why didn't you try to kill him?"

She twisted on the chair. Something she did not want to remember, those months before she had succeeded in running away. "It was his right —he kept saying that. He was stronger than me, and his weight alone would push me down. And it was his house, his family, his mother and father in the next room, his brothers down the hall, his country, his language, his courts, his law."

"Isn't it usually?" Natalie poured some peppermint tea, nudging the cup across. "Remember, I was raped at college."

"Raped? Oh." She remembered Natalie coming in with her blouse torn, carefully not opening her coat until she was in the room they shared in the dormitory, then sitting numbly on the bed's edge. For the first few hours Natalie could not cry. "That guy."

"Because he was Black and I was white, I thought it was my fault. It was our first date." Natalie tweaked her snub nose, squeezing. "In those days, we didn't expect trouble from men on the first date, if we were supposed to be nice girls."

"But isn't it like a racist cliché? Black man rapes white woman?"

"Most rapes are in the same race. Mostly white men rape white women—"

"My god, Natty, I hope you don't go around saying in your women's group that a Black man raped you! He was probably incredibly oppressed. That's like putting down Blacks because there's a high crime rate in the ghetto."

"When a man rapes a women, he doesn't do it to feed his hungry family. . . . He said, What does a white woman go out with a Black man for if she doesn't want sex? I said, I liked the way you talked in the meeting."

"Natalie, you've got to cool this. You want to sound like some Southern-belle racist?"

"Now, you listen, Davida!" Natalie clutched her hand hard. Her eyes were burning, and she looked close to tears. "I spent as much time getting my ass kicked in civil rights as you did. And I am not a racist! But I'm not going to lie about my experiences anymore. I'm not!"

If Kevin heard Natalie, he'd call her a fascist. She vibrated with anxiety imagining her sister running around New York telling everybody she'd been raped by a Black man. "That was years and years ago. It's ancient history."

"But you and I never let me talk about it." Natalie let go of Vida's hand finally. Her own hands sought each other, and again she twisted her ring, round and round.

Natalie was really angry, she finally noticed. Maybe she hadn't let her sister talk about it. If so, she was sure going to pay for it now. She could see herself explaining Natalie all over the Movement, and how could she rationalize something so . . . gauche? "That really scared you a lot," she said slowly. "You've been cautious with men ever since. You don't take the chances I do."

"No," Natalie said, calming down. "Why should I? It's not worth it."

"To be close to someone?"

"I have enough people to love, in my own way."

She wondered briefly if Natalie would include Jimmy among those. She noticed his striped engineer's cap lying on the radiator. Jimmy liked to dress in what he saw as workingclass clothes, such as white painter's pants and flannel shirts. Jimmy had been in love with her all through 1969, when twice they had attempted to make love, but he could not. Now he was more happily in love with Natalie. If at first you don't succeed, try the other sister. She did not think Natalie slept with Jimmy, because, after all, she had been faithful to Daniel for years and years, but that very fidelity might spare him the worry over whether he could or couldn't. Ordinarily she could have asked Natalie outright what was going on, but they had been getting on worse than they ever had in their lives. Besides, it was a little beneath Vida's dignity to inquire over a strayed lover or admit she did not know everything about everybody in her collective. She should gladly donate Jimmy to Natalie. After all, she did not love him except as a friend or as a pet, almost. Poor Jimmy. He adored too easily to be valued as he deserved. She tore her mind off Jimmy. "If you don't take chances on people, you don't get close to anyone. You don't learn new things."

"Vida, I do get close to people. Come on! I'm close to most of the women in my group. In a brand-new way, in fact."

She flashed on that tight circle of women on the floor. "When you work with a group, it's always like that. Struggling together, feeling a sense of *we*." Just like her with The Little Red Wagon. "It's just that with two kids, you haven't been able to get thick with the people you work alongside."

"It's not the same. They don't punish me for having kids. They don't stare at my breats when I talk. They don't come on to me and then walk off when they notice the ring on my hand and find out I have two children. When I express feelings, they don't call me hysterical.''

Hysterical. ''But Natty, okay, rape is something that happens to some of us—''

''Remember when Brenda got raped at knifepoint in her hallway? They only had to prove in court she's in SAW and lovers with Bob Rossi—''

''Natty, that doesn't make it political.''

''Terror exercised by half the population over the other half isn't political? What's more political than coercion?'' Sitting back tilted in her chair, Natalie looked at her. Vida had the sense that Natalie was suddenly tired of the conversation. Natalie, who had just spent an intense afternoon with her group, didn't feel like arguing any longer. ''You've lost weight. What is all this crazy hush-hush stuff? We never eat together any longer. I hardly see you.''

''That reminds me, I have to borrow onions and start supper.''

''Onions are hanging in a mesh bag in the kitchen. . . . Are you and Leigh getting along? I never see you with him. Always with Kevin. And I hardly ever get to sit down with Lohania. She's cold to me.''

''Political differences,'' Vida said. ''You know. Between Leigh and me. Between you and me. Between you and Lohania.''

''But not between you and Lohania and you and Kevin?''

''We're Marxist-Leninists.''

''Since when? And what for, sweetie? What's the point being a Leninist in the U.S. of A. in 1970? Everybody who made a revolution broke the rules by being entirely of their own time and place.''

''Exceptionalism. That the U.S. is so different, so special, we can't stoop to learn from what worked in China and Cuba.''

''Lenin wasn't what worked in China or Cuba!''

''The Cubans wouldn't say that. The Chinese wouldn't. They say study Marx and Lenin.'' She found herself getting angry. Natty was becoming frivolous.

''A revolution here has to come out of our situation, right? It isn't going to look like one anyplace else. You used to laugh at all those factionalists quoting their little red books. Bob Rossi looking for the peasants to lead into battle—''

''I'm more serious than I was then—''

''No! You're just more desperate.'' Natalie leaned forward, catching Vida's hand. ''Come on, don't let's fight. So what's wrong with you and Leigh?''

''Look, Natty, we're not a couple like you and Daniel. When Leigh and I are close, it's because we feel close. Right now we don't agree politically." She detached her hand. "To me it's not a job in itself to have a relationship with him. It's not the center of my life. As a woman, you ought to understand that. Making Leigh feel like he's in love with me and making him feel good isn't my big job in the world—right?"

"Right, Vida. You're absolutely right. I'm too traditional in my patterns—everybody says it. It's just that Leigh really loves you and you really love him. You're not happy when you're at odds. You look wrung out. You're not taking care of yourself. You sleep two hours a night."

"I'm stronger than I've ever been. I think that what women need to do about rape is not sit around with each other moaning and groaning but make ourselves strong. If we arm ourselves, nobody can rape us."

Natalie sat back, grimacing. "Sure, walk down Broadway with an automatic weapon. Take a grenade to bed."

"If we act strong, men won't try to bully us. We have to make ourselves strong." She jumped up and marched into the kitchen to take the onions.

"Black people always were strong, Vida, strong physically. Black women labored in the fields for fifteen hours—and were raped."

"But they didn't have guns!" She grabbed the onions and went out the kitchen door. "No slaves have guns." As she ran up the service steps, she met Jimmy with a bouquet of daffodils. Seeing her, he froze, embarrassed, on one foot.

"Those are for Natalie, right? Listen, she'll love them."

"I know it's bourgeois." Jimmy teetered on one foot, a stork with ulcers. "Don't say anything about it upstairs, okay?"

"Not a word. I think it's pretty, and American middle-class people hardly every bring each other flowers."

"I thought she might need cheering up."

She peered closely at Jimmy, exactly her height and probably weighing no more. "Cheering up from what, exactly?"

"Well. Daniel. That stuff."

She put an arm to stop Jimmy. "What about Daniel?"

"Didn't she tell you?"

"We had a pretty heavy conversation about priorities." She put her hand under his chin and gently turned him to her with his light brown eyes behind the aviator glasses. "I'm getting worried about her politics, Jimmy. We need to work on her. What didn't she tell me?"

"You know. Daniel's . . . well, he's having an affair with a student."

"I imagine so. . . . You mean he never did?"

"A one-night stand or something casual," Jimmy said awkwardly. Sexual slang came lumpy to his tongue. He was the only person she knew who said "fuck" with tongs if he said it at all. You could feel his effort to shape common sexual words. "But not seriously. Daniel say's he's in love."

"Does Natalie like her? . . . Is Natty upset?"

"Sure," Jimmy said looking miserable. "But nobody gives her any support. It's all Smash monogamy."

She felt a stab of jealousy that Natalie had told Jimmy, not her. Probably Natalie feared she would support Daniel and tell her to dissolve her marriage. She did think Natalie would be better off without Daniel, who was obviously holding her back politically. He was a mushy liberal, a self-styled socialist who was always talking about losing the masses by taking too left a line, without caring to do any mass work himself. Daniel and Oscar. Let them camp out on Long Island and lecture the sea gulls, who would shit on their heads. They had become irrelevant. History moved too fast for academics.

The moment she walked into her apartment, she felt Kevin's presence. She could not have said how. They were strongly attuned to each other; or at any rate, she was attuned to him. She chopped and browned the onions, pretending she did not know he was waiting for her. The door to Lohania's room off the kitchen was shut, but she could hear voices inside. Finally she added a bay leaf and thyme and stuck the pot roast back into the oven.

Slowly she walked into her own room. The apartment was a mess that she tried not to notice. She willed herself not to observe the sleeping bags strewn around the living room, the piles of pamphlets and cans for spray painting, the stencils, the molding towels and overflowing ashtrays. If the apartment was going to serve as a barracks, she began to understand the military insistence on neatness: she would like them to go under barracks discipline and each soldier clean his own damned space. She did not even know how many people were staying in the apartment that week, as the number varied and extra sleepers turned up snoring underfoot in the mornings.

Kevin, Jimmy, Leigh, Lohania and Vida were living here, although Lohania hung on to her job and her room in New Jersey. Only Leigh still had a room to himself. Nobody else could claim more than the space they slept in. When people had begun to borrowing his equipment and taking cassettes and tapes, Leigh had put a padlock on his door and locked it when he was out. He had tacked on his padlocked door a notice saying he would throw anybody out the window who attempted to saw through the lock or jimmy it. Lohania still slept in what had been her bedroom, but now it was the lab, and it too was kept locked. Every member of The Little Red Wagon had a key, but Leigh did not. Often Jimmy slept there, on the floor under the workbench he had built. In that room right now a box sat of electrical blasting caps that Kevin and Lohania had swiped from a construction site in Newark. There were also several alarm clocks, insulated wires, crimpers and batteries. What wasn't there—yet—was dynamite.

Somehow the rent on the apartment got paid every month, but she was no longer sure how. Only Leigh and Lohania were working, although money came to the rest of them through the largess of friends and through donations. None of them had the leisure to hold a job.

Kevin was sitting in bed naked with the sheet pulled up to his waist, smoking a joint. "Where've you been, damn you?"

"Getting some stuff for supper and putting it on."

"Don't play the good housewife with me. Save it for Micro." His new name for Leigh. "I'll eat beans out of a can. . . . Only one thing I feel like eating and that's pussy. Get your clothes off."

"Where's Lohania?"

"In her room."

"I heard voices. Who's there?"

"Dolpho." Kevin grinned. "Get your clothes off, I said."

Slowly she took her clothes off. "How come with Randy?"

"In the front way, I guess. Hey, no bra. I thought so. I dig that. I thought so when you came walking in."

"But why is Randy in her room?" She did not like it. Lohania did not want Randy. Lohania rarely wanted to have sex even with Leigh or Kevin. Last fall after Lohania had gotten pregnant in spite of the coil, she and Lohania had flown to Puerto Rico together for her abortion. Lohania had been upset by Puerto Rico—the poverty, the destruction of the land and of the people—yet she was excited to be in a place where everybody except tourists and rich people spoke Spanish. She had early memories of Cuba, and the landscape was the same and different, the same and different.

Vida had gotten pregnant about a year after she married Leigh. He had been strongly against having a baby; Vida had been balanced in desires. The job she had was no career, and she was politically involved but not yet consumed. That was before she had joined the Steering Committee, when she had been a member-at-large of Students Against the War—a little awkward because she was no longer a student, but drawn to them because they were the liveliest and fastest-growing of the antiwar organizations. She had almost thought of the baby as dues to Ruby, who had plenty of grandchildren but doted on them all.

Her abortion had been one of the usual illegal hasty jobs in a doctor's office with no anesthetic and no recourse from the later bleeding and pain, but she had borne it stoically and missed only a day from work ("I have a bad toothache and I have to go to the dentist"). Leigh had gone with her, waiting outside, and he had done what he could that night as she cried, not only for the pain but for the furtiveness of it, the coldness.

Lohania's abortion had been harder and the aftermath much more intense and protracted. Sex hurt her, and even when it stopped hurting, she did not feel pleasure. She did not want to be touched; she brooded on the injury to her body from the coil and the removal of the coil and the embryo taken from her with the coil embedded in it, the baby that could never have reached term. The pill Lohania refused to take, the diaphragm she said hurt her, leaving Leigh or Kevin to use a condom. Vida and Natalie had had an argument, because Vida felt Lohania was simply saying she did not want contact, she wanted the skin of the condom between her and any prick. Natalie rejected that interpretation, saying the pill caused blood clots, DES caused cancer, the coil did internal damage, and why shouldn't Lohania make the men worry about contraception? Natalie was on Lohania's side.

Lohania's sexual withdrawal had heated up the relationship between Vida and Kevin, and even as she fell headlong into it, she regretted Lohania's defection. She felt abandoned to Kevin—his drive, his rage, his energy, his power. She experienced him as pure energy. Now he summoned her and she fought a delaying action. "Why is she with Randy?"

"We're running a number on him. He's the hardest-working stiff in our cell. He got the plans, he taught us about munitions, he's getting the dynamite. He takes half the risks on himself. And we flaunt it in front of him. We got to share."

"We share food. Money. Danger. But Lohania is not a *thing*. She's not some resource. Why don't you lend him your asshole if he's so horny?"

"We had a struggle about it after you left. Lohania agreed."

She paced naked, holding herself over her breasts. "For more martyrdom. To humiliate her own body."

"He's a great guy. You ought to want to be nice to him."

"You too. Get down and suck his cock yourself."

Kevin grinned, not at all annoyed. "Come here, carrot cunt. I like it when you talk back. Let me give it to you."

He pulled her down on the bed, spread her legs roughly and stuck his hairy head between them. His lips and tongue felt good, and she sighed, but her mind was ice and with Lohania. She did not want to be in bed with Kevin; she wanted to be stopping Randy from blackmailing Lohania into having sex with him. Off her kitchen it was happening. She must protect Lohania better. How fiercely close they had been in Puerto Rico. As the anesthetic was wearing off, she had held Lohania's slim dark hand. Long, elegant fingers tipped with silver polish. Lohania was the only woman in the New York movement who wore nail polish. If she had looked whiter, she would never have got away with it. On her dresser stood bottles in ranks of Blue Jean Baby, Shanghai Express, Plum Passion and Café au Lay.

"Come on, Davey, suck my cock and then if you're good, I'll stick it in you."

She hated the way he talked to her in bed; it infuriated her and underlined her submission. The tang of humiliation fed the sense of being lost in him. It was as if he said to her, I'm coarse, I'm rotten, I'm powerful, and I'm strong enough to make you take it. He was fatally attractive lying on his back with a big grin, all the long lean hard-muscled planes of him spare and perfect and his prick standing out of the golden wiry pubic hairs so like his beard. He was not circumcised, and his foreskin fascinated her. He was the first man she had slept with who was not circumcised, although her father had not been. She had an impression of overhearing a fight between Ruby and Tom that centered around whether he washed or did not wash his prick enough and whether that was or wasn't what had given Ruby an infection. The walls of their house were thin as toilet paper.

The uncircumcised man was doubly not Jewish. She had listed to and fro in her life from Jew to goy and back, just like Ruby. Now she was completely hung up on Kevin; hung up as on a long hook that penetrated her through the breasts. When he touched her, she burned. She could not separate her raw sore craving for him from her desperation, from the war that raged in and out and around them. They were comrades in arms. Little tenderness, less gentleness, no playfulness passed between them, and they failed to spin a web of the small social acts and domestic pleasures that had defined much of her loving with Leigh which often, terrifyingly, felt over. It was as if the sharp blade that was Kevin had come literally between them and she could no longer feel Leigh. They fought too much.

When Kevin was thrusting high and hard into her, she stopped thinking, she stopped feeling anything except his weight and his violence and his need and his pleasure. Her coming was more emotional than physical. She felt like weeping. Since Lohania had stopped sleeping with him oftener than every week or so, they had sex at least once a day and sometimes twice. Often she was sore from him; yet she felt impelled. His touch aroused her even when she could expect and indeed desired no orgasm. This is real, she thought under him. The sense of compulsion convinced her.

Afterward they lay spent and wet. The windows were shoved up, letting the traffic concatenation of Broadway roar dully in the room. The curtains hung soiled and limp. The day was close to hot. It gave menacing promises of a long hot burning summer stinking of tar and tear gas. Weary, she slid down almost into sleep. Kevin was smoking, flicking the ashes into the sheet. He was not even conscious of making a mess. So unlike Leigh, fussy about everything, noticing every wrinkle. Once she had admired that concern with detail; now it felt petty and harassing. Who cared? Kevin's raging sharp beautiful contempt made Leigh stuffy and tame.

Against Kevin she dozed, his long sinewy arm around her. His gaunt profile etched against the window relaxed as he exhaled smoke rings to the ceiling, where dark red paint ran in a crazy pattern from an afternoon Kevin had got angry and spray-painted it in a random design from the hip, shouting, "Fuck your goddamned room, who are you to occupy so much space? It's my room too. We don't have any privacy. We're soldiers. No more private rooms and private property!"

Exhaustion rose, thick warm fog in her veins. How tired she was; how tired she always was. Fatigue made her feel guilty, so she drove herself harder. . . . She was packing. They had to leave. Smoke seeped from under the door. The living room was burning. The draperies were in flames. She was packing so that they could escape. She had to remember to pack everything they needed, because the fire would burn everything else, but always she kept forgetting things. Her good winter coat. Leigh's tapes and cassettes. His best Nagra. Her Cretan tapestry. Mopsy. She had forgotten Mopsy. She felt such a jolt of guilt it was as if she had been kicked in the stomach. Mopsy. Where was Mopsy in the smoke? She could hear her barking.

The walls fell in, fell onto her. She was suffocating, and the flames bit her arms and back, the flames scorched her face and eyes. She heard her own hair crackling into flames, and still she tried to cram Leigh's mother's antique lace tablecloth into the suitcase. . . . Mopsy was barking. Lohania walked in, Mopsy at her heels. For a moment Vida was terrified, seeing the room still flickering with black-and-orange flames. "Knock, man," Kevin said, "unless you be wanting some too."

Lohania was wearing the midnight blue wrapper Vida had got her when they went to Puerto Rico. Randy had his shirt off and padded barefoot after her. Vida looked at the ceiling, the ragged smears of blood red paint annoying her. Then she sat up, dragging the sheet around her shoulder. She did not want to lie supine in front of Randy. Lohania said, "Your mother's on the phone."

She simply refused to walk naked past Randy. She tore the sheet off the bed, uncovering Kevin, who would not mind, and sidled past them into the hall. "Ruby? How are you?" She glanced at the clock. Ruby called as soon as the rates went down. That meant Leigh's program was on. If she turned it on when she got off the phone, Kevin would be furious.

"Baby, are you all right?" Ruby asked in her fast thick voice.

"Fine, Ruby, fine. How are you?"

"Listen, I didn't call to be social."

"Why not? It's okay."

"The federal agents, they came around again. To the pharmacy. It's not good for Sandy, you know? They tell me, Do you know your daughter is living in the hippie commune with four men besides her husband? She calls herself a communist. And so on. They try to scare me. They tell me, You know, Mother—imagine an FBI calling me Mother? That made me mad. They got their nerve. I'm not old enough to be his misfortunate mother, I told him so. They said, Oh, you was born in 1916 in Cleveland, Ohio, to emigrant parents who came here to the land of the free in 1907. So, I said, If that's a crime, sue me."

"Ruby, you shouldn't talk to them. Don't confirm what they say. Don't argue with them. Don't say anything. Hear me?"

"Did I say anything? I wouldn't say a word."

"But you shouldn't get into arguments with them through the screen door."

"They're going to give your father Sandy a heart attack coming into the pharmacy. It's not right." Ruby always called it a pharmacy instead of a drugstore. That was fancier to her. "They went to your sister's too."

It took her a moment to realize Ruby meant Sharon. She never thought of Sharon as related to her or even to Natalie, although Sharon was Natalie's younger sister.

"She called me up spitting mad. Can't you make Vida and Natalie stop this stuff? she said. They're hurting my husband's career. I'm quoting her exact."

"So who else did they go to?" She amused herself by draping the sheet around her as a toga and admiring herself in the reflection off the glass door to the living room. A band of dirty sun lanced through the window and caught the ends of her hair.

"Paul. At the plant. It's not good, what they do."

"It's harassment. You call up your Congressman and complain. Tell them the FBI is telling you lies about your daughter and pestering you."

"My Congressman! What does he care?"

"Nothing, but why not complain? So how is everybody otherwise?"

She listened with half an ear, interested and bored at the same time and enjoying Ruby's voice and feeling a little guilty for enjoying it. Only Leigh had such a warm feeling for his parents as she and Natalie did.

"So when are you coming home?" Ruby was asking.

"Mama, my life isn't my own right now."

"So whose is it? Ho Chi Minh's?"

"Ruby, he's dead and don't make jokes. I have duties here. Make Nixon stop the war and then I can take pleasure trips."

"So at least I'm a pleasure to you."

"You are. I'd like to give you a great big hug."

"Are you taking care of yourself? Natalie says you run yourself ragged. You don't take vitamins, you stay up all night at meetings, you don't eat right. Didn't I teach you to eat right?"

"Natalie's a fussbudget. Don't I sound fine?"

When she got off the phone, she walked into a tense argument. Quickly she picked her clothes off the floor and went into the adjacent bathroom to dress, leaving the door ajar so that she could hear.

"I'm just expressing my doubts," Lohania said defensively.

"Well, step on them like roaches," Kevin said. "We got no time for doubt."

Vida waded into her pants and burst into the room still zipping them up. She had doubts too, secret snake pits full.

Lohania held the wrapper closed, frowning. "Maybe we're giving up on trying to reach people. I know, I saw *The Battle of Algiers* as many times as you all did, but we aren't in a colonial situation. It isn't like we have a Party. We're doing this on our own."

Randy was red in the face, shouting, "How long do you want to run around in the streets shoving each other? What do you think you are, a road-company *West Side Story?* You say you're at war. Well, start fighting. And I don't mean with slogans."

Vida said, "Slogans are ways of getting across what we have to say. They stand for solid analysis."

"They stand for solid crap. Ideology is a social disease. If you're not hurting the state, you're not doing shit."

"Without a sense of why they're doing things, people get confused," Vida said. "I want a movement that changes how people think."

Kevin sat up in bed naked, princely, with a calm smile listening to them haggle. He'd listen and then browbeat them to his way of thinking.

"Sure, Westmoreland's scared at night about how you think. Thought's cheap. Sticks and stones may break my bones, but names will never hurt me. All you chicks want is to crank out lousy pamphlets nobody reads but other college kids," Randy said

"Without politics, all you got is adventurism," Lohania said. "Without politics, what's the difference between us and a demolition crew?"

The outer door slammed, and they all froze. Kevin rolled out of bed and in one fluid motion grabbed his shirt, reached for his dope and got ready to swallow it. Jimmy burst into the room, and they all relaxed. "K-K-Kevin!" Jimmy stuttered only when he was extremely upset.

She was glad she was dressed. She did not like to rub Jimmy's nose in her lovemaking with Kevin. "Are you all right?"

"The radio. We were listening to Leigh—"

"A thrill a minute." Kevin turned his back.

"Leigh said the National Guard shot a bunch of students at Kent State. Shot them dead. Fired into a crowd."

"Where's Kent State?" Lohania asked.

"Ohio," Vida said. "We have a SAW chapter there. It's just an ordinary school."

"White?" Lohania asked incredulously.

Jimmy said, "They killed students, I'm telling you. Two men and two women. At a demonstration right on the campus."

"Jesus." Kevin stood up slowly. "They're killing us out in public now."

They had friends who died mysteriously in prison: She hanged herself with this piece of rope she got somewhere. Sure, he tried to escape in broad daylight right in the prison yard and was shot forty-eight times. Friends had died in automobile accidents coming back from Canada, on the underground railway that ran draft resisters and deserters out of the country: died in accidents where tire tracks showed they had been forced off the road. Nonetheless, this was the first time she could think of when white kids had been shot for protesting. She was horrified, and yet she had the feeling, underneath, of inevitability. What they had been saying about the repressive fury of the government was true.

The war brought home. Tears ran down her face as she clutched herself. "The war's starting here," she said numbly. Randy stared from one of them to the next, shaking his head in annoyance. "You look like zombies. You didn't know the kids. Besides, we're fighting back— right?"

Kevin crashed his fist into the wall, and plaster cascaded. Lohania put her arm around Jimmy's shoulders. He was shaking. Vida came to stand with them, and all three held one another. Official murder. The government shot unarmed kids and felt righteous about it. Maybe they enjoyed it.

Kevin lurched from the wall, his face bright, his eyes burning. "We'll show them a TDA! We'll blow them a TDA that hurts." TDA was Movement slang for The Day After: the demonstrations that immediately protested some new atrocity, a new escalation, new arrest, new entrapment, new weapon.

She hoped Leigh would come home for supper so they could find out more information. "Everybody's staying to eat," she declared with assumed matter-of-factness. "I'll get it on the table."

"No," Randy said. "I got to split."

"How come, man?" Kevin socked him in the biceps. "Thought we were running up to the Bronx, where they're picketing the hospital for a little action."

"Man, if we're going to move on this day after tomorrow, I got some hustling to do. Right?"

"You don't want company?"

"No, man, not for this. In fact, you'd be in the way." Grinning, Randy scooped up his pack from the hall and left. Kevin trailed Lohania back to the room where she put on her clothes. Jimmy began setting the table as Vida put together a vegetable plate from some frozen packages.

Kevin leaned on the doorjamb to Lohania's small neat room painted an almost blinding white with dark blue enamel trim. "Well, Lulu, did you fuck him?"

"Why ask?" Lohania examined her nails. As the copper paint was chipped on one, she repaired it, unerringly seizing the right bottle from the forest on her bureau.

"You saying it's none of my business? Because you don't fuck me anymore?"

"Shut up, Kevin." She turned her back on him, zipping her pants. "It was your bloody idea I should service him. Wasn't it?"

"That's what he wanted. Nobody made you do it."

"You made her do it and so did he," Vida yelled. "Get off her back."

"I didn't fuck him, if that's all you want to know." Lohania squirmed into her tank top, keeping her back to him.

"Oh? What were you doing? Playing doctor? You had your clothes off."

Quickly she raked her Afro comb through her hair. "I sucked him off."

"Oh?" Kevin drummed on the doorjamb. "And what did he do to you?"

Jimmy walked in and backed out immediately with an embarrassed grimace. She wanted to flee too. Hide in her room until they were done lacerating each other. If only Lohania would come out of her withdrawal; Kevin could not endure it and got meaner with each week.

"Nothing. I wasn't interested." Lohania marched past him into the kitchen. As she squeezed through the doorway, he seized her upper arm. They glared at each other, and then he let her go. "You made it happen! You let him make those demands!"

"He's crazy about you." Recovering his smiling mask, Kevin lounged against the refrigerator in Vida's way.

"I'm not 'crazy' about him. I used to be 'crazy' about you, but I get saner every day."

"Frigid! Your cunt is turning into concrete."

"*My* concrete. We got any bread? I mean bread to eat. I like bread with pot roast." Lohania came and stood close to Vida, smiling deliberately at her.

She heard the outer door open. "Leigh?" she called.

"Why, it knows its hubby's key in the lock scratching," Kevin drawled. "Hope it is Micro. We can get some use out of him for once."

When Leigh came strolling in wearing a new polka-dot shirt, he had a woman with him who looked and dressed as Vida and Lohania had a couple of years before, in sandals and textured stockings and a dark blue minidress with a fitted bodice covered with embroidery. Over her flaxen straight hair she had a hat wound with a scarf that dipped over her shoulder, in filmy blue, and she carried an oversized satchel that Vida recognized as a Peloponnesian saddlebag: not cheap. Standing in the kitchen barefoot in jeans and T-shirt, Vida was offended. That's what he wants, she thought: the way I was before. I haven't bought myself a dress in eighteen months. I should take the food money from the kitty and buy a dress?

"And Leigh, oh, Leigh, it was truly marvelous. I mean I'm just tremendously impressed by what all of you do with so little. You have absolutely fierce esprit de corps. But are all the engineers that rude and grumpy?"

"All of them," Leigh said heartily, guiding her through the apartment with his hand in the small of her back. "I'm afraid you're going to meet a lot of surly types in New York. Including here."

Kevin lounged now in the door to the dining room, blocking it, a cigarette dangling from the corner of his mouth and his shirt buttoned halfway down to where his pants would usually have been. He had not put them back on. Casually Kevin scratched his balls with his left hand as he extended his right to shake. "We wouldn't be rude, now. We like visitors too much. Females we like. We throw the men out the window. That's a long drop, and no one's bounced yet."

Uneasily the woman laughed, standing close to Leigh and carefully staring into Kevin's blue eyes so that she could not be thought to be looking any lower. Lohania shoved Kevin out of the way to give Leigh a quick perfunctory kiss. "Hi, baby. Listen, you had about forty-two phone calls. But this one cat, he made half of them his own self. Name of Angio, and he's been calling from Cleveland, Ohio, every five minutes, collect."

"I hope he calls back." He turned to the woman. "This is Karen. She's in the Washington bureau of *New Day*, down here on a story. Angio's our man at Kent State, so he ought to have something."

VIDA

Karen was giving Lohania a careful once-over, deciding she must be Leigh's girlfriend. She paid no attention to Vida, which Vida found infuriating. Vida and Leigh exchanged no word, no greeting, but glanced obliquely at each other. Couldn't he come home for once without dragging along some media jerk? It was as if he was afraid to walk into the apartment and confront her without a prop, a crony, an admirer. "How many do we have at table tonight?" Leigh asked airily of the whole hall. "One hundred, two hundred, many hundred?"

"There's just us," Jimmy said shyly. "Everybody else has gone to be on that hospital picket line." Jimmy was uneasy around Leigh because he had used to worship him, but had changed his devotion to Kevin and lately to Randy. Jimmy had been doing power-structure research on the oil companies. Leigh had met him when he was covering a demonstration at Con Edison on 14th Street and brought him home to share with the family, an awkward bumbling, undernourished genius who lived only for the moment and was fresh and ingenuous as a five-foot-six daisy. After a month, Jimmy had moved in. He needed a lot of loving, a lot of tending to flourish. But gradually Jimmy had come to feel that his brains, his ability to research a way through the labryrinthine maneuvers and institutions the ruling class had invented to obfuscate itself were pointless compared with Kevin's ability to act.

"Oh, the meat's delicious!" Karen said in obvious surprise as she tasted her food at the table. "Who did the cooking?"

"I did," Vida said drily. "*New Day*. I've seen that. It has left pretentions, but carries ads for Coke and RCA and Polaroid. The text says try something new and the ads say buy something new."

"If we supported it on subscriptions, it would cost five dollars an issue. A bit prohibitive, wouldn't you say?" Karen smiled at Leigh.

"No point doing research on the corporations if only people already in the Movement read it, is there?" Leigh said expansively.

"The fiddler fiddles, the boxer boxes and the intellectual puts out words." Kevin scratched himself inside his shirt. He did not itch, but did it to annoy. He never scratched himself when those he judged to be the bourgeoisie were absent. He put both elbows on the table and ate with his head down, acting the slob, swilling wine with loud smacks of his lips.

"How does anybody know what to attack? Because intellectual labor's been done naming names, naming corporations, fitting the links together. Marx didn't spend his time breaking windows. He spent it in the British Museum."

Lohania roused herself from her visible funk. "He didn't advise *us* to spend our lives there. Theory without practice is masturbation."

"And blind practice is a hole in the head. Why work at being stupid? It comes to some of us easily enough," Leigh snapped.

The argument had been going on for a year, Vida thought, eating her supper without pleasure. The parts of her life clanked like a machine needing oiling, whose parts no longer fitted. Never had any other woman she knew been blackmailed into sex in that nasty way Lohania had that afternoon. At least, Leigh would never have abetted that as Kevin had.

Jimmy and Kevin got up from the table to go to the Bronx. Vida caught Lohania in the kitchen. "Stay. Let's talk. They ganged up on you today."

Lohania gave her a tight wan smile, lifting her small chin. "Eh, what's the use talking about it? If I think too much, I get depressed. Better to go out and do something real. . . . We'll show *him* what women can do."

"Aren't you coming with us?" Jimmy asked Vida as Lohania slung her jacket over her shoulder and followed Kevin out.

"No. I better work on the plans."

That was the only answer that would work. She could not say that she had been to so many demonstrations and pickets in the last month that marching had become meaningless, leaving her with a desperate need to be alone. Loose ends welled up inside her. She felt too coerced by the group to know what she wanted or felt any longer.

Besides, she hoped that if Leigh saw she was going to stay alone in the apartment, he might get rid of the Seventh Sister and spend some time with her. He was stuck in an earlier phase of mobilization. He still thought that fighting the state could be assimilated into a comfortable existence —going to a job every day, going to the dentist twice a year, breakfast in bed and late suppers with the two of them snacking on sable on black bread or rich duck pâté from Zabar's.

As with Daniel, as with Oscar, his conscience permitted him little luxuries she had had to give up, and the tension between them sang through the air of the apartment like an air conditioner that ran all of the time with a flaw in its moving parts. She woke in the morning already haggard after four hours' sleep, her body raw, her mind sore, her nerves stripped, and she felt a stab of guilt that she was still living. So many had died that to be alive required that the stub of life be used to best advantage. She was a tool. A fighting machine, Kevin called himself. That was what she ought to be. Then why was she lying on her bed flat on her back staring at the ceiling Kevin had spoiled with paint, fighting resentment that the ugly dark red doodles made her feel aesthetically attacked?

I must try to be simpler. If I were a real revolutionary I wouldn't see the paint on the ceiling. Maybe Lohania doesn't want sex in her life because she wants to strip down to the bone. Maybe she's found a way to greater simplicity. Renouncing sexuality felt tremendously appealing to her as she glanced at the wreckage of her once cozy bedroom.

When she had met Leigh, she had judged him far more political than herself and she had admired him passionately. But he remained safely ensconced in his profession. She thought of Kevin imitating Leigh at a demonstration: "And I say, when the club descends on your head, how do you feel, could you tell us now for our listening public?" It was true: he came to record, to interview, to report. He had his press pass. While he had been roughed up now and then, he had never been arrested and never really beaten. Of course, someone had to cover the demonstrations; yet covering them kept him outside the fray. He did not change as they changed, who had more on the line. Now he was news director of the listener-owned station. He was famous in the Movement in New York and beyond. Last month he had sat on a panel on advocacy journalism at N.Y.U. Leigh's work made him more respectable as he covered their work, which drove them farther and farther outside the hedges of legality.

But part of her missed him all of the time every day and night. She was lonely in a way she hardly had time to notice. All along her side where she had grown used to a friendly warm body, to companionship, to give-and-take and good discussion, she was naked. She had not felt so deeply and constantly lonely in the midst of chaos since Greece. She did not feel loved.

Leigh was angry with her, too, and she felt guilty, as if she had let him down by getting too involved with Kevin. But she was angry at his anger too: he was punishing her for taking their mutual ideas too passionately and too far. He ought to try to change with her. Soon she would set between Leigh and herself an act that she could never tell him. Once done, no undoing. She mistrusted all decisions lately, because stopping to think, to weigh alternatives seemed fused with cowardice. Thinking itself was suspect, for it was the liberal rational heroes who had created this war. She had never kept anything from Leigh except other people's secrets. She would not tell him about Lark's leg or Oscar's occasional impotence; but she told him honestly what she did and felt. She was not permitted to talk to him about The Little Red Wagon, but that silence was becoming a lie.

Unable to rest, she went to her vanity. In the long May twilight, her hair shone crackling around the brush. For the first time in weeks she sat down at her vanity, pushed aside the litter of pamphlets and marking pens to put on a dab of Madame Rochas, her favorite perfume that Leigh gave her every birthday, even this year. Then she drew lines with the eyebrow pencil over and under her green eyes to set them off. She dabbed on a light coat of makeup from a bottle drying up from disuse. Then, as a last concession, she put on a pale green minidress she had always thought of as her doll's dress. It was simply cut, falling from the yoke like the dresses Ruby had run off on her machine for Vida's two dolls, Betsy and Marilyn. For a moment, she inhaled Ruby's scent: a little sweat (she did not use deodorant, believing it caused cancer), an inexpensive flowery perfume, violet or lily-of-the-valley, cinnamon, onions, ginger, all blended into Mama-smell. She wanted to rest against Ruby and weep. And sleep.

Slowly she strolled toward the light and voices. She had only the time when everybody was gone. Kevin would break up her little game if he got back too early. Leigh and Karen were sitting at the round dining-room table, where Karen had spread out photographs she was showing him. The Greek saddlebag purse yawned on the table, so that Vida could see it held two cameras and an assortment of lenses. Mopsy had come out of Leigh's room, where she had been spending a lot of time sleeping on his bed, and sat tight against his thigh, trying to get attention. Occasionally he rumpled her ears with a casual hand.

"Actually, that was Kenya," Karen was saying in that high cooing voice. "That's a Masai village. Those boys are all warriors."

As Vida walked into the circle of light, their unfriendly faces rose from the photographs in one motion. "Hi," Leigh said. "Thought you'd gone."

"No. Everybody else is off to the picket line in the Bronx."

"What'd you think of the coverage we gave that tonight?"

She debated whether to admit not hearing his show. "Actually, the news about Kent State shook me up so much, I don't remember anything else."

"I have a theory about that," he said to Karen. "When you come on with a blockbuster story, you might as well shut up then. Nobody listens. I'm going to try working up to big stories."

Karen laughed in a high tinkly burst. "Like those old-fashioned British papers that used to have lost doggies on the first page and The Queen Assassinated on page twenty?"

"Somebody bombed Dow Chemical with an incendiary bomb at dawn in Rockefeller Center," he said. "Not unlike napalm, although nobody was there. But they must feel like their products are coming home."

"How awfully clever," Karen said. "It's all very Robin Hood, all these merry bands blowing up a different corporate office every night. The insurance companies must be ticked."

If you think it's so cute, you can both come along. Look at me, damn you, she addressed Leigh silently. How can you dote on that caricature? She strolled to the window to push it up. "Warm tonight." Mopsy came to her, grateful for the moment's attention. Every time she looked at Mopsy lately she felt guilty. Now she felt united with her dog in trying to capture Leigh's attention.

He did look at her as she raised the window, the dress rising on her long legs. "Where are you going all dressed up?"

"No place. I thought I'd run down and get some cold beer at the Dominican grocery. Then I thought I'd just take a night off and hang out here and read. Take a long bath. Relax." How seductive can I be, with her sitting glued to him?

"They have that Mexican beer I like, Dos Equis."

"I'll get a six-pack." She could not continue watching them look at Karen's photographs. Maybe if she went down for the beer, Leigh would catch the hint and get rid of Karen. She could not remember the last time they had been alone together in the apartment. "Come on, Mopsy, old girl," she said gently. Mopsy forgave her with passionate wriggles and bounded after her to the door.

But when she came up, having for once properly curbed Mopsy and given her a little run, the light was still on in the dining room as she put the beer away, but only the photographs remained on the table. She rifled them briefly. Aesthetic poses of the picturesque Third World. How would you like it, Karen baby, if some photographer from Kenya marched into your kitchen and your bathroom and snapped photos of you at your colorful native pursuits? American woman wearing hair dryer. American woman at appendage-coloring rite. American man shortening grass in ritual area.

Resisting an urge to throw Karen's photographs out the window to snow as confetti on Broadway, she walked slowly back toward her room. Mopsy's claws ticked on the floor behind her, wet nose against her dangling palm. The lights were on in Leigh's room, and she could hear music from within, but the door had been shut in her face. Leigh was always on his private unlisted phone, chatting, flirting, arranging interviews, part work and part play and part seduction, and for a moment she listened, hoping. She heard Karen's tinkly laugh and did not hope any longer.

She slammed the bedroom door, tore off the dress and flung it on the floor. In the heat of the stuffy night her teeth chattered. Her bed was filthy. Roughly she yanked the used sheets off and rummaged in the hall closet for clean ones. Did nobody ever do the laundry? That was how she was going to end up spending her stolen night: doing the laundry in the basement with Mopsy for company while Leigh screwed that simp. She lay on the stripped bed with her face against Mopsy's warm flank trying to make herself move. She was glad when the phone rang, and she went to answer it and heard Lark's voice.

"Listen, Asch, get down here. Am I glad I caught you! We're having an emergency meeting of the Steering Committee. We have to respond to the shootings."

"When?"

"Right now. Pelican just went up to the Bronx to pull our staff off the picket line. We have to get on the streets fast."

"I'll be right down." She hung up to step into her jeans and yank on her T-shirt. With great pleasure she banged on Leigh's door. "So long," she yelled. "The Steering Committee of New York SAW is meeting. We're going to knock through a TDA for Kent State. Tell everybody where I am. . . . And have a ball!"

The hell with him. On impulse she dashed into the dining room, grabbed a photo and wrote a note to her roommates in purple marking pen on the back of it, then stuck it near the door where they'd see it. A little vandalism for the Vassarette she hoped would give him syphilis. "No, Mopsy, stay! Stay, girl." Maybe he'd like a job with *New Day* too. Off to greener pastures.

"We aren't his brothers and sisters anymore, we aren't his comrades, we're his fucking material," she said as she burst from the elevator and raced across the lobby, waving to Julio, their friend who tipped them to surveillance, and then into the street. She felt like Wonder Woman streaking through the city. Fast, fast she went down the block, too fast for any man to give her trouble. Running lightly in her sneakers. Into the subway, she vaulted over the turnstile and bolted into a train. That was Movement style, perfectly executed. Show the people they can do it too. An example to other women.

Tomorrow she'd tear that dress up and make a rag of it. Tomorrow she'd be on the streets; they'd bring the city to a halt. They'd show the government what it meant to shoot down kids and try to terrorize the Movement. Then the day after that, The Little Red Wagon would roll. Leigh didn't matter. She had wanted to break security to talk their action over with him, she had wanted to break the faith of their group for the sake of telling Leigh what she was about, but he had stopped her. She would show him. He didn't have enough respect for her. He didn't know how serious she was. So much the worse for him. He'd see.

13

The SAW demonstration took a day to mount, and all their plans got kicked over another day, while two Black students were shot in Mississippi and Randy fumed. When Vida stopped by the apartment to change for the streets, Randy and Kevin were head to head in the dormitory living room.

"Man, your priorities are screwed up," Kevin snapped. "Why does it matter exactly when we act? We can't make a direct connection between that induction center and Kent State or Jackson State."

"Suppose you get busted fighting cops? That ruins everything," Randy said, exuding sulkiness thick as cold gravy.

"What's the difference? It's all the same war." Kevin slapped Randy on the back and strolled off. "We'll see some fine action."

Randy slammed out of the apartment. Kevin grinned at her. "*It's* here. Stored in Lulu's room."

"It?" Then she understood. It was as if he had shoved his fist into her abdomen. "Oh."

Together they went in and looked at it, packed neatly in the box. Her hands were sweating. She could not find anything to say. They locked the door, locked the dynamite in. Then Vida had no more time to think. She ran from one meeting to another—the teachers' group, the welfare mothers, the city planners, the taxi drivers. By the time the demonstration came, she could not whisper without pain. Her voice was entirely gone. Lohania, Jimmy and Kevin were in the streets, the Steering Committee of SAW, kids from the fifty-odd chapters, people from all the off-campus

221

antiwar groups. She noticed Oscar, Natalie, Jan, Bob Rossi in a separate Maoist contingent, his ex-girlfriend Brenda with some bikers, Pelican. Everybody was out and running, while the police were rioting and breaking heads. She did not see Randy.

He disappeared completely until after the demonstration, whereas he was usually one of the busiest street fighters, always calling for a charge, the first to pick up a rock or toss garbage cans into windows, to rock a car over, to set a fire in a trash basket. Vida, who was always trying to keep action directed against political targets, did not miss him, but she was surprised he could stay away.

She could remember the peace parades down Fifth Avenue dressed in their respectable best, marching with agreed-upon placards along the negotiated route. Always they had been pleased how many old people turned out. Yet in such legal parades she had been beaten the first, the second, the third time. Always the newspapers reported half the numbers, and the war went on. Gradually the activists had grown tired of standing and being beaten on, and they had begun to run, to regroup, to taunt; gradually they had begun to fight back, to pick up the tear-gas canisters and return them, to come back at the police with clubs. Usually they got beaten anyhow. They were not often outnumbered, but they were outgunned, and the police tended to attack many on one.

Now when they went on the streets they expected to fight. Beforehand she was in terror, with an ache of fear growing stronger and stronger as the moment approached. It seemed to her that for years she had been forcing herself into the streets into more and more danger, and yet the war went on. First it had been a matter of moral courage, to pick up a sign and march against your own country's war; but it had become a matter of brute physical courage.

The night after the demonstration, Randy came back, chastened and ready to make up. She sensed that he felt like an ass for missing the big action, and she put herself out to be nice to him. Brought him coffee and a plate of the chicken-and-barley soup she had made left-handed and even forced herself to smile at him.

"What happened to your arm?" he asked.

"A cop grabbed me." She had an Ace bandage around her right wrist. "I got free, but my wrist is a little sore." They were tending their injuries and feeling that deep mutual sense of relief. These rest periods after a demonstration were the most peaceful times she knew now. They had gone out and fought and they had all come back: no broken bones, no broken backs, no bashed-in heads, no blindness, no maiming, no one shot. They never guessed before they went on the streets a particular day or night what level of response would be dealt them: clubs and gas only, tear gas or Mace or the fancier chemicals, rubber bullets, shotgun pellets, lead bullets. Would the cops just bust, or would they bust and beat, or would they beat to maim?

She grew weary and sometimes disgusted with the efforts to prove herself again and again and again, as if they were all earning some sort of revolutionary merit badges. Now, at least, they had all tested their courage, they had all tested their commitment, and they had survived. The mood in the room was easy and loose; they were warmer together than they acted at any other time—the bond of people who faced something and helped one another through. She loved frail Jimmy, who had slipped through unscathed; she loved Kevin, the brawler, the scrapper, the hero of every fray, with his right hand bandaged and a Mace burn on his ankle from kicking a canister. She loved Lohania, her head in a bandage from a scalp wound, eating soup with a broad smile. Two of her beautiful green nails had been broken, but she was carefully building them back with an ill-smelling chemical from a bottle, layer upon layer, to match the other daggers. She ate with her left hand only while the artificial nails dried on the right hand.

Vida loved even Randy, eating soup with a checklist on the table of everything they must remember, listed only by abbreviation or careful initials. If it were not for his dedication, they would probably have chucked the whole idea, she thought as she slowly ate her own soup, for their satisfaction had a lining of stupor and masked a craving just to let down and relax for a while. Lark had talked to Kevin just before the demonstration, asking him to come to a factory in New Jersey where SAW was holding talks with the more militant workers. Kevin was not a member of SAW, but Lark wanted to draw him into workingclass organizing. He was sure Kevin could talk to the workers. Maybe he could. Vida would have liked to see Kevin drawn into regular organizing and made responsible for more than his big mouth.

Without Randy, no doubt they would have talked a lot but let the bombing die. They were overcommmitted organizationally. She would have to steal the time tomorrow from hours supposed to be spent collating pamphlets and meeting with representatives from high school papers. Lohania and Jimmy would be defaulting on other obligations. For their common act of war.

Jimmy and Vida prepared the bomb except for attaching the clock and set it out next to the briefcase that would carry it. They could not attach the wires to the alarm, since clocks know only twelve-hour cycles. Then they all went for a brief walk in Riverside Park to review their plans. Randy left them there to head home. The whole family retired early, before Leigh came home. Kevin followed Lohania into her room to give her a back rub and change the dressing on her head and never came out. Jimmy went to sleep on the living-room floor.

Vida was glad Lohania and Kevin were together, sleeping in there with the dynamite. She hoped they would rise happy with each other. She did not undress, but lay on her bed with the light on going over the plan of the morning, hoping Leigh would come home. She wanted to talk to him. So many things could go wrong; she needed to feel close to him again, at least briefly, fleetingly.

When she awoke in the middle of the night, he had got past her. Standing outside his door, she could hear him snoring, but she did not know if he was alone. She pissed and returned to her room, undressed and got into bed properly, nudging Mopsy over. She did not sleep again. She watched the hands creep in their slow inevitable descent toward six and watched them begin to rise again, up to seven, when she shut off the alarm as it began to ring.

When she got to the kitchen, she put on coffee. Moments later, Kevin stumbled in groggy with Lohania behind him. "Go shave, my dearest," Lohania said to him more tenderly than she had in months. "Show Vida your haircut that I laid on you. You got to look respectable today, if you can make a pass at it."

"Yeah. Sure." Yawning, Kevin shuffled off to the other bathroom to use Leigh's razor. His pants hung loose around his hips. With a scissors Lohania had cut not only the hair of his head but his beard down to the stubble ready for the razor. Vida hoped he would curse and make a lot of noise while he shaved off his beard to rouse Leigh. She still wanted desperately to see him before she left. Suppose she were killed this morning? Suppose she were busted or shot down on the spot? Suppose they really didn't know what they were doing and the bomb exploded in the briefcase, and that was the end of them?

She felt distant from Leigh as if a deep rift valley had grown between them, as if an earthquake had opened a fissure and their continents were shoving apart. She could not go and wake him. She did not know who might be with him, and the others would be upset. But if he woke and came out, she could snatch a moment. After the water boiled and she started the coffee dripping through, she ran back to dress, slamming the door intentionally.

A beige linen dress just three inches above the knees, demure and proper, that she had not worn since she had been fired from her job. Gold nonhippy earrings. She piled her hair into an expert French twist. Her hands remembered, for she had worn her hair that way in Greece. She put in the amber comb that had belonged to Grandma, to hold the twist in place. Ruby had always worn her hair short. Shoulder bag. Panty hose. Passable sandals with a little heel, almost matching the bag. She eyed herself. Put on makeup carefully, not to stain the dress. She had forgotten to put on makeup first. To protect her dress she had to borrow a towel from the bathroom where Kevin was with fierce concentration and some blood shaving off the remains of his wiry golden beard.

On a final inspiration she fumbled in the back of her vanity drawer, among lipsticks and curlers of past styles, for a small jar of eye shadow. Lavender eye shadow. A few Movement women used eyebrow pencils or eyeliners, but nobody in the Movement ever wore eye shadow. It was one of those magic lines of demarcation. Eye shadow was what her sister Sharon wore in suburbia. Married ladies with Black maids wore eye shadow. There! She finished by applying makeup to her hands, covering chemical burns that might attract attention.

Seeing one another in their bourgeois finery was disquieting. Jimmy looked as if he were about to graduate high school or attend his mother's funeral. He had a narrow maroon tie tucked into the neck of his navy suit and striped shirt. "Oh, Jimmy, you cut your hair!" He had. A mortal sacrifice. Without it his ears stuck out, red and naked, making him appear seventeen.

Kevin did not look successfully bourgeois. He emerged a working-class hustler. The madras plaid sports jacket he had borrowed did not quite fit, tight in the back for his musculature. The shirt was open at the throat. He had held up his khaki pants with a leather belt, borrowed at some point from Leigh probably without permission, because Leigh hated to lend his clothes. He had combed his hair neatly and slicked it back with water.

"Lohania cut my hair," Jimmy said. "But wow, Kevin, you look different without the beard."

Actually, she had had a moment of fantasizing that perhaps he would have no chin at all, but Kevin was handsome without the beard, although less interesting-looking. Almost blandly handsome. A young man who'd sell you a can opener in a hardware store. Lohania looked every inch the secretary on her way to work, in a blue-and-white print dress the same length as Vida's with a straw bag and little heels. As a last touch she had put on a wedding ring. "Natalie says this makes every woman invisible," Lohania said giddily. "We haven't seen you looking like the New York Career Girl on the Go since you worked at Kyriaki, Vida. Like that you could walk into the Pentagon."

Randy was the surprise. He had just arrived, in time for breakfast. He too had his hair cut short, like Jimmy. "Did Lohania cut your hair too? Last night before you left?"

"I got it done at a barber. Thought I might as well do it right. There's one open till late on Columbus."

He looked so straight she could not get over it. He wore a lightweight brown wash-and-wear suit, a striped shirt, a square-cut tie with a print of tiny anchors, polished dark brown shoes. He even had a crisp white handkerchief in his jacket pocket. In these clothes suddenly class is with us, she thought: he looks like he could be Kevin's cousin who's the striver and strainer. He had in fact gone to some little Catholic college in prelaw.

"Okay," Randy said edgily, holding out his wristwatch. "How do we divvy up the tasks? Three with the clock, two to give the warning and distribute the communiqués. . . . Jimmy has to go with the clock because he set it. He knows it the best."

"And I go with the clock." Kevin did not argue. He announced.

"Sure, man," Randy deferred. "Okay, the ladies have been complaining about women's lib. Let one of them go with the clock. The other can do the phoning of the warning and the delivering of the communiqués with me. Let's flip a coin. Heads, Vida goes with the clock; tails, Lohania goes."

"Come on, come on, tails!" Lohania chanted. "Show me tails!"

Vida said nothing. The shiny coin gleamed in Randy's hand. She knew it was coming down heads; it did. "Okay, let's move out," she said. The longer they hung around, the longer she had to feel scared.

As they rode down in the elevator, Randy and Lohania giving them a fifteen-minute head start, she said to Kevin and Jimmy, "Did you notice that whenever Randy flips a coin, it's a shiny quarter and it comes out heads? I didn't say anything because I'd rather go."

Kevin chuckled. "Yeah. It's a trick quarter—heads on both sides. I didn't want to say nothing either. Better for us to take the heavy risks. She's had enough grief in the past year."

At the moment she loved him, taking his hand between hers, the hand not carrying the briefcase. "She has!"

"But she has to heal herself, you know? Got to come out of it herself."

"But Kevin, sometimes a person can want a little coddling, a little tenderness. Need to be gentled."

"Not in a guerrilla situation. Lohania's tougher than you think. She's coming through."

"I'm surprised Randy didn't fight to take my place," she said.

"Didn't turn out for the demo either." Kevin stopped on the street corner as if sizing up the weather, the day, and completed a leisurely inspection. "Getting soft. Chickening out. We got to run some discipline on him when we get through with this."

"Oh, you didn't buy his sudden conversion to women's lib?"

Jimmy spoke up suddenly, his voice high and choked, "Y-y-you don't really think Randy is scared?"

"Why not? I am." She stared up at the brown-blue sky of polluted sunshine between the buildings on Broadway. She imagined woods, the hills of western Connecticut along the Housatonic where Leigh and she and their friends used to go hiking on a Sunday, easy walks in the boulder-strewn woods. One spring Sunday porcupines had been chasing each other, indifferent to them.

"Yeah, but we're going. K-K-Kevin's saying Randy's too scared to go." Jimmy fell into anxious step beside Kevin. "You don't mean that! Not about Randy."

"Shut up," Kevin barked. He was gazing intently into a store window.

"What is it?" She felt cold metal in her.

"We're being tailed."

"Are you sure?" She tried to stare past him for reflections.

Jimmy started to turn, and Kevin gripped him by the arm. "Keep walking. Never look back. We'll shake them in the subway."

"Sure," she said. "They can meet us down at Rockefeller Center."

"Do you mean that?" Kevin said. "Think they been tipped?"

"Let's lose them first. Then we can consult." She picked three tokens as if casually from her purse. "Don't let's get busted with the clock on us."

"What do you want to do?" Kevin barked. "Drop it in the trash? They'd see us." Kevin ambled along, waving his free hand as if in relaxed conversation. "They already seen us with the case."

It was next to impossible to go on walking slowly. She wanted to turn, she wanted to turn and look so badly she could scarcely control herself. To turn and face their pursuers. To break into a run. Dash for it. To grab the case from Kevin, toss it into a doorway and make a break. On they strolled. As they came up to the first entrance to the 96th Street station, Kevin said, "I hear a train, now run for it. We'll take *any* train."

Vida pressed a token into Jimmy's hand and then one into Kevin's. She then fell in behind Kevin, who was a good battering ram through rush-hour congestion. Jimmy, after trying to slip through on his own, fell in behind her, and they thrust for the gates. Kevin went over the turnstile; Vida and Jimmy used their tokens. "The local's in," Kevin shouted. He got into the train first and forced the doors to stay open as they slid under his arm and in. The doors slammed shut and the train started. They collected together, hanging from straps. The briefcase was clutched between Kevin's legs.

The express passed them just after 72nd. They got off the local at 59th and trotted into Central Park, watching carefully, circling back, watching. They were no longer followed. Finally they sank on a bench and stared at each other. "Stay here," she said. "I'm going back to a phone booth and call the house."

"No, we'll stick together. There's a phone booth at the zoo. Let's haul ass over there." Kevin stood. He had a need to keep moving that she could feel.

"Why would they have followed us today?" She asked argumentatively. "It can't be chance. They *knew*."

"Did any of us say anything on the phone?" Jimmy asked.

"Don't be funny." Kevin walked faster. They had to trot to keep up. "We're a year past saying anything real on the phone. Maybe they got the kind of tap on us that picks up room conversations. How about that?"

"Maybe," she said slowly. "We've talked a bit in the apartment. But not much. Not enough for them to put it together." And I didn't tell Leigh: I never did.

"How do we know they put it together?" Jimmy's hands kept knotting in the pockets of his suit jacket. He shoved his hands into the pockets, where they twitched and struggled like captured birds. "They knew we were going to do something today. So they followed us."

"I don't buy that," Kevin said. "We did all the arguing in that room or in the park. We never discussed target or timing in the apartment."

"Could the SRO room be bugged?" she asked.

"That's one possibility," Jimmy said slowly. "They've been waiting for us to act so they could grab us with the clock."

They marched across the park, pushing themselves. They were all three scared. But they were used to being terrified and acting in spite of terror, used to forcing themselves to fight fear and transcend it into courage. She felt proud to be with them. "I wonder if Lohania and Randy got followed too? They have the statements on them. It doesn't matter we have the bomb. They're in the same conspiracy. I hope they paid attention!"

"Dolpho's not so street smart, but Lulu is. She'll spot them. . . . There's your phone."

She dialed Leigh's unlisted number. Since the chaos in the apartment, he had had his own phone put into his room and would not let anyone else use it. He claimed he needed a phone kept free to reach the station and to be reached, and that the regular phone was in use eighteen hours a day.

"Leigh Pfeiffer speaking," his voice came through.

She felt an enormous relief. Now let him catch on for once. "Leigh, this is your old Greek friend. Vasos' ex-wife."

"What?" But he recognized her. "What's up around here, anyhow?"

"Never mind. When did Lohania and Randy leave?"

"They haven't—"

"Great. We can warn them. Why haven't they left, do you know?"

"They're waiting for you to come back."

"Waiting for *us* to come back? Why?"

"Didn't you call a while ago and say for them to wait for you? What's going on around here? What's all the mystery?"

"Who answered the phone when I am supposed to have called?"

"Randy. He said it was you. The other phone."

"Leigh, something's rotten. I can't explain. Lohania will, afterward. Get Lohania, but don't say in front of Randy that I'm on your phone. Just get her into your room."

"Sure. Hey, someone's at the door. I'll get her."

She waited and waited. Vaguely she could hear occasional dim sounds, but nothing she could identify. She waited and waited. "Deposit ten cents for the next five minutes," the operator said, and she did and waited. Nothing. Why couldn't he get Lohania in there? Then she thought they might be tracing her call, and sweat broke out on her hands as she gripped the receiver, straining to hear. Why didn't he come back? Five minutes and more had passed. Then she heard voices. Not Lohania. Men yelling. She could not make out any words. Then she heard a voice close to the phone say, "Hey, Sergeant, this phone's off the hook." She quietly replaced the receiver and backed away from the phone.

When she turned at first she did not see Kevin or Jimmy and went faint with panic. Her sight was riddled with black spots as she forced herself to breathe slowly, not to hyperventilate. They had walked toward the entrance and stood watching her. Kevin was drinking coffee from a vendor.

How did she walk toward them? How did she keep from running? "Let's get out of here. East. Keep walking. They busted the apartment." She took Kevin's arm and Jimmy's arm for comfort, but then let go. Their strides were too dissimilar; Jimmy stepped twice to Kevin's once. "Listen, Randy told Lohania it was off. To sit tight. That we were on our way back. He told everybody I called and said it was off. Then while I was talking to Leigh, somebody came to the door. Cops. I'm telling you, I'm sure they were raided."

"How could Dolpho think it was you?"

"Either they imitated my voice. Or he's an agent."

"Dolpho an agent? I might as well suspect *you*. Or me. It was his idea. If we ever had a hothead, it's Dolpho."

"Kevin, we can't go on with the plan. They have the communiqués. They know where we're going. They know what kind of action this is and the target. They know how we're dressed."

"What do you want to do? Turn ourselves in? Fuck that." Kevin walked even faster. The shiny new briefcase banged against his hard calf muscle, bulging through the thin material of his pants.

"We can't just quit," Jimmy said. "If Randy is an agent . . . If they grabbed the communiqués, they have us for conspiracy."

"We might as well bomb something," Kevin said reasonably, changing arms with the briefcase. Now it hung between Vida and him. "What else can we do with this Tinker Toy? Unless it's set to go off and get us."

"I set it," Jimmy said. "I'll vouch for it."

"Man, your life depends on it." Kevin laughed, a barking sound. "So what the fuck do we do with this live one?"

"We had other targets. Let's hit one," Jimmy said.

"No," she said. "If they know about Rockefeller and Whitehall, they know the others."

"Great. Some random place. The politics of that makes perfect sense!" Jimmy's face was flushed dark red as he sweated in the navy suit.

"Slow down. We're getting soaking wet," she said. "We can't walk in someplace looking as if we ran two miles. . . . How about a police station? Headquarters?"

"With an APB out on us, think again," Kevin snorted. "Come on, Jimmy, get us a war criminal. You did all that bloody research. Let's lay a fine on some damn corporation."

"See, Leigh was right," she said almost cheerfully. She felt numb and brisk; this was what it was like to be dead. It was all over, all over but a bullet in the back. "Research has its political uses. Let's have a cup of coffee and pick a target. We have to write propaganda. Jimmy and I can do that in half an hour while you scout." Move, she thought; we have to do something because they have us anyhow. They can send us up for twenty years on conspiracy, even if we never set off this damned thing. Besides, they'll try to pin every unsolved bombing in New York on us, and if Randy is an agent, he'll back them.

"The East side," Jimmy said slowly. "Chase Manhattan's all the way south. Union Carbide. Du Pont's on Fifth. IT and T. Sylvania. Mobil Oil. All good war profiteers. I'll give you a rundown on their games at home and abroad."

"I could do with some breakfast. Some coffee shop on Third, maybe," Kevin said.

A splash of stomach acid bathed her throat at the mention of food, and for an awful moment she thought she would vomit. "We have to be sure the timing won't fail," she said. "We have to give enough warning to clear the building."

"It's built right," Jimmy said stubbornly. He looked like a miserable high school student late for graduation.

"Make it snappy," Kevin barked at them. "I doubt we got all day."

"You're wrong," Jimmy said, cold and serious. Connections were being made in his head, that she did not understand, concentrating as she was on not showing her panic. "For whatever time we have, that's what we have to do in it. Our lives are over. We're only weapons now. It's very simple.''

With her credit card she outfitted them in different clothes at Altman's, putting the rest into a suitcase she also charged. Kevin checked the suitcase at Grand Central while Jimmy and she made appointments by phone at 150 East 42nd Street. She was applying for a secretarial job. Jimmy was a junior high teacher wanting materials for a unit on Developing Our Natural Resources. Kevin elected to try to enter at lunchtime through Shipping and Delivery, around on 41st Street.

They stood across 42nd Street, taking a last look together before splitting up. Mobil Oil was housed in a massive misshapen aluminum skyscraper that occupied a square block. Blue glass was used in the lower few floors. The windows above were small in the dull metallic walls decorated with wedge-shaped bas-relief like cuneiform inscriptions. The front entrance was squat, a mouth under a big brown marble moustache. ''It sure is ugly!'' Vida tried to sound cheerful. ''Too bad we can't demolish it. We'd probably get a medal from some architects' association.''

Jimmy had taken the bomb, since he argued the briefcase was most congruous with his persona. ''Meet you on the 34th floor. I was actually in there several times, when I was researching the oil companies.'' They had mailed the communiqués explaining their action to the press; no way they could drop off the other copies as planned.

''Well, here goes.'' Kevin sauntered away.

The building had heavy security, not one but five guards standing around the lobby, watching everyone and frequently challenging for business and identity, but Vida walked in at one o'clock in a stream of secretaries returning from lunch. She started a conversation with two women, and strolled in between them. She did not need her appointment, but rode up and promptly salted herself away in a women's rest room to give the others time to arrive.

By two they were all upstairs. Vida took the bomb from Jimmy, and in a stall in the women's room she painstakingly disconnected the wires, working on the toilet seat. With such a large building, the bomb must go off during the night, as the occupants during daytime could never get out in half an hour. They could not after all call in a warning to evacuate only the 34th floor, or the bomb squad would be right on the job. Finally she reset the clock for eleven and connected the wires again. When she had finished at three, she was exhausted, wet and shaking. Her hands trembled. She gave the briefcase back to Kevin and Jimmy. They had decided to place it in the wall in the men's rest room. She could not help them. It would take them a good while. She kissed them both, briefly, dryly, and rode down.

As she walked out of the large but stark marble lobby, she noticed an American Express travel office to her right. Ought to march in there and book passage for Calcutta. It was like a joke the building was making to her. Up above her, Kevin and Jimmy were working like mice in the walls. She felt faint and realized she had eaten nothing since the night before. Walking toward Grand Central, she bought a hot dog with sauerkraut from a vendor. After she picked up the suitcase, she sat on the platform of the IRT waiting.

Their communiqués were traveling now through the bowels of the post office. She passed the time by addressing more notes to radio stations and underground papers. They were all in her or Jimmy's handwriting: no time today for fancy messages cut out of newsprint like the communiqués Randy and Lohania had been supposed to deliver.

Socony-Mobil is one of the biggest corporations in the United States. Its annual profit would feed the hungry and clothe the poor and warm the elderly from Bangor to San Diego. Yet like the other parts of the Rockefeller family empire, the men who run it never feel they have enough. Oil companies profit immensely by war, because every machine that moves on land, sea and air uses their product. But Mobil's interest in Southeast Asia is not on the surface: it's under the water. Offshore oil drilling in the shallow waters off Vietnam is one of the places Mobil plans to pump oil to sell to the Japanese, always oil-hungry and willing to pay high prices. We are just showing them what war feels like, since they appreciate it so much. Let's bring the war home to Mobil and other war profiteers.

She felt it would be almost a relief to feel a heavy hand on her shoulder and be carted away. She wanted to cry; she wanted to sleep. Instead, nervously, she copied the communiqué, sealed it in an envelope, addressed and stamped it and started the next one, to the *Roach,* Leigh's paper. Was he in jail? Was he out?

Where would they go? Where in the world could they run to? The funny white gloves she had bought for the job interview she had not needed were growing grimy and stained with blue ball-point, but she kept them on. Even if the handwriting was hers, at least she wouldn't leave fingerprints. Those precautions felt like a joke, because she was damned sure by now that when Lohania came to trial, Randy would surface as an agent.

Finally she saw them coming down the steps together, small Jimmy and tall Kevin, and rose to meet them. They all looked at each other and they could not help smiling grimly, a twist of the dry lips, but with genuine relief. "Into the train," Kevin snapped, and gladly she obeyed him, grateful for his command, for something to shore up against the mudslide of hopelessness inside her. "We go to the end of the line and grab us a car. They'll be looking for us all over the city. We got to make some distance fast. We can call in the warning." They sat huddled together, the suitcase against Kevin's knees, taking the subway off the map into what she could not begin to imagine. What happened to people who ran away? She had helped deserters and draft resisters to get to Canada. But they would be just as wanted and just as hunted in Canada. No safety there for the three of them. She was glad she was not alone, glad for their company and the animal warmth of their bodies, one on each side, as all three sat staring glumly and riding in silence through the noise and the dark.

PART V

The Present, November

14

The two cars were parked at the entrance to the trail, the old black Chevy Joel had bought and the truck from Hardscrabble Hill, where Kiley and Lark were staying. When they met in the parking lot, the sun was poking feebly between scuds of cloud. Kiley embraced Vida, reaching up for her; then with no difference of expression or emphasis, she embraced Joel, who blinked and blinked, staring at her. Lark kissed Vida and shook hands with Joel. Then they began to climb. A few people had climbed this way since the last snowstorm, probably on the weekend, making the trail easy except where ice filled the ruts.

"One thing for sure." Vida's breath blew out before her over the snow. "We don't meet in smoke-filled rooms any longer. We may not be safe or centrally located, but we sure are healthier."

Kiley gave her one of those famous icy pale blue glances. Vida was trying to figure out if Lark and Kiley were a couple. Lark had grown even thinner. She was unquiet about his health, but he shrugged off her questions, limping a little, restraining a worse limp.

"We must strike back," Kiley said, slamming her small fist into her gloved palm. "We can't let a defeat remain in people's minds. We must follow it with a positive breakthrough."

"You mean Kevin getting busted?" Joel asked. "But he wasn't even in the Network anymore. Was he?"

Lark went on as if Joel had not spoken. "We need to put our politics out to people. People think of us as stuck back in the '60s. It's important for them to know our line on current problems."

"People mostly don't think about us at all," Vida said dryly. "But a way of reaching people, yes. Remember that idea Eva had of comic books? I saw a wonderful Marxist comic book the other day done by a Mexican—"

"We need to clarify our position," Kiley said. "We're projecting a long position paper. The energy crisis, racism, Puerto Rican independence, apartheid, the woman question, neofacism. We can run it off on the press at Agnes' house. That would knock them on their heels."

"Kiley, no!" She banged on her arms to keep warm. "A long position paper? To be read by nobody but the ten thousand hard-core nuts who read everything we put out."

"That's no way to talk about cadres—" Lark began, but she blundered on.

"Kiley, Lark, how can you think what people crave right now is a couple of hundred badly inked pages of our inimitable rhetoric? By the time we run it through the collective, it comes out stirring as a list of spare parts for a '74 Chevy. The Sears catalogue is written in more moving language."

"Jargon turns people off," Joel said. "If ads were written the way we try to talk to people, nobody would buy blenders or leisure suits."

"Some jargon is necessary," Kiley said stubbornly. "You can't talk about imperialism without saying imperialism."

She had hoped that Lark would support her about the jargon; sometimes he did. Roger and Kiley were the two people in the Network who wrote the worst, in Vida's opinion, and thus were charged with grinding out most of their propaganda. But Lark was not talking much. He seemed to be concentrating on putting one foot ahead of the other as they walked up the snow-covered fire road.

"Lark," she said in direct appeal. "Remember the Vietnamese telling us in Montreal to shut up about imperialism and talk about suffering and bread and butter? What's imperialism to my mother? But if you tell her how jobs move out of the country, she'll understand. She used to work in a shipyard."

At the mention of Vietnam, Lark's face relaxed from the grimness of controlled pain. "I remember the woman who talked to us that way. She was a company commander from Quanh Binh, and she hadn't seen her husband in seven years. . . ."

"We must correct the course of the left. We can clarify weaknesses of certain key sections of the Movement," Kiley said. "Our words matter to people."

"Sure," Joel said, his head down, "The sound of one claque clapping." He was mad at being ignored.

"Do we need this negativism?" Kiley turned and looked him in the face, blocking the woods road. Four inches shorter than Joel, she vibrated annoyance, her eyes wide and pale with anger when most people would narrow them. Her hair in a blond Afro stood out around her head. She alone wore no hat, no cap, and her hood was cast back on her slight shoulders. Her nose did not run, as Vida's did. Her skin shone rosily pale, blood through porcelain.

Can he still want her? Vida wondered. Very likely Lark had her now. This coupling had been under construction for a long time, she suspected, ever since she had broken up with Kevin in 1974 during an upheaval in the organization. At that time Kiley had been with Roger. Vida had chosen not to work with Lark that year. It had not been that she was rejecting Lark so much as that she wanted to be without any man except and unless she could be with Leigh.

She felt a tinge of regret. She did love Lark, not passionately but fondly. He was a more serious person politically than Joel would ever be. She trusted Lark even when she disagreed with him. She felt involved with him, his rattletrap body, his pain, his frailty, his driving will. He was a cold man. Yet when she had suffered through the infection from a metal chunk in her leg, he had been the best nurse of all, even better than Eva. That was the most recent period when they had been lovers for more than an occasional night. He alone had understood that even though she was an invalid, she needed to make love to feel herself still involved and alive.

How strange to walk a fire road arguing about things that had no connection whatsoever with the landscape, knowing that nothing would so prick up the spirits of the FBI and the right, more militant daily and wealthier, than if the four of them were suddenly surrounded by police. Forever Jimmy and Belinda died in her head in black-and-white flames. The television had not been a color set. And how strange to argue as if their mutual histories had no influence on the positions they assumed and the anger and heat with which they hammered at the others.

"I suppose you two think we should go back to bombings," Kiley said, striding on. "For a long time we expected people to follow our politics from our targets and the communiqués. But the *Times* can't get the issues straight. They don't want to. They botch it."

"No, I don't think we should go *back* to bombings," she said, striding ahead just as rapidly. "Bombings made sense when they were bombing too. When a lot of people cheered us on and felt, Hooray, *we* hit them again." How to introduce her own inchoate project?

"What I saw in Angola convinced me, bringing down apartheid is the first priority," Larkin said. "American banks and corporations are fattening on slavery. And the party for an Africa war of intervention is growing. Another Nam in the works."

Vida said, "But what about racism here? That's our business. Plus, at this stage of things, it's teach-ins that are needed. Yes, American banks profit from South Africa, and South Africans are buying into the American economy—"

"We recognize your America-is-no-longer-the-center-of-the-empire thesis," Kiley said. "Have you finished that paper yet?"

"Not yet. I've been on the move. It's coming along."

"We have to raise money," Lark said. "We're nearly broke."

"You could have a bake sale," Joel said.

"What's wrong with you?" Kiley snapped. "I can't stand cynicism and pessimism. You've been a negative force all afternoon."

"What could be wrong?" Joel rolled his eyes. "You'd never guess. You're shitting all over me."

"Oh." Kiley's eyes were expressionless. "Is this a personal issue?"

"Is anything personal left in you?"

"Are you not with Peregrine? What do you want from me?" Kiley used Vida's nom de guerre.

"I guess only some stupid recognition we were together for two years. Something really wild like that."

"This is a political meeting, not an encounter group."

"Aw, fuck it," Joel said. "It's a bunch of people walking in the woods."

"Maybe we've walked far enough." Vida was watching Lark. The set of his thin mouth, the tension in his shoulders registered like muffled screams. "Let's turn around now."

Larkin glared briefly at her. "I can go on."

"But why should you?" She took his arm. "You don't have anything to prove to me. Or anybody else here. It's close to zero and my face hurts, and so do my sinuses."

"You know that's not what's bothering me." But he let himself be turned. He even leaned a little on her, surreptitiously.

"Did you hurt your . . . self in Africa?"

He nodded.

She wanted to carry him down the mountain on her shoulders. How hard he pushed himself.

"But it was worth it!" he said strongly. "Our international connections are vital. That's what keeps me going—the sense that if we're stalled, in other parts of the world, on other fronts, people are fighting and winning."

"We have to endure until the time is better for us." In front of them Kiley and Joel walked together, a distance apart. As Kiley turned to speak to Joel, Vida saw that she was smiling. She had a small smile that bared her white teeth in their orthodontically correct bite but left the rest of her face unmoved. Kiley's purer, stronger, simpler than I am, she

240

thought. How can I call her a fanatic? Most people would think I'm one. Kiley is incorruptible, as Lark is. They never hesitate from fear, from desire, from any motive of profit or greed. "Leigh thinks Kevin may be talking." She spoke up. "Randy and Lohania are both around him."

"Kevin." Larkin drew out the name as if it filled his mouth with mud. After a minute he said, "If you hadn't stuck with him so long, I think we'd have thrown him out earlier."

"That's not accurate," Kiley said over her shoulder with measured fairness. "The first years under, Kevin was a source of strength. His anger and his energy pulled us through the paramilitary phase. He simply couldn't evolve politically. His adventurist tendencies came to the fore."

"Sounds like something more dangerous may be coming to the fore now." Lark stumbled and leaned harder on her. Why had Kiley let them all walk so far? She had to know about his leg; you could not sleep with Lark without finding that out. It was a small elite club; all the woman who had been Lark's lovers knew about his leg. The government did not know. It was on none of his Wanted posters. When he came into the movement he had taken a new name, Larkin Tolliver, because his father was an officer who disowned him, and changing his name was a way of disowning his father right back. The name Tolliver was from a teacher who had been kind to him. Larkin was his mother's maiden name. The government had never busted Larkin, never got his fingerprints or his real name. His family did not know what had become of him. All the women in the Movement who had made love to Lark held his secret and held it well, but Kiley did not take good enough care of him. He stumbled again and cleared his throat. "Sounds as if the desire to save his dirty neck may be taking over," he went on stubbornly.

"We must discuss this at a meeting of the full Board," Kiley said. "Soon as we can get together."

"Where's Roger and where's Eva?" Vida asked after the other Board members.

"Roger's in Rochester," Lark said testily, "living with some schoolteacher. We should talk some about that. Eva's in Montana on a reservation, where she had friends from the old days." At one point Eva had been a public-health worker with Vista.

Kiley continued, "Anyhow, you should produce a draft of your work on the changing nature of imperialism. We'll meet near Agnes'. Can you hang around Vermont for a while? Three weeks, say."

"We can get back in three weeks. My mother's sick, and I have to travel."

"Be careful." Lark stopped her, peering into her face with his intense cornflower blue nearsighted gaze. "If Kevin's chattering, we're all going to have to move our covers."

"Kevin doesn't know anything after '74," she argued.

"He knows about your mother. He knows you see Natalie. He knows you see Leigh. Let's just try to keep a sharp eye on which way the hounds are running. On what scent and after what game," Lark said almost sweetly, leaning on her without seeming to.

"You take care of yourself too." She touched his face. "Kevin holds you responsible for his ouster."

He smiled briefly, nodding ahead. "Isn't *he* a little young?"

"Aren't I a little old?" She let her hand drop.

"Vida, you never age. I think you're more beautiful now than you were when I first met you. The hard edges are gone."

"In the SAW office, when we stayed up all night to write the pamphlet. Oh, my."

"I let you write it. So you'd sleep with me."

Briefly they kissed. His lips felt cracked, feverish. "Lark, are you well?"

"I'm fine." He pulled away. They limped on after the retreating backs of Kiley and Joel. Lightly, lightly snow began to fall in tiny crystalline shards that glittered on her arms.

"Wait," she called ahead. "Wait for us. I have a small action to propose. There's been a lot happening locally against the nuclear power plant they're building on the river. Why not do something minor? Remember how Eva told us that the Crees kept sabotaging the earth-moving equipment at James Bay?"

"Antinuke stuff?" Kiley turned, her eyes wide. "Isn't that awfully . . . liberal? All the old Ban the Bomb marchers."

"You're too young to remember," Vida said, more crossly than she intended. "Issues don't go away because people have to work on something else. Ghettos and unemployment still exist when we forget about racism. Fifteen years ago it was nuclear testing. Now it's power plants and the neutron bomb. Seabrook was a surprisingly big action—and think of all the others in the South, in California, Germany, Austria, Sweden. Energy issues are involved, health issues, farming, labor, public safety, genetics—"

"Whether there'll be a world to bother trying to make better," Joel blurted out. "I want a future."

"Are you going to introduce an antinuke proposal at the Board?" Kiley asked as if she couldn't believe it.

"I sure am," she said, deciding on the spot. "Anything's better than another unreadable position paper written by a computer programmed to reproduce the style of literal translations from Sumerian. I'll make a formal proposal in three weeks. Right now I'm making an informal proposition. Let's do something. Together. Use our painfully acquired skills."

"I'm totally opposed to mushy politics that come from counting heads and saying, Well, the Friends of Ducks have forty thousand members, let's support the Friends of Ducks. . . . But a little action would be neat," Lark said. "I'll compromise on the action if you drop the silly proposal."

"No deal on my proposal. I'll win you over, I swear it. But let's agree on a small action. Even guerrilla theater—real guerrilla theater, by us. You know that coup we pulled in L.A. Or a spot of sabotage—local, not too fancy."

Joel was staring at them, puzzled she knew, because suddenly all the tension had evaporated and they were happy together. We're old soldiers who feel better about ourselves when we're fighting, she thought but could not convey the thought to Joel, who saw her suddenly close and acting like a family with the others with whom she had worked for years.

"Hi, kid," Natalie said from the phone. "How're you doing?"

"How's Ruby?"

"You got the word. Well, she's in the hospital. I'm going back next weekend. It's hard with things upheaved with Daniel. It's not like he's living here anymore. I'm going to take Sam again, but I don't know about Peezie this time. She has a meet."

"Natalie, answer me. How's Ruby?"

"Not so good, really."

"Not so good how?"

"Well . . . she had another attack in the hospital."

"*Another* heart attack?"

"That's it. A wee bit worse than the first."

"What's the use being in a hospital if they let her have attacks like that?"

"Sweetie, I don't think they know how to stop them. She's cheerful —but there she is sneaking into the bathroom to smoke. She's impossible. It's like she can't take care of herself."

"I've got to go out there."

"Maybe we can smuggle you in. I didn't see any security around the hospital. . . . But listen, there's a grand jury convening in New York that has us nervous. Investigating a conspiracy to shelter and harbor fugitives."

"That sounds dangerous. Who are they calling?"

"Nobody yet. But we're waiting."

"Give me the information on the hospital. I'm going out there."

"Be coolheaded for once in your life, please! You watch your step. Will he go with you?"

"Yes."

"He's a nice boy. You be good to this one and he'll be good to you."

"He's jealous because I love you so much."

"He'll grow out of that nonsense," Natalie said grandly. "Just bring him along a step at a time. Now, in Chicago I got a friend who can take messages for me and you. Here's her number. I'll clue her in when I arrive. She's used to all this stuff. She won't ask questions. She's a Frenchwoman in her sixties, and she was in the Resistance and then active against the Algerian war. She runs a boutique. In fact, I'll arrange for her to give you a dress."

"You mean you'll pay for it. You don't have the money. Especially with Daniel out of the picture."

"Ill get the money from Sandy. Don't worry. How are those boots?"

"Wonderful. I wear them all the time now."

"Take your time and take it easy. Ruby's going to be in the hospital for a while, I'm afraid. Here's my friend's number . . ."

"Should we claim this one?" She was dipping condoms in black dye. They were all at Hardscrabble Hill, where in 1973 Kevin had got a case of condoms, which had been moldering in the basement ever since. Hardscrabble Hill stood at a halfway point in Vida's mind, much neater and more livable and closer to being a successful working farm that it had been when she'd left, but a long way from the prosperity of Agnes' farm. Of the inhabitants in 1974 only Tequila and Marti and their children re-mained, along with Belinda's baby, no longer a baby, who had fake I.D. at age six.

"With a simpleminded leaflet like that? Not on your life," Kiley said. "We have reps to maintain."

"Besides, we have no line on this." Lark was attaching leaflets to dyed balloons of former condoms. "It isn't an official action. Just us having fun."

That they were, in spite of her own edginess at Hardscrabble and having to soothe Joel down every hour like a pot that kept boiling over in the middle of canning. She remembered canning tomatoes and apple-sauce, the women except Belinda—Alice, Eva, Marti and herself—closeted with increasing irritation in the hot moist kitchen like a Turkish bath while the men smoked dope—Kevin, Tequila, Bill—and Belinda—on the big front porch. . . . "I wish Eva was with us!"

Tequila, dark, with a low-slung muscular build and surprisingly light gray eyes in his round face, winked at her. "Soon. We'll party together after the Board meets late this month."

She was glad she was with Joel: he stood between her and Kevin's ghost. The walls were scarred with their battles; their hard sour words could suddenly seep like poison gas from the cracks. She had lived here, yes, but she had fled. Every room in the wandering house on its hill, every shed, every table and chair evoked a time she preferred to forget. She was fond of Marti, Tequila, the kids, but she was restless in their house. Marti and Tequila were legal, and they were buying the farm. Tequila was essential to their small action because only he could fly a plane.

Tamara, Dylan and Roz were all playing with the balloons. She tried not to stare at Roz, to look for Belinda in her chubby face and sturdy legs and little potbelly. Belinda had had hair of corn silk, her skin almost albino, but her daughter had hair the color of clover honey, and her eyes were dark brown and shining. Roz thought she was Marti's kid, along with Tamara and Dylan. Vida did not approve of that falsehood, but she was no longer helping raise all three. She had fled Hardscrabble and returned only on short visits, except for two years before, when she had been mending from an accident. When Eva, Lark and she had bombed IT&T on the anniversary of the overthrow of the elected regime in Chile and the institution of terror, the bomb had gone off early and sent a piece of metal into her leg.

She was glad they were spending only one night here. If Joel came back with her for the Board meeting, she would try to arrange for them to stay with Agnes. Joel felt awkward with Lark and Kiley, but he seemed to warm up to Tequila, Marti and their family. When he got tired of blowing up balloons, he lay on the floor playing with a Lego set alongside Roz, Dylan and Tamara. They climbed over him pulling and hauling, resentful when he spoke to the adults. "Jo-ul, Jo-ul, Jo-ul!" Roz chanted, pulling at him with doting gaze and fierce pudgy hands, treating him as a mixture of Prince Charming and a floppy dog.

Vida and Joel had had a brief but vital time alone upstairs in the afternoon when Kiley had been off with Lark printing up the simple half-page statements, some to be attached to the black balloons, some to float free: if there were an accident, this would be radiation. You'd be dying along with your children and your cows and your chickens. If it were a small accident, your milk would be bad and your land tainted and in ten or fifteen years you would have a good chance of getting cancer. The back told in smaller print about accidents, contained and not contained —Windscale and Brown's Ferry, Idaho Falls and Monroe, Three Mile Island. Tequila and Marti had been experimenting with CB radio for putting out political ideas, and they planned to follow up after the action to lay down some explanation and pick up reaction.

An hour before dawn, Tequila, Joel and Vida were dropped outside the tiny airstrip where Tequila meant to borrow a plane. Kiley and Lark roared off in the farm truck to release propaganda and balloons from the ground and meet them where they would land.

"Not that one, it's too fancy," Tequila said as they walked along the mooring strip, looking at the tied-down planes. "Here's a good one. A Cessna 172." He took a stick and tested the gas in the wing tanks. "It's a good size. Easy to drop things from because the wings are high. And I learned on it." Before getting inside, he tested the wings, the propeller, pulling and hauling on the plane in a way that alarmed her, suggesting that the wings were only lightly attached and might at any moment fall off. Then he jimmied the door and hopped in to jump the ignition. Vida bundled the balloons and leaflets inside with Joel's help, and then Joel untied the plane and got in himself.

There was no reason for anyone to stop them, even if anyone had been around so early in the morning. The little strip had no tower, and takeoff was a matter of Tequila's craning his head to look around and then taxiing into position. Vida loved small planes, and as they finally took off down the dark runway, which Tequila insisted he could see, she felt a surge of delight: a stolen plane, an action and a pearl gray dawn coming out of the gloom of the night.

"We're really doing it," Joel said over his shoulder. He was sitting up front beside Tequila. She was wedged in behind with the black condoms and the papers. "I didn't think we'd just do it!"

She squeezed his shoulder through the pea jacket. "At our best, we act rather quickly. Hey, Tequila?"

He nodded, squinting into the gray twilight. "It's a good thing today, to get out and play a little."

They did act well and easily together: that was one of the best legacies they carried on from the '60s. Joel had come in on the tail end, so he didn't know the wine-tart pleasure of believing you could act and change things and going ahead. The act as theater; the act as pure joy. The act as collective art, improvised and sensual. Yes, he had missed that, but he was getting a taste here and now. Simple but nice, she thought. The air was bumpy as the plane chopped on, droning busily across the fields, the woods where the snow lay thatching all, the fields where it had melted and the pastureland where it still spread. The sun was up now, behind an overcast in swirling shades of gray on gray, and the land tilting below them was broad and beautiful. The mountains lay in ranks with plumes of cloud trailing along the ridges. Tequila banked, getting ready to come in low, as Vida began handing the propaganda up front to Joel. Joel had been good on the airstrip, helping to pull the plane out, nervous but together.

It was a gesture that she continued to find small but pleasant, flying low over New Hampshire and Vermont, circling the power plant to drop their load in small clumps. At ten thirty they landed at an abandoned fairground where there was a stretch of cement just long enough for Tequila to bring them in. The landing was jarring, the plane bounced hard, and for several moments she was scared. They bumped to a stop at the far edge, surrounded by weeds growing from the wide cracks. "We'll call the airfield for the owner," Tequila said. "We might want to borrow it again sometime."

Kiley and Lark were waiting with the truck. Joel and she sat in back in the open bed, clattering toward Hardscrabble and their own Chevy waiting for them to set out for Chicago that afternoon.

15

The obvious route from Vermont to Chicago across Canada was too risky. They stayed off the turnpikes, in part to save money, because they had little left after buying the car. "But I'm glad we bought it. You were right," she said, driving. "It gives us the flexibility to make this trip and get back when I have to."

"Why go back? You don't believe in their position paper."

"The place to say that is with them."

"Let them write their stupid paper." Joel was slouched in his seat with his feet up on the dash. He had put three days into working on the car, a two-door black Chevy sedan they called Mariah.

In the Finger Lakes region of New York, from a roadside-table turnoff they watched the sunset, vast and roseate with grandiose bands of crimson clouds. They had a bag of apples from the Hardscrabble Hill orchard and the remains of a Hardscrabble chicken they had been eating all day. The eggs were good and plentiful by now, but eating the chicken required a lot of chewing. They were athletic chickens, lean, muscular, always in training for a flight to the trees.

She felt stretched, as if her feelings were forcing themselves open inside her, forcing the skin of her mind to expand like the walls of a balloon. She was wildly happy to be sitting in the car beside him, a small metal world encapsulating them. She was wildly happy to be allowed to love him. A license had been given her to lavish feelings and desires and all the riches of her soul on another person after years of measuring her reactions, of concealing, of declining, of pretending not to recognize signals, of turning aside and turning off and turning down the volume. Years and years of carefully damped responses had alternated with periods of permitting herself severely limited connections. Now she was licensed to be in love.

At the same time, she vibrated with fear for Ruby. She felt like her old spaniel Mopsy with one ear cocked toward Chicago (Worry, worry, is Ruby all right? What's happening?). The other ear was cocked back toward New York. Strange squeaks of hidden gears grinding came to her as the apparatus of the State prepared to try to crush her and hers. She was afraid, she was worried, she was overjoyed. She felt like a cave of the winds where violent emotions were suddenly unleashed from heavy leather bags to blow in contradictory irresistible gusts in the sinuses of the mountain.

Her absorption in the orchestrating of her rich emotions ended abruptly when they got back into the car and it wouldn't start.

"An old car, an old car, it's trouble," she fussed.

"Aw, shut up," he said, leaning into the engine. "You thought it was a great idea an hour ago."

She had to stand holding a dim flashlight while he poked and prodded the battery. Finally he said, "The terminal connector is too corroded. It's not making contact." He took the cable off the terminal and by the light of the flashlight carefully scraped the terminal and then the cable connector. When he finished and tightened the contact again, at length the car started.

"Why should you go work on some stupid paper you don't care about?" Joel pursued his argument at the wheel. "Let them do it themselves."

"We're bound by collective decisions."

"What's the use of the collective? You thought there was going to be a revolution. Too bad for you. Now you're stuck out here—"

"Well, so are you," she snapped, clutching herself. What did he know? He was just a kid, with no political perspective, no viable analysis, no long-term strategy. Just an impulsive kid who had been buffeted by moral qualms into bolting and running, and now he was stuck, as he put it.

"But we're stuck together now." He beamed. "How's that for a pun?"

He was light and she was serious about the discussion, a discrepancy that annoyed her. How could he imagine that telling her to sit out a decision of the Network was a joking matter? "I can't just negate a decision."

"What do you need them for, anyhow? I'm serious. It's passé. You're not doing anything that means shit to people."

"Then we have to survive until things are moving again. In any revolutionary struggle, there are off periods, defeats, times of apparent inaction."

"Then why not sit it out for a while? We could pick some safe place. Some little town with a lot of ex-hippies. In Northern California. In Colorado. Oregon. Or back in Vermont. We could just settle in. Find a house with some land. We could rent a house cheap and put in a garden. I could get an off-the-books job and so could you. Then you could think about politics and write your paper. But we'd be living like human beings for a change."

She was astonished at the wave of, was it nostalgia that came over her? A couple in a little house with a view. Fruit trees, a garden, she could elaborate it endlessly, opening at once before her like a hobby, a piece of knitting, a daydream that could be carried on for months and even years: Add bees, slowly, add a couple of hives. A strawberry bed. A couple of simple chairs and a rough table out back. An asparagus bed: Dig it deep and shovel in aged manure. Mulch it well with dead leaves. Simple possessions from the secondhand store selected because they liked them. A country bureau, hefty but simple, with white shelf paper in the bottom of the drawers. Shelves put up for books they would accumulate.

"Why not?" he asked softly, turning to glance at her face.

"Because I didn't go underground to hide, only. If I live in a little house with you and the two of us keep our noses clean and raise bees—"

"Oh, you want bees, my honey." He was grinning.

"—then they've won, you see? They've forced us out politically. Made us innocuous. Taken us out of action."

"No, Vida. If we survive, we've won!"

"Survival is not enough!"

"Even together? That's not enough?"

"It can't be. We can't let it be. We can't settle."

He reached over in the dark to put his hand on her belly. "We'll see about that."

In the long November twilight of the late fall, the land was beautiful. Snow flowed over the hills, white under the blue-black sky. Around ten they slept at the side of the road for two hours. Then the car refused to start and once again Joel got it started finally. At the only all-night gas station they passed, he stopped and got the battery charged up, but it should not be running down in highway driving. "It could be the voltage regulator or it could be a dead cell in the battery," he mumbled. "It's not charging right." Fatigue burned behind her eyes, fatigue pushed on the thin membranes of her brain, fatigue sat in her stomach like an ill-digested meal; yet she could also enjoy the lightness it gave. It reminded her of an earlier life when she was always too busy. Fatigue was a drug she had used to be addicted to, that rang on her nerves familiarly.

All night one or the other reached out in a passing caress. Constantly she wanted to make love, but they could not. It was too cold to simply pull off the road and go into a field or even to remain in the car with the engine off, and would it start again? They were nervous at the idea of pulling over and letting the engine run. "Lovers found dead of carbon monoxide," Joel intoned. Whenever they saw a patrol car in the rearview mirror, whenever they saw a police car approaching, whenever they passed the state troopers parked on the margin of the highway, they fell silent and watched. They drove cautiously, crawling along. The car had a hole where a radio had once been. When they got tired of talking, they sang.

She remembered childhood trips. Vacations had freed Ruby and Tom from the press of daily quarrels and troubles and let them enjoy each other. Tom was never in as good a mood as when he was at the wheel of a big old American car like this sailing down a highway with all the windows down and Ruby rattling the maps in the front seat and Paul in back with her eating, nervously cramming into his mouth some kind of candy. In childhood Paul had been overweight. Of course, he was big-boned too, like his father, and when he hit sixteen he shot up and filled out. But earlier Paul was fat and pimpled, and if he was not eating malted-milk balls or Good & Plenty or Raisinets or peanuts, he was chewing gum. She had grown up without a sweet tooth because the sight of Paul endlessly chewing and sucking on candy had spoiled sugar for her. She loved her brother, but she didn't want to be like him.

From a fairly early age she had been convinced she was the only one in her family with any hard sense, any intellect to spare. Tom richocheted from catastrophe to disaster. His temper got him fired; his impulsiveness kept him in debt. Ruby had more practical sense day to day. She could be trusted to budget the available cash and put supper on the table; but she had no long-run strategy for getting them out of trouble. Vida was her mother's conspirator. Paul was always in hot water with his father and often with school as well. When she was furious, she told herself she did not belong to them. She was a foundling. Her real mother was a lady doctor like the one who came to school and tested their tonsils and their hearing. Her real father was a war hero who had gone on to be something great like a movie actor or a politician.

As she drove with Joel snoring beside her across the snow-encrusted fields under the rising moon, its light coming over her shoulder like mild headlights from behind, she mused on her mother. Never had she really been able to persuade herself she was not Ruby's daughter, not for long. She had her father's red hair but her mother's body: a good one for both of them, trim but lush at the same time. Why was it letting Ruby down now? Ruby the romantic. Ran off with a tall red-haired stranger with whom she had nothing in common but intense sexual attraction and a hot temper and a working-class background.

Ruby had fallen in love other times; Vida had always known. Ruby couldn't keep anything from her. While Tom was off in the Army of Occupation in Japan, Ruby had fallen in love with her foreman at the shipyards, Gene Cornutti, but had resisted. They went bowling with chums from the yard, they had a few drinks and made eyes at each other and once in a while they necked in the car. Ruby was being faithful. Then she was laid off, with the other women. Gene got married. That was that.

Then in Chicago Ruby fell in love with the man behind the counter at the drugstore. Sanford Asch. A nice widower with two daughters, Jewish, doesn't drink except for a little wine with dinner, a good man and steady and what heart he has. Vida had known every step of the way what was happening, even what Ruby did not tell herself. Ruby fabricated excuses —and stories to make it look good to herself. Vida felt as if she was slipping and sliding in the mud, but she kept her mama's secret and she abetted her. She chose her mama. Her mother wanted what was good for her and Paul, and her dad didn't. She knew that. He could win her, he could turn the house upside down with his fury, he could turn the house right side up with his good humor coming in with a turkey he had won, coming in with a half gallon of maple-nut ice cream, coming in with a bottle of Four Roses somebody had given him for a favor he'd done and a bouquet of yellow roses picked down the street. She chose her mama, and Ruby became Ruby Asch and she became Vida Asch. Natalie chose her. Natalie had been trapped playing little mother. She was tired of being so very good. She wanted to run off with Vida and play.

Actually, their mutual wickedness got its real kickoff when they were both fifteen and Ruby had a baby. At her age! Sharon, Natalie's baby sister, was nuisance enough at ten, but Michael Morris Asch, called M and M by them, was too much to endure. To be expected to baby-sit for a screaming baby, to have their house turned into a large playpen and that little monster spoiled silly sent them into revolt. They cemented their own lifelong conspiracy as they fought their wars of independence side by side.

Sandy was a good-hearted liberal Democrat, against machine politics, for civil rights, devoted to Adlai Stevenson. At age sixteen, studious Natalie had already moved to his left, where Vida followed her. They collected clothes and canned food door to door for the voter-registration drive in Mississippi, where sharecroppers were being starved into submission. Mounds of bagged clothing took over the entry hall of their house. They were nonviolent but militant, and their heroes had been beaten, jailed and maimed in Alabama and Mississippi. They went to rallies with the air of prayer meetings where men on crutches and women with their arms in casts told of events on that battlefield and planned local wade-ins, swim-ins, to desegregate parks, pools and beaches in Chicago. They picketed Woolworth's on Saturday mornings. That was their rebellion against Sandy and Ruby, who kept asking, But what are you doing outside Woolworth's in the rain? They marched, Vida flirted and Natalie argued with the boys in the picket line and they began to live in a wide world, they began to live in history.

I can't make a romantic folly out of Joel, she said to herself, staring at the road, the walls of darkness to each side slipping under the car. This is my life, what I have made of it. I can't give it up for anyone. My integrity is to go on.

Joel moaned in his sleep. His snoring stopped as he drifted up from true sleep into dreaming. His fingers convulsed in his lap. Once his whole body shuddered. Headlights behind her maintained a distance but were persistent. The same car had been behind her for close to twenty minutes. She slowed down more and more and put on her turn signal, waiting. The car hung back for a while. Then it speeded up and passed her. She remained at her slow pace until it had gone far ahead. Okay.

Why wasn't she angry at Joel for trying to deflect her? For trying to get her to settle for survival? When he suggested flouting the will of the collective, she was angered because scared. What had they but their frail organization, thrust from a common history and built if at times jerry-built of a common politics? However, when he suggested the two of them going to ground together, she was flattered. It was a temptation to be resisted, but one whose very existence she appreciated. After all, Leigh had never suggested he give up his job, sneak out of New York and meet her in Dubuque, Iowa, to set up a new life together. . . . He hadn't, had he? Well, he had his political duties too. He was more serious than Joel, but less serious about her, perhaps. She could not help being struck by that observation and wounded by it. Perhaps Leigh had never thought of the possibility. Either people imagined the fugitive life as romantic—robbing banks, meeting with vanished celebrities, escaping ahead of the posse with a pistol in your teeth; or they imagined that you must be hidden in a room literally underground (like Laura's Newton cellar), confined to a safe cell or spirited out of the country. Few people could imagine the limited options that existed, but the fact remained that there were always options and daily problems of something to eat, something to wear, someplace to sleep, somebody to talk to, somebody to sleep with, work to do and rest to seize.

But Leigh had lived with her in Philadelphia, going back and forth each week. It had been as it was when they were first together: he had the interesting life, she worked as a secretary and he brought the news of the world to her. His being in what he called Filth-a-delia was a mixture of sacrifice and retreat. If he had wanted to be with her again, full time, why had he never brought it up, at least as a daydream?

With a muffled grunt Joel sat up. "My back hurts," he grumbled.

"Let's stop at the next coffee shop that's open. We can stretch our legs, one at a time to keep the car running."

"Where are we?"

"Just passing our old hometown. Erie, Pennsylvania. I have some bad news to report: you've been fired from your siding business. Absenteeism."

"Good. Now I'm an ex–siding man, for sure. . . ." He yawned. "Want me to drive?"

"After we stop. Watch for a place. Something has to be open."

"Oh, for a bed. A nice big bed with clean sheets and some blankets. We'd hold each other and cuddle. In the morning we'd make love."

"To be with you makes me glad. Do you know that?"

"Why not? Am I not the greatest lover in Erie, Pennsylvania? And all points east and west and in between? At least, that's the line you hand me. I'm beginning to believe it. All these houses of sleeping women, women lying awake beside fat and snoring husbands, they don't know what they're missing as we go by."

"You were snoring a while ago yourself. . . ."

"Hey, watch it. What's wrong?" he shouted.

"I don't know." She gripped the steering wheel tightly, bringing the car slowly over to the side of the road. "It's a tire. We got a flat."

They did. The right front tire was utterly flat. She had pulled off onto the gravel shoulder, where ice stood in the ruts.

"Damn bolts seemed to be rusted on," Joel said, trying to turn them.

"I thought the tires were supposed to be new?"

"Pretty new. Probably picked up a nail."

She looked at the worn tread and hoped they did not encounter weather of the kind that had hit them when they'd had Tara. With a yell he finally got the bolt loosened.

After the tire was changed, his hands were too cold to drive. On they went toward Ohio, the waxing moon bright on the ice-glazed snow, the pale ribbons of highway. She felt as if she could drive forever under the moon. Fatigue was burning in her veins like Benzedrine. They were two ghosts in a private afterlife driving on. Her eyes felt full of ashes.

> You are my sunshine
> My only sunshine,

they both belted at the top of their lungs. Joel had a fine deep singing voice, much deeper than his speaking voice. She sang in a wobbly contralto that sometimes came upon the melody and draped itself there in relief and sometimes wandered away lost, but remembering, always remembering the words. She was always the one who sang the words to the third verse when everybody else gave out after one and a half. What a waste of brain cells.

> As I walked out on the streets of Laredo,
> As I walked out in Laredo one day,

they warbled, more or less together. Coffee soon, by the light of the brillig moon.

> Una mañana del sol radiante,
> Bella ciao, bella ciao, bella ciao ciao ciao,
> Una mañana del sol radiante
> Saldré a buscar al opresor.

He didn't know the words to that or to the other Spanish-language songs. "How come you know them?"

"Because of Lohania. She coached me in Spanish. We planned to go to Cuba together on a Venceremos Brigade in the spring, the next spring." She rubbed her nose which had begun to itch. "She didn't get to go either. I was under, she was waiting to go on trial. . . . Lohania wanted to go to Cuba so bad, but she was scared silly they wouldn't let her in because of her parents. We were still waiting to hear when the ceiling fell in."

"But she's out now? Do you want to go see her sometime?"

"She started using drugs inside, and I don't know if she ever got clean. With a drug bust hanging over her, she's too vulnerable. That's how they recruited Randy. They sure got their money's worth. He had real talent. And they expunged his record, too."

"You talk about him awful cheerfully."

"We shouldn't have let him penetrate us. We were too stupid and too naive. God, how he hated us! Except for Lohania. He got her a deal, I think. He wanted her."

"Did he get her?"

She bit her lip. "I hope not." The past was pressing too hard. "Look at the moonlight on the fields. Isn't it beautiful? Maybe nobody loves this country as much as fugitives running before the wind, back and forth across it." Moonlight on ice. Kevin was driving the stolen car, she was riding shotgun, Jimmy called out instructions from the back seat. That was the first year; they had no rules for survival. They drove across Pennsylvania to the town, the street, the house. Ice in the driveway. Jimmy fell. Then a flashlight caught them in its beam and they halted, feeling the bullets they anticipated. "A fucking trap!" Kevin grunted, and Kiley's cool voice came out of the dark: "Well, it might well have been, with you lunkheads barging in without even scouting. Really!" On the moonlit ice they had met and embraced; Vida had wept tears of joy. No more alone. Lark's frail body in her arms, the chiseled miniature features of Kiley. Roger, tall and shuffling, carrying a rifle was the only stranger to Vida, although she knew him by reputation from his work in the anti-war movement in Seattle. Jimmy, like Vida, knew Lark from New York SAW and Kiley from Boston SAW, but Kevin knew only Lark. They had founded the Network that night. Joel could not understand her loyalty to the structure that had kept her from utter despair and given her an organization. She said to him, "Nobody knows this country like those who hide in its folds and crevices. Our land. Our country. That's what the screeching paper won't say."

Joel grimaced. "Sure. Let's have a parade. First float, man branding a runaway slave. Second float, soldier bayoneting an Indian baby. Third float, Pinkerton shooting a striker. Fourth float, flyboy dropping napalm on pregnant woman."

She tapped his knee. "There's something in what you say, Mr. Bones. But it also produced us. This country is a long war. It's our history too, Tecumseh and Mother Jones and Ida Tarbell. You must love who you are to love anybody else and to make good politics. Natalie always understood that. It took me a long time to see it."

"You take yourself so seriously. How come you love *me?*"

"Just bad karma, I guess. Want to sing old Beatles songs?"

"Doo doo doo." He thumped on the dash. "All you need is love, right? You guys didn't dawdle in that stage long. When I started hanging around the Movement, all the guys had tossed out their love beads. They were wearing buffalo plaid shirts and carrying long knives. They had hair down to their belly buttons, they were all seven feet tall, they were always talking guns. 'Nah, that Marlin 62 Levermatic is a piece of crap. Lousy four-shot clip.' Always saying, 'Let's go heist the Bank of America.' Wow, I thought they were gods walking. They pissed all over me. Treated me like a little boy. Till they found out I'm a mechanic. Listen, in the Movement if you can screw in a light bulb, that makes you a genius. If you know how to jump a car, you're on your way. All of a sudden they accepted me. My feet didn't touch the ground. If DePeuw—he was the honcho of our scurvy crowd—had told me to go spit in some cop's face, I would have marched out and done it. Know what brought me into the

Movement? Sex. Obviously the guys there were getting more. Those people were having *fun*." He laughed. "Can you imagine anybody thinking that about little Marxist-Leninist study groups now with their paper *The Worker's Crutch?*"

"Like that Crumb character saying, Remember, boys and girls, keep a smile on your lips and a song in your heart when you go out to smash the state. ... . But we've been having a pretty good time, love."

"I didn't know you'd been lovers with Larkin."

"Oh. Not really." So he had overheard her talking to Lark on the fire road: he had eavesdropped.

"What does that mean? He never put it in?"

"Come on! I mean we were never that serious as lovers. We just slept together a few times."

"So if you don't care about him, why did you sleep with him? Were you that hard up?"

"We were working together—"

"God keep you from ever working with a German shepherd."

"Joel, stop it! It was years ago."

"When was the last time you slept with him?"

"How would I remember?" She remembered perfectly. It was just before she had gone back to California after last year's Board meeting. On the anniversary of Attica, she and Lark had been delegated to carry out a memorial reprisal, planting a bomb in the Department of Corrections office in Albany. Knock out some records. The fewer records the state had, the better for everybody. They had spent two weeks together, living as husband and wife in a rented trailer. Strangely cozy, like a ship.

"Oh, there's so many men you fuck now and then you just can't keep them all straight, right?"

"You used to have a relationship with Kiley. I'm just comrades and friends with Lark. Why bring this up now?"

"I saw how you looked at him. Touching his face. Hugging him."

"I saw how you looked at Kiley. So what? I know you loved her, and maybe you still do."

"She's as lovable as a pickax. I don't know what I ever saw in her. Just a way to get hurt. The way you'll hurt me too."

"What is all this?" She had to pass a truck, straddling in to the oncoming lane. Her palms were sweating. "What are you suddenly upset about?"

"You didn't tell me you were seeing Leigh. You told me you had some kind of meeting. Then you tell everybody you saw Leigh and he told you blah blah. Why did you lie to me like that?"

"It wasn't *lying*." She was clenching the wheel too hard, treading on the accelerator. She forced herself to draw breath deeply, to sit back in the seat. Her neck ached. "It's dangerous to go around telling people who we see. You don't have to know I see Leigh. Knowing jeopardizes him without doing you any good."

"I don't have to know? Bullshit. What else don't I have to know? Who else do you see that I don't know about? How many lovers do you meet?"

"None, you asshole. I'm with you just about all the time!"

"That's where you got the money, isn't it? We spent all our money on the car and then you had sixty bucks. He gave it to you!"

"Why shouldn't he give me money? He makes a good salary. He's comfortable." She tried not to sound bitter.

"Services rendered. Does he know the money went to me too?"

"He doesn't know about you. Why should I risk telling him? He has no need to know."

"I'd like to confront him. I'd like to meet him. The next time you go have a rendezvous with him, I'm going along."

"No!"

"Why? So you can fuck him?"

"Why shouldn't I? I was making love with Leigh before I ever met you. In 1965 when you were in junior high, I was living with him. Come off it, Joel. He's been important to me."

"More important than me?"

"I'm with you. I'm not with him. He's living with another woman. Susannah."

"Does she know about you?"

"No. And I don't want her to."

"So you do fuck him?"

"Sometimes. Of course."

"Why? How can you do that with him?"

"How could I not? I still care about him. There's a connection between us."

"If you love him and you want to be with him, what are you doing with me? Just because I'm available."

"I love you. You know that!"

"I don't know what you mean by love. I don't think you mean very much."

"I think I love you a lot! I think I'm good for you! Not like Kiley, who didn't give a damn about you and wouldn't fuck you and made you feel like a clod. That's what you like. I bet you didn't give *her* a hard time."

"Hey, a pig pulling out. How fast are you going?"

"Oh, god!" Her foot instantly came up off the accelerator and gently pressed the brake. "Over. I think about sixty, sixty-two."

The cop did not turn on his lights but drove just behind them. She was going 51 now, and she slowed to 50 just in case there was a discrepancy between their speedometers. Right on her tail he sat. Her hands slid on the wheel with sweat.

"If he doesn't bust us, I'm taking over the driving."

"Fine. My neck aches. . . . But baby, you shouldn't start on me that way when I'm driving."

"Oh, what am I supposed to do in the car? Make conversation about the weather? Discuss Mao *On Contradictions?*"

The cop tailed them and she drove sedately, sweating. How had she been so careless? How had she let herself speed? She could spend the rest of her life in prison for getting excited during a fight. His vast rotten jealousy, it would end up killing them both. On they went, on and on together, the cop stuck to their rear bumper. She had trouble believing in his jealousy, that he could not simply stop that nonsense. That it was not somehow put on. Could he not simply observe to himself that he was attracted to her because she was who she was and that involved a sharp appetite for others? What was the cop doing, anyhow?

Then a car came up from behind in the outside lane, driving much faster. As it caught up to the cop and saw him, it hit the brakes and fell back, but the cop put on his lights, the beacon on the roof slashing its beam. Her heart lurched. He pulled over the second car. She could not stop staring in the rearview mirror to see if he was going to pull her over too. Joel was squinting at the map with the aid of a pocket flash. "If we can just get two miles up the road, we can get off. Drive into town. Maybe something will be open." Slowly she drove on, afraid to speed up, watching the rearview mirror more carefully and more often than the road.

"That's the junction," Joel said. "Hang a right. Then pull over and let me drive."

"With pleasure." The energy of fear was ebbing along her veins, leaving her sick with fatigue. Besides longing for sleep, she was hungry. A sandwich, a cup of coffee and she could hold out. "That was close," she said.

16

Joel and Vida camped at night in the back room of Madame Florian's Couture. It was fine and private among the stock of dresses, but they had to clear out before the store opened and return just at closing. This morning when they stumbled out, a wet snow rushed horizontally off Lake Michigan, sandblasting their faces as they tried to walk. As soon as the Art Institute opened, they went in to get warm.

They used the rest rooms, located the pay phones, and then Vida selected a room with American surrealist paintings of the '30s she felt were underrated. They were good company, and the room did not receive heavy traffic. She sat down on a bench and blew her nose. "I'm coming down with a cold," she said to Joel.

"I better go rip off some Vitamin C."

"Don't. Buy it. Don't take unnecessary chances. If you tell the guard you're coming back, they'll let you in without charging you again."

"Don't get sick, it'll be awful."

She smiled at him. "I can't get sick. Where would I have to be sick? The alley?"

"I'll be right back with the Vitamin C. Maybe I'll get some B vitamins too."

"See how expensive they are." Crossing the country in the old car, getting the tire fixed, the terminal replaced, paying out for gas and more gas had left them strapped. After he left she tried to work on her essay, but her head felt heavy. Blood pressed on the backs of her eyes. She was tired from the trip, tired of traveling. Since the week and a half on Cape

Cod, they had never stayed anyplace. If only they could establish a base, settle in for the rest of the winter. Maybe she'd volunteer as printer-in-training to Marti to stay put in Vermont for a while. She wanted to have a bedroom, a kitchen, a bathroom with her towels hung in it, a closet with her clothes on hangers, food in the refrigerator and food in the cupboard.

Every night she would lie in Joel's arms. In the morning she would put on fresh-ground coffee. With her pots and pans and sauces she would make love to him, and he would cause everything in the old house to work smoothly; pumps and furnaces and all finicky machines would purr for him like well-fed cats. She did not want to move them into Hardscrabble Hill, that was the truth; she wanted a place of their own—apartment, house, cottage, ski cabin, trailer.

At the archway into the hall she caught sight of Sam peering in. With elaborate caution he sauntered in, but then lost his cool and grinned at her. Oh, he had Natalie's big grin exactly, although he was already a head taller than his mother. "Sam," she cried, "you're bigger than ever. You've grown a whole foot!"

"Two inches," he said. "I grow an inch a month now."

"You have to stop." She kissed him.

Sam blushed. That embarrassed him more, and he glared at the nearest painting. "What's that supposed to be?"

"I think of it as capitalism, myself." She could not take her hand off his shoulder. She knew she had to. "But where's my sister?"

" 'Your sister' is downstairs," Sam said gravely, recovering his composure. It was necessary for him to remain calm; he was at the age when surface composure was more important than almost anything and harder to achieve than A's or orgasms. "She sent me to find you. She didn't want to run all over looking."

"How come she's so lazy?"

"She never likes to climb stairs. You know. It's her knee."

She pulled Sam back. "What's wrong with her knee?"

"Remember, since she was pushed down the steps at Columbia? Her knee hurts in cold weather. . . . She's got a touch of arthritis," Sam said confidentially and importantly, leaning toward her. He was repeating somebody's words: "a touch of arthritis." "But she won't admit it. She says it's just stiff."

"That's not good," she said. "I'll speak to her. Has she seen a doctor?"

"Mama? You know better than that! She never goes for herself. If I have a sore finger, it's off to the doctor. If she has a sore finger, it's What do they know? And she doesn't go."

Did he really appreciate his mother? She was half envious of him. At the same time she was struck by how much the pattern he described was

Ruby's too. Ruby thought of herself as the strongest, able to endure, but the rest of her family she fussed over. "Sam, will you grow up as wonderful as you are? Promise me you will."

"Oh, I get better every year." He was grinning again. "She says I do, and she ought to know. I can see it with Peezie. She was a real creep when she learned to giggle, but she's human again since she won the hundred-yard sprints. She's training all the time. She couldn't come along because she's running indoors in a meet."

She tried to imagine her flesh and blood an athlete. Natalie seemed so proud of Peezie. "Maybe she'll go to the Olympics."

"She's not that good. But she can run pretty fast for a girl."

Like Joel, Sam seemed more angelic than he was. "For a girl? Can you outrun her? Madame Curie discovered some neat radium—for a girl, huh?"

"You sound like . . . your sister. Okay, okay, she can run faster than me. You want me to get Mama?"

"Please. Right away."

As soon as he left, she laughed at herself. Why hadn't she gone with him instead of sitting as if she were receiving in her boudoir? She was slow today. Sam's presence, the expectation of Natalie excited her. Now she was condemned to wait and wait while she burned a bright orange with impatience and need.

She loved Natalie more today than she had a decade before. Time and age only made Natalie rarer. Would she have cherished her as much if they had lived normal lives? If she still shared the apartment on 103rd with Leigh while Natalie lived out on the Island, they could not meet daily, but they would talk on the phone. They would talk and everything she thought she would share and Natalie would comment on every event and he said/she said and every project would be worked over in their busy mouths. That would be pleasure keener than sex, healthier than gluttony, more lasting than wine: to share your life with a sister who knows all about you and with whom you discuss and debate and dissect everything.

Natalie trotted in behind Sam. In her forest green down jacket she looked like a pigeon and walked a little stiffly on red-booted feet. Her skin seemed drawn and sallow with fatigue, even though her face was cut wide open by a beautiful grin, both Sam and Natalie like pumpkins with candles shining out through their strong ivory teeth, both their heads curly, cropped, asking to be petted and stroked.

"Where's Joel?" Natalie looked around anxiously.

"Gone out for vitamins. He'll be back soon." She could never say something like that without a twinge of superstitious and yet fully rational fear. Every statement of intention and probability in her life was part prayer. Let him come back soon. Let us be able to go to the hospital. Let us be able to return safely to Madame Florian's, who told us to call her Claire.

"Good. Then we can go downstairs and have lunch." Natalie no sooner took a look at her than she started wanting to feed her.

She did not mind. She wanted to be fed soup. She wanted taking care of. Joel and she could eat a full meal now; then after Madame's boutique shut they could boil an egg on the hot plate for supper. "How's Ruby? When can I see her?"

"She's about the same. You can't." Natalie took her hand between her own, still cold from out-of-doors.

"Can't what? I have to see her. They don't have a guard posted at the hospital."

"I wouldn't bet. Sam and I were followed this morning. . . . No, don't jump, we were careful. We shook them hours ago."

"Why are you being followed? What's up?"

"I'm followed in East Norwich. It isn't to learn anything, because they're doing it openly. They stand outside staring at the house."

Sam was bouncing and weaving with the desire to speak, making little noises, until Vida and Natalie turned to him. "I went outside and took pictures of them," he said, "and they chased me. One of them grabbed me and broke my Kodak. But the next time I took Dad's Pentax and I used the telephoto lens. So I didn't have to get real close, and I ran in the house before they caught me."

"Wonderful, Sam." Vida sank on her bench, too tired to stand long. "Lucky they didn't smash Daniel's camera."

Natalie blew her nose. "Yeah, we may have to pawn it."

"How come?"

"Money. He's cut us off. We're in the middle of a big battle over the kids, custody, the bank accounts, everything."

"He called up and told Con Edison to cut off the electricity," Sam said. "Mom was making toast. Peezie was using the Water Pik. I was watching the *Today* show, when *bam!* It all went off. We had to get them to turn it back on!"

"Take him for every penny he's got," she said, surprising herself. "He can always make more money, like he can always get more girl-friends."

Sam was embarrassed. He made a noise and stared at the painting again, leaning to peer at it.

"He's got a lot on me," Natalie whispered. "Suki, for openers."

"He can't use an old love affair now if he didn't leave you for it at the time."

Natalie chewed her finger. "Tell that to his lawyers."

"Hey, Natalie, maybe it's Daniel who has the dicks out front."

Sam swung around. "They're Feds. They interviewed the neighbors. They even followed Peezie and me to school twice."

"Frankie's with Daniel in town," Natalie explained.

"Are they following Daniel?"

Natalie shook her head no. "They take pictures of everybody who visits me. We don't meet at my house anymore. I had to take a leave of absence from the shelter. Every time I'd walk in they'd photograph everybody coming and going and take down license plates. Women were afraid to use our shelter. They subpoenaed my long-distance calls for the last year—as if I'd be stupid enough to call you from the house! They're harassing everybody I called."

"Can this heat be from me? I thought they'd cut back on chasing us."

"A grand jury's been impaneled in New York, and I'm sure to be called. I've had warning. Maybe I should come under too?"

"Natalie, no!" She spoke too loudly. "It's a dead end for you. They'll only put you in for six months at worst. Then you're free."

"I didn't mean it," Natalie said mildly. "I have my kids to worry about."

"*I* could go underground," Sam boasted. "I'd be good at it."

"Besides, I'm not fond of your companions. Joel's the best of the lot. . . . That cop whose wife we helped made trouble for us with the town. But Kevin's the source of my sudden importance, I'm convinced."

Vida shook her head. "Kevin would lie to them. That might do us some damage, because nobody's clever enough to talk without giving away something they need. But he would never fink."

"Kevin hates you. Don't you know that?"

"Here's Joel," Sam piped up. "He's got a package."

The guard was watching them, idly, because they were the most animated group in the room, making it time to move on. "Come on, gang," she said, warming Joel's cold hands between hers. "How come your thumb's frozen?"

"Let's find a water fountain and you take your vitamins. The C's are chewable." He pushed one into her mouth.

It was sour but endurable. She chewed busily. She squeezed his thumb again, asking with her eyes.

"The glove's torn. They were good gloves. I found them on a bus three years ago."

"Listen, we'll get you gloves," she said. "We'll stop at the Lost and Found. We'll ask for men's fur-lined brown gloves. I bet they have a pair. People are always losing gloves in the winter." An old trick of her childhood from Ruby, the great improviser.

Sam wanted Joel's attention, bobbing alongside him clumsy and puppylike but already taller. "Uncle Joel," Sam said and then stopped, embarrassed. "I mean . . ."

Joel smiled, that twist of his lips denoting pleasure. Sometimes when he was happiest he did not beam or grin but gave only that little smile, as if afraid his pleasure would escape from a big grin, or that to show the full extent of his joy would invite hardship or cruelty. "That's fine. If we could get married, I'd be your uncle. Someday we'll run off to Cuba. The Cubans are nice and they'll marry us. Then we can have monogrammed towels and matching sheets and curtains and those things that make life a gas."

My family, she thought: my new family. So good that Sam and Natalie liked Joel.

Natalie took her arm above the elbow. "You could get married now if somebody'd do it."

"My divorce came through?" She tilted her head, seeking a change of subject. "Do you like Monet?"

"So they got married."

"Who?" She knew immediately, but refused to. She felt weak and tried to stand straighter in Natalie's grasp.

"Leigh and Susannah. They were married last Sunday."

"Oh. Was there a big party? Did you go?"

"You know I was here. Monday when I got back Leigh called me."

"I'm glad you didn't go. I have to say that. But I could use a spy in the enemy camp."

"Don't feel that way. It's over and done. You have your own life."

Her own life, her own death. For a moment she wanted to die on television on the evening news, as Jimmy and Belinda had, where Leigh would have to eat it with his beef Stroganoff. What was going on in him? From one marriage to another. Joel had turned to watch her carefully. Natalie was observant too. Only Sam was talking on, about how he had gone on a real fishing boat overnight when they went scalloping. Would Leigh persist in seeing her? If Susannah and Leigh shared a joint account, how would he explain the money he gave her? She needed that money; she needed it to survive. What would he honor of her old claims?

It was not right for him to marry while Ruby was in the hospital; but he had not stayed close to her parents. He was uncomfortable around them, bored. He was used to his mother, with whom he could argue politics, one kind of leftie to another, swap gossip, share a sense of history and embattlement. He could not comprehend her link with Ruby, based not on politics but on a shared hard-luck childhood; on shared complicity; on shared bodily continuity—the same breasts, the same legs and green eyes; the same deep driving energy, in Ruby dissipated in endless chain smoking, cleaning, pacing, in Vida harnessed but the same force. Everyone was watching her now, and she had to summon the strength to pretend calm. She wanted to drop on the marble floor and scream. She wanted to weep and be comforted. She wanted to feed Leigh rat poison and watch.

Elaborately she shrugged, detaching her arm from Natalie's nervous hot grasp. "Why, that man sure does like to be married. You'd think he'd enjoy being legally free for a week or two. He's compulsive as Henry the Eighth, just got to have a wife. 'Course, I haven't done a lot of cooking or cleaning or mending these past years. I guess he felt a little neglected, but you know how it goes when one's work keeps one on the road constantly! Just another marriage broken up by professional demands." This mocking performance was Ruby too. She could see her mother, her eye black from a fight with Tom, toughing it out, standing with one hand on her hip, a pose Ruby never struck except when she was putting on an act. "Now, you know that man is clumsy. Stuck his elbow right in my eye as he was turning over in the bed. I swear, I might as well walk into work and tell the girls my husband beat me, because then they'll know I'm really covering something up, like I got drunk and walked into a door."

Natalie glanced sideways with narrowed brown eyes and probably recognized the performance, although not necessarily. With Sandy, Ruby had not needed often to summon that tough lady out of her bruised innards, so that Natalie had seen only a few times that Ruby with a few touches of Bette Davis in her gamier roles, of Joan Crawford, of Lauren Bacall. Her mother had loved those strong ladies and gone to all their pictures, she and Mama at the matinees before the prices went up. Tom fell asleep in the movies and so did Grandma, who had trouble following. That interfered with Ruby's concentration, so that she preferred to go with Paul, until he would no longer go to silly women's pictures, too much of a man at thirteen, and Vida, who loved sharing the tears and the talk afterward. They gossiped about the characters as if they were neighbors, about whom they also gossiped constantly. Do unto the neighbors as they do unto you. The neighbors in South Euclid pointed to the Whippletree family as an example of what happened when you married outside your own kind: she's a Jew and he's an American, and look, they fight all the time. You can hear them down the block. She makes eyes at all the men, and he drinks like a fish. Stick to your own kind and you don't get into trouble.

"Natty, I have to see Mama. Make it happen! I'm good at disguises. You check things out at the hospital. Even if it's only five minutes, I have to see her!"

"Shvesterlein," Natalie said in a lugubrious voice, "nohow. If you get busted trying to see her, Ruby'll have another heart attack. I'm not kidding.''

"You wouldn't have to tell her. Natty, check things out. Draw diagrams. Look at exits and entrances. Steal me a white coat. Watch the schedules day and night. I need to see her.''

"I'll see what I can do,'' Natalie said. "Now it's time to eat.''

"Yeah, I'm starving,'' Sam said.

"Look at him!'' Natalie said proudly, "He eats like a bull—like a bull elephant. He's going to grow up to be one of those basketball freaks, fourteen feet tall and you have to send him telegrams to tell him to wash his ears. I have to get a bank loan to take him to lunch. . . .'' Then, realizing that mentioning cost when she was about to treat them was tactless, she barged on, "but it all turns into brains and muscles. This is my pride and joy. And Peezie! I wish you could see her racing. With my short fat legs, who'd think I'd give birth to a gazelle? Peezie should have been your kid, Vinnie. She's got your legs. Racehorses, both of you. You could run like the wind.'' Natalie turned to Sam and Joel. "She was wonderful in demonstrations. Me, I'd get mad and I'd march around, but I always felt lumpy. Like the cops were going to look at me and say, Get that one, she's a sitting duck. A marching duck.'' She shepherded them down the stairway toward the cafeteria.

"You're upset that he got married?''

"A little bit.'' She was lying on the cot in the back room of Madame's boutique. She could not call their hostess anything but Madame. The image in her head had been of a petite charmer with blue hair dressed in ruffled crepe de chine. Madame was a mountainous woman who spoke with an odd British accent and told them she weighed thirteen stone. Stones seemed the right thing to measure her in as she stood towering over them. Madame's shoulders were broad, her hips broader, her hands large and squared off. Her hair was short, crisply curled and shiny black. Her face was wrinkled into long drooping folds, but her walk was brisk and her voice loud enough to hear across the street. Madame called all of her customers by name and inquired after the health of their grandchildren and dogs. A simple little thing you could wear to a luncheon that looked to Vida like a jersey housedress went for about $160 and was the bottom line. Natalie's idea of getting Vida a new dress there cheap had quietly perished.

They saw Madame only as they arrived and she left, hurrying off to supper at a special table in the kitchen of the restaurant her husband owned. Every night she ate there except for Mondays, when the restaurant was closed and so was the shop; that night, she told them, she

267

cooked wonders for him. As Madame prepared to get into her nightly taxi, the same driver coming by for her at six, she often gave them a little present: English tea biscuits somewhat stale; bonbons, which turned out to be filled chocolates; a tin of macaroons. Everything she gave them they ate with puzzlement. Where did Madame get the little goodies, and why?

The back room—in sharp contrast to the store with its floral carpeting and white Venetian chairs—was dusty and bleak. Racks of dresses stood waiting to be shown among sewing and pressing apparatus, a cot, a couple of broken chairs, piles of boxes to be folded and formed, a hot plate and a sink and toilet.

Joel did not press the issue of how upset she had been until he had finished heating the canned soup and served it in plastic containers from which they had emptied straight pins. After he had supervised her swallowing the soup—she was feverish and did not want to eat—he frowned. "Are you starting to lie to me on a regular basis? Or do you just think I'm stupid? About politics, about Marxism, about the theory of economics, maybe. About you, no. I can tell when you're ready to fall down. Why do you think you're sick tonight?"

"Because I'm tired and run-down. I've been fighting off a cold for three days."

"You're telling yourself it's okay to be sick. You want to collapse and lie in bed and suffer. You think it'd bother him? She's no competition to him, this one. She probably falls on her knees and admires him. Can I suck your electric prick? She expects him to save her from boredom and Long Island. Listen, you're well rid of him, but you're too caught in your old patterns to figure that out. I love you ten times more than he ever did."

"I believe you. It's just depressing. And he didn't tell me he was going to. He let on to me he wasn't."

"Why should he ask you before he marries her? How come marriage means so much to you? Big revolutionary broad."

"Because it was a real commitment. Then we had a lot of work getting out of that married box. It was hard to get people to stop relating to me as somebody's wife. For a woman that's deadly, because you really do lose autonomy, seriousness. Miss X can lead an army, but if Mrs. X tries to be a general, everybody says, 'Where's her husband?' "

"Baby, so you're free at last." He put his hand on her belly. "But you aren't glad."

"Now he officially belongs to this woman. She's involved in all his decisions."

He frowned. Then he raised his eyebrows. "Oh. You're scared he won't give you money anymore?"

For an instant she was angered, because she was worried about that but didn't want to mention it, and because that wasn't the source of the pain. It was simply more dignified to acknowledge the crass motive. "So? We're broke. I feel entitled. When I ran, he ended up with everything, Joel—our checking account, our savings account, our dandy rent-controlled apartment, our china, our furniture, our stereo, our comfort and standard of living. . . . The last year we lived together I wasn't making money, but earlier I was the real breadwinner."

"Fuck his money." He swaggered to the hot plate to put on water for tea. "We'll make our own. We've done it before."

"Since we bought the car, we've been living on what he gave us."

"Your alimony checks. Big deal. Tell Natalie to get us some other gig."

"Natalie has a lot of heat on her. But there are other sources. I'll think about it." She looked at him and he looked back at her with the dead weight of fact. "We have twenty-four dollars left. Not enough to get back East. I don't want to hit Natalie. She's broke."

"Yeah, she's in a lot of trouble. I like her better this time."

"You like her because she likes you. You don't see her as a person yet."

"She's so much older than me it takes time."

"Joel! She's only six months older than me!"

"Are you kidding?"

"Joel, she is."

"That's weird," he said. "You seem closer to me and she seems closer to my mother. Don't be so upset. It's just that she's a mother and she's overweight."

"You should have seen her when she was taking karate and got into her only affair with her instructor, a Japanese-American woman named Suki. She dropped twenty pounds."

"I bet she was attractive that way."

"To tell you the truth, I like her better plump and a balabusteh. A little sloppy in her person and curly and feeding everybody."

"How come she got involved with a woman?" The kettle whistled, and he went to make tea.

"Why not? That's who she mainly meets. Imagine big Daniel on top of her. She must have felt smothered."

"Is she still involved with that woman? Smokey?"

"Suki insisted she leave Daniel. Daniel said he'd go to court and take the kids. I think she feels it's not fair in her situation to get involved with anyone again."

"Nobody?"

"Joel! Don't get that tone of voice on your face. You aren't Freud's gift to Natalie. She sets her own priorities. They aren't the same as mine. You just love and respect her as she is. You hear me?"

"Are you jealous? After weeping and screaming about Leigh all day?"

"I neither wept nor screamed!"

"But you wanted to."

Her sinuses were draining, forcing her to spit delicately into a crumpled paper handkerchief as she huddled in the doorway of a doughnut shop. Paul's Malibu was parked across the street. She had to hope he came out of the bar, The Brass Monkey, alone. Her plan was to intercept him, but she was freezing to death waiting. Before flying back last night, Natalie had given her Paul's schedule. The sisters had decided Paul would be the new go-between, but that he could not be consulted in advance. Natalie felt sure Paul was not being watched; it was Natalie's observation that the right believed their own myths about the working class being solidly conservative and acted on such presumptions.

Four years ago Paul had been in the process of divorcing Joy and wedding Mary Beth, and she had got sucked into family squabbles and had risked a sudden appearance from underground to put in her lively and unpopular opinions. It was getting dark and harder to see men's faces as they pushed out through the padded door, their heads ducked into the fierce wind. She thought she saw him and started across, only to stop and turn back in the middle of the street when she got a better look. Pacing in the doorway, she beat her hands together to fight numbness.

Suddenly Paul pushed out the door with another man. What should she do? She immediately knew it was him: not because he looked exactly as he had four years before, but because he looked too much like Tom to be anybody else but his son. She was almost afraid at the resemblance. Not that Tom would have turned her in. He had a rough patriotism and a pride at having served in the Pacific, but he had a strong sense of class. He hated politicians and the rich. His anger was undependable, turned as easily inward or against his family as out into the world. She'd come running up to him when he entered the house saying to him, "Here's Daddy's little girl!" and he'd swing her up in the air, but the seventh time he might knock her across the room shouting, "Don't jump on me like a puppy, you noisy brat!"

Maybe it was that memory of violence which paralyzed her. Now Paul was slapping the other guy's shoulder and they were both ritually laughing at some ritual joke. The guy turned and walked down the block to his car. Paul waved after him, then turned to his own. She let him start unlocking the door before she crossed. Coming up behind him, she took his arm as a bus whooshed past close enough to stir her jacket. "Don't jump, big bro. It's me. Don't yell. Can I get in the car with you?"

VIDA

"What? Jesus, it's you! Vida, what happened? Did they give you amnesty or something?"

"No, and please, let's get in the car. Could you not use my name, pretty please? Call me Cynthia, remember?" She went around the car and got in the other side as he reached over to unlock it. Then she gave him a kiss, his face crinkling up in a big beery smile.

"What a surprise! You almost gave me a heart attack. You can't just come up behind somebody in Chicago and grab them and not give them a heart attack. . . ." He realized that the reference was tactless. "Er, well, have you seen Mama?"

"Not yet. Natalie says they're watching the hospital. That's what I'm here for, to see her." She had a scheme, but she had to work on Paul to get him to agree. She owed it to her mother to see her no matter what the risk, to be clever and able enough to pull the visit off. That was her daughterly duty.

"Hey, you want to go back in and have a drink? It's not a fancy bar—"

"We can't go anyplace where you're known. Let's get a bite to eat somewhere they won't wonder who you're with."

"Mary Beth's getting supper for me at home." He eased the car out of the tight parking space and into the rush-hour traffic. "I'll call her from where we go. She'll think I'm seeing Joy, but I can deal with that."

"But you do see Joy and the kids. Don't you?"

"Yeah, but Mary Beth don't like it."

Paul had four kids from his previous marriage. The eldest, Marsha, was . . . twenty-three? Only the two youngest girls were still living at home with Joy. With Mary Beth he already had a baby that she had never seen. Paul sure had multiplied. He had had his share and hers too of babies. Mostly they were stuck in her head in little home movies of toddlers and ten-year-olds long out of date.

Vida and Paul were both half Jewish. Paul had fought with his Christian father all through adolescence, and yet he did not consider himself Jewish. She had gotten on much better with Tom, yet she had always thought of herself as a Jew: like mother, like grandma. When she had learned that rabbinical law was matrilineal, she had thought, Of course. Both Paul's wives were lapsed Catholics.

"Listen." The lines cleared from Paul's heavy brow. "I know where to go. Not a dump, either, like this place. It's a bar, but they got good food. Italian. I been in there once or twice with the guys, but they don't know me."

Paul ordered manicotti and meat balls and spaghetti and salad for her, while steadfastly insisting he wouldn't have a bite to eat and eating all the bread on the table as he talked, tearing it in his big scarred hands. He had heavy, bony brows like their father's but Ruby's brown hair turning gray. He was heavy now, his paunch heaved against his pants, yet she still thought of him as a kid. She loved him, she pitied him, she felt guilty sitting across the table. She felt as if she had stolen something vital and decamped; escaped and left him to their class fate. Ruby had married into the middle class too late to do Paul any good. Already he had quit school and gone to work in the mills. Jobs were easy to come by then. Steel production was booming. Now he wheezed as he laughed, he was short of breath, his hands and face were scarred, and he was stuck.

"Don't worry about me, blood's thicker than water," he was saying. "I think you're crazy, but you're my own sister. Fuck 'em all. But don't try to see Sharon. She's got a bee up her ass. She'd turn you in quicker than you can say Cincinnati. She thinks you're to blame because that asshole she's married to never got promoted. But anybody else can see it's because he's such an asshole even those jerks can see through him. . . . But you know you're killing Mama."

"Don't lay that on me. If Tom didn't kill Mama, I sure couldn't."

"We all worry about you. What's gonna happen to you. . . . I think of you every time they put it on the TV about terrorists and shoot-outs and skyjackings."

"Paul, I am not a terrorist. I am not. We don't go after individuals, we don't terrorize. We go after corporate targets, governmental targets, landlords, IBM, the Department of Correction. We do what we do carefully and we never hurt anyone physically."

"Yeah? What about these guys in Italy that are offing all those people?"

"We're not connected, you know, with every little group in the world. . . ." Should she attempt to defend them? He wasn't understanding. Her head hurt. "So how is Mama?"

"Not good, to tell the truth. I don't know what's going to happen. . . . I think she's been in trouble with her heart for a couple of years and she just kept it to herself."

She felt scared. She excused herself and went to the women's room, where she had diarrhea. Then she washed her hands and face and collected herself. I'll see her, I have to see her; then I'll *know* how she is. That ox Paul has never been right about a thing in his life. Don't talk about it at the table.

She came back bright and determined to change the subject. "How's Mary Beth?"

"She's pregnant again."

"Wow, Paul, do you want another one?"

"Sure we do. . . . It's going to be hard. Jacky's fun, but I've got five kids already. . . . Mary Beth wanted it. She feels outdone by Joy."

"How come she's so threatened by Joy? After all, you left Joy to marry her."

"I left Joy because she was fucking that dumb Polack Fred. Making a monkey out of me. Playing around behind my back."

"Then why is Mary Beth jealous?"

"I'll deny it, I'll deny it to my dying day. But what can you do when you lived with a woman for twenty years? I mean, I go over to see the kids. I'm glad to see her. You know, we have a little fun together. For old times' sake."

"You go to bed with her?"

"What harm is there in it? We were married for twenty years. It's not like she's married to anybody else. . . . She's always got boyfriends. That woman's older than me. She's forty-two and fat, and her teeth stick out. But she's always got boyfriends. It's the way she laughs. When you hear her laughing, you can't help thinking about it, you know, sex."

"You miss her, don't you, bro?"

"She's a slob, but she's an easygoing woman. She likes to cook, she just don't like the cleaning up. She's a good mother to the kids. She's always horsing around, ready to go bowling or out for pizza or see a dirty movie or watch a game on TV. She's no alkie, but she likes her beer. She doesn't make you feel like you're some kind of jerk for drinking a beer at night."

"Oh, Paul, you're not so happy with Mary Beth. Are you?"

"She's okay." His face closed up. "Always wanting something. When are we getting a new couch, when are you going to get the stairs carpeted, when are we going to take a real vacation? . . . meaning no vacation for me, not relaxing or taking it easy, but pissing out money in some dude place. . . . Joy always had a job on the side. She liked to get out of the house. Maybe she did it because she wanted to meet guys, it'd be just like her. But it took some of the weight off my back. Mary Beth is a good wife. She stays home with Jacky and she keeps her nose clean. . . . But she's driving me to the poorhouse. I was moonlighting weekends driving a delivery truck for a liquor store, but the doc told me I can't do it. Like Mama, I got high blood pressure. Runs in the family, I guess. How's *your* blood pressure, Vida?"

"Steady as she goes." Actually, Dr. Manolli had told her she had to keep an eye on it when he had dealt with her infected leg. Paul should never have left Joy. He'd been much happier with her; only his useless male pride had convinced him if she went to bed with somebody else, he had to get rid of her. "Do you ever think of going back to Joy?"

"I think about it. But now Mary Beth's knocked up again. . . . Joy says it's better like this, we appreciate each other. . . . How could I live with that slut, anyhow? I'd always be scared what she was doing behind my back. . . . So Leigh's got his girlfriend knocked up, huh? They got married, the three of them. Won't be the first time in our circles, right? I guess you must have been expecting it?''

"Sure," she said automatically. "How do you know—what makes you think Susannah's pregnant?''

"I heard Natalie and Ruby talking. You didn't know?''

"Naturally he told me they were marrying," she said, toughing it. "But he didn't say Susannah was pregnant already.''

"Three months. I guess they been fighting about it and she won. Joy was bigger than that when we tied it. She was starting to show.''

Three months. September. When they had gone to Montauk together, Susannah had been carrying his child. In New Hampshire he knew; he'd had to know. She could have broken his head in. She hated him. Say something. "Hey, you want another drink? Do you have time?''

"Not really, toots. I told Mary Beth I had to get the battery checked, the car didn't start when I came out of the mill. She'll believe anything about the car, she won't look under the hood. But if I come home tanked, I'll have to listen to her screaming about Joy all night. It gives me heartburn.''

She must pull herself together; from the floor, the table, the ceiling. She felt exploded. On to her plan to penetrate the hospital. "Listen, Paul, has Marsha been to see Mama?''

"No way, Vida. She's living in Houston, and that's a lot of dough to lay out for a plane ticket. Her husband's a pipe layer, but she's pregnant now. Mary Beth, Leigh's girlfriend, Marsha—it's a regular epidemic!''

"Listen, I want you to take me into the hospital as your daughter Marsha. Make sure Mary Beth doesn't get wind of it. I don't want Mama hassled.''

"But . . . Marsha's blond and six months pregnant. She's twenty-three.''

"I'll be wearing a blond wig and I'll be pregnant, don't worry. I'll dress for the part. Just take me in real calm and don't act nervous and don't call me Vida.''

"Okay. It's your funeral. When do you want to do it?''

"Tomorrow night.''

"That's kind of hard. What can I tell Mary Beth?''

"Just say you want to see Mama alone.''

"She doesn't care for going to the hospital, anyhow. The smells, and seeing the people on stretchers.''

"Paul, you're an angel. I'll meet you at seven where I met you tonight. Okay? I appreciate it more than I can say. I just have to see Ruby. . . . But don't say a word to her yet. Just walk in ahead of me and whisper it to her. Natalie told her I'm going to try. . . . You just march in ahead and whisper in her ear. Okay?"

"She's been asking where you are. I'm supposed to bring her some photos of Jacky, anyhow. She asked for them yesterday."

"Okay. Bring them. I'll meet you at seven."

As Paul took out his wallet to pay for her food and his beer, he folded a bill and slipped it to her discreetly. His caution amused her, if it was that rather than a code of manners; she could never get him to call her anything but Vida. "Just for you to take care of yourself."

On the bus she unfolded it. It was a twenty, and it would help, though not much. After her visit to Ruby, Joel and she had to solve the cash problem. Maybe Natalie would have a lead. They had a phone call scheduled tomorrow morning at eleven to "her" pay phone in the Art Institute. She was sitting at the back of the bus, where she could turn her head to the darkness outside the dirty windows and let herself loose, like unchaining a pack of tugging howling wolfhounds. How she longed to bay at the low dirty sky, ruddy with the glare of neon: Susannah was having Leigh's baby, and Leigh was choosing that too. Oh, Vida had gotten pregnant about a year after they were married, and then it had been, Kids get in the way. Leigh had said, Who wants a kid tying us down and crimping our lives? Then Lohania's abortion later. Why was Susannah's growth more precious than hers or Lohania's?

Leigh was married, about to be a father, founding his line in another woman. He was no more hers, not at all. She felt herself cast off. The phantom ex-wife. Leigh Pfeiffer and his wife Susannah Pfeiffer and baby, a complete unit. No room for Vida. Her place had been usurped entirely. He never thought of Vida any longer except when she forced him to, and then he felt a twinge of annoyance, a twinge of guilt. Oh, that one still there, a tooth he should have fixed.

The pain was in her pride. The pain was in her sense of sexual worth. She was not the great love of Leigh's life. She was an earlier stage, a folly, a displaced person, an old flame guttered out and the wick trimmed. Why had he bothered going to bed with her? Nostalgia? Pity? Casual lust? And why hadn't he told her the truth? He had to have known he was going to marry Susannah. She felt a pang of hope that he had not wanted to marry his girlfriend but finally (after three months) had done so out of obligation. But she didn't quite believe. Women had longed to marry Leigh, and at least one of them had claimed to be pregnant. He had told them he was already married. His excuse had been that if Vida was caught, as a husband he could not be forced to testify against her. He had hugged that excuse to save him from what he did not want. Obviously he wanted Susannah. That was the cup, and she must drink it down. A cup of lye; the bitter truth.

She almost missed the El stop. Up the slippery stairs she climbed to the windy platform, hugging her jacket around her. She must tell Madame Florian what she needed for her masquerade. On the half-empty train she found a seat easily. Rush hour was over, most people had sat down to their supper. Behind her a drunken old man told a litany of curses sometimes in English and sometimes in a language she did not know, although she knew it was Slavic.

She wanted to stop and buy a bottle of wine when she got off the subway, but she could not afford it. One more taste left over from her life with Leigh; incongruous now. She must come to Joel without bringing her wild grief.

She ran into the dark, frightening alley full tilt and raced for the back door, to pound on it with the rhythm they had worked out. As he opened it, she slung her arms around his neck.

"I saw my brother. He gave us twenty dollars—"

"Is that all?"

"He's got too many kids. I wouldn't take that off him if we had any choice. I'm going to see Ruby tomorrow night."

He peeled off her jacket, took her by the shoulders and sat her on the cot. "I have bad news for you."

"Ruby's worse?"

"No, I haven't heard anything from the hospital. . . . Sam called. Natalie got served with a subpoena when she got off the plane. They called her before the grand jury today. She refused to answer. She's out now, but she's afraid they'll get transactional immunity and call her back. Anyhow, she gave Sam some money and told him to take Peezie back here."

"Sam and Peezie are coming to Chicago?"

"Sam called from O'Hare half an hour ago. He was waiting with his sister for your stepfather, Sandy, to pick them up."

"Why did she do that?" She was frightened for Natalie; yet irrationally and terribly, she was relieved because it took her mind off her pain. She was galvanized into fear for Natalie and released from the obsession with Leigh's marriage and fatherhood. She did not have to force herself to pretend to think of something else.

"She's afraid she might have to go to jail. She doesn't want the kids terrorized anymore. She figures there'll be less heat on them at Sandy's. And she's afraid if she's busted, Daniel will take the kids and she'll never get them back."

"I didn't think he wanted the older kids."

"He wants to improve his bargaining position." Joel smoothed her hair. "As Sam explains it—that kid is cool—if Daniel has the kids, he might not have to pay Natalie any money at all."

"Family wars. The vengeance of fathers." She leaned against his arm. Then she took his face between her hands and kissed him again and again in gratitude. He was there, he existed, he loved her. "Hey, you haven't shaved."

"Aw, Vida, I haven't got any new blades. It's like shaving with a brick."

"Now it's like making love to a bed of nails. At my age I'm entitled to a little comfort." Suddenly it occurred to her that at her very age Ruby had left Tom, making her big leap from one life to another. Here she was changing men and profound allegiances also. But her life had not been structured by Leigh. Joel was not her work, as Tom and the children and Sandy and the children had been Ruby's no matter what jobs she had held. Perhaps the only time Ruby had felt differently had been during World War II when she had been intensely proud of her work in the shipyard. "It's a man's job," she told Grandma and Paul and Vida in the evening when she came home in her overalls and changed into a dress. "My foreman, Gene Cornutti, says I'm faster than the man I replaced."

"What happened to him?" Paul asked.

"He's with your father, fighting the Japs. And I'm making ships. Even our baby Vida can do her part by stepping on the tin cans, can't you, baby?"

She could see herself crushing the cans by jumping on them with both feet, before they were collected for scrap metal. Her early-childhood memories of wartime were warm and happy; it was almost obscene, she thought. No European Jews could have such memories. Grandma, Mama, Paul, baby me. We were never as happy again until she married Sandy, and then Paul was already quitting school to work.

All the time she was making love with Joel and afterward as they talked each other to sleep, odd flashes of childhood lit the insides of her lids. Tomorrow she would see her mother. No matter how and at what cost, she would succeed.

The blond wig was the one she carried for disguise, used with Tara; the pillow was from the cot in the back room at Madame's; the maternity pant suit, a hideous turquoise with dozens of shiny buttons, was provided by Madame from who knew where. She painted on a heavy mask of makeup. Paul arrived late, while she almost froze in the pant suit. Her nose dripped freely, and all the makeup wiped off it into her handkerchief. She had stuffed cotton batting into her cheeks to distort her face to a round fat-cheeked look.

As Paul's impulse was to lope, she had to drag on him as they left the parking garage and went into the hospital lobby. "Slowly, slowly, Dad.

Do you want me to lose my baby? Remember, you have to act solicitous. You don't make pregnant women run."

"Aw, come on, Vida. We can playact upstairs."

She dug her fingers into his arm. "What is my name?"

"Marsha. Marsha. Damn it, you have a grip there."

"Damn it back, Paul. Don't forget my name again. Not when you think we're alone, not anytime. Okay, lead the way, Dad."

When they reached the floor and entered the nurse's scrutiny, the nurse behind the desk said, "Only two in at a time."

"Oh? Who's with her?" Vida asked, smiling.

The nurse looked at the list. "Her son. Her other son, Michael."

"Listen, I'm going to take this time to run downstairs and call my husband. I'll be right back." To Paul she said, "Get him out of there fast. Make sure Sharon's not around, too."

"What am I supposed to do? Boot Mike out?"

"Tell him you have something private to discuss with Mama."

"Yeah, he couldn't be more bored with my life. He thinks I'm a slob."

"I think he's spoiled. I'll be back in ten minutes. Get Mike out by then. I don't trust him."

"You just better hope Sharon don't show up tonight."

"If she does, you belt her and I'll run." She grinned at him. "I know you'll watch out for me, Daddy dear. Ten minutes."

She did not want to hang around the lobby, so she simply hid in the women's room. When her watch read ten minutes, she gave Paul an extra five and then returned. If M & M was there—Natalie and her old name for Michael Morris Asch—what would she do? She would go on instinct. A man was sitting in the area near the nurse's desk leafing through sports magazines. As she got off the elevator he scanned her carefully and then lost interest. It felt as if a naked electric wire had touched her, but she strolled toward the nurse, chewing her gum as if bored. "Did my uncle leave yet? You know, he's my uncle even though he's younger than me. Mike."

"Yeah, you got a big family," the nurse said. "He left just now. He's in his second year of medical school, huh?"

"Yeah, doing real good." She panicked as she realized she had no memory of where he was going to school. "Well, I'm going to see Grandma. I take a plane home tomorrow, so this is it."

"First left around the corner. Then it's the third door on your right. Put on this gown. Your father will show you what to do."

Ruby lay cranked up in the bed, but she was staring at the door, waiting, her cat eyes bright in the haggard face. "Vida, is that *you?*"

Vida winced, glancing at the woman who lay on the other bed watching a television set overhead. It was loud enough, she hoped, to screen their talk if she spoke softly.

"Yes, Mama, but you have to just call me Dear or Honey, please. Okay? Anything you want to. Even You little stinker. But not my name," she whispered as she came to kiss Ruby, who looked years older than she had the year before. The skin hung. She was still fleshy, but her flesh seemed to be withering; her skin was pale and her veins distended. She gasped for breath, and her breathing rasped in a way that scared Vida further. Vida drew the curtain between her mother and the next bed.

"I knew you were coming. I told Natalie so. She said you couldn't. She's a worrywart. But Sandy said you would. He's right, the way he always is. When I listen to him, it turns out. . . . He's eating his supper now. He eats real late so he can see me when nobody else is here. Then at seven—"

"Mama, you're not supposed to talk too much," Paul warned.

"I'll keep her quiet," Vida said. "Paul, watch for me. Go gossip with the nurse and keep an eye. Okay? I promise I won't stay long." She pulled the cotton batting from her cheeks, letting her face back into its normal shape behind the curtain.

"Are you having a baby? I know Leigh's new wife is. You didn't go and get pregnant too?"

"No, I'm supposed to be Marsha," she said softly, sitting on the edge of her mother's bed. Ruby looked a little like Grandma, and that was frightening. She had never seen a resemblance before. Grandma had been a stout dumpy woman who wore shapeless clothes. After Grandma was left a widow, she had never wanted to remarry. "Once is enough," she had said. "Too much sometimes." Ruby was the same age Grandma had been when she had her fatal heart attack. Vida's stomach bunched tight in her, painfully.

"You don't look anything like her in that awful wig. Get a better wig. It breaks my heart. Your hair is such a wonderful color. Only thing we ever got from you-know-who that did us any good."

"How are you, Mama? Are you in pain?"

"I'm fine. They're keeping me here to get me fat on their tasteless food. Upstairs, downstairs, upstairs again. They move me around but they won't let me go home. It's all a racket."

"Get better, then. Do what they tell you."

"Ha. Oh, the nurses are nice, mostly, especially the night nurse. But my doctor lies in his teeth. And they won't let me smoke."

"But Mama, that's bad for your heart."

"So the damage is done. Now it's hard on my heart to want a smoke, right?"

"You have to get well!" Vida insisted. She felt a pang of anger toward Sandy that surprised her. Then she realized that somehow she blamed him. She felt as if she had handed her mother over to him and then she didn't have to worry about Ruby any longer and was free to grow up into her own life. Now if Ruby was sick, she wanted to blame someone.

"Sure," Ruby said without interest. "He's younger than you, this man you got now?"

"Natalie has been blabbing?"

"She shouldn't tell me? How come?"

"Well, he's not as young as Leigh's new wife."

Ruby laughed—that deep gravelly cackle which ended up as a cough. "That's telling them. Why not? You marry an older man and you're a good wife and mother for fifteen years like your sister and what does it get her? Child support, if she's real lucky." With the animation of gossip Ruby looked beautiful again. She was only sixty-three; she had twenty years to live. Her hair hadn't started to gray until she was in her fifties, when she had immediately reddened it. Her eyes gleamed, sea green with their long fluttering lashes. Ruby could not help flirting with her. Ruby could no more keep from flirting than she could levitate. "Isn't it nice Natalie sent the kids to be with me? I know she shouldn't keep them out of school, but I love having them. Isn't Sam a darling? He's going to break hearts. He yatters Spanish with all the Puerto Ricans in the hospital. And Peezie's going to be a knockout. She's going to shoot up way taller than Natalie, taller than you and me."

On the night table photos were standing up jammed together like rush hour: Natalie's three children, Paul's five, Sharon's two. Vida felt a burst of relief that she had not had any. Enough! All those childish faces. She saw a picture of herself, but it was not dangerous. Vida at age ten stood outside a brick apartment house on Montrose. One hand was missing: it had clutched Tom, who had been sliced off.

Ruby gripped her arm. "Does he love you?"

"Yes, Mama. A lot. In fact, a lot more than Leigh did."

"Why don't you marry him?"

"Mama! That won't make *me* legal."

"Well, one thing at a time. You got to start somewhere."

They hadn't told Ruby about Natalie's being in jail, obviously. So much went wrong in their family all at once, she thought, it was practically normal. Her childhood had been a series of accidents and bumps in the night. How did they, her responsible relatives, Sandy and Sharon and Paul in committee, decide that Ruby could be told about Natalie's impending divorce and Leigh's remarriage and Vida's new lover, but not about Natalie's bust? Maybe they had a proper sense of what was a disaster and what wasn't, for losing Daniel was no disaster in her book.

VIDA

More likely, however, Natalie had told the truth until she was off the scene and then the others lied steadfastly.

"Are you worried about Natalie for breaking up with Daniel?" she asked cautiously.

"That shlemiel chasing after young chickies? He can't keep his hands off his students. . . . Listen to me, precious, don't ever marry a college professor. They stand up there showing off year after year to a new crop and always some young girls are going to be bowled over. Daniel could always argue circles around her. . . . You think I didn't tell Natalie all this twenty years ago?"

"Twenty years ago Natalie was in high school, Mama."

"I told her after that, too. I never liked Daniel. He looks down his nose at us. So did your husband. New Yorkers all think they know everything. They think us Jews in the provinces lack culture and eat with our toes."

"Now you're saying you didn't like Leigh?"

"Well, he was better than the mad Greek. . . . Better than Daniel too," Ruby said, relenting. "You got a picture of the new one?"

"Now, Mrs. Asch, are we getting too tired? We aren't supposed to be sitting up in bed, now, are we?" The nurse settled Ruby back down. Ruby looked indignant and gasped for breath again. "Time for our meds now."

When the nurse finally left, Vida said, "Mama, I ought to go now."

"But you'll come back tomorrow." Ruby seized her hand.

"Mama, I have to get out of Chicago. Don't tell anybody I was here."

"I have to tell Sandy, precious. I don't like to keep secrets from him. That was one of the troubles with you-know-who—having to hide the food money, not telling him when Paul was in trouble. . . . Do you think God's punishing me?"

"Ruby, don't be ridiculous. You love Sandy."

"I thought it was the best thing for you."

"Okay, tell Sandy, but nobody else."

Ruby pouted. "Paul knows. I bet you'll tell Natalie."

Who hadn't called this morning at the Art Institute. "Okay, Mama, but not Sharon and not Mike."

"You've always been jealous of your younger brother."

"You think he's real proud of me and eager to have a chat?"

"Vida! How could he be proud?"

"Shhh. Why not? A lot of people think I'm exemplary." She pulled herself together and kissed her mother. "Bye-bye, Mama. I'll be back soon." She doubted it, but she had to say so as she stuffed the cotton batting back into her cheeks.

"Stay. Just a few minutes." Ruby clutched at her.

She kissed her mother. "Okay. A few minutes. That's a pretty bed jacket," she said to make the mood light again. "I never saw one outside the movies."

"Ritzy, huh? Sandy got it for me. He shouldn't have. . . . I mean that. Things aren't so good for us. You know we wanted to retire and move to Arizona? Ever since that time, remember when we met you there? At that cute adobe restaurant, sweetheart? But Sandy can't retire at sixty-five. We're feeling the pinch. And now look what I've gone and done. Every day in here, you could fly to Japan and back for the price. . . . He's Jewish? What does he look like?"

Paul came bursting in. She quieted him until she had dragged him out into the hall. "Softly, bro."

"Sharon's there by the desk!"

"Okay. One moment while I say goodbye." She dashed back into the room, holding her pillow in place. "Mama-love, I got to move it. Don't tell Sharon I was here. She's on her way."

"Take some fruit!" Ruby sat up, waving at the centerpiece of fruit between the photos, the pitcher of water, the yellow roses.

She marched out, taking her gown off and dropping it on the counter. "Bye-bye," she called to the nurse. "I'm leaving." After all, Sharon had no reason to assume she was coming from Ruby's room, around the corner. Sharon had lighter curly hair than Natalie's, processed to be less kinky. She wore a short brown fur coat. Even though she was not Ruby's blood daughter, she had picked up chain smoking from her. Sharon smoked exactly as Ruby did, the same jaunty twitch, and now she was stubbing out her cigarette in annoyance as the nurse insisted, a scene that probably happened every time she came onto the ward. Was it Sharon who was sneaking in cigarettes to Mama? Vida wanted to corner her and ask, but she had to march on, quickly.

"Hey, Sharon," Paul bellowed. "How are you doing? Where's Si? Hey, you look like you gained a little weight, huh?"

"You should talk! How dare you talk to me about fat? I have *not* gained weight!"

She could hear Sharon's high indignant voice yapping behind her like a furious small dog as she dived into the elevator and rode down. She would wait in the garage near Paul's car for him to appear, distant enough to flee if any trouble arose. As she crossed the lobby, Joel rose from a chair. "Hi!"

"You!" She was startled and relieved at once. "Fast, out of here."

Outside the doors she said, "How did you get here? Why?"

"I took the car and followed you."

"You're an idiot!"

"You're not so good at watching for tails as you think."

She flinched as if he had struck her. Then she thought, But he knew which hospital Ruby was in. She did not believe she had missed a car on her. "Is the Mariah here?"

"Sure."

"Let's get out of town. I just had a close call and I think we'd better hop it. I'm not sure I made it out without tipping them. Sharon arrived just as I was leaving, and I wouldn't put it past her to say it wasn't Marsha who just visited Mama."

"She hasn't seen you since you went under, right?"

"I don't trust her. She's told things to the FBI. I hope Paul doesn't get in trouble. . . . Sometimes I feel all we do is cause trouble. To Natalie. To Paul."

"I brought all our stuff."

"Excellent. Did you wipe the place clean?" She meant fingerprints, paper handkerchiefs, everything.

"No. I didn't realize we were going to take off."

"Let's hope they can't trace us there."

"What about telling Madame we're leaving?" He put his arm around her as he unlocked the car.

"When we're gone tomorrow she'll know. And be relieved." She fell into the front seat, leaving him to drive.

"Well, where to? Back East?"

"Yeah, but we need money." She felt feverish, drooping against the bench seat. "Joel, did you really follow me?"

He stopped to pay the attendant, then pulled out into the street. "You think I'm no good at these games."

"But you knew what hospital she was in. . . ." She'd find out later. The idea that anyone could tail her unobserved terrified her. It was suicidal not to pay attention.

"Where to?"

"Where indeed?" She sank back again. "I'm exhausted. We need money. Cleveland, maybe. How about Cleveland?"

"More relatives? I know you were born there."

"No relatives. Shelter. A friend. Maybe a money connection. Time to reach Natalie at eleven tomorrow. Oh, god, she's supposed to call me. Okay, I'll have to use the mail drop. What a mess."

"Why don't you get that pillow out and the wig off?"

"Jesus! I should have done it when we got in the car. I hope the parking-lot attendant didn't look at me. I'm not functioning, I'm not functioning at all." She discarded her props into a bag.

He said, "Why not lie down in the back seat?"

"I'll sit up to keep you company. . . . Okay, maybe I will lie down. I can't believe I forgot to change before we left the parking lot. I'll put on my own clothes in the back seat. I'm not functioning!"

He pulled to the side and quickly she ducked into the back. After she had changed and lay down curled awkwardly on the seat, she heard him singing to himself in his deep resonant voice:

> Well, I been long gone!
> Well, I been long gone!
> Like a turkey through the corn
> With my long clothes on,
> Long gone John. . . .

PART VI

February 1974

17

Both mice and salamanders had crawled into the well housing and chewed the cabbages, she discovered. She carried armfuls of the injured and partially decomposed cabbages up to the house, sliding on the ice that had formed when the temperature had gone above freezing the day before just long enough to melt an inch of snow and then to freeze it at sunset. On the way to the well she had slipped and fallen on her side and she still ached as she picked her way stiffly, an armload of heavy stinking cabbages and two more loads to go.

She put the vegetables on a table in the unheated shed outside the kitchen door and went downhill for another load. As she toted the final load to the table where she would have to separate the edible from the spoiled, she thought that the month of February, like Dante's hell, should have written over the entrance, Abandon Hope All You Who Enter Here. Or was it Abandon All Hope, You Who Enter Here?

She had never studied Italian: rooms not entered, lovers not taken, a pleasure on the tongue never tasted. In another life, born in less interesting times, she would have been a scholar. Instead, here she was acting as nemesis to dormant spotted salamanders; nevertheless, she felt glad to be out of the fetid overcrowded house. The men grabbed most of the outdoor jobs, and only a recent revolt of Eva's and hers had won the women the right to cut wood. The men still monopolized work on the cars. She, who was proficient at building three types of time-delay bombs, lifted the hood of their old blue Saab and saw a mass of Medusa snakes that turned her brain to stone. Whenever Kevin said he would teach her, he meant he would browbeat her, rattling off terms so fast she had no idea what he

287

was referring to, turn from her sullenly and at last lose his temper, stalking off. Starting one of the two cars or the truck the folks on Hardscrabble Hill shared was an hour's occupation on a frosty morning. Life revolved around the preparing of food, the serving of food, the washing of dishes and interminable laundry, the care and feeding and washing of babies, the heating of the house with its variously cranky and voracious wood stoves, the starting of the cars, the fixing of the cars, the going out with the cars over the icy ruts to the town road, sometimes plowed, and into town and back. When they had a political discussion in the house, it was only a means of displaying and acting out their mutual hostilities.

Whack, whack, the heavy iron knife chopped deep into the rot entering the pale savoyed hearts. Her hands were red and chapped, scarred, discolored, a map of farm labor learned as it was awkwardly done. Plowing, sowing: once those had borne romantic connotations to her; once they had been political metaphors. Separate the wheat from the chaff, the little left ideamongers quoted who had never seen a sheaf of wheat in their lives, let alone been presented, as the woman had, with a fifty-pound sack of hard red winter wheat berries Bill had won in a poker game and the injunction to make bread of them. Whack. The savoy cabbages were pale green brains, huge with the ideas of ideas.

She did not want to return to the house looming over her. Two and a half stories tall it wobbled down the hill—dairy barn, storage barn, chicken house, toolshed, woodshed, garage, tractor shed, all connected by walkways of rotting wood or joined end to end against the six-foot drifts of snow that had lain against them up to a week before. Now only four feet of snow humped against the old wood; but there would be more, and more, and more. Beyond stood the maze of house, the oldest part with low ceilings and wide floorboards, the Victorian rooms with high ceilings, the part from the twenties with more low ceilings—hard times had come again.

She had first seen the white farmhouse among its maple trees a year and a half before, in September of 1972. She and Kevin had driven all night from Detroit, arriving exhausted and desperately glad to find haven. In the late summer the picturesque rambling white house had seemed idyllic, topping a small hill on rolling land with a view of the long razorbacks that closed in the valley on both sides. It was the week after Labor Day, the air warm and still as honey. Old-fashioned scarlet roses bloomed against the porch; in beds along the foundation pastel asters sprawled, fuzzy lavender and frail pink. They had occupied the house with carefully chosen people, most of them fugitives, all in the Network. Tequila and Marti, legal and married to each other, had been living in the area long enough to be familiar with it, and they had located the farm for rent with the option to buy in a year.

VIDA

Coming up the walk leaning on Kevin with his long arm around her, she had felt like a bride. The first year under had been hell, with them hunted from hole to hole. It had taken a year to put the Network together, to gather in political fugitives, to learn how to survive, to give workshops in counterfeiting and establishing I.D., to learn to carry out bolder and better raids, attacks, guerrilla affronts. Now she and Kevin would live together for the first time. Their relationship would become solid and homely, less violent. That night, September 9, the first frost had struck. The temperature plummeted from 59 to below freezing. Ice stood in the yard. In the kitchen garden every plant perished except for parsnips and cabbages. The roses hung brown.

She struck at the last cabbage so hard the knife sank into the old wood and held fast till she wobbled it loose. That fucker, she muttered. The thought of Kevin hurt, a bruise the size of a clenched fist in her chest, a bruise that never healed. Staggering out with her arms full of rotten leaves, she threw them into the compost barrel, then wrapped the salvaged portions in newspapers for storage on the porch, where the mice would surely find them again. She was filthy and stank. If Marti was done washing diapers, she would take a bath. She did not care whether it was her turn.

She took a last breath of fresh air and plunged in: stale milk, sour baby smell, smoke from the stoves, stale tobacco and pipe smoke. She went up to the bathroom over the kitchen and strode in to start the water. Alice was throwing up in the toilet. Hastily she backed out, waiting. Alice emerged, looking yellow. "Are you sick?" Vida asked unnecessarily.

"I'm pregnant," Alice wailed, rubbing her nose.

"What?" But she had heard. "How far along?"

"I don't know. I should have had my period four weeks ago."

"Why didn't you say something? It won't just go away."

"Bill and Jesse want me to have it."

Jesse was Kevin's underground name—for Jesse James.

"Bill and Jesse could take off tomorrow for a year. You know that. It's February. They're bored."

Alice started to cry. Vida held her. "Come on, you want to talk to me?"

But Alice pulled away, looking yellower. "You smell just awful. I'm sorry."

"I was just on my way to bathe. . . . Look, I'll get cleaned up and then come and talk to you."

"I have to get the bread started. . . . We need more wood chopped. You're still chopping wood, right?"

"Right." Should she chop wood first? It made her sweat. No, she couldn't stand the smell. Each bathroom had a small gas heater, and while the supply of hot water was finite, it was renewable. She had only to light the gas and wait, scrubbing the tub in the meanwhile. No matter what she said, no matter how many signs she put up saying Please take your own dirt out of the tub with you, she could never persuade Kevin or Bill or Tequila to clean the tub after he used it. One of those slobs had left a used condom hanging on the back of the toilet like a squashed slug. With toilet paper she picked it up and dropped it into the wastebasket. From hard experience they had learned not to put condoms down the toilet, where they backed up the septic tank. Damn them, pigs were cleaner.

She saw Oscar's pink carcass slung up with the blood streaming. Kevin's idea of a joke was to call the pig Oscar. He fancied he saw a comparison. She thought that in a way there was a likeness to her old lover Oz, because Oscar the pig had been at least as smart and considerably better-tempered than the humans around him and had remained sweet and useful for four months after his death. Their neighbors had done the butchering for half the meat, showing them how to cure and freeze and salt down. They were subsistence dirt farmers for real.

After her bath, she chopped wood in the last dying light. Eva came out to watch her companionably, sitting on the fence with her arm in a sling. She had fallen and broken it three weeks before, chasing a terrified chicken. Eva was her ally in trying to change the balance of power in the house, as was Larkin, who had arrived the week after Eva broke her arm. He stayed in his room most of the time reading, writing, going over reports and communications.

Kevin, Bill, Belinda and Tequila hung together, although Tequila was not so much hostile to her as loyal to Kevin. Eva, Alice and Vida formed another mutual-support group. Marti tried to remain neutral, although she would support her husband, Tequila, if she was forced to take sides. Basically Marti functioned as child-care worker and main mama, even to Belinda's baby, Roz. Belinda did not like the sexual division of work either, but she solved the problem individually by becoming one of the guys. Belinda had not slept with anyone in years—since Felipe, the father of her baby, had gone to prison. Jimmy was torn. He and Belinda were close as friends, close politically, but his older loyalties were equally to Kevin and to Vida, and he banged and knocked back and forth between them in growing misery.

Eva was singing something she had written a little while back, before the TV had broken. The men had not been in a good temper since. Vida rested on her ax, unzipping her down jacket as heat billowed out. Her body steamed on the clean chilly air.

VIDA

Let him turn, let him turn
Like a torn imperial flag
On the dirty air and burn.
Let him flutter like a rag.

Eva sang in her strong cellolike contralto. Vida chopped until the light was gone. At moments like this she loved Hardscrabble. Then she stacked the wood and put away the ax and bit. Her shoulders ached pleasantly. While she stacked, she and Eva heard the truck arrive, but neither turned her head and nobody spoke to them. The women's chopping wood represented an uprising and would be ignored by Kevin and company, coming from town where they had got a day's work on a road crew cleaning culverts and drains.

Eva got down off the fence to put her good arm around Vida, still singing:

Let him see his henchmen buzzing
to the committee like scared flies.
Let the hangman hang himself.
Let him choke on his own lies!

Rubbing her hip where she had landed earlier on the ice, Vida ambled reluctantly toward the house. "Alice is pregnant."

"Aw, shit," Eva said, but then cheered up immediately, tossing a black braid over her shoulder. "I can go with her to the clinic. I'm useless for the moment, anyhow. It'll be nice to talk to some activists and find out what's happening in the women's movement here."

"She's thinking of having the baby."

Eva snorted. They climbed the ice ruts in silence for a moment. Then Eva poked her gently. "Whose bright idea is that?"

"Jesse and Bill."

"Sure. They do a lot of child care now. . . . Wouldn't it be nice if we could put them in the deep freeze for the long winter? Or send them into hibernation like bears or woodchucks?"

"Why would we ever thaw them?" She smiled at Eva.

"Oh, my." Eva was startled. "I'm sure it's hard on your relationship being shut up here together all winter long. . . ."

"What relationship?" She kept smiling. "We seem to be in the relationship of permanent opposition. What have we agreed on in the last year?"

"That we need another wood stove for the upstairs."

Vida laughed, stomping the clotted ice from her boots before they entered. "Why does it scare you—Jesse and I falling apart?"

"We're stuck. You can't get a divorce underground. We have to get along."

"The Board meeting should clear the air. We've a lot to thrash out." In the entryway she paused, hanging her jacket. "Jesse and I may have to sit on the BOD together, we have to go on living in this house, but no matter what policy we lay down at the Board, I don't have to sleep with him. Anymore."

"Has it come to that?" Eva blew her nose.

"Come and gone and gone some more!" She projected at Eva a strong desire not to discuss it, and Eva fell silent. She remembered Jimmy, of all people, coming to her room a few nights before to try to reconcile her to Kevin.

"But he's miserable," Jimmy had said. "Under it all, it hurts him. Why can't you make it up?"

"No!" she had said to Jimmy. "I don't want him that way."

"For the group," Jimmy pleaded.

"I am not a thing to be given him to keep him happy. I will not fuck him for political reasons." Her bluntness had shut Jimmy up.

Vida and Eva entered the kitchen together. Kevin was watching the door, leaning on the newer of the refrigerators scratching himself under his wool shirt. That hard lean hungry look, the fury under fraying control: once that had caught her on fire. His gaze raked them as if accusing them of conspiring. "How much wood can a good fuck chuck, if a good fuck could chuck wood?" he asked loudly. "Where's Lark?"

"Upstairs, I imagine," Eva said. "Are we ready to eat?"

"Larkin went off in the Saab," Marti said, carrying Tamara to her high chair to insert her. Tamara kicked hard without real malice or disapproval, simply exhibiting the habit of always struggling against the high chair. Tamara was robust for a two-year-old as Marti was robust for a woman, both square, chunky, broad-faced, a little dour around the light eyes with their light lashes that often seemed stuck to the fair skin. Sleepy dust, Ruby used to call that exudation from the eyes.

"Without explaining himself," Kevin said, glaring at Vida as if she were responsible for Larkin.

"I assume he had business," she said evenly. "Board meeting soon."

"How much wood can a cold fuck chuck, if a cold fuck could chuck wood?" he chanted.

God, he was an idiot. How had she managed to overlook for years how stupid he was? Nothing in that magnificent tall horsy skull but sinuses for resonating that loud know-nothing voice. When Leigh had called him an ignoramus, she had had the blindness to disagree. Now he was hung around her neck like an idiot child.

Lark slipped in quietly as they were sitting down to supper—everybody but Alice, who was being sick again upstairs. If we have a little luck, she'll turn out to have flu or mononucleosis instead of a baby, she thought, glancing at Lark. He was looking better lately, not as drawn and exhausted as when he had arrived. Maybe the house was helping him, although she had trouble imagining that anyone could experience Hardscrabble Hill in February as a rest-and-relaxation furlough.

"Board meeting set for Sunday. Roger's on his way," Lark said. "Perry, you and I got to pick up Kiley in the Bronx."

The central committee consisted now of Kevin, Roger, Kiley, Lark and herself. Vida had been elected to replace Belinda, when Belinda insisted on having her baby. Belinda had felt it was all she would ever have from Felipe, who was in Sing Sing on a forever sentence and with the word of the system over him that he would be killed inside. Belinda had insisted on giving birth over all arguments, and that had precipitated the Board ruling that no fugitives could bear children. Yet when Roz was born, Belinda had had trouble accepting her baby—blond like her and female like her, with only Felipe's dark eyes. Felipe was a Puerto Rican independentista Belinda had loved without requital for years in the New York political scene, until fugitive life had brought them briefly together. When a sympathetic lawyer had brought him news of Roz's birth, he was more upset than pleased; he had a wife and family in Brooklyn.

When Belinda had heard his response, she had gone into a depression. She stared at her baby. "It's all a mistake," she said.

"No, it's a baby," Marti said. "A healthy one. A good baby."

Belinda loved her baby, but almost surreptitiously. She would run into the nursery and seize Roz up and hug her and then run off.

Vida had been to only two meetings of the Board, and they still made her nervous. To be on the Board was a big responsibility.

"Why the *two* of you driving down?" Kevin asked. "What for?"

"If we take alternate shifts, we can drive without stopping. We leave in the morning." Lark cracked his knuckles. He would never admit he couldn't drive that many hours.

"Man, you could walk there and back by Sunday."

"We have fund raising to do. The doc to see."

What was Lark doing? Something was up. Kevin pulled at his chin, where the beard used to be. "Real chummy, the two of you in the truck."

"We'll take the blue Saab."

"That don't start half the mornings," Tequila chimed in amiably.

"I had it worked on today. A deserter down in Tunbridge can make anything run. Calls himself Terry. Kiley told me about him. . . ."

"I know him," Jimmy said resentfully—jealousy? "He's my friend. Kiley just met him when she was here last month."

"Faggot," Kevin said softly and almost fondly to Jimmy.

"He said it had the wrong spark plugs and the ignition cable was frayed. He tuned it, and it's perky now." Lark spoke in his flat Midwestern voice, casual and almost without affect, but his bright blue eyes never left Kevin's face. "I think you ought to take the black Dodge over to him. The cars are Network property, not your high school hot rods. Don't touch the engines, guys, if you can't do better than you've been doing."

"Who said it was the wrong spark plugs?" Bill boomed. "He don't know his ass."

"Then why is it running so good? He's a real mechanic. You ought to be glad we've got one."

"How the hell would you know?" Bill watched Kevin to see if he should attack Lark further. "You never tried once to work on those cars."

"I'm not into proving anything on a car. Only interested in getting it into shape to be used. I'm surprised how you guys have lost political steam up here. You need to refocus. Where's Alice tonight?"

Tequila and Marti, husband and wife, exchanged a guarded glance at the question, and both became very occupied with their plates. Jimmy stopped eating and stared at his knuckles. He looked pinched with worry.

She was sure the question was not as innocent as it sounded, Lark's thin face waiting blandly. Anyhow, she was going to answer truthfully. "Upstairs having all-day morning sickness."

"Morning sickness?" Lark repeated. "What from?"

Kevin guffawed. "If you don't know by now, it's too late to give you a description."

"Why hasn't it been taken care of?" Lark asked gently. "Has no one volunteered to go with her to arrange it?"

"I have," Eva said. "I'm useless with my arm broken anyhow."

"Eva, with both arms off, you wouldn't be useless," Lark said.

Jimmy made a noise of assent, glad of a friendly word at the table. A bit of blame and a bit of praise, Vida noticed: Lark took his leadership role seriously, one reason he had been on the Board since it had been organized out of panic and early chaos. When Kiley and Lark had chosen to go underground in the fall of 1970, Vida told Jimmy she thought they were crazy: imagining doing voluntarily what the three of them had been forced to. Kiley and Lark had expected an imminent revolution and were preparing. So much for that guess, she thought, but what a relief to have him in the house. Such a different kind of man. She had matured these last years, and she had no female masochism left. Lark was asking, "Some kind of problem with the clinic? How good is Alice's I.D.?"

"Good," Jimmy started to say, when Kevin cut in.

"Why should she have it out? We're doing fine with Marti's two kids and Belinda's baby."

"Marti's not a fugitive," Lark said softly. "We agreed last year fugitives have no right to bear children. Nothing has changed."

"Aw, dig yourself, man, a lot has changed. They're not on our tails night and day. They got their own troubles. Hey, when are we getting that fucking TV fixed so we can see them impeach him?"

All through Watergate, everyone except Jimmy and Vida had been mesmerized by the set. They watched the action, they watched reruns, they watched the nightly recapitulation of what they had watched during the day. Since the TV had broken, tempers were booby-trapped among the fugitives and friends. She could not share their obsessive satisfaction. For her it was Eichmann punished not for mass murder but for being caught with his hand in the till, and sentenced to exile from the Elks and having his American Express card cancelled. Jimmy agreed and hated the spectacle. He accused the rest of the snowbound house of believing in the ultimate justice of the system and expecting to see it on TV like the shootout in a Western.

"I'll talk to Alice after supper," Lark said, laying down his knife and fork. He ate a third of what Kevin, Tequila and Bill put away. Often he fasted. He did eat fish; perhaps, she thought, because the Vietnamese ate a great deal of seafood. He was partial to a fermented fish sauce called nuoc mam that nobody else could tolerate when he produced it—except Jimmy, who never tasted his food anyhow and ate it as politically correct and to please Lark. She had the feeling that the sight of others wolfing down hunks of chicken made Lark squeamish. Eva too was a vegetarian. If Kevin could have made it happen, they would have had meat every night as much to affront Eva as because he liked it. Since they could rarely afford meat they had not raised, that possibility for discord was muted.

"Alice knows what she wants: to have that baby," Kevin said.

"I didn't actually think so," Vida said mildly, aping Lark's approach because it seemed to work better than her own of bluntly screaming at Kevin.

"Me, I'm the father," Bill said. "You got to talk to me."

"If you're the father, I'll talk to you. About contraception," Lark went on without raising his voice. "Do you think a woman who may go to prison at any moment has a right to bear a child? Do you realize what it's like giving birth in prison? Did you pay any attention to what they did to Erica Huggins? Giving birth in chains? And then what? You want 'our' child raised by an orphanage? Adopted by rich jerks?''

''What kind of cowards and, defeatist creeps are we to live thinking they're going to catch us?'' Kevin wiped his mouth, sneering.

''Where other lives are concerned, we have to assume that. As was decided in council. Who are you to set yourself up to change rules on impulse?'' Eva cried, her voice hard. ''You think rules are for us, but not for you.''

Jimmy looked in mute appeal to Kevin, who stomped into the living room. She could almost feel Jimmy crushing his doubts as he followed.

Lark went up to talk to Alice, who cried in his arms awkwardly, because she was a long and lanky woman four inches taller than frail Lark, complaining about the long winter and Bill and feeling politically lost and useless and pushed around, caught between the two factions that had polarized in the house. Kevin, Bill, Belinda, Jimmy and Tequila sat around the busted TV drinking local moonshine, a form of vodka from potatoes distilled in the next township by some freak ex-chemists who were doing a roaring business. She went upstairs and locked herself in, going quietly past the room where Alice lay weeping in Lark's arms.

She looked around at the room she had labored to fix up and she wanted to scream, to shut her eyes hard and wake back in her own room in New York: her room where as far as she knew her clothes, her jewelry, her books and art objects were still stored. She wanted to return to her life. Enough of this already, enough! She was weary of it. She wanted to give up. She wanted to cry and collapse and give up and go home. She wanted to be Vida Asch again. She missed everyone she really loved. Oh, she'd take Eva with her, the one close friend she'd made underground.

Despair crushed her until she lay on her stomach and wept and wept until her eyes were swollen and the quilt soaked and her head ached and she could not breathe except through gasping mouth. Then she lay panting, and still she was trapped in that cold room she had painted white, not understanding how much white she would see in Vermont in the long winter, that room with old-fashioned sheer white curtains and white shades. The wedding-ring quilt she had found in the attic—worn and washed out, with some patches tearing loose—every month or so she took needle to repair. On the walls were paintings, acrylic on paper, Eva had made during last winter and this one: views of another world. They showed a blazing cobalt-and-gold landscape where women walked in threes and fours with small children and sturdy animals. Fountains, stone arches, mountains, but not these beautiful low green mountains. Red stone. Volcanic rock. Eva's painting had gotten much better in the last year. The earliest paintings Vida had put up because they broke the agony of the too-white walls and because Eva was her best friend here. Of course, Eva should have been working on her music; she had been a serious musician until she had been set up by an agent in a bust on the G.I. coffeehouse where she played and sang. But what can a serious musician do as a fugitive?

The drawing had got better, as had the use of color. All around Vida's room the box-sized paintings marched (nothing too big to be moved fast), windows on someplace else. Lately Eva had been painting a series called "We'll Go to California" 1, 2, 3, 4, 5. Eva came from the West Coast. Eva was saying, We'll leave this loud house and go to California together. Imagine, the paintings sang, a tree full of oranges like miniature suns, a sea the color of a blue jay, palm-tree lollipops.

Vida recognized in herself no California dreams, but she was at a dead end. What point was there living in this broken-down farmhouse chopping up cabbages and banging heads with Kevin, as if the puttering and maintenance and bickering were political acts? She had to get out of here, and without Kevin. What she had seen in him was a bad joke. She did not know whether he had changed or whether she had or whether she merely saw more clearly. Perhaps fugitive life had brought out the worst in Kevin. She knew she could have marched back and forth across his fresh grave with no other emotion than relief and a lingering hostility.

Why could she not persuade Lark to argue in the Board that for two of the leadership to occupy one isolated house was absurd and she would be ten times as useful anywhere else? That would be her humble approach: send me where I'm needed. Let me organize an action in Toledo, in Houston, in San Diego. Let us open a new front. But save me from rotting in this house in a rotting bond with someone I have grown to loathe. On the trip to New York she would work on Lark. He was stationed in Buffalo now.

She felt exhausted with weeping but too lethargic to do more than undress and creep under the covers. The sheets were so cold they felt wet. What she ought to do was get up and put on that ugly flannel nightgown from the Thrift Shop, but she sprawled flipped on her back like something fallen, unable to sleep, unwilling to get up. She had run out of willpower. She wanted someone to call her Vida; she wanted someone to hold her and love her and coddle her; she wanted to be herself again! Voices rose through the floorboards, harsh laughter that jarred her as if it had been twice as loud. Anyone else's voices would not have scraped her raw.

Yet she must have dozed, because she woke when someone banged on her door. "What is it?" She hopped up instantly, stepping into her pants. Rammed her feet into boots without bothering with socks.

"Damn cunt! Open up." Kevin was hitting the door with his fists.

Bastard. She had thought it was an emergency, a raid, but it was just nincompoop Kevin pounding her door as if he wanted to break in. "Lay off the door! I'm asleep!" she yelled.

"Open up, you hear me? Come on, cunt, open up!"

She pulled off her pants and boots and put on the flannel nightgown to climb back into bed. Warm this time. "Go to bed, you shithead. I'm asleep. I'm not opening the door."

"Damn you, open it!" He gave it a terrifying whack and the door shuddered but did not break. She heard him cursing and hoped he had broken his hand. Probably he was kicking it; the worst he would get was a sore toe. She could hear Marti's voice saying, "Cool it, Jesse. You're scaring the kids!" The baby Dylan and Tamara and Roz were crying down the corridor.

"All right, I'm coming in," he bellowed. The blade of his hunting knife thrust into a crack in the old jamb and forced the bolt of the lock inside. In the drawer of the old nightstand by her bed she had a knife too. She reached for it and sat up, switching on the reading lamp clamped to the headboard.

"This is my—my room!" She sputtered with anger. "I don't want you in it! I never want you in it! I locked the door to keep you out!"

He slammed the door back against the wall to the trickle of falling plaster. "I'm coming in. We're getting things straightened out, Davey. You're mine and you're going to start acting like it."

"You don't own me. Get the hell out!" She felt too exposed in the bed and leaped out on the far side, flashing the knife. "Get out!"

"You think you know how to knife-fight, little punk?"

"I think I can cut you some."

He stood laughing, but he was not amused. He was scraped raw with desperation. "My reach is a foot longer. You need a lesson who's who around here."

There were no guns in the living section of the house; she had been responsible for that. She had argued at length against storing guns around the living quarters, but her real reason had been that she thought Kevin with a gun would shoot her. But she had not anticipated that a gun would make them physically equal, as a knife didn't.

"Stop it!" Lark stood in the doorway zipping his pants. "Nobody gave you the right to threaten one of us."

"Keep out of this. This is between my girl and me."

"I'm not your 'girl,' " Vida shouted. "I don't want you!"

"The fuck you don't!"

"Get out of her room! You can settle arguments between you with mediation. Things are going to pot here. We mean to intervene, and we're going to get everything straightened out even if we have to break up this house to do it." He walked by Kevin, calmly.

"Let her alone," Eva sang out. She blocked the doorway with an ax in her good hand.

Jimmy stood in the hallway blinking with sleep in his rumpled pajamas. Vida saw him as a child. Yes, she had played Mama and Kevin had played Daddy and he had made of them his family. The trauma in seeing them fight so viciously paralyzed him. He could only stand blinking, his hands clasped behind him as if tied.

"Who the fuck are you to tell me how to treat her?" Kevin said to Lark, ignoring Eva, but he was watching the ax out of the corner of his eye. "She's mine. You'd like to get your hands on her, wouldn't you?"

"I won't try it with a big jackknife, you better believe that." Lark walked over to her, still crouched by the bed with the knife hanging loosely in her hand, feeling ridiculous. "Are you all right?"

"My dignity's bleeding. I don't like scenes. I don't like my door forced. And he'd better believe, *I* won't be forced either. I'll kill him."

"We aren't in this to kill each other. You cool it too, Perry."

She wanted to cry. Did he expect her to take it calmly? Reprimand Kevin mildly as he raped her? Eva pushed in past Kevin and knelt by Vida, still holding the ax. Marti crowded into the room too and for once took Vida's side. "The kids are bawling. They're terrified. What kind of shit is this? Jesse, don't you wave that knife around here. I've told you not to bring sharp knives into the house and leave them around where the kids can hurt themselves. I cleaned and washed all day, and I'm bone-tired. I won't put up with this!"

Jimmy had not spoken a word. Silently he followed Kevin. Kevin retreated in a sulk to his room. Slowly the others dispersed. Vida spent the night in Eva's room with the door locked and a chair wedged under the knob. In the morning she did not even see Kevin as she packed her knapsack to leave early with Lark.

"What's our business in New York?" She was driving. With his artificial leg Larkin could drive, but it tired him. He would spell her one hour in four. Off to New York! That was her secret mecca, not Eva's luscious sunbaked orange-grove California dreams. The fugitives had learned how dangerous New York could be; yet it remained The City to her, pulsating source of energy.

"You want a mediator to negotiate between you two?" Lark asked.

"I can't stay in the same house with him. It wastes everybody."

"Politically you don't seem a compatible team any longer," he said tentatively. "But you've always worked together."

"I've worked with a lot of people," she said. "I used to work with Jimmy. I work well with Eva. You and I work well together." Would he suggest she leave the Board to avoid fights with Kevin?

"Yes, that's what I think," he said. "But you will admit things have been stagnating.

"Absolutely," she agreed fervently. "We're holding each other back politically."

"I have to fund-raise in the city," he said. "And I wanted us to have time to discuss program for the coming year. . . . Besides, I can't drive alone to fetch Kiley."

Leigh! She must see Leigh. She felt as if she had just been offered a vacation in the paradise of her choice. Three months had passed since their last meeting, and while things had been much improved between them in the past year, she could only hope he would want to see her as much as she wanted to see him.

"First we'll have to drive into Manhattan while I see Dr. Manolli," Lark said. "You wait. Then take me up to Co-op City. We have a shelter there. . . . You want to see the doc?" Lark needed help from the doctor, and besides, he had all the fugitives' problems to relate and prescriptions to collect.

"I'm fine! I'm wonderful. . . . So you think maybe it would be good if I left Hardscrabble?"

"What do you think of Eva?"

"Eva? I love her. She's very just, Lark, sweet-tempered day to day. But she's not afraid to take action or stand up to anyone."

"I've been quite impressed with her politically," he said gravely, cracking his gaunt knuckles. "You know, at first I think some of us looked down on her because she was framed. Most of us acted, as you did, or chose to come under because of our analysis. But Eva got pushed."

She wondered if she should say she thought that some of them looked down on Eva because she was a lesbian; but she decided not to cross words with Lark. He was unprejudiced toward gay people as far as she could tell and opposed to taking political positions on gay rights at the same time, because he was always terrified of offending the Cubans, the Chinese, the Albanians. "Eva's tremendously hardworking. And she's bright. She reads everything."

"She seems serious," he said. That was one of his key words—she remembered that. Why was he asking questions about Eva? "Maybe we didn't respect her so much politically because she came in late, and because she's a musician. You don't think of musicians as cadre."

"But Eva's really cadre," she said nervously.

"I think so." He nodded. "She must take a greater role."

In what? Kevin and Eva were bitter enemies, and she had not helped them get along together, always running to Eva with complaints. At ten she stopped to call Natalie and set up a meeting for the next morning when all Natalie's kids would be in school or day care. Obviously she would have the car, so she chose the Bronx Botanical Gardens and asked Natalie to contact Leigh and arrange a rendezvous out of Manhattan with him. Maybe a motel on the Island or near LaGuardia.

After the call she was flying. Feeling no fatigue, she drove on past the scheduled shift change. She was soaring, grateful to Lark, solicitous of his comfort. At the same time, she recognized that if he had been warmer to her the night before, more consoling, she might have ended up in his bed instead of chastely in Eva's. Now she was glad she hadn't. Really, Lark would be a tremendous improvement on Kevin, and she could feel his interest as a hum of suggestion between them. She wasn't the best fund raiser in the group and knew few contacts to scatter big bucks on them. No, Lark had his reasons, both political and personal, which she would decipher with time.

February in New York felt almost tropical. She and Lark visited Dr. Manolli in Washington Heights. Then she dropped Lark in Co-op City, towers on reclaimed garbage, where they were to make their headquarters for the next couple of days. She parked near the Mosholu Parkway gate to the Botanical Garden. No snow lay on the ground except for granite-hard patches of ice beside the paths. Her feet touched pavement and bounced, springy. The temperature was a balmy 37 degrees, with a wan sun trying to burn its way through a yellowish haze.

At once she picked out Natalie's old green VW bug. Natalie was sitting inside, reading a book of whose title Vida, leaning against the glass, could see only WOMEN, which made her smile. What else would Natalie be reading about but WOMEN? Women in World War II. Women in the Work Force. Women of Ethiopia. Women of 16th-Century England. Women in the Construction Trades. Women Writers of Provence. Women Healers of the Upper Volta. Women in the French Commune. Natalie's hunger was vast. She tapped on the glass. Natalie put down the book and hopped out to embrace her.

"Natalie!" Vida hugged her and then frowned. "Where are you?" Natalie felt slight, like Lark.

"Great, huh? I weigh 115 exactly. I haven't weighed this little since high school." Natalie unzipped her down jacket to show off. She was wearing a maroon warm-up suit striped along the side.

"But . . . you're awfully thin."

Natalie beamed. "Peezie wanted to learn karate. We've been going."

"Isn't she awfully young?"

"Six, and strong-minded. Er, what do I call you?"

"Peregrine at the moment. Stick to that."

"My sister, the falcon. Endangered species. It's fun galloping around the gym at the junior high Monday and Wednesday nights. Really, it all started because I confronted Daniel. I said, Okay, you just broke up with your girlfriend. What would it take to get you to pay that kind of attention to me? He said, Lose weight."

"He's stupid. If I was a man, I'd like fleshy women."

Natalie squeezed her shoulder. "I don't notice he's any more interested, but my instructor's an angel. Speaking of husbands." She rummaged in her shoulder bag. "I guess you read this and then eat it or it self-destructs, right? Honeymoon in Queens for you!"

"Oh, Natty, when?" She grabbed the paper to read off the motel. "Did he seem glad to hear from me?"

"Glad is no word for it. He got so excited he dropped a coffee cup all over my shoes."

"Really? He wants to see me?" She hugged Natalie. "Let's walk. It's so gorgeous here."

"Gorgeous?" Natalie looked around, puzzled. "Tonight. At seven. He's coming straight from work."

"How can I wait that long? I'm sorry. Of course I can wait. I'm just as happy to see you, really and truly."

"How're you doing in your life? You look a little tired."

"I've given up on Kevin. How could I ever have loved that bag of wind?" They passed the white metal–and–glass conservatory.

Natalie nodded toward the building. "Want to go in?"

"No, let's stay outside. It's so springlike."

"Springlike?" Natalie shook the curly hair out of her eyes. "Kevin isn't only wind. He's a man of action, and you were into action, shvesterlein. You were the action-faction. Kevin's a street fighter. Like falling in love with a police dog, but then, I don't see much in most men besides privilege and arrogance, or privilege and self-pity."

"Natalie . . ." She licked at the ice. "Do I have lousy taste in men?"

"Yep. Oh, wow, yes!" Natalie giggled. "I suppose a Freudian would say your own daddy was a real bummer so you think real men are real bummers."

"Well, Leigh isn't. Was that just blind luck?"

"He and I are on the outs. He's a smirking sexist. Listen . . . Peregrine, long after the truck drivers and construction workers are working side by side with women, male journalists and male writers of all stripes will be clinging to their contempt for women. They need that contempt. What else would most of them write about?"

They climbed a short neat hill with pines planted on the slope but not on the broad plateau which offered them a view of distant Bronx towers. "Maybe I shouldn't have relationships with men at all?"

"The one with Kevin might well give you cause to say that." Natalie wrinkled her nose. "Are you considering women? Or is it just that you lack suitors today?"

"I got one. I'm considering him."

"I should have guessed! I can't remember a day from the time we met you didn't have a man on tap."

"He isn't exactly on tap." She did not understand what compelled her to choose one man rather than another: to love Kevin more than Oscar; to run off with Vasos; to run off from him as vigorously and a whole lot more sensibly; to reject Pelican as a lover and relish Kevin. "Natty, be serious. Tell me what to do with my life. I've made such a mess I'm ashamed."

"You mean, the bombing?"

"No, the sex and love part." Vida bridled. "We've done okay down under. Survived and learned to strike hard and to communicate—"

"I think you could use a few lessons in basic conversational English for those doughy communiqués, actually."

"Actually, yes. I don't write them. I'm not allowed to. I don't grind out dense enough M.L. jargon."

"Peregrine . . . hold off. Don't jump into bed. Why leap from one man to another? Try to feel more complete in yourself. Try to draw some strength from the women around you. There are women, aren't there?"

"More than half of us are women. . . ." She mistrusted what commanded her love, what triggered her sexuality. Kevin had proved such a baldly bad choice, such a lingering foul mistake that she doubted herself through and through. Maybe Natalie was right. "I don't mean to break off with Leigh. I love him, but maybe I should try not to get into anything new and serious with a man. . . ."

"Why not stay clear altogether?"

Within reason, she thought, because her life was not exactly Natalie's. She thought of Lark and she did not know.

"Try." Natalie put a kiss on her finger and pressed it to Vida's nose. "You have the world's classiest nose."

Leigh too was thin, as thin as when she'd first met him. He fussed about his weight and dieted sporadically and broke his diet whenever anything especially tempted him, so that he was always somewhat dieting, but the truth was he looked better with some flesh on him. When he was thin, he looked not lithe but bony—the stoop-shouldered sallow intellectual rather than the Movement media star. His nose stood out like a request, and the request worked on her as guilt: she should be feeding him, she should be making him happy. One of the foundations of their marriage had surely been that both of them believed strongly that Leigh had a right to whatever he needed to make him happy and functional, so that he could get on with his important political work.

They made love in the motel bed violently, compulsively, too rapidly. She was left still wanting to hold him, but he moved back from her, eager to talk, blocked somehow. Patiently she probed for the knot. His hazel eyes focused as if on something hidden in her belly. "How could you go off with that shmuck?" he blurted out.

"Leigh, I'm not involved with him. I haven't slept with him in a year." It had been at least a couple of months.

"You'll go back to him."

She stroked the curly hair off his forehead. A metallic white hair shone over his ear. "Never. I detest him." Another hair gleamed and she plucked it, unable to resist.

"Ow! Why did you do that?"

"Look." She showed him the silver hair like a hook in her palm. "Isn't that beautiful?"

"I'm getting old. I'm falling apart. Why did you leave me?"

"I didn't!" Gently she shook him. "I'd never have left you. I'll never find another man I'd rather talk to my whole life."

"But you liked making love with him better?"

"Never," she lied bravely, remembering stickily that there had been a time when she certainly burned for Kevin. She had felt possessed by him as she never had by Leigh, obsessed. Not that Kevin made love better than Leigh; in fact, his ram-in, bang-on style did not wear well. But that very pain of their coupling had convinced her it was more real; pain was real, difficulty was real. Every step they took politically was harder, so what was hard and against the grain must be good. "Leigh, remember history! I didn't leave you. I was forced under. I had the choice of going to prison for thirty years or vanishing. This way, at least we're together sometimes."

"I'm glad you didn't go to prison," he said with such harsh vehemence she was startled. "It would've destroyed you too!"

Too? "You've seen Lohania? She's out? Is she living with you?"

"She's changed. Completely. She doesn't want to see me."

"Is she bitter about doing time?"

"I can't get far enough with her to find out. She doesn't even say she doesn't want to see me. She just doesn't show up when we make a date. Sometimes when I come over, I know she's behind the door but she won't answer. She makes excuses. . . . When I manage to be alone with her she tries to get me into bed as fast as possible, but I know she isn't feeling it . . . you know?''

"What's up?" She felt frightened. "What's she into politically? Does she have to keep her nose clean till she's off parole?"

"She's not supposed to go to meetings or join organizations. But she doesn't want to talk politics. . . . She's nervous. Jumpy."

"Lohania's always been high-strung."

"This is different. Something's broken. She's asked me questions I don't believe. Like she asked me right out if I see you. . . . I said No, before I even thought. People just don't ask those questions if they're a little political."

"Leigh, maybe she wants to see me. Maybe she needs me."

He shook his head. His mouth thinned. "I'm telling you. We'd just fucked. Practically a dry fuck. I knew she hadn't come, and I felt sick because she faked it. She never used to do that."

"Never. Lohania used to tell the truth even when it hurt. When I was mad at her, I'd think she'd do it especially when it hurt."

"She used to get mad when she didn't have an orgasm. Sometimes she'd make me feel guilty, like I was a real loser to let her down. . . . But anyhow, she was lying there examining her nails. . . .''

"What color? Oh, Leigh, I miss her."

"How do I remember what color? She said, 'Do you see Vida? Do you meet her?' The hair stood up on my nape."

"Leigh, she'd never hurt me. Next to Natalie, she was my best woman friend. We shared lovers, we shared our politics." She smiled. "Even our clothes."

"I'm telling you, I can't trust her."

She lay staring at the white motel ceiling, the neat moon of light cast by the lamp next to the bed. Sometimes when she was driving down a highway and saw a sign winking MOTEL she would think abruptly and painfully of Leigh. Now she must puzzle through Lohania. Finally she asked, "What's Randy Superpig doing these days?"

"He graduated law school. Working in the Kings County D.A.'s office."

"He initiated the plea bargaining for her, I know it. . . ."

Leigh frowned. "Haven't run into him in a long time. Not face to face since that demonstration where I caught him getting kids to burn cars and I confronted him and he knocked me down with a club. But I unmasked him in the *Roach*, and then he had to surface for Lohania's trial. Admit he was an agent." Reminiscently Leigh rubbed his head. "You think he's into Lohania somehow?"

"I'd look for him."

He plucked at his wiry beard. "No. Not Lohania."

"Is it easier for you to think she'd ask for information for the FBI than to believe Randy is running her?"

"Running her how?"

"That's for you to find out." She took his bearded face in her hands. "But Lohania isn't all that's eating you."

He let himself fall back against the heaped-up pillows. "Why, don't you know the news?" he asked rhetorically. "Just Friday I was ousted from the *Roach* collective. The women have taken it over and decided I'm not worth struggling with. . . . Things at the station are stagnant. Nobody listens to us. From a hundred thousand listeners we're down to ten fans, all phone-in freaks. Basically we provide a service for people who need to talk into a microphone."

"One thing at a time. You got kicked off *Roach?* But you helped start it!"

"So? Nineteen sixty-seven is ancient history to these kids. The women have gone crazy."

For a moment she was acutely uncomfortable, because she could hear Kevin saying the same thing two months before to Roger, who was traveling through on his way west: the women have all gone crazy. She was reminded enough of Kevin in the wail of outraged hegemony for her to remember Natalie's sour appraisal of Leigh. "Things are changing between men and women," she temporized. Of all things she did not want an argument with him. "A lot of even the slow changes hurt."

"Slow are they? Lucy and I called it off less than two months ago and now she's a rabid dyke. She stands across the room surrounded by her coven and glares at me. They look like a motorcycle gang—"

"Lucy's five feet four! You weren't . . . sympathetic when she thought she was pregnant."

"I won't be pushed. If I want something I know it. You didn't have to push me, did you? What crime is it not to live with somebody just because they think they want to latch on to you?"

"But if it wasn't a crime for you to want to live with me before I wanted to live with you—"

"I know what I want," he reiterated, angry. "I'm not going to let some . . . woman move in because we balled a few times."

. "But you went on working together on the editorial committee. You got on well enough for that."

"No, she was voted off. We couldn't work together."

"Leigh! She was voted off because you broke up with her? No wonder she's pissed. That was . . . not smart and not very political."

"I was the one who put her on."

"In 1968 you could get away with that," she said. "But it always made us mad."

"Us? Nobody ever put you on a committee for that. I bet breaking up with Kevin won't slow you down politically."

"We're on opposite sides of every issue." She realized he was flattering her, the exception, the perfect woman with whom all others shall be compared only to be found wanting. "But you're really off the *Roach?* Or just off the editorial committee?"

"If I don't have any say-so, why hang around?" Reaching toward the bedside table, he put on his glasses; it was as if he were no longer naked, as if the glasses were clothing. "I want to play you a program I aired last week. . . . I'm going to look for a mainstream job and let those losers hang!"

The tape was a report on the COINTELPRO penetration of the New Left by the FBI. Leigh read Hoover's directive: " 'The purpose of this program is to expose, disrupt, and otherwise neutralize the activities of the various New Left organizations, their leadership and adherents. . . . We must frustrate every effort of these groups and individuals to consolidate their forces or to recruit new or youthful adherents. In every instance, consideration should be given to disrupting the organized activity of these groups and no opportunity should be missed to capitalize upon organization and personal conflicts in their leadership.' "

"But in 1968 we weren't doing anything wrong. I mean anything violent. We were doing a lot of student organizing and regular big demonstrations and starting to have women's stuff, and that year we had our first demonstration about mass transportation and pollution and subway fares."

Leigh grinned at her. "They had you coming and going. Infiltrated, recorded, guilt-tripped." He flicked the On switch again and began to play her exposés and confessions by former agents. "The FBI paid for the dynamite caps which I brought into the defense office. I had volunteered for the committee in order to clandestinely and illegally rifle the files and report on the defense attorney's plans. I purchased chemicals for Molotov cocktails and taught a number of the youngsters how to manufacture them. I supplied one activist with a .22-caliber rifle. I passed out formulas for making explosives and incendiary devices. I was hoping to get people involved in this activity. All these actions were within FBI guidelines. The Bureau paid for my purchases." "Informers are contract employees paid on salary or on piecework, as they provide information. I was a special penetration agent. My duties also included fomenting dissension in the office—a task that was extremely easy."

After he had played the tapes she felt depressed, while he brightened up, listening to his own program. It was a good one. It was excellent. And several years too late.

"You were had," Leigh said.

"But think of all the money and manpower they spent on us. At least, they took us seriously. Hoover really thought we might change things."

He set his glasses back on the bedside table and leaned forward, resting his head against her shoulder. "Babes, I've been feeling kind of lost. I'm not getting support for making hard decisions about whether I should take a straight job or not. . . . Listen, with the heat dying some, think we could see each other regularly? Do you have to live so far away?"

"I can't risk New York, but it would mean the world to me if we could be together again. . . ." Tears stung her eyes. She was too critical of him; being with Kevin had hardened her into an adversary stance. "Have you forgiven me for ruining our lives? Maybe if I was nearby we could live together. Like an hour or two out of the city. Just a long commute."

"I miss you a hundred times a week. Every time I walk into the kitchen and see your pots hanging on the pegboard. Guess what: I'm hard again. I haven't had sex all week. All the women I know, they're lesbians or they're having babies. Maybe you could live in Queens?"

"I had in mind something a little farther." she smiled. "You may not think so, but that's still New York. . . . We'll be married again. We'll have a real life together. We'll eat together and sleep together and have a home and share our lives." Still smiling, she began to weep silently on his shoulder. "I'll make it happen, I promise!"

18

The Board met Sunday in a ski cabin Roger had rented for the weekend half an hour west of the farmhouse. Kiley had spent the night at the cabin with Roger. Vida and Lark had got back to Hardscrabble too late to do more than say good night to each other, turn in and then collect Kevin in the morning for their meeting.

Kiley was speaking, as precise and clear as always, yet electrifying. Vida experienced her appeal even as she wondered at it. Kiley's pale ash blond hair stood out in a modified Afro, an aura of exclamation marks. "And we must avoid the pitfalls of a tendency to left adventurism we have been sliding toward, pitfalls that can undermine our mass strategy." All that jargon, and yet her high eager voice galloped along passionate and cold, glinting like her ice blue eyes. Her forehead was high, smooth and pallid, her mouth small, her chin and nose narrow, her brows thin and angled out and down. Kiley was small and wiry, built like a well-coordinated little boy. Next to her at the round oak dining-room table, Vida felt oversized, cumbersome. She had long ago recognized that Kiley could plot rings around her. In a way, meetings of the BOD consisted of watching Kiley try to get her way politically among a minefield of hot smoking male egos and jealous hegemonies and massive differences tilting into each other like plates of the earth's crust, causing volcanic eruptions and earthquakes.

Only in the last year had Vida learned how ineffective she was in meetings, how often she missed the real portent of what was happening and charged off a cliff expecting agreement. She had come to know well that dreadful sense of space yawning under her after she had spoken. She had not the skill and patience to manipulate consensus beforehand. She relied heavily on being right. Kiley never made that mistake, and if they took to open warfare, she would want Kiley for general. She respected Kiley thoroughly: cool under fire, yet with a streak of pleasure in danger that carried her through like a racehorse going on spirit and nerves and the fine tune of its muscles rather than brute strength. Never had she seen Kiley panic. She could not say that about herself and she could not say it about Kevin. Kiley was simply not paranoid.

"Whenever I hear that left adventurist shit, I smell a dead rat," Kevin drawled. "Somebody turning yellow, all it ever means."

"The phrase comes from Lenin," Roger said brusquely, knocking out his pipe. She had never hung out much with Roger. He was a tall gangling, loose-limbed man Vida's age who had taught English in a high school in Seattle until the antiwar movement had roused him to take action that had finally driven him from his job, his wife, his two daughters. His daughters were growing up in Seattle, where his wife had married again, and Roger would always seem a little uprooted in their life. He was Kiley's lover. Probably the two leading theorists of the Network, they had been growing in influence as the frequency of bombings diminished that winter and the fugitives began to wonder what the hell they were doing with a mass movement becoming invisible.

". . . and I don't give a shit if Lenin carved it on a stone tablet, are we making a revolution or are we making paper?"

Experiencing a moment of déjà vu, Vida decided to speak. "Gee." She looked straight at Kevin. "That reminds me of Randy. Same damn rhetoric. Act now, pay later. Last one in's a coward. Hoopla, over the side and don't watch to see if anyone follows."

Kevin rose in his seat, the cords standing out in his neck. "Are you calling me an agent?"

"Of course not. I'm saying you didn't learn from our errors."

"Good point." Lark flexed his fingers, cracking his joints mechanically. "We must learn from our errors, all of us."

They were ganging up on Kevin: maybe he represented an earlier phase they were rejecting as vehemently as they had embraced it. Even the quarrels between the ex-lovers were held against Kevin as they might as easily, two years before, have been laid to her. Lark and Roger did not exactly share a style, but they were not street fighters. Lark was too influenced by the Vietnamese to charge around waving his prick. He wanted to speak quietly and persevere for the long haul. He thought of himself with pride as an organization man. What went on in Rhodesia and in Angola was as important to him as what happened in this room; distant battles fed and drained him. He read long articles on the latest ideas of

Kim Il Sung and Enver Hoxha. Since he had awakened in the hospital behind the lines minus a leg, he had viewed himself as a dead man. To a cause he had grown to despise he had given his leg; he would give his body, his mind, his life to a cause he respected. His personal life was only mortar between carefully fitted blocks of theory and practice.

Roger adopted a working-class style, dressing in baggy work clothes her father would never have been caught dead in when he wasn't lying under a truck. But Roger wrote poetry and read Neruda with more passion than the *Guardian*, and she had seen him stop dead in the street upon catching sight of a child with brown braids down her back, stop and swallow and swallow as his Adam's apple bobbed with pain. He watched sports programs with the other men as if it was a discipline he was forcing on himself; always when he talked about some basketball player, he sounded self-consciously folksy. In Seattle he had been beaten by the police in relays, handcuffed to a radiator and beaten unconscious. When he had come to, they had beaten him again. Six months later he had enjoyed placing the bomb himself. Of course, they called in a warning first, but the records went up, and Roger was satisfied.

"You're all turning yellow. Now, when we have them on the run, you're getting scared. You want to let the troops down!" Kevin was fighting, but not with his head. He pounded on the table, he threatened, used to getting his way; more used to it than anyone else at the table, because he had been king of the mountain at Hardscrabble and had become habituated to giving orders and being obeyed. Kevin had never been a member of SAW, a wildly democratic organization—passionately, agonizingly on all levels democratic—but the rest of them had. The four of them had been trained to argue for a position, to lose gracefully, plotting to rise again in a parliamentary motion, to compromise for support by accepting a friendly or even moderately hostile amendment, to shift support from one candidate to another and withdraw it behind the scenes. They were used to counting votes in their heads. That had been the purpose of sending Lark to Vermont and fetching her to New York. Lark had been feeling out the lie of the land. Kiley, Roger and Lark were allied against Kevin. Now would she be ousted from the Board?

". . . time for outreach," Roger was arguing. "We're not a military organization exclusively. We must put out propaganda. We must influence the direction the Movement is taking. In short, we have to work on our mass politics."

"Sitting on our ass makes us more of a mass," Kevin sneered. "People respect us because we act."

"People mostly have forgotten us," Vida said coldly. "They're worried about Nixon and making a living and getting laid off and welfare cutbacks and losing food stamps and prices still going whoopee."

"Fuck them, we'll make them remember us." Kevin stood, his face shining. "Why draw in our horns? It's time to strike at the heart. People's justice—suppose we offed Nixon?"

"We've never injured a person, never," Vida said. "I don't think ordinary people respect assassinations. All they think is, Jesus, one more gun-happy nut. People are sick of assassinations. I'm sick of assassinations. It's always the right that does it, anyhow. Why borrow their rotten weapons?"

"We broke with old forms of terror," Kiley said icily, "because of our analysis. Attacks directed at leaders are individualistic. They further the myth that presidents make history rather than executing the policy of the corporate ruling class."

"We've aimed our attacks at corporations—the invisible government," Vida argued. "Every time we attack IT and T or Union Carbide, we make them visible. We define their crimes. We've always made a sharp distinction between the corporate enemy and employees." For a moment she heard Jimmy saying those words. She had not seen him since she and Lark had got back from New York with Kiley.

"We've never tried to do significant damage," Lark said. "Why should we? Our aims are political. Blowing up one liquid-gas tanker or storage facility or a gas pipeline would make an incredible mess out of a city—someday that'll happen through corporate stupidity and corner cutting. But they're *our* cities."

She was helping things along without a clear notion exactly what was afoot. A deep and thorough shift in Network policy was being effected by Kiley, Roger and Lark. They must have decided the Network was isolating itself from aboveground politics. The women's movement had shaken them. The disappearance from public view of the New Left worried them. They were responding, too, to discontent in the organization; she was sure of that. If Alice cried in Lark's arms that she didn't know what they were doing, many must feel the same. She found those fears in herself, but she had thought she was alone in doubting.

"I think what's been going on is that most of us in the Network are secretly scared we don't know what we're doing anymore," she said slowly, nervously. Kiley could mow her down, but the time had come to speak truth to each other. "We go on bombing. We're better at it. But the purpose is lost. The war's almost over, the Vietnamese are finally winning. We have to get back to work building an indigenous movement. We have to change or we're relics. Remember that fossils are also located underground."

Roger actually smiled. "I agree. We need to have an impact again. Repeating ourselves, the sixtieth bombing, is to persist in what we do only because we've learned to do it well—"

"We need direction," Kiley said briskly. "And I think we need a BOD weighted toward analysis. We need to put out a document that will move us forward. Jesse, you're out of touch politically. Perhaps you've been leadership too long. Cadre is cadre because it serves the people. The arrogance of power is beginning to cloud your judgment."

Vida realized at the same moment as Kevin did that he was being ousted from the Board. She felt like giggling, and yet she was astounded and even frightened. Kevin had been leadership from the first day they had run upstate, the first night they had slept in a car Kevin had stolen. A BOD without Kevin was inconceivable. Kevin, Kiley and Lark had been the original and lasting power figures from that cold night in Pennsylvania when they had begun to forge the Network. From the time they had met during a full-scale armed manhunt into which the government had thrown hundreds of agents and millions of dollars, when their Wanted posters had adorned every post office until supporters tore them down, Kiley had been the brains; Lark, the conscience; Kevin, the energy, the fist. Vida felt too startled to speak. She was disqualified by personal rancor, and yet she was not as pleased as she would have expected.

Slowly Kevin rose, towering over them. "What are you motherfuckers trying? I am the Network! You can't sneak around behind my back. Don't get funny with me. Vida's behind this!" he roared.

"Wrong as usual," Lark said almost amiably. "We didn't take her into our confidence. We have the votes." He put a pile of petitions on the table. "The membership's behind us. Eva's been elected."

"Eva! That dumb dyke!"

"We agreed to support gay liberation," Roger said. "That's what's wrong! You've become increasingly individualistic. You've encouraged a cult around you. You need to spend more time with the rank and file and pay more heed to the line we hammer out."

"We have a majority of women," Vida said wonderingly, wishing she could tell Natalie. See, that would show her sister they were changing; but Board membership was secret.

Only Kiley heard and glared at her as Kevin bellowed, "I'm not getting off! We'll see who the troops really support!"

"You're off, as of right now." Lark also stood. He was six inches shorter than Kevin and weighed half as much, but he stood up without hesitating, without diffidence. "You've been voted off and you're off. No one has a *right* to be leadership—no one! We earn it by being responsible revolutionaries. We keep it from the trust of those we lead. You've lost that trust."

Kevin clenched his fist and took two steps toward Lark. Kiley rose in his path, tiny and furious. "What do you think you're doing?"

He stopped. Then he picked up a chair and threw it at Lark, who ducked. It slammed into the wall.

"If you don't leave the meeting, you'll be thrown out of the organization as well as the Board," Roger said quietly as he stood also, facing Kevin.

Vida did not believe the threat, but Kevin shouted, "You can't throw me out! I'm quitting! And you'll come on your bellies to me begging me back before the month is over!" He slammed out.

The silence was complete for several minutes. "If he really quits," Roger muttered, "could be awkward. He knows a great deal."

"He's shooting off his mouth," Kiley said, sitting down firmly and reaching for her pen. "A fugitive alone is a sitting duck."

"I wouldn't care to see him arrested," Roger continued. "We should send a delegate after him to soothe the battered ego and get him to back down from what has to be an uncomfortable position. Peregrine, how about you pour oil on the troubled waters?"

"He already tried to stick a knife into her this week," Lark said. "I'm afraid you'll have to go after him yourself, Roger, as the one he has the least against. We should fetch Eva from the farmhouse and resume tomorrow in full session of the new BOD Agenda: new priorities. Relationships to liberation struggles abroad. Relationships to liberation struggles inside this country: Black, Puerto Rican, Chicano, Native American. Union organizing and strikes. Oh, and women."

"And gay," Vida said.

"We'll have to soft-pedal that for international consumption," Lark said. "Peregrine wants to leave Vermont. I'm not even sure Eva should remain. It seems to have been a hotbed of political inactivity. People come up to this farm and vegetate."

"The whole BOD ought to be active in the field," Kiley said briskly. "We aren't in the business of growing cabbages and potatoes. Peregrine has not taken any political initiatives or carried out tasks of leadership since the last action. You aren't on the BOD as decoration, you know."

I hate that stupid name, Peregrine, she thought; she had found it romantic-sounding that first year, when Kevin had taken Jesse for Jesse James. Roger and Eva had the names they had first used underground; Kiley's name came off a building, probably in ironic reaction. Lark kept his previous made-up name. "I don't mean to be," she said evenly, wanting to give Kiley a hard kick. "Fighting with Kevin has drained my energies, and we've been locked in political battle inside the house."

"I'll stay for a while," Lark volunteered. "I'll straighten up the house before I go back to Buffalo. I could use Perry there. A lot is happening."

Kiley lowered one of her thin sharply angled eyebrows. "Interesting. But I think we should spread our cadre more widely. I was about to suggest Philadelphia, where we could use some intelligent liaison with local groups. Also, there's a fight about women's issues that needs mediating among our people.''

"Buffalo or Philadelphia—which do you prefer?'' Roger asked.

"Wherever I'd be most useful,'' she said humbly, keeping her eyes on Kiley and ignoring Lark's glance of appeal. Nobody here knew how involved she was with Leigh and how involved she wanted to be. Philadelphia was only two hours away from him. They could even live together again and her real life would resume.

She did not want to become involved with Lark, she knew it through and through; she only wanted to keep him from guessing her decision. "I haven't been effective politically. I've let personal turmoil cloud my judgment. I want to make it up.'' She sounded humbly fervent, and she was not lying. She was truly ashamed of how little she had used her leadership role. She also guessed that Lark would take her decision at face value. After all, he had not made any overt suggestions that they become more intensely involved; he had expected working together to accomplish that for him, and he was not accustomed to examining personal motives closely. She thought of his face as he pushed away his plate after eating a little mound of rice and a few brussels sprouts; she saw him in the car cracking his knuckles and staring grimly ahead. No! She saw Leigh toasting her in the squat motel glasses, the wine red as his lips against his curly beard. Yes. She wanted to be free of sexual entanglements and she wanted Leigh, both, passionately and at once. Free in Philadelphia but secretly married to New York.

Roger went ahead to reason with Kevin, but when the rest of them arrived at Hardscrabble, they walked into a house turned upside down. Kevin was leaving. He had loaded the black Dodge with his few things. Belinda, Jimmy and Bill were going with him.

"I won't let you take the baby!'' Marti said, arms folded on her ample bosom. "You've all gone crazy.''

"Leave her,'' Kevin ordered. "We'll have to travel light till we knock over a couple banks. We'll come back for her by summer.''

"I can't leave her,'' Belinda wailed. "I can't!''

"You can't take a baby along,'' Kevin said. "Come or stay, but you can't do the kind of fighting we have up the road with a kid on your back.''

"She's just a baby, Belinda,'' Marti said stubbornly. "She'll get sick. She'll be scared. She'll miss me. She'll miss the other kids.''

Belinda stood with stooped shoulders, worrying folds of her army jacket in her gaunt hands. She could not move from the front hall. She looked from one to the other and down again. Bill was sitting in the Dodge, warming it up. Vida knew he was running off with Kevin because he was angry at Alice for deciding to get an abortion, but he would not admit that was his reason. Alice sat on the stairway weeping.

"Jimmy!" Vida took him by the arm. "Why are you going? Why? Kevin's not right!"

Jimmy was smiling a wan twisted smile. His gaze stayed on Kevin, who held himself aloof in the doorway with a casual yet military bearing. Kevin looked less crazy, less crazed. He was jaunty poised there, burning with energy. He did not bother putting pressure on his comrades to stay or go. She felt a flash of the old attraction. It was not right for him to go off! Something had gone awry here. Or maybe it was right for Kevin to go and right for her to go with him: almost she felt that. Inaction had poisoned them both. They had scapegoated each other for their impotence. He was using the fight in the Board to pull free of an apparatus that was holding them back. She felt a burning of sorrow in her throat, yet she could not speak. She still wanted to be free of him.

"Jimmy, why are you going?" she whispered, turning his face so that he would look at her with his mild brown eyes.

"He needs me," Jimmy said softly. "If he can't have you with him, by him, at least he has me. I do, sometimes."

"Jimmy, don't sacrifice yourself!"

His lips jerked, and the awkward smile deepened. "Why not?"

What had happened here in her absence? She doubted if anyone but Kevin or Jimmy could tell her. Jimmy was not angry at her, but he was closed to her in some new and final way. He had given himself over to Kevin absolutely. She remembered the feeling of that abandonment, and involuntarily she let go of Jimmy's shoulder.

Jimmy stepped past her and took hold of Belinda, still fingering her coat, crouched over. "Come on, pal, let's get moving. We'll show all these jerks what guerrilla action is. We'll show everybody."

Belinda let herself be tugged along. "I'm coming back in the summer!" she called over her shoulder to Marti. "Take care of Roz. I'm coming back for her by summer!"

By summer only Bill had returned, and Jimmy and Belinda were dead.

PART VII

The Present, November

19

A woman in muslin pajamas whose head was shaved admitted Joel and Vida, telling them in a little voice to be seated on cushions in the room decorated mainly with posters about the Master Sajarahata of the Holy Darkness. Joel raised his eyebrows at her. She was having misgivings herself. The last time she had seen Brenda—in 1975—Eva and she had been traveling through Cleveland together. Brenda had been married to a big surly accountant whose passion was a refurbished Harley-Davidson. Brenda was no longer political but was happy to see them. She introduced them to her husband as her old college roommate (Eva) and her former teacher (Vida).

Brenda had been living in Shaker Heights and taking care of her six-month-old child. Her only outside activity was a Chinese cooking class at the high school one evening a week, and she was delighted to see them, more out of boredom than out of any sense of what they were doing as fugitives. She loved having two women home with her during at least part of every day to share child care and housework and above all, to talk to. At that time, Vida had been in between well-established identities and had used her general Movement pseudonym Peregrine or Perry. In the intervening years Natalie had received several change-of-address cards from Brenda and had passed along the new addresses to Vida. This address had turned out to be a two-story house on a residential block in Cleveland Heights.

Whining music came from below, and a smell of frying oil made the air heavy. An older man with shaven head, dressed in a long unbleached robe and clasping his hands before him, took up lotus position on a mat facing both of them. "You wish to see our sister who was called Brenda Warburton?"

That was Brenda's married name. "I'm an old friend of hers. From college," Vida said, beginning to get an uneasy prickling sensation along her skin. "Peregrine Nash. Doesn't she remember me?"

"We haven't asked her yet."

"Would you mind?" Joel flashed his brightest smile. "We're only passing through Cleveland."

"And what kind of relations did you have with our sister Brenda while she was in the world?" The bald man made a steeple of his hands. He spoke as if English were a foreign language; yet she did not think so. Kick him and he'd curse in fluent Cleveland American, she was sure.

"Me?" Joel hesitated, unsure whether he should claim to know Brenda or not. "I never met her. Peregrine's her friend."

"You are not from her ex-husband, Frederick Warburton?"

The biker. "No," Vida assured him. "I'm a friend of Brenda's only. Er, are you Master Sajarahata? Brenda and I have been friends since 1967."

"Our Master is in New Delhi," the bald man said. "We are only the poorest of the ashrams that study His way. What *kind* of friends?"

She glanced at the exit nervously. "Not extremely close. But good friends for many years." What was this?

"You were lovers?"

"No," she said, barely suppressing a smile. Brenda had been almost tediously heterosexual, loving a series of large and macho men—Bob Rossi, a lump named El Ratón and the biker.

"Our way does not encourage such attachments, and often those who come seeking our sisters and brothers are those bound to them by old chains of sensuality and ignorance."

"This is my wife," Joel said.

"I see." The bald man rose gracefully. "Sorry if I have offended you. I will find out if our sister wishes to see you."

When he left the room, a girl, also with shaven head, brought them a plate of flat wheaten breads and chick-pea mash, which they ate greedily. "Should we get out of here?" she whispered.

"It don't look good," he muttered back. "No money here."

"Come on, let's get out." She rose. "I'm afraid she may decide to save us."

"One second." He scooped up the rest of the chick-peas on the flat bread and rolled it into a napkin provided them. "Picnic by the side of the highway. The romantic swoosh of diesel trucks, the scent of burning rubber."

VIDA

As they turned to flee, a woman waddled in, looking round as a beach ball in muslin pajamas. It took Vida a long moment to recognize the beach ball as Brenda, bald and grossly overweight. Her face was moonlike in shape and pallor. Where was her child? Vida was afraid to ask. Shaved and bound someplace? With the biker? Probably with Brenda's long-suffering mother in Jersey. "But Vida, wait!" Brenda howled, as Vida did recognize her voice and broke into a trot, leaping over the cushions. "I have to talk to you!" Fumbling with the door, Joel got it open, and they rushed through. "Come back! I've found peace and tranquillity. Inner peace! No more drugs! Vida! Vida Asch! Come back and listen to me!"

They ran into the snow where their old car, Mariah, was parked at the curb. For a moment the engine would not start. Brenda appeared in the open doorway to wave eagerly to them, beckoning them back. The woman who had served them leaned around her, giggling behind her hand. Since Brenda was barefoot she did not come outside, but waved wildly, shouting something. As the ignition finally caught and they barged off sluggishly in a wake of badly combusted oil, Brenda was still beckoning hopefully.

"Where the hell do we go now? It's 9 P.M. Who else do you know in Cleveland? Anybody who's really crazy?"

"I'm scared about hanging around. Do you think they got a good look at the car?" She wrung her hands nervously. "I have a headache."

"She's enough to give you one. Calling you by name out loud. Where's she at? I don't think anybody looked at the car. Where to now?"

"I know a guy, if he's still around . . . Mason, he was called. He camped out in my living room for a month while he was in New York. Let's see, I heard he went back to school . . . in social work—that's it. He was going to social-work school in '75. Next phone we see, let me try."

"I better keep the engine running. The battery's dying. We've put a couple of thousand miles on the car already, so we can't complain of the old darling. But she needs some help, and that means time and money and tools." He let her out at a pay phone.

Mason was in the phone book, but when she dialed his number, intending to hang up if he was home and go over to scout, she got a recording saying that the number had been changed. Moved, probably. Nothing to do but call the new number and talk to him on the phone. "Hello, is Mason home?"

"This is he speaking. Who's this?" A little flirtatious.

Difficult moment. "Why, Mason, once you slept on my living-room floor for a month. . . . Do you remember . . . Peregrine?"

"Your *floor?*"

"In 1968. In the fall, in New York." Come on, slowpoke. Connect a little. "On the Upper West Side."

"Holy shit! Oh, my god. Oh, no!" He hung up.

She stared at the buzzing phone. Gee, thanks, Mason. I hope your teeth fall out right now, one at a time and starting in front.

"That was a ringer," she said. "He hung up on me."

"Well, imagine you answer the phone some dumb night. You're drinking Colt 45 malt liquor and feeling like a he-man watching the Browns on the TV and suddenly the phone rings. Hi, there, it's me, Jesse James. Thought I'd come by with the boys and hang around your living room. Don't worry, the posse's at least a mile behind and we can take them easy. We'll put the horses in the john."

She laughed and felt better. "That exhausts my Cleveland contacts. I know somebody in Cincinnati. . . ." She thought of Saul and Dee Dee embedded there with good I.D., real jobs. She envied them because they had come underground as a couple and they were still a couple. They never seemed to get lonely or strung out.

"Listen, we got to score soon. The car's in trouble. The battery's dying. We got less than fifteen bucks, and every time I look at the dash, the gauge sings out Fill me up again." He took out the napkin gooey with chick-pea mash. "Let's eat!"

"In four days I contact the Network." She pushed away the proffered food, feeling nauseated.

"Sure, they're rolling in dough. We need a plan. Listen, nothing is easier to steal than cars. I mean, they got wheels, you just get in and off you go. Always a market for newish Caddies and Lincolns. You run them south."

She chewed her nails, then stopped, feeling age ten. She had a moment of fearing Joel would suddenly turn into Kevin. Money. That was always the sticking point. "Going into New York makes me nervous as hell . . . but we can come up with money there."

"Oh. From Leigh? A reverse wedding present?"

"My love, I know a lot more people there than Leigh! I lived in Manhattan most of my adult life. Somebody will tide us over, and I bet we can pick up a job. Contact the Network and report in. . . . It just makes me nervous."

"Not eating makes me nervous." Joel licked his fingers, searching for the last taste of their last food. "All we need is for our car to break down. From now on, no money for anything but gas till we hit New York."

"Then we're going there? If only the car didn't drink gas."

"Baby, we're lucky to have Mariah. Don't knock her. Yeah, why not? I've never been there for longer than overnight. The Big Apple. Why do they call it that? Like, L.A. is just about as big, right? Only it don't have a center. Why be scared of New York?''

They had another flat in Pennsylvania, near Harrisburg. They stayed off the turnpikes, but there was no free way from New Jersey into Manhattan. Every dollar hurt. They were both exhausted past safety. Vida was driving, and whatever Joel said, whether it was Turn left at the end of the ramp or Hang a right, struck her as intolerable meddling. They were snapping at each other till she wanted to burst into tears, but a voice in the back of her head knew it was fatigue and they must plod through safely to a haven and sleep.

"They drive like maniacs," Joel said, giving the finger to a cab.

"No. That's Boston," she said wearily. "It's precision here. They drive like manics." Nevertheless, at 6 A.M. she must find her way across Manhattan to Brooklyn. When she had told Natalie she could not trust Hank Woodruff to put her up again if she had to visit New York, Natalie had given her the address of Pelican Bob and Jan, who were married and living in Park Slope in Brooklyn. Natalie had not seen Pelican and Jan in a while, but had felt sure they would take Vida in. Natalie had been supposed to check the idea out with them, and it occurred to Vida that she had no idea if Natalie had ever managed to do that. You didn't exactly call an acquaintance and say on the phone, Hey, how would you feel about putting up a fugitive now and again for a couple of days? My sister wanted to know. Natalie and Jan had stayed in touch ever since they had been in that rap group together. Vida could still see the circle of women.

Joel had dozed off, his head fallen on his shoulder, his mouth open. He looked beautiful to her with two days' stubble on his face and his eyelids swollen with fatigue. She was feverish—she felt it. When she looked sideways, the corners of her eyes hurt. She could feel fever burning in her mouth and forehead, her hands dry and throbbing on the wheel. She had to concentrate on every movement. Push the brake in. Let your foot up. Kick the gas. She felt as if she were reaching through some thickened sludge to the gears, the brake pedal, through air turned to warm mud.

Over the Manhattan Bridge and up Flatbush, on and on toward the park. As she finally passed Grand Army Plaza, she woke Joel.

"Listen, love," she said. "I don't know how this is going to be."

"What? Where are we?" But he couldn't listen to the answer.

Always she was astonished how slowly he woke. In an earlier life she had wakened groggily, lain long in bed and gradually stirred, but years as a fugitive had honed her nerves to the first faint sound. She could not understand how Joel had preserved his youthful somnolence. Perhaps he had never been hunted as she had in the first months after they had bolted, pursued from temporary shelter to shelter one jump ahead of the FBI, the police, the red squads. She had no transitional state of sleepiness, but came directly from sleep into utter wariness like a cat, like a fox.

By the time she turned onto 3rd Street he was barely awake, yawning sonorously. Around the corner from the address Natalie had given her, long since memorized, she left the car running and got out, motioning Joel to slide over. "I'll see if they're home. If they're willing." She stood in the street with a pasted-on smirk meant to give reassurance. "If so, I'll be right back. If I come running, be prepared to get us out of here fast."

It was 7:35 on November 20, her Timex said, under a streaked gray sky, with the temperature just above freezing. The streets were clear of snow, although gray wedges of ice compacted with grit lay along the north sides of buildings. The street was lined with brownstones, the stoops lined up in a gray row coming down into the tiny front yards except where renovation had produced an apartment-style ground-level entrance.

The number from Natalie matched a fading number high above a thick windowless door. The steps were cracked, but in the middle of the wee lawn someone had planted a rhododendron whose washed-out tag proclaimed it Blue Peter. Its base was bound in burlap, giving it the look of being partially and badly dressed, like a poodle in rags. She tried to peer up at the parlor-floor windows, but the shutters were drawn tight. The names on the mailbox of the ground-floor apartment, reached by a brick path between stoop and rhododendron, were S. and B. Williams. She felt a pang of dismay. Maybe they'd moved.

She climbed the stoop. Only one mailbox outside. This town house was only three stories in all. The upper two floors must be a duplex. The names were Hamilton and Sforza. She moaned aloud with relief: Pelican and Jan. Leaning her ear to the massive old door, she pressed the bell. Couldn't hear a thing. Again she thumbed the bell, wondering if it was working. Next door a man was starting his car. If everything was all right, she could run to fetch Joel and he could grab the parking space. Already she was slipping into New York mode. A parking space first, everything else later.

Nobody seemed to be home. In despair she leaned on the buzzer, banging it vengefully. Was it working at all? Maybe they'd left town early for Thanksgiving. Where now? She could not think of an alternative. Suddenly the shutter moved in the window and a man's face glared at her. "Pelican!" she yelled, waving. He went on glaring at her. She mimed begging and pointed to the door. He slammed the shutter closed and she waited, leaning on the bell. Come on, you lazy bum, let me in!

At length he unlocked the door, glaring over the chain. "Who the hell are you? What do you want? I'm sleeping."

"It's not that early, Pelican. Let me in. I think you can recognize me if you try. Please."

He went on glaring; then suddenly he did recognize her. "Oh!" He did not say her name. Quickly he fumbled at the bolt and chain, opened the door and drew her inside, shutting it again. "What do you want? I mean . . . Jesus, you almost . . . Am I still asleep?"

"No, it's great to see you." Lightly she kissed him. He had put on some weight and looked all the better for it. His hair was medium short, just below his ears, rumpled with sleep. His glasses, shoved on crooked, were caught in his fine brown hair. "I need a place to sleep, and a mutual friend suggested you and Jan."

"Who? Of course. Come on in."

"Is it really all right? I'm with a friend. He's in the car, around the corner."

"Yeah—I'm just a little blown away. Do you live in New York?"

She shook her head no. "Is Jan home?"

"It'll be fine with her. She's sleeping. She can sleep through anything. . . . If you hadn't leaned on the bell so long I'd never have got up. I didn't climb in bed till an hour ago."

"How come such a night bird? Look, I'll go back and get my friend. We've been driving all night ourselves."

"I work at Kings County, in a geriatric ward. I'm a nurse."

She fetched Joel in time to seize the parking space next door. All she wanted to do as they stumbled inside was sleep, but Pelican was already scrambling eggs and making toast. Joel was starving. She was burning, too dry with fever to eat, but she said nothing because she wanted to settle in before she admitted she was sick. She did not know if the nurse really wanted to come home to a sickroom. Besides, if she only got some sleep, she'd be fine . . . fine . . . fine.

"What is it, Vida?" Pelican was staring at her.

"Don't call me that. Vinnie. Please." Then she blacked out.

When she woke or came to, she was on a couch upstairs in what was normally Jan's study. Jan was in medical school, and the room was full of books and papers, with a big chart from *Gray's Anatomy* on the wall showing the nervous system of the human body. The sheets, the quilt were soaked with sweat; her hair was plastered to her. Her flesh steamed. She felt too weak to get up. Joel was watching a small TV, lying on his stomach and eating potato chips. She knew she had been out all day because Walter Cronkite was talking about the Middle East.

"Yeah, they seem like nice folks," Joel said. "Settled, but nice. You know they own this house?"

"Really? Own it?" Her tongue was stuffed with feathers.

"Yeah. When they got married, Jan's dad gave them the down payment. They're buying it. Planning to remodel. It wouldn't be half bad. Not as big as it looks—two rooms down, two up, a bath on each floor. The fixtures are from back when but you could fix it up nice if you worked on it."

Now he wants a brownstone. "Do you feel safe here?"

"They seem cool about us. Pleased, even. I think they're too busy to entertain much. We're excitement. Jan had to be kept from waking you to talk. . . . I been carrying the ball."

"Thank you." She sank back. "I'm thirsty." She had a ridiculous desire to weep. Indeed, as Joel padded off barefoot to get some orange juice, fat tears ran along her nose. She did not question them. She waited in timeless limbo for the juice, drank it and fell back asleep.

The pipe bomb in the handbag began to tick as she was crossing the slippery floor, newly waxed and shining, ticking louder and louder. She knew the officers at the desks could hear it, the tocking ringing in her ears, but they did not look up. Each was sitting with an earpiece on, typing directly into a computer; they glanced sideways at her as she slid along the aisle, heading for the master computer behind glass doors. But she kept slipping. Her feet would not move. Not fast enough. It was going to go off early. Something was wrong with the mechanism. It was going to go off at any minute in her purse, killing her and the others. Ahead somewhere she knew Ruby was waiting for her. Behind the computer room she could hear the sounds of domestic battle, muffled in the night. She must get to Ruby, get to her and pull her out, but the computer was making time run faster and faster, so the bomb was screeching now like a bomb falling in a movie. . . .

Thanksgiving she sat up. Joel and Pelican had shopped, and now Pelican and Jan were off to New Jersey to spend two days with her parents and the rest of her Italian clan. Vida could scarcely call to mind what Jan looked like now, she had so little recollection of the past days. Her first adventure consisted of sitting in the living room watching the beginning of a detective movie on the color TV while Joel cooked his chicken dish. She was sick and Ruby was sick; it seemed right that they should be sick together. They were attuned root to root. Sleepily, feverishly, she thought that as she got better, Ruby would improve. She was getting sick to help Ruby and she would magically make Ruby better with her. She stayed up long enough to eat.

"Do you want to watch the little TV?" Joel asked as he changed the sheets, damp again from her sweating, and tucked her in.

"I can't remember anything I saw before, so what's the use?"

. . . "Jimmy," she said, shaking him. "Jimmy!" But the top of his head was missing. Inside was black and sticky, like burned cereal, she thought, and let him fall back. She was crawling on her belly among the burning wreckage, the fallen roof, the smoldering timbers of the house. When she saw the next body, she could not turn it over. She could not. She did not want to see. She kept crawling. Somebody was moaning. Somebody still must be alive in the wreckage, if she kept crawling and could get to them. But when she came to the protruding bloody leg and dug at the rubble with her hands, uncovering first the torso and then the broken head, it was Jimmy again. The top of his head blown away. The burst jellies of his eyes. She could not bring him to life or escape from him. Then she heard footsteps coming on the rubble, wavering. . . .

Gradually as the weekend passed she stayed conscious more, as pieces of their situation began to return to her. Joel was sleeping on the floor in his sleeping bag. She knew she was something of a nuisance, occupying Jan's study, but Jan seemed to survive studying in the bedroom. She became aware that Joel was working hard to make himself useful. He cooked several meals—his chicken again, lasagne, spaghetti —took out the garbage, shopped, did the dishes every night, carried the laundry off to Seventh Avenue to be washed. She was aware she had surrendered to inertia. She welcomed the flu that Pelican told her she had. Her body ached, she sweated, she coughed and wheezed, she was miserable and yet content to be ill. Here in the heart of the enemy camp she had collapsed to let her will recuperate. She was in no hurry to get back on the road. She wanted to relinquish, to be taken care of, to remain passive.

"Listen." Joel drew up a chair to the couch. "Our problems are over. I'm getting us money."

"You got a temporary job?"

"Only me and a million others are looking for that. . . . No, I got a great deal cooking."

"What kind of a deal?" Gasping for breath, she sat up. Suddenly she remembered Ruby. She had let them all go—Natalie, Leigh, Ruby, Paul.

"I got a chance to make three, maybe four hundred."

"What kind of a deal?" she repeated.

"A little snow."

"Cocaine."

"Pretty good, too. My friend Mel gave me a snort."

"Who is Mel?" She straightened her back. Her side stabbed, but she set her feet on the floor.

"I have friends in New York too, see. You think you're the only one with friends in the Big Apple, but I know him from Berkeley."

"Friends in the drug trade." She felt a flash of anger at having to come back to life. She was not ready to resume the work of living; but she must.

"Don't be supermoral. You smoke dope. What's wrong with coke?"

"That world swims with narcs. We can't afford to deal with drugs— we can't take those risks."

"The battery's dead in the car. We need a new battery. Pelican and I have to shove Mariah across the street to keep her from being towed. How many times can we do that? We're running on our spare. When another tire goes, we've had it. We need money, we need it now."

"Money won't help if they catch us. No more of those friends, Joel. We can't afford them."

"It's just acting as courier. Running a shipment to Springfield and another to Worcester. Nothing could be simpler."

"Don't call them again. Don't get in touch. Don't see them. Just hope they didn't trace you here."

"Not a chance."

"Many chances." She rose, had a spasm of coughing and sat again, her knees giving way. "I better start eating." From that moment she began to recover. She fought her weakness, but her convalescence dragged on. She could not stay out of bed for more than two or three hours before she had to lie down again for an hour; further, she was still running a low-grade fever. She began to want to leave the house, but Jan had objections. Finally Vida focused on her. Jan's hair was brown, as it had begun to be in Natalie's old consciousness-raising group, but it was waved becomingly around her face. She was more confident in her mannerisms, louder and jollier in her voice. Now she wore sweaters and tweedy pant suits and looked healthy and brisk in them. Jan was in her third year of medical school and had begun hospital work.

"V . . . Vinnie, you can't march around Park Slope. Half the old New York Movement live around here. No chance somebody won't recognize you."

"You don't think I look different by now?"

"Sort of . . . but then you stare, and if you stare enough, you figure it out. . . . Joel can go out. But you have to stay in the house."

"Jan, I'm going to have to borrow money from you to get our car fixed. If I can't walk out of the house, we're going to have to get the car fixed before I can get us on our feet financially. . . . There are people I have to see."

"Borrow our car. I go into Manhattan on the subway. Bob needs it for work, but he's on night shift. During the day, borrow it. . . . I'd loan you money if I could, but we've been sinking every penny into the house just paying off the mortgage. We're a couple of months behind on the bills. . . . Once I'm through school, we'll have less of a problem, but in the meantime I spend rather than earn. . . . So we're short. If my father didn't help us, we couldn't make it month to month."

Both Pelican and Jan were always telling her, as if they were still arguing with themselves, how important it was for political people to go into health care. Pelican as a nurse seemed more secure; Jan as a potential doctor, more nervous and eager to justify her choice. After breakfast with Jan, Joel drove Vida into Flatbush, where she found a booth. She could not yet drive. Even walking to the parked car exhausted her, and she lay back against the seat of Jan and Bob's orange Honda. Calling Leigh felt onerous but she had to get money from him. In the whole last year she had had only about three hundred sixty from him. That hardly represented a strain on his finances. What would he say about his marriage? Would he assume she knew? She dreaded the moment she heard his voice, her heart thumping in her throat. She had not told Joel she was calling Leigh, because she lacked the strength for an argument.

She called the first of the numbers. It rang and rang. She checked her watch. Should have called Time this morning to set it exactly. Then she tried the other number. After it had rung about seven times, she heard it answered. "Leigh?" she burst out.

"Lady, you got the wrong number. This is a fucking pay phone." The man slammed down the receiver.

Shit. She waited five minutes by her watch. Then she knew she was past ten. He was punctual usually; what could be holding him up? She dialed the first number again, and again it rang and rang until she did not dare let it ring longer. She waited two more minutes and dialed the second. It was answered on the third ring. "Get off of here," the same voice said. "You bozos are ringing into a pay phone."

Three more times she tried the first number. Then it was a full quarter after the hour of ten and she knew that Leigh had not made the rendezvous. That was the first time he had ever missed an appointment with her. Once when they were to meet he had not shown up because he was being followed, but never had he failed a phone connection. Now she could do nothing but wait till the next day and try again, same time, same numbers. She dreaded more confrontations with the loud nut who kept answering the second number. Attracting that kind of attention was dangerous. Why wasn't Leigh on the spot? Because of heat? Trouble? Or was he backing out? She found herself shaking, but she did not know whether it was with fear or with anger as she stumbled back to the orange Honda and Joel.

"Jan . . ." She cleared her throat. "I wonder if you could call my sister Natalie? I have to find out how my mother's doing."

Jan's full face grew long with some suppressed reaction. "How can I call her?"

"Really, it's all right. Don't say anything about me. Just ask about my mother. Ask if the appointment for next Monday can go in the other direction. Have you got that?"

"But—Natalie's in jail. . . . I thought you knew."

"In jail?"

"They gave her immunity, and when she wouldn't testify, they cited her for contempt. Her lawyer's appealing on some fancy ground that the whole grand jury's illegal, but she sure is inside. I thought you knew. Joel does."

He had been protecting her in her chosen isolation. "No, he didn't tell me."

Jan patted her arm. "He loves you a lot. He's much nicer than Kevin, that you ran off with."

"I didn't run off with Kevin any more than I ran off with Jimmy. We just ran. We had to."

"Of course, Leigh's a wonderful speaker. But he's a little cold. You know."

She could not resist asking, "Did you go to their wedding?"

"No. Leigh's a bit of a star. When he was doing that series on health care, he called us for some leads, but it wasn't social. . . . I never met her. I saw them together at a big benefit party."

"Is she pretty?"

Jan nodded. "But Leigh looks around, and she looks only at Leigh. That scene."

They were pushing the dead Mariah around by hand, living in fear of a neighbor's reporting it abandoned and the car's being towed. They had to get money—she knew it. "Jan, what have you heard about our old friend Oscar?" She had a moment of wondering if she was sticking her hand in a sore place, but that was a very old fracture. "You don't mind me asking?"

"He's gay now, you know?" Jan made a small face. "It's hard not to think, maybe we turned him off women?" She laughed then. "We're friendly, but we don't bump into each other a lot. He's got tenure at Richmond. I remember a battle about it. . . . Gee, I ran into him in the Village in September. Every so often I see him on Channel 13 commenting on the balance of payments or the banks' takeover of the city, but I can't say I know much. Bob and I don't get a lot of time to socialize, and mostly we see other people in health care. . . ."

"Is he still living on Avenue B?"

"Far as I know. He's been there forever."

She called the college and got his schedule. Now all she had to do was borrow the Honda and intercept him at the ferry when he came over from Manhattan. Jan was silly to lend her the car, which would link them if she should be caught. She had figured out by now that Jan could give her anything—her apartment, meals, a bed, her car, medication—but money. Jan's squeamishness about her coming professional status took the form of an unwillingness to admit she was no longer dirt-poor. In fact, her family was so happy she was married and respectable that they sent monthly checks, and Pelican made a decent living. Jan would lend them the Honda, but she would not give them two dollars to put gas in it.

She wanted to argue with Jan that her penury with money and generosity with things was irrational and even dangerous, but when she was sponging off someone, she walked around their eccentricities rather than through them. She skirted areas of disagreement. Joel was much better at smoothing over than she was, and gradually he had taken over most negotiations, such as when they would get the Honda and for how long.

She had no idea whether Oscar would respond to her sudden materialization with pleasure or horror, but she would have to risk his reaction. She had not been chummy with him the year before she had become a fugitive; in fact, the last time she had seen him at a regional meeting, she had called him whatever insults they were laying on everybody they considered cowards that year. She took Joel along to Staten Island, mostly to keep an eye on him, for she knew he was still brooding about the cash to be made as a cocaine courier. She had only to exaggerate her weakness slightly. The fatigue of years seemed condensed in her limbs. Joel agreed to come because she had let him know that Oscar had been her lover; let him know as she was trying to sleep and he was interrogating her: "Oh, you wrote stuff together. . . . Did you find him attractive? . . . Did he ever try to make you? . . . How often did this happen? . . . Why did you sleep with him, if you didn't love him? . . . Oh, you did: *love* him. My, my, you've certainly 'loved' thousands, haven't you?"

Off to see the Wizard, the Wonderful Wizard of Oz. Oz was what she had called Oscar, while she loved him. After Kevin she had given no one a pet name. He had soured her on nicknames. Almost she wanted to address everyone as Mr. Pfeiffer or Ms. Sforza. In bed he had been more of a Teddy bear than a passionate lover, but the affection had been real.

Would he still be angry about 1970? As they drove across the Verrazano Bridge, the day bright and glittering, ships at anchor in the bay, a tanker steaming under them out to sea high in the water, sea gulls among the cables, the question was not idle. Some old acquaintances once comrades hated the Movement people who had turned to direct violent action. Many had disagreed with them, but some hated them passionately for the very challenge they had thrown to the others to fight against the war with every means possible. Vida had been warned that Bob Rossi had said he would beat the shit out of any of them who dared show up. Great, she thought, I hope he sends out public challenges like that to David Rockefeller. Until she made contact, she never knew. It was best to send a go-between to test the temperature, but she had no time to work out safe passage.

They parked near the ferry and waited. He was not on the next two. Obviously Oscar was not arriving excessively early for his classes. It was approaching ten, when she had to try her call to Leigh. From the phone booth she kept an eye on the ferry exit. Today the first number was busy, and she felt a pang of hope. She kept calling the second. At least today no one answered to yell at her. Finally the first was not busy and rang. Nobody. Today her watch was exactly on time; she had called N-E-R-V-O-U-S before leaving Jan's. Nevertheless, she kept calling the two pay phones until she saw Oscar strolling toward her. Quickly she slipped out of the booth, then halted. He had a young man with him. They had stopped walking and seemed to be arguing, not in anger but vehemently. Oscar waved his arm back toward the ferry, laughing. The young man kissed him and then returned to the boat, waving over his shoulder and stopping to blow a kiss.

Joel came up from behind her, where she had stationed him, having guessed from her expression that she had found Oscar and was watching him. "He's gay, huh? You didn't mention that little fact."

"But Joel, what difference does it make?" She wasn't sure herself. Once his friend was back in the ferry building and Oscar began walking briskly, she moved to intercept him. Approaching on the sidewalk, she caught his eye. At once he looked away. Then, startled, he looked at her again. Looked away. Looked back. His pace slowed and he went on walking from the knees mechanically, staring again. What fun to be a walking ghost, she thought. Hi, there, Oz, thought I was in heaven or hell? No, here I am, the ghost of revolutions half past, come to haunt your academic peace. She forced a tentative smile, keeping eye contact. "Good morning, Oz." Was that a bad move, the old endearment? Looking for the right button to push on a stranger once your friend, once your comrade, once your lover, on a cold windy street in uncertain times.

Many minute events were happening behind Oscar's broad forehead. His hair was still curly and dark beneath a jaunty suede cap. He had an unlit pipe clenched in his teeth, drooping awkwardly. She hung back, waiting. "Hello," she said, stopping in front of her. Peering into her face. "I know I know you. . . ."

"Not for many years. Not since 1970."

"I thought so." He looked a bit glum, sucking on the cold pipe. "What brings you back to the city?"

"I'm only here briefly and, of course, unofficially. I am still enjoying an unofficial existence, you might say."

"I wasn't sure, what with half one's notorious old friends popping up nowadays." His gaze flicked past her to Joel, hovering. "Is he with you?"

"My friend. Terry, meet Oscar." She did not give her current name, waiting to judge his attitude.

Oscar shook hands with Joel, looking slightly more relaxed. "It's good you're not traveling alone." Had he been afraid she had sprung up from the past to plague him in a personal way? An old lover demanding blood sacrifice? "I can't put you up," he said. "I'm still in my tiny pad on Avenue B, and I have someone staying there with me."

"That must be the friend I saw saying goodbye at the ferry." She was sure Oscar must be out of the closet. "We have a place to stay."

He looked further relieved, pausing to light his pipe. "Yes, we're in the stage of things where taking the ferry with me is a romantic venture at this ungodly hour. Of course, by next month it will be Don't make so much noise when you get out of bed, you're giving me a headache. How are you?"

"And what do I want, turning up in your path?"

"Well, yes, that too. Of course, I'm delighted to see you alive and well. I'd heard that you were in Cuba, that you'd been shot in Mexico and that you'd had a sex-change operation and married a princess."

"All true, of course. We're only in the city for a couple of days, Oscar, and my name is Vinnie. We're having some trouble. . . ."

"Money?" He raised a thick eyebrow.

"We're looking for a job," Joel said. "We can do anything somebody might need. Any ideas?"

"Could be," Oscar said. "What kind of work?"

"You tell us," Joel said. "We need money and we need it bad."

"I don't require any banks robbed," Oscar said teasingly, and strolled on with one of them on each side. "However, let me think about it."

"Is there a pay phone where we can set up a call?" she asked.

"Don't be melodramatic. Just call my office at the college—you don't think they have the college tapped, do you?"

"It makes me nervous to call a radical's phone."

"I'm an academic radical, quite respectable. I even have tenure, though they tried like hell to withhold it. But I have three books out, and

The Political Economy of the New Banking has gone into its third edition. Have you had a chance to glance at it?''

"I wish I could," she said, never having heard of it. "It's expensive for me." She hoped she was guessing right. "I've looked at it in bookstores."

"Well, at seven hundred pages, no way it can be cheap. Because we use it as a text, I can get extra copies. I'll pass one along to you. The other books, of course, I merely had the standard number of author's copies, and they're long gone to my mother and uncles. . . .''

"The other thing—I'd love a copy of the book, I really would . . .'' They were approaching the corner where he'd get his bus. "If you have any cash? I've had the flu for two weeks and we're broke."

"That's why you look pale."

He didn't realize her hair was different. He simply thought she looked washed out. He plucked his wallet from the hip pocket of his tweed pants and peeled off a twenty. "Here you go." Then he was running for his bus.

"What can we do with this?" she asked Joel.

"I'm going to have to steal a battery. And we're going to have to use the Honda for the operation. No argument, Vida: we've had it. Either let me run the show or let me swipe a battery. We can't hang around here waiting for it to rain money."

"It's not fair to Pelican and Jan to use their car."

"Tell them to report it stolen if anything goes wrong."

"Joel, I'll get money from Leigh, I swear it."

"No! I'll get the battery in the very early morning." He slid into the driver's seat. "Stay away from that shithead announcer. He's liable to turn you in."

"He'd never do that," she said, furious. "Don't be ugly."

"You just want an excuse to see him."

"Believe me, I don't!" She lay back against the seat, weary. "That's the last thing I feel like. Would you control your jealousy?" She had trouble believing in it; at times she was convinced it was all a show he put on. There was always an element of self-parody in it, as if he were acting out an old vaudeville routine.

They did not alert Jan or Pelican to their plans, but went out together into Brooklyn Heights in the predawn, taking the Honda, until they found a new Chevy that Joel said would have the right kind of battery. It took him ten minutes to get it out. A man came by walking a German shepherd, glanced at him working on the car, nodded, kept going. Either he thought Joel was trying to get his car started or he did not care. At seven they were back on 3rd Street. Someone had taken their parking place. She hopped out to grab the note left on the kitchen table telling Jan to call the police and report the car as stolen if they weren't back by seven thirty. Joel remained in the Honda going round and round the block looking for a parking space. He installed the new battery before he came inside for breakfast.

She did not bother going out to a pay phone to try Leigh again. He would not be there. He had never failed her before, but she did not guess he was in jail, or laid up with a broken leg. She did call Oscar.

"Sure, old pal," he said, almost audibly putting quotes around the phrase. "I'll keep on it. Sure. No, nothing yet." She couldn't tell if he had in fact asked anybody for leads.

"I'll call again tomorrow," she said ominously, hoping to budge him.

"Um, yes," he said. "Well, I'll ask around. Hmmm."

She spent that day back on the couch, her fever up to 101. But she did not withdraw from fact this time. She contemplated Natalie in jail. Down to Centre Street. It was vivid to her. Then the Women's House of detention, she assumed—not the old one in the Village where she had been locked up, but out on an island now. How the women used to scream from the windows, yelling happily at demonstrators below. For *her* Natalie was inside; yes, but also for herself. Natalie was a political woman. She did what she had to. She followed her own conscience and her own judgment.

The next morning her fever went down to 99.2 and she called Oscar again. Let him find her a pest. But he was brisk and cheery.

"Well, old bean, I do in fact have something for you, could be."

"Maybe we shouldn't do this over the phone. Can I come to meet you?"

"No, just go see the lawyer of a friend of mine. In fact, the lawyer will meet you in a bar on Third Avenue tomorrow at two, if you can make it."

"Third Avenue in Manhattan?"

"Well, perhaps there are others, but isn't that generally what one means by Third Avenue?"

She hesitated. Dangerous. "What kind of job?"

"Clean and nice, but a little risky. She'll tell you."

She did not want to go into Manhattan; but they could not move on without money, and she was sick and tired of begging from old friends. In a short while she would give in to the cocaine running if she could not provide a better alternative. If she insisted on meeting outside Manhattan, the lawyer might object. People who lived in Manhattan always acted as if you were asking them to visit Toledo if you suggested they come to Brooklyn or the Bronx. To hang around Park Slope longer was risky too. Every day increased the chances of someone's recognizing her.

"I'll meet her. Where's the bar?"

Joel had a lot of work to do on the car; it would eat up Oscar's twenty and his whole day. "We got to be ready to roll," he said, and she agreed. Pelican needed the Honda, and Vida was left to take the subway into Manhattan. The day was bleak and overcast. Wearing dark glasses would make her look too conspicuous. Every time she saw anyone from their mid-twenties up to forty coming toward her she tried not to look into their face, but stole glances, fearful of accident, fearful of acquaintance, old friend, cop, passerby with a good memory for a photo that had been in the papers again not long ago. Twice she thought she was being followed and took elaborate cutbacks and detours, but each time it proved a fantasy of her special New York paranoia.

On the corner of Union and Eighth Avenue two women were chatting, each pushing a stroller in a different direction, coming and going from the park, a block to her right. One woman was standing hand on hip, gesturing with the other and using her knee to block the stroller in a way that made her think, with a pang, of Natalie. But the woman's hair was straight, shingled, black. . . . Natalie, yes, that was the connection. The woman had been in Natalie and Jan's consciousness-raising group—one of that circle of women who met in Natalie's apartment and had made Vida jealous and resentful all through her last year in the free world. What was her name? Glenda? Gloria? Gail? She had been the youngest, their college sophomore at Barnard. Something about the woman whose back was turned to Vida was also familiar, but she could not dawdle to find out. Turning on her heel, she retreated a block, then resumed her march toward the subway down President and along Prospect Park West.

She bought a *Times* and folded it in the conventional subway manner to block her face as she skimmed. Fortunately, she got a seat. Partly she stole quick eye reconnaisance of the car; partly she went through the paper methodically looking for news of Kevin, of Randy Superpig, of Natalie. Nothing. Not a damned thing. All the news they saw fit to print. Nevertheless, she kept the newspaper as she changed at Nevins for the East Side IRT. Who knew how long she might have to wait for this lawyer?

The bar was well occupied but not crowded at two. Her description of the lawyer was that she would be wearing a gray pin-striped suit and a raccoon coat, that she was tall and, to quote Oscar, "Oh, pretty in a sort of rawboned way. In fact, she looks, I hate to say it, a little like Kevin." With that description she stared at every woman in the bar, but nothing matched. Damn Oscar's comparisons. He would rather be witty than right. Nervously she paced from front to back of the bar, used the women's room and returned.

While she had been feverishly ill she had missed her phone call to the

Network. They must be worried. She must check her mail drop and make the next phone call, to give reassurance. But now they ought to have picked the day for the Board to meet. Eva should be East. She felt a rush of tenderness and that tinge of acid worry that always colored her thinking about any fugitive of whom she had not had recent word. Let Eva be safe.

She was just trying to decide whether she should leave the bar, take a walk, bolt and run or wait it out when a tall blond woman in a raccoon coat sauntered in. The lawyer did not look at all like Kevin, she thought in annoyance; she was a fine-boned Scandanavian type with flaxen hair. She was obviously looking for someone. Vida kept back, let her look awhile, then select an empty table and face the door. Vida went on watching to see who else might enter. Finally, after several minutes, Vida walked over and sat down.

"I think you're expecting me?"

"A woman? Well, Oscar didn't tell me." She laughed. "I'm Johnson."

"I'm a woman and a man. We can handle whatever you have in mind. If we choose."

Johnson laughed again—as before, a brief coughing laugh that crinkled her face but left her eyes watching Vida appraisingly. Her voice was low and theatrical. She lit a cigarette, coughed and asked, "What would you like to drink?"

"Ginger ale."

Johnson laughed again. "Come on. I'm buying."

"Ginger ale with coffee on the side, then. Do they have anything to eat here?"

"I haven't the faintest. We can ask the waiter." With her finger she summoned him. They had cheese and crackers for an outrageous price, but then, Vida was not paying. "All right, a tequila sunrise," she said, to get them off her back.

The lawyer drank Chivas Regal. "It's a domestic problem," she explained, her voice brisker. "The week after my client started divorce proceedings, her husband took the children. A little boy and a slightly older girl."

"How old?"

Putting on glasses for a moment, she consulted a card in her snakeskin purse. "The girl is nine, the boy, six. The problem is that the abduction is legal. He has taken the children out of state, where we believe he's planning to secure custody. Frankly, he has more money than my client. He's the owner of a chain of fast-food shops called Dog Houses."

"You want the kids back?"

"Have you done this sort of job before?"

"Sure," she lied happily. "What're the special problems in this case?"

"What makes you suppose there are any?"

"Otherwise, if you know where they are, she'd just go get them herself. Right? Or the detectives you have watching him would have done it."

"They won't," the lawyer said bluntly. "He has used physical force against my client numerous times. That's one of the reasons for the divorce." She motioned to the waiter. "Another. For you too?"

"Another cheese and crackers, actually. The drink is fine." She sipped at it for effect and to keep it from slopping over the top as the ice melted. She had no intention of ever drinking it. "Where are the kids? Is he armed? What will you pay?"

"We don't believe he's armed, except with a hunting rifle. That's legal where he is."

"Except for a rifle. That's great. Maybe a shotgun too?"

"Perhaps," the lawyer said noncommitally. "But he certainly has no handguns."

"Or howitzers. Or airplanes."

"Actually, he has a light plane," the lawyer said with a moue of amusement. "That's how he transported the children out there. But the plane is at an airstrip fifteen miles away. It's not a serious problem."

"Any helicopters? And how much?"

"The standard fee is fifteen hundred. My client is prepared to pay that."

"Fifteen hundred plus expenses," she said quickly, before she had a chance to react to the sum. That would save them; that would set them up high and fine for a winter of comfort. Even with the tithing to the Network, they would do just fine. Images of little houses in Vermont jogged through her head. Joel would be delighted.

"What kind of expenses did you have in mind?" The lawyer raised her eyebrow, knocking off the Scotch.

"Where is this . . . hunting cabin? The Arctic Circle?"

"A good guess—the hunting cabin. No, it's in Michigan. Standard mileage or air fare plus car rental?"

"Plus twenty-five a day for each of us to cover expenses while we're in Michigan. We could have to hang around for a week, and you know it. In the dead of winter? It won't be easy. Twenty-five a day for two plus ten days' car rental."

"I'll have to discuss your offer with my client."

"Take it or leave it. We can get the kids back for her. Tell her that."

"I have to make a phone call." The lawyer rose.

VIDA

She sat at the table sweating. It could be a setup. She was angled to keep an eye on the door, but she swung to watch the room too. A man was looking at her, and as she caught his eye, he smiled. She looked quickly away. In her nervousness she sipped the tequila sunrise again, but was careful to stop. She could not be fuzzy. She envisioned a log hunting cabin standing on a vast snowy plain with a maniac inside stalking from window to window with a hunting rifle and a shotgun. Oh, just hooray! They had to be crazy to do it.

As the lawyer came toward her, surreptitiously she wiped her forehead. She was still a little feverish. Stay calm but wary. "What did your client say?"

"She wants a meeting set up."

"Why?"

The lawyer elegantly raised a bony shoulder. "They're her kids. She can't accept the idea of somebody carrying them off who might abuse them the way she thinks he's doing. She insists on meeting you before she gives her okay."

"Where is she?"

"Roslyn Heights."

I might as well move to Long Island; I'm sure economically dependent on its problems lately. "How soon can she get here?"

"She can't. She's at work. She would like us to come there."

"When? It has to be settled today."

"Why are you in such a hurry?"

"I have another project that I have to fly to the West Coast for."

"She was thinking of the weekend."

"Ask her to think again. We can meet her for supper tonight."

"You like to eat food over decisions."

"Right. Break bread together." I like to be fed; that would never occur to you, would it?

The lawyer sighed. "I don't know if I can make it. . . . I'll have to get her back and make a few other calls."

Johnson was gone for twenty minutes. The bar was filling up, and the waiter asked twice if either of them was wanting another drink, even though she had her tequila sunrise barely touched before her. She sipped it, watered down with the melting ice, and ordered more cheese and crackers.

The lawyer came back, motioned to the waiter. "The bill, please. I'm running late. All right, we meet at eight in a restaurant on the North Hempstead Turnpike. That's 25A, just after you cross Glen Cove Road, on the left. I won't be eating with you, but I'll be there long enough to close the negotiations or end them." She sighed. "Now I'm in a rush." She paid, still standing.

"How about an advance?"

The lawyer laughed. "Advance for what? Eating crackers? You be there at eight with your partner. If we agree, we'll talk money then."

Joel had better have the car fixed. Money, money. Desperate, she glared at her watch. Leigh left the studio every day at four, unless he really was out of town, laid up, hospitalized. On his honeymoon in the Dry Tortugas. If she walked at top speed she could get there in time to catch him. Or should she wait near the apartment? No, that was even more dangerous. Midtown was marginally safer.

She strode uptown. Normally the mild walk would not have bothered her, but she was weak. The strains of the day etched into her, acid eroding her strength. She did not want to force herself to this confrontation, but he was her last chance. After this, petty crime. Running coke was not what she had bent her life to do. Survival is not enough. I could die now, she thought, of fatigue, of weariness, of vexation. I'm sure many have died of vexation. It breeds the carelessness that makes you step on a mine, walk into an ambush, miss surveillance. I must look where I am going.

Would Joel be able to fix the car? She saw him bending over her, carrying juice to her, sponging her face with a washcloth, rubbing her sore back. Last night they had made love, the first time she had felt well enough. She could feel his hands on her thighs. . . . Forswear sexual reveries on Manhattan streets!

The studio was on the 50th floor of an office building and the lobby the only reasonable place to wait, on the side where elevators from 31 to 50 came down. Let's hope Miss Susannah isn't meeting him. She did not dare loiter in the lobby too long. Building security men were always about in Manhattan. She stood at the candy counter skimming the magazines, trying to position herself where she could appear to look for a periodical and keep an eye on the bank of elevators. She realized she still had her *Times* crammed under her arm and discarded its mangled mass in a wastebasket. When she turned again he was exiting from the elevator, chatting to a younger man who bounced at his elbow nodding. She kept her face turned from him and then fell into step a little behind. Leigh and the younger man walked out through the double doors. She moved up behind them. She had never seen the other, and neither of them had any reason to look back.

"Well, take care, Stan. I'll see you on Saturday."

"Yeah, Leigh. My best to Susannah. We'll be over at seven."

Behind him she walked a block, keeping close but not too close. He was whistling a rock song whose words she recalled as "skin full of trouble, head like a bubble . . ." Slowly she moved into step beside him. "Greetings. You've been too busy to make our appointments."

He jumped, flinching, and whitened over his beard. "What in hell are you doing here?"

"Hitting you for money. I need it. I'm in some trouble."

"I'd guess so. With Kevin . . ." He censored himself. "Your sister's locked up tight, you know."

"I plan to get out of town tonight, but I haven't the money to leave."

"Er . . . have you had a chance to talk to Natalie at all?"

"Congratulations, you mean?" She sounded tight as a drum. What did she feel? Pain and anger with exhaustion over it all in a numb layer like blubber in a mammal that must make its living from the Arctic seas. Inside, the hot blood boiled far below. "Name it for me, and I guess you're doing what you want, hey, Leigh? Only I expect you to keep our appointments."

He rocked on a boot heel. "What's going on—some kind of blackmail? Showing up like this."

"Don't be an asshole. It's me that's in danger. I'm only here because you weren't on your end of the phone calls."

"I can't go on paying you. You seem to know I'm married and Susannah's having a baby. She'll have to quit her job in June."

"New commitments do not cancel old commitments."

"Face it, damn it, I'm married."

"Quite. For all you know, so am I. But you owe me, Leigh."

"For how long?"

"For how long I continue to fight. You get paid for your work. If we're on the same side, I'm entitled to be paid for mine."

"How am I supposed to give you money on the sly? I can't sneak off to see you any longer."

"I'll give you a contact you'll pay. You can call it professional expenses, paying an informant, booze money, dope money, anything you want. But I'm not evaporating because you got bored with clandestine rendezvous. You don't ever have to see me, but you have an obligation."

"I didn't say I don't want to see you. I never said that!"

"Give the money to Oscar. Eighty a month."

"I can't hack that, Vinnie. I just can't."

"Fifty, then. I think you can afford it." She smiled. "Call it alimony."

"I knew you'd be pissed."

"Then why didn't you tell me face to face?"

"When?"

"Leigh, there was time to discuss your program, time to talk politics, time to walk in the snow, time to fuck. But no time to be honest."

"Are *you* honest? You just said you might be married."

"What have you asked me the last year? You act as if you don't want to know, Leigh."

"Maybe I don't."

"Rather watch it on the television some night?"

"You're getting nasty. . . . Suppose I do give Oscar fifty a month. For how long?"

"How long will I be under?"

"Look, it isn't as if I begged you to go underground. It isn't as if I was involved in that harebrained scheme."

"We were all involved. You had limits. You were a professional journalist. You could say to yourself, I have to stop at such and so or I'll lose my job. What was my profession? Fighting the war. Making a revolution. Where was I to stop? At death? We each carried out our duties, but the wages have been different."

"Is that how you really see it?"

"Isn't that how you see it?"

"I'll pass Oscar fifty a month." Leigh glanced pointedly at his watch. "Oscar? How is he mixed up in this?"

"As an old friend, not as fickle as you. I need cash *now*, bad, whatever you have."

"What am I supposed to do, pretend I got my pocket picked? I don't go around with a fortune in my wallet."

"You seldom have less than a hundred. It's your habit. I do remember your habits."

Grimacing in his beard, he peeled off two twenties and a ten. "That's your fifty this month. That's all I got, and I don't know where it's coming from."

"Sell some of our furniture."

"Aw, come on. Susannah redecorated the living room in the fall. She bought out Bloomingdale's. She didn't like the old stuff."

"My red Cretan hanging. Where is it? Give it to Oscar. I don't want it over your bed."

"Christ, Vi . . . nnie, Susannah took that down ages ago."

"Where is it?"

"How would I know? I remember her sending it to the cleaner's."

"You give that to Oscar. I'd rather have it over his bed." Beginning to cry, she turned and charged blindly along the crowded sidewalk, bumping passersby, heading west automatically. Roughly she scrubbed her hand across her eyes. She could not afford tears; tears blinded. She had humiliated herself for what? Fifty dollars would hardly get them to the Vermont meeting of the Board. Perhaps this encounter was like scrubbing out an infected sore with strong lye soap, or the iodine that Ruby had always favored: it hurts because it's helping you. It burns because it's killing the germs. The infection. Leigh had become an infection. Burn it out.

She felt like a fool marching to the subway, fever rising in her forehead, her body heavy with fatigue. Joel thought she loved carelessly and casually; he did not see she loved too long and too well. She did not know when to give up, but stuck to a bad bargain. She could try men, taste them, feint, withdraw, but once she had begun to love someone, she let him into her own space, her center, and could not easily pry him out. Endings were bitter to her. Why not? They were deaths. Leigh was dead to her. He had become a fifty-dollar-a-month annuity. Nothing more. She trudged into the subway mouth with the rush-hour crowd.

20

Joel and Vida met the lawyer's client Mrs. Richter, a square-built woman of Vida's age with big bones, a little voice and a perpetual crease of worry between her soft brown eyes. Joel charmed her, and she agreed before dessert to hire them. They were supposed to appear to do the job within ten days. Vida figured that that gave her enough time to attend the Board meeting, launch her antinuke project if she could steer it through the Board and get back to pick up the advance.

At her mail drop in New York she found a notice from her lawyer about the divorce, a note from Leigh and one from Eva. The note from Leigh went:

> *December 7*
>
> *Baby,*
> *You caught me by surprise and we both said things we don't mean. You know I still love you. Remember New Hampshire. I'll be expecting a call Tuesday at the old numbers. Be seeing you.*
>
> *Love, Leigh*

She read it, reread it and tore it in little bits. She would not call. Oscar was amused at his role of go-between and would provide any link with Leigh that might prove necessary, besides what she hoped would be the regular flow of that small amount of money.

Eva's note said she was on her way East for the Board meeting and was stopping to chat and politic along the way. She would like to meet Vida early and suggested Rochester:

Perry, love, I'm migrating but slowly toward the powwow. Stopping to test the breezes. Suggest we meet and plot in Flower City 2nd week in D.

She smiled. Eva couldn't say anything outright, but the code was so transparent that no one would take more than five minutes to figure it out. Even when Eva was leaving a shopping list on the kitchen table, she obfuscated it. Vida felt a little pang of nostalgia. After so long on the road, she felt sentimental over the four-room house with its gas heater and gasping refrigerator. Mostly she missed Eva.

Roger was living in Rochester with a woman who was not a fugitive, causing some gossip, some controversy, some anxiety in the Network. Was Eva proposing a possible coup: that Roger, Eva and she try to find a common ground before the Board met? Something was up. She felt a stir of fighting spirit.

Joel and Vida set off for Rochester, the black Mariah once again functioning at her own chosen speed, chugging them down the byroads as they drank coffee from Natalie's thermos and ate roast beef sandwiches packed at Jan and Pelican's house.

"How come this Eva wants to see you?"

He wasn't supposed to know who was on the Board, but how was she supposed to box him or freeze him on demand? Really, some of the rules were just not realistic any longer. "The Board is meeting. She wants to talk first . . . and we haven't seen each other since I left L.A. She was one of my roommates." She was conscious of underplaying her feelings for Eva. Why did she let his jealousy dampen her even before he expressed it? Why assume the worst? And what good did trying to conceal her feelings do? They would be with Eva soon enough.

"Is she the dyke you were lovers with?"

"You use that word awfully freely. I am the dyke she was lovers with. Do you like to be called a faggot because you had sex with Jimmy?"

"It was lousy sex."

"Does that make it less real?"

"Sure." But he was grinning. He handed her back the empty thermos cup. "So she summons you and you come running?"

"She's my friend. She's been my friend for years. Long before we were lovers, and I imagine long afterward."

"So you're not lovers with her anymore?"

"You're driving me crazy!" She turned from him and glared at the snow-covered Catskills. She would not speak and he did not speak until she began to feel silly. "Joel, maybe you'll like Eva. Did that ever occur to you?"

"Great. I can fuck her too. We can all get in bed."

"You reduce everything to sex! Eva's my friend. She stood up to Kevin when nobody else would. She's my friend and my ally, and all you can think about is that when we lived in L.A. together we made love sometimes."

"So it's not important. There's no danger you'll do it again."

"Damn you, Joel, it depends on her too, don't you see that? I have to be free to feel what I feel when I see her. I don't dump people for other people. I won't! I won't forget her because I met you. If I did that, wouldn't I trade you in on somebody else? You know I love you!"

"Only because you can't have the Voice of Radical Radio you were married to."

"Leigh wrote me a note, wanting to make up."

"Yeah? Are we meeting him in Rochester too?"

"I tore it up."

"I don't believe you. How come?"

"It's over, and I don't want a game to go on. . . . . I'm with you and I want to be with you."

"Yeah? You got lousy taste in men. We'll see what kind of taste you have in women."

She was silent for a while. Then she burst out, "Joel, with Natalie in the can, how can I find out about Ruby?"

"Call the hospital. Say you're somebody else and ask about her."

"But would they tell me straight? I'm afraid to be Marsha again."

"Call your brother. He's on your side, right?"

"I don't dare call him at home. If we got caught out that night, if Sharon blew the whistle on us, then Paul's phone is tapped. I can't chance it. . . . . I'll call him at his bar. He stops there every day after work. I know where it is. If I can just remember the name." She shut her eyes tight. The street, the rush-hour traffic, the snow, the early darkness, Paul pushing out of the heavy door . . . She kept thinking instead of the name of the chain of fast-food places the lawyer had mentioned, the Dog House. "Something to do with animals."

"The Cat's Meow. The Elephant's Trunk. The Hair of the Dog. The Cock-a-doodle-Doo. They ought to ask me to name bars. The Tiger's Paw—"

"That's it! The Brass Monkey."

He patted her head. "How did you get there from tiger's paw?"

"A story on the radio we all listened to when I was little: "The Monkey's Paw." I remember how scared we got—all but Grandma, who couldn't follow the English and kept asking us. But what's wrong witchu?" She heard herself imitating her grandmother for the first time in twenty years. "And Ruby was just as scared as we were! Paul and Mama and me, all hugging each other, and Grandma thinking we'd gone nuts."

She called from a pay phone at a time she hoped Paul would be in the bar.

"Brass Monkey."

"Is Paul Whippletree there? He comes in every day, this time. A big guy—"

"Sure, sure, I know Paul. Who wants him?"

"Just say a friend."

"Sure, sure."

About a minute later Paul picked up the phone. "Joy? What's the big deal? It's not cool for you to call me like this."

"It's not Joy. I'm calling long distance, never mind from where, and don't say my name, bro, please!"

"Jesus, Steve told me it was Joy calling. What's up? How're you, toots?"

"How's Mama?"

"Better, some better. I think she's getting her act together and she's gonna make it. She's back upstairs and they're letting her out of bed."

"Bro, that's wonderful, that's perfect. I love you!"

"Hey, I guess you know the Feds got Natalie, and Sandy has her kids. Peezie's a real little champ. She's talked my daughter Marla into running every A.M. And Sam, he's got Joy and Mary Beth fighting over him."

"He takes after you."

"Go on, they lead me around by the nose and the you-know-what. I can't talk too long on this. You okay? Are you coming back?"

"Not real soon. Take care, bro. Tell Mama I called, but don't tell even her where I called you. Okay?"

She got back in the car grinning so hard her cheeks felt as if they would tear. "Ruby's better!" She remembered her superstition when she was feverish that since she had gotten sick like Ruby, when she got better Ruby too must grow healthy. She would never admit that belief to a soul, but she was convinced that somehow she had helped. She was superstitious about few things, but she was superstitious about Ruby. Ruby was basically irrational, so why shouldn't irrational forces work for and against her? Now Vida felt ready to take on the Board.

They met Eva in a Howard Johnson's on the edge of town. As they walked in, she saw Eva at the counter, her black braids hanging straight down her back. Eva's old shearling coat was slung over the back of the stool so that the curly side showed. She wore a faded red shirt, jeans and high-heeled Western boots. When Eva saw them and passed to the cashier to pay and leave, she was taller than either of them by two inches of her own and two of the boot heels. As she walked by, one eyelid almost fluttered, a ghostly wink. Vida ordered an orange juice to go; Joel got a mocha chip ice cream cone. Then they strolled back to their car.

Eva was waiting in the lot. "No wheels. I'm Eva."

"Joel. How'd you get here?" he asked.

"Hitchhiked. I don't like to, but now I have a nice ride back."

Vida got in back, tactfully and to let Eva give directions. Please let them get on, she begged. Please. I'll do everybody's dishes all weekend. Why did she have to feel as if she were maneuvering a battleship by straws when she had to be with Joel around people from her old life?

Eva, nodding, waving, giving overprecise directions, was physically maternal. She held, she rocked, she caressed. Sex between them was not so much passionate as soothing—entirely different from Vida's lovemaking with Lohania so many years before: not violent, not ecstatic, not smolderingly orgasmic, but relaxed and dreamy. Eva and Vida had been friends a long time before they had been lovers. Underground, Eva, who came from an Iowa farm family of many sisters, had discovered other women and became tentatively and then vehemently a feminist and a lesbian, in whatever order. By the time they had both lived in Hardscrabble Hill a few months, Eva was defining herself in opposition to Kevin and Bill and Tequila.

As Eva gestured to Joel, her long black braids held by pieces of embroidered blue ribbon swung to and fro over the seat. Gently Vida tugged one, and Eva threw her a broad warm smile over her shoulder. Joel, who missed nothing, scowled in the rearview mirror. "No—there!" Eva cried. "You missed the turn. That was our right."

Joel said sulkily, "You have to tell me before I'm on top of it."

"But I did. I told you two blocks ago and I told you again just now. . . . No, don't U-turn. Just go around the block."

Please behave yourself, please, she said to the wavy black hair on the back of Joel's head. "You could be brother and sister," she said almost pleadingly. "Black, black hair." She caressed the back of Joel's neck, to balance the equation. "Maybe I should have black hair too?"

Eva was looking closely at him, not having missed the hint of the caress. At long last they pulled into the driveway of a single-family home with an overturned bright blue sled on the lawn, the stumpy remains of a melting snowman. On the front storm door a Christmas wreath of plastic holly was tacked up. Joel shut off the engine as they sat in the car.

"This can't be it," Vida said.

"It can be because it is." Eva hurriedly added. "You know she's *outside*."

"Is this safe?"

"Tim thinks so."

"Tim?" Joel asked.

"Roger's name now."

He turned to ask Vida blandly, "Another of your lovers or ex-lovers?"

"No," Eva said, bending toward him. "Only me. You met Roger under the name of Bud—when you aced him out for Kiley. Remember?"

"We're all one big happy family." Vida lolled back. "Good, great, wonderful. We'll get a lot done. Roger/Tim can glare at Joel and Joel can glare at you. Maybe I can work up something to glare about."

"It shouldn't take long the way it's going." Eva knelt on the seat to face her. "Then Kiley can pick up the pieces at the Board. You know she's been campaigning to kick me off. Alleged separatist tendencies."

"I don't think she can swing it," Vida said. "You have a lot of support. People trust you."

"You have a hefty amount of support too. I've been out politicking myself, all across country." Eva rested her elbows on the seat and her chin on her hands. "You and I are seen as the feminist block. Also, believe it or not, you have some of Kevin's old followers—irrational as that may seem. They see you pulling for action. Then some folks are just pissed at Kiley or Lark for some decision—like getting sent to Des Moines or Toledo. Your seat is secure."

Vida sat up, catching Eva's gray gaze. Eva's face was broad and girlish. She wore big round glasses with a faint bluish tint. Her skin was smooth and ivory with cheeks so pink she looked, except for the blackness of the braids, like a Gretchen doll, a big-boned calm lovely slow-moving and slow-spoken woman with a voice that suggested some of the range and power of her singing. Vida said, "You know I'm pushing an antinuke action."

"I heard via the grapevine. I thought we'd parley on it tonight. I'm open to reason, though I admit I was startled."

"Eva, we're living in might-have-beens. We have to move where people are, even if it's a retreat."

"You can grasp at relevance too and end up with no politics. People who were charging barricades with us went chasing the Maharaji Moo and then chased just as hard after security or big bucks," Eva said.

"To serve the people you have to have some contact with them. Being pure may get you in good with God, but it doesn't move molehills down here."

Roger was rapping on the car window. Beside him an alarmingly large and floppy puppy bounced, barking wildly. Guiltily Eva hopped out of the car, and more slowly Joel and Vida followed, bringing their small luggage with them toward the house.

"Perry, you look great," Roger said, hugging her. "Hi . . . Terry."

"You might as well call me Joel," Joel said. "It's my name, and I'm no celebrity in Rochester or anyplace. Besides, with Terry and Perry I'll start feeling like we're Donald Duck's nephews."

"Come on in," Roger said. "Have you eaten? I've got a big pot of chili on the stove. Gwen made it before she went to work."

"Gwen's your girlfriend?" Vida moved a ray gun to sit on the slip-covered couch. "This is her house?"

Roger beamed with pleasure, more animated than she could remember seeing him. He wasn't embarrassed by the Play-Doh on the floor, the puppy galloping around with ears flapping and tail swinging in the air like a length of chain, the mustard yellow wall-to-wall nylon carpeting that gave her little shocks when she touched everything, a litter of plastic toys and socks and Golden Books from the supermarket. He radiated satisfaction. "Gwen's at school right now—she teaches English in the high school."

"Like you used to." She watched him carefully. No, he would never agree to an action. He could not be an ally. He would favor another comfortably rhetorical position paper.

"Yeah, but she's a better teacher than I was," he said, chuckling, "Jamie's at day care and Jane's in school. About four everybody hits the house, but we have a little time. This is Rudolph. Named by the kids for the reindeer."

"What about that chili?" Joel asked. "I'm starving. He looks half spaniel and half elephant."

"Yeah, look at his paws," Roger said. He and Joel were awkward with each other. At the doorway to the kitchen both stopped and each stood waiting for the other to proceed. "I figured out last night, they say a dog will grow up in proportion to his feet. Rudy's going to be six feet tall lying down."

They were still not looking at each other, but some silent agreement to get along had been reached between the two former rivals for Kiley's favors. They both roughed up the puppy, who fell on his back, shaggy belly up, and had puppy giggles of wriggling and yelping between them. Vida looked at Eva, who winked. They all squeezed into the kitchen around the Formica table, eating chili out of blue plastic bowls. Joel tasted his and then began adding pepper and chili powder from the rack over the stove. Vida took the spices from him. They were bland too, the strength cooked out of them by the heat of the stove. Could she advise Gwen when she arrived not to keep her spices and herbs over the stove?

Jane got home first, pouting as Rudolph barreled into her. "There's a dirty old black car in the drive," she announced sulkily.

"These are friends of mine, Jane. They're going to stay with us for a couple of days."

"Oh." She stared at them briefly, a lanky brown-haired eight-year-old who could have been Roger's daughter: tall for her age, skinny, long-boned as he was. For a moment she thought, could it be? Then she remembered that Roger's daughter had been seven when he went underground. She would be fourteen now. "Daddy . . . don't you want to see what I did today? You didn't ask. Look Daddy."

Crayon drawings of snowflakes—red snowflakes, purple, green, drawn with a fussy detail Vida found a little scary in a child. How had she made each snowflake precisely symmetrical? "Why, they're beautiful, Janey, beautiful!" he crowed. "I'm going to put them right up. . . . Where should we put them?" A good question. The refrigerator and cupboard doors were plastered with drawings of houses and trees. "How about we take down a couple of the old ones?"

"No! You don't like them anymore?"

"I love them, Janey. They're beautiful houses."

"I made them for you! 'Cause you didn't live in a house for a long, long time."

"I love them, Janey. But I'm not going to throw them away. I'm going to take your old drawings and put them away in my desk. . . . When you take off your red dress and put it away you don't throw it out, do you? It's like clothes. It's more fun if you change them. Then sometimes we can take out the old ones, when you've almost forgotten you made them, and we'll put them back up and say, Hey, look what pretty houses Janey made."

"Okay," she said slowly. "But in your desk. In a drawer, like putting clothes away."

In rapid explanation he said to the rest of them, "I told Janey I'd been traveling a lot in recent years."

"But now you're tired and you're going to live with us forever and ever and ever. That's what you promised."

Again he glanced at them over Janey's head. "I'm Janey's daddy now," he said in a furry voice. "Come on, Janey, we'll put the snowflakes up."

Jamie came into the house first, trotting. "Daddy! Rudy! Daddy!" He was a chubby six-year-old with a big voice who stumbled awkwardly across the kitchen to fling himself against Roger. "Daddy!" he bellowed, paying no attention to them.

"Jamie goes to a facility for special children," Roger said quietly, and swung Jamie into the air. Jamie grabbed him and held on, squeaking with pleasure. "Daddy! Daddy! Daddy!"

Gwen came into the kitchen still wearing her coat and carrying her purse and attaché case before her as if to ward off being bumped into. She was plump and freckled, her face pinched with worry. She glanced at them all and looked immediately away, as if frightened. Did Gwen think they would attack her? Or take Roger away? Vida could not believe what he had gotten himself into: a wife, a house, a family with a retarded child. Gwen took off her woolen gloves and put her hand on Roger's arm. Over the squealing Jamie and the leaping puppy they looked at each other.

As the after-school snacking got launched, Joel and Vida shut themselves in the bathroom. "He'll never agree," she whispered, sitting on the closed toilet seat. "An action is the last thing in the world he'll want. He's got instant family."

"You're off, again. Jesus, Vida, you can't tell the good guys from the bad guys without a scorecard, can you? He has to prove himself. To show he can have family and still be just as revolutionary. He's happy, and he doesn't think he ought to be, so he feels guilty. He'll be for anything chancy."

Someone knocked on the door. "Hey," Joel called. "We're almost done."

"It's me," Eva said. "Can I come in for a minute?"

Joel opened the door. "Want to watch me piss?"

"I didn't figure that's what you were doing." Eva carefully shut the door, taking a joint from her cuff. "Toke time."

"How the hell are we going to have a meeting in this house?" Vida asked.

"We'll go for a walk after supper." Eva lit up and drew, passing.

Vida opened the bathroom window a crack, automatically. "It's ridiculous, hiding in the john. . . . But we got to make our nuke presentation to you and R . . . Tim."

"I want to be persuaded." Eva sat on the edge of the tub next to Joel, who took the toke, dragged and passed it along. "This document: I couldn't stand to read it, let alone write it."

He said, "Another document—wow, it'll fall on the world like a mouse's fart. How come Kiley and Larkin are sold on it?"

"How come you're discussing Board business?" Eva waggled a finger at him. "If you keep giving me dirty looks, your face could freeze that way. That's what my mother used to say to me when I'd throw tantrums. Peregrine-ace, I can see you invented this, a, to get us moving again, and b, you want an issue you can work on with him. Am I right?"

Feeling silly sitting on the closed toilet in the position of shitting, Vida nodded. "In that order."

"You," Eva said to Joel. "Did you leave Kiley or did she dump you?"

"She dumped me. She froze me out," Joel said sullenly, refusing to look at either of them and hogging the joint.

"What will you do if she changes her mind?"

"Yawn," he said.

"How come? I hear you were crazy about her."

"Crazy is the word." Joel finally released the dope to Eva. "She"—
he pointed with a nudge of his shoulder at Vida—"she likes sex, she likes
me. Think I'm stupid enough to risk that for the Ice Queen?" He actually
looked at Eva. "What do you care?"

"You think I don't care about her?"

"I don't know what to make of all this honesty. I think it's a bad idea
all the way round. Why don't we go back in the other room and try to
manipulate each other the way real people do?"

"Actually, we can't hide in here, the three of us, smoking dope till
supper," Vida said. "We'll freak them out. I'm going to volunteer to set
the table or something."

"I'll volunteer to get a little hot sauce," Joel said. "Her chili tastes
like cornflakes."

"Be good," she said. "How would you like to be her with us arriving?
She's probably terrified for her kids."

"Aw, shit," Eva said, ruffling Vida's hair and sauntering toward the
door. "We haven't eaten kids in years."

Supper passed, mercifully. Then Gwen took the kids to visit a friend.
"It's good I should go and see her," Gwen said earnestly into the air. She
would not look at them individually. "I used to see her all the time before,
you know, and now I hardly ever drop in."

"Of course I trust Gwen," Roger said after she had gone. "She'd do
anything for me."

"But if you leave, what will she do to you, to us?" Vida asked.

"She knows what could happen. She says any time we have together
is better than none. Every day is one more for us. She means it. A woman
like her, Perry, she knows how to love."

"Is the kids' father around?" Joel asked.

"Her husband walked out on her when Jamie was two. He wanted to
put Jamie in an institution and try again. Can you imagine, wanting to
throw your kid away and pretend he didn't happen? Gwen's a good
woman. . . . I've never been so happy. Is that awful? I'm ready to leave
whenever I'm needed. She's behind what I do, one hundred percent."

Eva asked, "Aren't you afraid what may happen to her?"

Roger rubbed his pipe against his chin. "I wouldn't let this house get
shot up. I'd surrender and take a prison term. I don't think they could
hang anything on her. No way they could prove she knows who I am—
she doesn't even know my real name."

Eva crossed to the window and peered out through two bent venetian
blinds to the street. "It's snowing. . . . Alice and Bill turned themselves
in this week. Roger heard today."

"What?" Vida rose out of her chair. "They got caught?"

"No. They got a lawyer in L.A. and turned themselves in." Eva met her in the middle of the floor and they looked at each other.

Roger sucked hard on his pipe. "Why?" he asked. "Why?"

"Alice has been sick a lot. She needs an operation on her sinuses. They're always infected and she gets a 103-degree fever every couple of weeks. . . ." Eva's voice trailed off.

"If we don't develop political momentum soon, we'll lose more. The ones who don't have heavy sentences hanging over them," Roger said.

Vida glanced at Joel. "After all these years . . . We'll never see Alice again. Never. She just went and left us, like that. I trusted her. And Bill. I'd got close to him in L.A. In Cincinnati in September he seemed in good shape."

"No use dwelling on it and getting depressed," Eva said. "Let's get on with our business. Why should we mess around with nuke stuff? Basically it's an ecology issue, middle-class, quality-of-life."

Gathering her energy, Vida stood. For a moment she remembered the old excitement of addressing a crowd, her words bouncing back at her in waves of energy. Never again. "Basically, power is power. The same folks that gave us the military-industrial complex, utilities that charge more and more for less and less, dirty air and rotten cities, a fifty-percent unemployment rate in the ghettos, agribusiness where the price of grain sold goes down and the price of meat goes up are pushing nukes." As she spoke, she paced. Her familiar style of oratory gave her confidence. "Nuclear power involves public safety: What happens to people who live nearby? To their kids? Downstream? Why does it make power cost more? What happens to wastes nobody knows what to do with? How does government interlock with industry and the same families who own banks? If the plants always cost more to build and more to run and produce less than they say beforehand, who gets rich off building more and more?"

"Jimmy walks again." Roger wore a sad smile. "He always said, Keep naming the enemies. Put faces on where the money goes. But where's the anti-imperialist base to your project? Clamshell doesn't have any class politics. A lot of antinuke stuff comes out saying Save the rivers and fuck the cities and too bad if you need a job."

"Look, it's like sitting back with a good Marxist analysis in New York in 1957 and saying, What's all this busing stuff? What does it have to do with the means of production? All this Black religion, phooey. When what happens doesn't match our preconceptions, we get annoyed. Annoyed we aren't leading. The E.R.A., abortion, tax revolt, gay rights and nukes are causing more heat than anything, and we keep out."

"Don't you see?" Joel burst out. "It could wipe us out. Wipe out our ability to have kids and a place for kids to have kids. It's too dangerous to leave to those shmucks. We have to stop them.''

Roger turned to Eva. ''Kiley was trying to chase you off the Board. Did you know?''

''Basically dyke-baiting. She can't swing it. She's been testing the support behind everybody,'' Eva said. ''Including Perry. Including you.''

He sucked on his unlit pipe. ''Including me. That was her next logical step.''

''Why?'' Vida asked. ''Can't she expect you to support her position?''

''Kiley knows how my mind works. She's extremely bright. I've never been sure which has the better mind, Kiley or myself. If I spent less time manipulating and more time in serious work, I might know. Kiley is afraid I might support you.''

Eva asked, ''Will you?''

''I haven't decided,'' Roger said mildly. ''I have questions still. Besides, she may have got rid of me.'' He was looking at Joel.

''Sometimes I think if she could press a button she'd get rid of me,'' Joel said. ''Some people like their ex-lovers, like our sassy friend here. She'd keep every last one. She'd live with them all in a big house, right? Then there's people like Kiley who'd like to have your head off the morning it's over. She's done with you and she'd just as soon never see your face. You're a mistake that reminds her she ain't perfect.''

Eva cocked her heat at Vida. ''I'm going to make coffee.''

After a moment she followed Eva into the kitchen. For the first time they had a chance to hold each other. ''I missed you,'' she said. She had.

Gently Eva kissed her eyes. ''I'm worn out with traveling. After the Board I can't wait to get home. . . . Without Alice, I was thinking maybe we could rent a house a little farther up in the hills. Maybe Glassell Park? Think how warm it'll be back home.''

''Eva, Eva . . .'' She felt a little ill. ''I don't love L.A. the way you do. I feel in exile out there. East is home to me.''

Eva let go of her and stepped back. ''You're not coming back with me?''

''Eva . . . I'm an East Coaster. I understand the politics here. I work better. Out there it's just too much scenery for me.''

Eva crossed her arms. ''Scenery as on a sound stage or scenery like the Grand Canyon?'' A cool voice, a closed facade.

She wanted to touch Eva, to break through, but she felt guilty. ''Both. I like cities that have been around long enough to accumulate a history of corruption and struggle. I like seasons. And my own history is here. I can't stand being so far from my life.''

''Aren't I in your life?''

"Of course you are!"

"And him?"

She pretended not to understand. "Oh, he'd go West. He lived in Sacramento."

"But is he a permanent part of your . . . history? Scenery?"

"What's permanent? You and I have been friends a long time."

"We were living together. Now you seem to be with him!"

She touched Eva's smooth cheek. "Don't withdraw from me. Please. I feel close to you. It's beautiful to see you again. I've missed you."

"You want me to feel good about not being wanted? No, I can't manage that."

"But Eva, the sex between us is part of our affection. We were friends for a long time and lovers as part of that ongoing—"

"Don't continue or I'll get angry. You're comparing me with something or somebody and I feel it and it hurts!"

"Eva, please don't punish me. I feel as deep friendship and warmth for you as I ever have. Please don't make me feel bad for loving him."

"I wish I was in a lesbian community. Then I'd be done with this jarring. What you're saying is that you're straight and he counts and I don't."

"We didn't either of us love each other passionately. And I did choose you over a man. I chose you over Lark just as I chose you over Kevin. I chose you over every man in the Network. I feel closer to you."

Eva held her knuckles to her mouth. "I'll think about it." At least, she was no longer standing as if cast in bronze.

"Eva, stay friends with me. Stay close. I need you."

"I'm slower than you are. Slower to feel, slower to know what I feel, slower to act on it, slower to recover. It's like you're done and summing up when I'm just starting to deal with it. . . ."

"It's as a friend I loved you and as a friend I still love you. My feelings haven't changed. Be my loving friend still, please."

"I was happy when we lived in that funny house, even with Alice sick and whining. I thought you'd be happy too once you got used to it. But after you left I began to suspect you'd never come back."

Vida leaned on the well-scrubbed yellow stove. "I wasn't happy. For years I haven't expected to be happy."

"It was what I'd wanted."

"Eva, I tried. But it didn't become what I want. I'm sorry it isn't, but I'm telling you, I felt in exile. I wanted to please you, and I tried."

"Why is it good with him? Because he's a man and you think that's real."

"No! I didn't pick you out because you're a woman. Because he's fast too. Our emotions, our reactions work at the same rate. You know how you get tired with me because I want to talk about everything, to chew it over. My sister's like that. He's like that. I'm not lonely with him."

"How could you be lonely with me?"

She felt a bellyache seizing her. How could she hurt Eva so? "Eva, I was happy. Of course I wasn't lonely!" The image came to her of the two of them lying in the white-painted bedstead. Eva was sleeping on her side with her black braids pinned on her head, her sweet even breathing like the song of a muted cricket, her hand holding Vida's. She saw herself stark awake beside Eva wanting to talk, wanting to discuss Alice's depression and why they should all study Spanish harder for the neighborhood and what they could do politically to relate to the undocumented workers who got the same kind of off-the-books jobs they did. Eva spoke most deeply through silences and smiles and gestures, through her music, through her guitar and her rich satiny voice, through the paintings she had stopped doing in the last year. Vida needed to talk in words. "How many times does anybody really fall in love?"

"How do I know what you mean? As you say, I don't have a passionate nature." Eva turned her back, taking the percolator off the flame and pouring four cups of coffee. "Why don't you carry a couple of these and we'll join the men?" Eva stalked into the living room.

She leaned on the stove feeling sad. She had failed Eva, who had stood by her; but in order not to fail her she would have to lie or turn into somebody else. She had trouble believing that the couple aspect of their relationship could mean much to Eva, but that very inability to believe was a further failure. In order to please her friend she would have to lie, and there she couldn't. To please Eva she had eaten brown rice casseroles and vegetarian soups watery as tears, but she could not tell herself she preferred them to veal scallopini or Ruby's Jewish pot roast spiced with cinnamon and cooked with apricots. The gentle holding acting between them was not a love that engaged her. If she and Lohania had come underground together that day, she believed they could have been lovers as Joel and she were. Lohania instead of Kevin. She needed someone who compelled her, who seized her in a fierce and conversational demand. She could not take passion lightly, for it did not strike her often and yet she valued it.

Carrying a cup for herself and a cup for Eva she entered the living room, where Roger and Joel were forgiving each other for Kiley by arguing about the Knicks. They looked relieved at her entrance. Eva sat in the straightest chair with her arms folded. Vida stared at Eva and then at Joel, asking for forgiveness. However, she had more arguments to try out on Roger and Eva, and that must come first.

21

Eva declined to drive with Vida and Joel, going on ahead with Roger. Vida was sorry she would miss the little shock of surprise that must hit Kiley when Roger and Eva arrived, as theirs had to be an unsuspected alliance, although whether for or against her proposal she could not tell. Vida dropped Joel off at Agnes' farmhouse to wait, while she went on to the meeting.

The Board was meeting in a borrowed A-frame cabin on a small frozen lake, midway between Agnes' farm and Hardscrabble Hill. She was the last to arrive, walking into a glum silence. Five folding chairs had been set up around a card table; an ashtray for knocking out Roger's pipe; cups and a coffeepot; mint tea and antacids in front of Lark, whose stomach must be upset. Some journals and papers were on the table. Lark gave her a bleak searching look and nudged a medical journal which lay open before him toward her. She took it. A boxed notice called the attention of orthopedic surgeons to the case of a single amputee, Frederick Walter Burns, a.k.a. John Larkin or Larkin Tolliver or Lark Tolliver, armed and dangerous. A complete account of Lark's condition was appended.

She sat down hard. "How did they get it?"

"You tell me," he said.

"Well, how many women have you slept with?"

"I don't exactly burn with suspicion of you or Kiley," he said. "But Alice came into my bed after her abortion. In 1974, you'd left for Philadelphia. Kevin ran out and Bill went with him, although he came back in June. I was reorganizing our cell there. Now Alice has turned tail."

"Alice turned herself in just six days ago," Eva said matter-of-factly. She sprawled in her chair, arms folded. "This journal came out a month ago. Assume it was *at least* a month in being printed. Two months ago Alice was unhappy, but she was not talking, and she hadn't talked when I left L.A."

"How do you know?" Kiley asked, tapping a pencil on the card table. "It takes time to work out a deal."

"Alice told me when she started to think about it. We argued about it every day, every night for a month."

"Why didn't you inform us?" Lark asked coldly.

"Maybe *you* never talk about turning yourself in, but I hardly know anybody else in the Network who doesn't have fantasies about pardons and short terms and going home. Alice wants to have a baby. When she went to the lawyer, I told you."

"You shouldn't dismiss me," Vida said. "I'm a possible source."

"You told Joel?" Lark said.

"I did not. He wouldn't tell anybody if I had. Which, I repeat, I didn't."

"What do you mean, you're a source?" Eva said. "Don't talk in your sleep that I recall."

"Lark, we first slept together in '67. When I was living with Leigh and Lohania."

"You told them?"

"Not Leigh. I never told him details like that. But Lohania. We used to tell each other everything."

"Vida!" Lark forgot for the first time in years to use her underground name. "How could you take those risks?"

"I think it's disgusting," Kiley said. "Going home and giggling like adolescents."

"We didn't giggle." She drew herself up in her chair. "May I remind my comrades that in 1967—you were a little young then, Kiley, unless you've read about it—we were wide open. We had just more or less amalgamated with hippiedom. Everything was love and bright colors and beads and feathers and openness. We had less security than the Girl Scouts. Lohania and I shared everything in our lives." Especially information about men.

"You were lovers, weren't you?" Eva asked.

"Yes," she said gratefully. Eva was making her confession easier. "None of us guessed we might ever be fugitives. What would it have meant to us? A TV program? Escaping from the posse? Remember, '67 was the year we had a workshop in bombing and sabotage at the national convention to draw the agents out of our real workshops, because we knew nobody else would go and it was a joke on them. By '70 it was no

joke. Anyhow, I'm afraid Lohania has a good memory. She's thick with
Kevin, Leigh tells me, and Kevin is talking. Randy is in the middle of it
all. So I'm your leak, and we can date it and trace it. Until Lohania and
Kevin got together in New York after he was busted for gunrunning, she
had no idea you were in the Network.''

''Well, that's better than suspecting Alice, isn't it?'' Eva said brightly.
''We can hardly trash Perry for telling her best friend and lover in 1967
about sleeping with a man. It's only amazing it took them this long to put
your fingerprints and name on you.''

She caught Eva's gaze for a moment, beaming thanks. Eva still would
not look her in the eyes, but uncrossed her arms.

''What exactly did you tell her?'' Lark asked, still staring.

''Oh''—she smiled slightly—''I was very taken with you. I told her
you were fascinating. You seemed different from any man I'd been with.
You were more serious, more disciplined, honed by suffering—I believe
that was the romantic phrase I used. I described you physically and I
talked about the sex. Lohania loved good oral sex, and I said you were
the best.'' She felt wicked as Lark blushed to his fingertips and Kiley
tapped the pencil furiously.

''Oh, that's why. . . . When we were penetrating the Hilton together,
she was . . . flirting heavily with me and I didn't know why.'' Lark
moved around in his chair. ''Anyhow, I don't think you can be blamed
for what happened way back then. I just wish she had forgotten.''

''No doubt my advertising was too persuasive,'' she said, teasing. She
could feel that she had got out from under it. ''If I know Lohania, she put
you on a list to be tried and there was never a chance she would forget.''

''Can we get on with program?'' Roger asked in a bored voice. He
was not feeling warm and friendly toward Lark. No doubt somewhere in
his head he was wondering if Lark was that good a lover and if Kiley
preferred him and did she really like oral sex that much? Sex could get
you in trouble, but sometimes it could get you out, Vida thought. She had
flattered Lark to the core. He could not quite look at her, but glanced and
then withdrew, glanced and withdrew. If they were alone, he might coun-
terattack by asking why, then, she had chosen not to live with him in
1974; but they were hardly alone, and he could not expect a chance to
question her. How much could what she said matter now, with Kiley at
his side? She was protected from the consequences of flirting with him.
Why did she feel that way, as if he embodied a chilling fate, the grim, in
some ways helpless, ascetic man she might end up with? For all Lark's
virtues and Joel's weaknesses, she preferred Joel. Flesh and tsurris; hot
bothersome kvetchy talk and sex.

''The antinuke movement is nonviolent,'' Roger said when she finished her presentation. "What makes you think they'd welcome our intervention?"

"In the antiwar movement we had pacifist groups and revolutionary groups. In any viable movement there's a vast spectrum of politics. Same with civil rights, women's issues. They can't exclude us if we don't join their groups. They can't judge what issues we choose to work on any more than we can choose their strategies."

"So you don't think they'd welcome us?" Eva asked.

"Hell, no," she said. "Do you want to be welcomed?"

"Sometimes." Eva did look at her briefly for the first time that day. "We have to be clear what we're doing and why. Good propaganda this time, folks. And antiproperty only. No antipersonnel stuff. We have to be extra careful of that in this context where we're arguing about saving lives in the future. There's no saying we're fighting a war at home now."

Eva was supporting her! Vida let herself sit back against her chair, her tension loosening a bit.

"A revolution is a war," Lark said. "It's hot enough war in Africa right this moment."

"But we're here," Roger said. "And it's tepid."

"Are you arguing for or against this proposal?" Kiley barked.

"I'm making up my mind." Roger puffed out clouds of smoke as Eva and Vida moved back surreptitiously. "Not all of us are visited by the truth instantly. Some of us think till we reach it."

"Then I take it you're undecided on this proposal and the proposal for a new global position paper?" Kiley persisted.

"No, Kiley. I've made up my mind on the paper. I'm opposed. I think we've taken quite enough time playing academic in the last two years. We could do that as well in prison. The Network exists for two purposes: one, to service fugitives; two, as a political expression for fugitives. We can't do political education well from underground. Anybody with a job at a college, a high school, a trade union, a newspaper can do that fifty times better. Our specialty has to be propaganda of the deed."

"Then you intend to vote with Eva and Vida?"

"I intend to work on the only proposal for action I hear coming out of this meeting. I don't care who proposed it—I wouldn't even mind if you had, Kiley. I want us moving again. I doubt if my decision shocks you. You had to have reached the same analysis, or you wouldn't have been trying to maneuver me off the Board." Roger puffed more furiously.

"Oh, I don't know." Kiley gave a thin smile, a crescent of even white teeth. "Your recent choices of how to live your life are disconcerting in a Board member."

"I don't think cadre should relate only to cadre. I think that's elitist.

If we want to serve the people, we have to have some contact with them."

"Oh. Are you recruiting your schoolteacher, then?"

"I was a high school English teacher myself, Kiley. Don't be a snob. Your class background is showing."

"This context is an odd one for waving class banners," Lark said with annoyance. "This proposal is basically opportunistic. It doesn't grow out of our politics."

"Our politics have been growing mold," Vida said. "We slowed down our corporate and governmental raids because the war ended and there was no constituency out there for them. There's a hundred issues, but you have to look to people to tell you which of those hundred terrible things move them. . . ."

"A Marxist analysis should tell us what to move on, not the evening news," Kiley said.

"Lark, remember in the SAW office in '68 when Oscar, Lohania and I launched the Con Edison project? It had everything: Labor troubles we could relate to. The consumer getting screwed. Pollution. Alternative energy—yes, we were talking about that in 1968. Public health—the incidence of respiratory diseases near generating stations. Regulatory agencies. Governmental corruption. Control by the rich and powerful. Demands for public ownership. But there was one problem: it was boring. The project died a slow, dreary death. People crept away from it and didn't answer their phones. Fewer people came to every meeting. Finally Oscar, Lohania and I had a fight and we buried it. An absolutely correct project with no sex appeal."

Kiley stood. She met every pair of eyes. "You have the votes. I'll work on it."

Lark frowned. "I can't go along. . . . No, I'd better resign from the Board."

"Don't be foolish. Accepting the temporary will of the majority is good discipline," Kiley said to him. "It won't hurt us to carry out a successful action. I am convinced the position paper doesn't move the troops. This project is weak-minded and opportunistic, as you agree, but we can put together a proposal for a set of actions based on a sounder analysis by February or early March."

According to the prevailing etiquette of the group, Kiley and Lark could not go into the next room to confer privately about whether he should resign from the Board in protest to what was obviously going to be their decision. Kiley could only glare appeal to him with her eyes and ask him to maintain discipline.

Lark cracked his knuckles in the silence. "My disagreement is too strong."

"I don't want you to quit, Lark. Neither Eva nor I went along with the omission of a strong gay-rights section in our last position paper, and that struck close to the bone. Neither of us resigned." Vida asked with her eyes also. She had a moment of relief that Joel was not present to reduce her maneuverability. "Continuity is important to us. You and Kiley provide that. We built this Network in the teeth of a government at war with us, and we've survived everything they could throw at us. Let's survive our occasional disagreements with each other. They're minor compared with all we share of work and politics and history." As if tremendously moved, she took his hand: a rhetorical gesture, but meant. She did not want Lark quitting. What kind of victory would that be? A Board without Lark would lack legitimacy.

He let her squeeze his hand while he frowned into space. "I don't know. . . ."

"Well, I could hold your other hand if that would help you decide," Kiley said sarcastically. "Vida likes to put a little body English on her arguments."

Vida noticed that Roger was not joining the persuasion attempt. Either he wanted Lark off the Board, leaving him clearly the dominant male, or he couldn't get rid of resentment about Kiley.

Eva said, "If you think we're wrong, shouldn't you retain the maximum leverage to affect our judgments?"

Vida gave Lark's hand another squeeze and let go, smiling at Kiley. "Communication works on a lot of levels. Between comrades, argument should be aimed at communication. What I was trying to communicate is the depth of my respect and affection."

"Do go right ahead," Kiley snapped. "Borrow the couch."

"Kiley is having an emotion," Eva said smiling. "It's big and green and covered with long spines."

Kiley glared. Vida thought that Kiley was a woman who did not take nonsense or interference from any man, including her lovers, but refused to identify with other women, who annoyed her simply by being women.

Lark drew himself up. "This is unnecessary. Of course I'll remain on the Board. I strongly disapprove of this decision. I can't even imagine how we'll explain it internationally. But I'll stay on and fight with you. I'll work on a counterproposal. I admit, I'm surprised by Roger's position. I'm beginning to think the time is wrong for a long analytical project. I accept responsibility for producing a counterproposal by February 28 centered on corporate profits from South Africa."

"But you agree we proceed with this project in the interim?" Roger asked.

Lark nodded. "I understand. I don't approve."

"But do you cooperate?" Eva asked.

"Of course," he said. "That's group discipline."

"Now, down to specifics." Roger opened his ancient leather brief-case. "What and where? No functioning plants. That's just too bloody dangerous. We could do more damage than those blockheads that build the awful things. I understand Peregrine has some concrete ideas on construction sites, and so do I. Let's take a look at the various sites and possibilities and check them out."

"We have two construction sites to choose from. We should scout them both tomorrow and then begin surveillance on the target we pick," Vida said. "We can figure out what kind of action to take once we've got our site and know it reasonably well." She unfolded a map of northern New England and spread it on the table as the others moved closer to look.

22

They spent a week scouting the possibilities before they decided on an initial site where the Mohican Nuclear Power Plant was under construction on the Connecticut River on the New Hampshire side. Then surveillance began around the clock. Joel, Tequila and Marti were involved now that the Board had finished meeting and the action had been launched. Every two days they met to correlate observations and get on with the planning. They planned a small local action soon and then a bigger action later focused on the corporate offices of the electric company.

"First off today." Kiley rapped the big sheet of butcher's paper taped to the plate-glass window. There weren't an abundance of available flat surfaces in the A-frame where Kiley and Lark were sleeping and the meetings took place. The A-frame was located in between Hardscrabble Hill and Agnes' farm, where Roger, Eva, Joel and Vida were staying. "A timetable. And the wherewithal."

"Money?" Eva asked. She had pointed out to Vida how squeamish Kiley was about naming sex and money. "We have a contact for dynamite, but they won't do it on the cuff."

Roger laid out his pipe, tobacco, ashtray and pipe cleaners on the table before him like tools for an operation he was commencing. "Do we have anything in the kitty?"

Lark was treasurer. "We're broke. A lot of our sources have dried up. My last trip to New York was wasted."

"Maybe this'll loosen them," Roger said cheerfully. "But we need money soonest to prime the pump. I think we have enough cash between us to get a small load—enough to blow that earth-moving equipment. But for a more major effort we need a modest pile."

"Joel and I have a possible job that could bring in something," Vida said. "A contract for a lawyer in New York."

"What kind of job?" Lark looked suspicious, his eyes narrowing.

"Kidnapping two children back for the mother. The father took the kids to Michigan."

"How do we know this is politically correct?" Roger challenged.

Eva shook her head at him. "You identify with all fathers."

Joel sat by the window unraveling a length of old rope. He tended to place himself at the edge of the room during meetings. "We talked about doing that job, yeah, but to live on. We been broke for months. We can't go on like we have. It's too dangerous."

Lark asked, "How much money is involved?"

"Fifteen hundred," Vida said. Joel threw her a dark fuming glare. Did he expect her to lie?

"That's great," Roger said, gaining enthusiasm. "We can split it down the middle. It's enough to finance our action and you can live on it for a couple of months besides."

"I don't think it's fair," Joel said. "The risk is all ours. For months we been on the road. Constantly hitting people for money. Both dog-tired. Vida was sick for weeks while we holed up in Brooklyn. I want to live someplace with her. It's our right."

"We're not in this for comfort and our rights," Kiley said. "Where do *I* live?"

"You thrive on it. She doesn't." Joel glared at Kiley.

Eva was frowning, hugging herself. Vida could feel Eva's inner buffeting. Finally Eva burst out, "We're not in this to burn ourselves out either. Haven't we long ago passed the stage of trying to prove we can each take more deprivation, more loneliness, more danger, more tension, more fatigue than anybody else? We're the survivors. Let's give each other a little room."

"Peregrine proposed this action," Roger said. "I'd have thought she'd be ready to support it all the way."

"The whole group agreed," Eva said. "It's not hers any longer. . . . And you don't seem to lack a desire for a little stability in your own life. How can you deny it to them?"

Joel got up awkwardly and came over to Eva. "Thanks," he muttered. "You really care about her too."

Eva gave him an exasperated glance. "Too! You're the one still to be tested and proved."

Vida wanted to put her arms around both of them. "I suggest a two-thirds/one-third split," she said. "We can ask for half the money as an advance. We'll take the one-third split for the Network out of the advance. Five hundred should cover our expenses on the power-company action. Then Joel and I will take the second payment to live on."

"How soon can you get the advance?" Kiley asked.

"The lawyer's waiting for us to get back in touch. We were okayed by the mother."

"Do it at once." Kiley was jotting on a calendar. "Get the money before Christmas. We can start the New Year with our broadcast."

Vida had not heard that old slang in a couple of years: a broadcast: an action. She smiled. "I'll call the lawyer today. But we have enough cash for dynamite to take on a small action at once. We know we can place a bomb at the Mohican site, where there's only one watchman to get out of the way."

Tequila stood, grinning. "We can get the dynamite today."

"Let's jump right on it. By tomorrow at the latest. Tonight if we can." Roger cleared his throat, rapped with his pipe. "I'd like to go home—I mean to Rochester—for the holidays. The kids will be disappointed if I don't show."

"If Tequila leaves now and brings the sticks back, we can pull it off tonight," Kiley said, beaming at everybody. "It'll be neat."

"Go just for Christmas," Eva said. "If we're going to do a major bombing at the utility offices, we need to do surveillance for a lot longer and a lot more carefully than on the construction site."

Tequila left with what money they had between them to get the dynamite as Marti arrived, with Dylan along, to take the next shift of surveillance with Roger. Marti's daughter Tamara and Roz were in kindergarten, but her son Dylan was too young and had to be parked in the A-frame for the rest of the day. Joel rose to the occasion as the one most sensitive, in Roger's absence, to the demands of a bored and lonely little boy. Lark, looking up from his hand calculator and running column of figures, instructed Vida, "Get it in tens and twenties. Leave the day after tomorrow. We'll proceed on this end assuming you can get the money here by Tuesday night."

"So we'll drop off the money before we do the job," Vida said.

Kiley, working at the card table on logistics, refused to admit that children existed as children. When necessary she addressed Dylan formally. "Dylan, if you persist in kicking in the couch, you'll scuff it. Then the people who own this house and who have been generous enough to lend it to us will be annoyed." Dylan pouted and kicked the couch harder. He had been doing it unconsciously. Now he was seriously engaged in kicking the couch.

Lark was uneasy around Dylan, although he had lived with him. Lark was more afraid of children. She wondered why. She was not much interested in them unless she knew a child personally, as she did Sam and Peezie and Roz, but what did Lark fear? Perhaps he thought the child would leap on him suddenly, like a large dog. Perhaps he hated to remember his own childhood. Perhaps something concrete disturbed him when he looked at children.

When Lark talked about being in Vietnam, he always referred to the visit he had made as a representative of the antiwar movement. He almost never meant the years he had spent there in the Army. She was curious, but a deep inhibition restrained her from questioning him. Either you stayed out or you went in and took responsibility for what you might stir up, she felt. She divided her time between studying the topographic and site maps and playing with Dylan on the floor to spell Joel. They had an old squeaking duck pull toy and a new fire engine with a horrible siren to amuse him.

Finally they got home to Agnes', a forty-minute drive west. Agnes sheltered the East Coast press of the Network in her chicken house. The house, gray with dark blue shutters, stood among dark drooping Norway spruce whose trunks were as big around as Vida. You came into a stately entrance hall with a loop of stairway climbing and a parlor to each side. Agnes, who ran a working goat farm that sold cheese to an organic wholesaler, was a fiercely antiwar Quaker and sheltered political fugitives. As a pacifist she had serious political differences with the Network but over the years had come to view them as her children. Like Eva she wore braids, but hers, gray-streaked and sandy, were bound around her head with its blue eye and darker blue glass eye, her own put out by a stone in a civil rights demonstration in Selma years before. Her eyes were set in crinkles over jutting cheekbones that formed pouches in her cheeks. Agnes was as tall as Eva, but thinner. She wore clothes well and with an unconscious, almost incongruous flair going among the goats and puddles in a long green woolen Irish cape with a high collar. Her clothes were old but elegant still—tweeds, silks, linens of chaste but unmistakable quality. Agnes had an opulent swinging long-legged stride across the rocky pasture, up the hill, across the wide-boarded floors of her old house studded with bright rag rugs she braided. Vida thought of Agnes as always in rapid but fluid motion. Even when Agnes sat in a rocking chair by the Franklin stove her gaunt hands were busy piecing one of the quilts she made for use and sale.

Besides the goats, Agnes had several cottage industries going into which the fugitives who came through her household were easily if not always comfortably fitted: maple sugaring, apple growing, cider making, quilting and of course the production of cheese, not to mention the ongoing tasks of cutting firewood, mending fences, shooting woodchucks, plowing and planting the kitchen garden. Now everyone stayed in the big house, but Vida longed for the summer shack up in the sugar bush on the hill where she had hidden all by herself for a month the second year she was a fugitive. She imagined sleeping with Joel up there in lofty privacy; but of course, the shack was unheated and inaccessible in the deep snow.

"I recall," Agnes nodded. "I had to put you up there by your lonesome, as I had the Puerto Rican children. That's when you made the Star of David quilt. The stitching was too coarse to sell it—you have no patience, dear. But the design was pretty and nicely worked out. That being so, I never minded keeping it around. It's on Eva's bed."

By your lonesome. But she hadn't been. That July of 1972 had been the first time since the early days of her marriage to Leigh that she had been thrown back on or escaped to her own company. The first night on the mountain she had not been able to sleep. At once it was deadly quiet and furtive with small mysterious sounds tickling the woods. The grinding gears of trucks, the growl of horns, the artillery of cherry bombs would not have disturbed her sleep in New York; here two dry branches rubbing tortured her. Yet by the third night she was accustomed to the small rustles in the silence and slept soundly. She walked long distances, bushwhacked to the top of the rocky trailless mountain, explored compulsively. She had to haul buckets of water two hundred yards uphill from a spring. Otherwise she kept busy with thinking. She realized that second week she did not miss Kevin, off in Montreal. Instead she experienced a sense of expansion, as if a rock had been lifted off her chest. The realization had frightened her. She did not see what she could do about it. Not that Kevin loved her. If he had ever loved anyone, he had loved Lohania. But he was dependent on Vida. Sexually he was obsessed with her body, her skin, her legs, her breasts—who knew? It had nothing to do with her as Vida the person, yet she had taken three years to understand that, for his need felt intense. Sometimes she thought that if she died leaving her body intact, his sexual attraction for her/it/the thing would be the same. Perhaps not. Perhaps he needed that element of resistance her being alive provided.

She had told herself it did not matter whether she loved him. She felt clear and hard on her mountain. They were a team. They were one, politically. Better to have no irrelevant personal fog welling up, no romantic distortions. Kevin and she were tools. Love was a bourgeois distraction. On August 2 Kevin had arrived and they headed for Detroit where they planned to organize some support and to make contact with militant Black labor groups—if they could.

Shaking off her reverie, she followed Joel to his room. Agnes had given them separate rooms, over their protests. "I don't care what you do if I don't have to know about it," Agnes said down her aquiline nose. Vida was astounded as always. Agnes did not approve of sex outside of marriage, and she did not much approve of marriage. Under her roof the usual pairing and unpairing went on, but Agnes managed to remain ignorant. Vida sat facing Joel on the swaybacked bed. She said, "My problem is I seem to think I can adjust to anything at all if I have a strong reason. For a political reason I can talk myself into agreeing to chop off my arm."

"You mean this afternoon. Split the money down the middle?" He pulled her hair. "It's getting pretty again. You lack imagination."

"That's what Natalie always tells me." She craned to look past him into the mirror on the dresser. "That time again. I'll run into town for dye and do my hair before we hit New York."

"I tell you, you lack imagination. Dye your hair black."

"Black?"

"To match mine. And show off your pussy-green eyes. We'll both have black hair and green eyes."

"Oh, you want to be my brother."

"Your baby, your brother, your lover, your sugar daddy, your soul mate." He pinned her to the bed, nibbling along her neck. "Eva really cares about you. I'd never do that—argue in favor of something that lets an ex-lover of mine enjoy her new lover?"

"Hello? Hello?" Agnes rapped on the door. "Is Peregrine in there with you?"

"Sure." Joel grimaced.

"Tell her I need help with supper."

"Tell me yourself." Vida slid grumpily out of bed. "Agnes has an instinct."

It was a matter of peeling and chopping. She worked as fast as she could and then made a quick trip into town. She needed to pick up a bottle of hair dye, and she wanted to catch Paul at The Brass Monkey; she could do both from the local drugstore.

"Brass Monkey," the same bartender's voice said.

"I'd like to talk to Paul Whippletree? He comes in every night around this time after work."

"Yeah, but not this week. . . . Fred!" he shouted off phone. "Paul ain't been in, has he?" A moment later he spoke into the mouthpiece again. "Family troubles. You got to get him at home."

"Thank you." She frowned at the dial of the pay phone. She certainly could not call Paul at home, though she was worried enough to be tempted to try it. What kind of family troubles? She hoped that Mary Beth was sick or had caught him in bed with Joy. Not that she liked wishing hard luck on her brother, but she just wanted the trouble not to have anything to do with Ruby. She stood several moments longer trying to think of someone else she could call to get word of Ruby. It was time to get back to Agnes' and set the table. In New York she could think of some way to hear news.

Right after supper they all met back at the A-frame. Naturally, Agnes was to know nothing of their activities. Vida argued, "But since Joel and I will be off in Michigan and we could even get stuck there awhile, we ought to get the lion's share of the action tonight."

Lark nodded. "But not together."

Roger said, "We've noticed some tension between Eva and Joel. We want them to work together calling in the warning and putting out the communiqués."

"Munitions will be you and I," Kiley said, "with Tequila standing by. Roger has prepared a bomb with an hour delay after placement."

Kiley, Tequila and Vida got into their night clothes, dark with ample pockets inside and nothing that could catch on a wire. All five of them piled into the most reliable car, Marti's relatively new dark green Saab, and Tequila drove slowly and carefully, avoiding bumps, toward the construction site.

She sat in the back seat between Eva and Joel. Eva was singing softly, hunched, as if to pull her extremities out of reach by contracting her body. In danger Kiley grew manic. Tequila affected a bluff front, all combat boots and elbows and hearty chopped-off laughter. He and Kiley kept up a brittle nonsense argument about union organizing, work none of them had ever tried. Roger, who had long ago been active in the teachers' union in Seattle, was, of course, not in the car to hear them. Vida doubted they were listening to themselves, let alone to each other.

Joel held her hand hard. She wondered how he would do in the action. She felt responsible for him, uneasy and then guilty for the lack of trust her unease suggested. As if to apologize, she squeezed his hand. It was not sweating, whatever that meant. If he grew rattled or panicked, he would endanger them all; moreover, he could deeply embarrass her before her peers. She felt a stab of annoyance that they had refused to let her work with Joel. She was convinced that if he did blunder, she could cover for him. Eva was a good soldier but a little phlegmatic and not the fastest to improvise in a tightening vise.

The two in the front seat chattered and the three in back were silent, except for Eva's soft singing. Darkness had come early and thickened. "It's the solstice," Vida said suddenly. A small slice of moon hung in the windshield just over Kiley's head.

"That's an ancient witches' holiday," Eva said. "We're celebrating."

"Midwinter's Eve fires," Vida answered.

As they approached the spot where Kiley and Vida were to get out of the car, everyone fell silent. Standing on the road's edge as the car sped away to drop Eva and Joel in a nearby town, Vida thought of her mother. Family troubles. Don't let her be sicker. Turning then on her heel, she followed Kiley along the shoulder of the access road.

They both walked softly, not hurrying, light on their feet, Vida with the bomb, Kiley ahead with the wire cutters. The site was surrounded by a high wire fence, visible ahead of them now. They struck off on a path through the woods Marti and Roger had trodden for them that afternoon. It brought them up on the far side of the construction site from the watchman in the construction-company office at the gate. There were lights at the entrance and around the office, but they approached across the excavation. Nothing but a vast hole and machines for making it vaster yet. Vida felt weightless, almost giddy. It was cold with no wind stirring, as if the night were frozen up to the sharp stars. The air felt dry and crisp against her face. Vida made her way slowly. She must not slip on the ice. It would be a rotten idea. Invisible ahead of her, Kiley must be kneeling at the fence.

When Vida stepped out of the woods, Kiley had the hole cut, the wires bent back and was through, waiting to take the bomb before Vida wiggled after. Then Kiley laid a piece of newspaper against the hole as if it had blown there, impaling it on the edges to hold it in place. They padded on carefully, Vida taking back the bomb. Right at the fence the snow was unbroken and the going difficult, a glaze of ice over a foot of snow. Near the equipment the ground was churned into deep frozen ruts of mud and ice.

Kiley pointed to a power shovel and a Caterpillar side by side. Vida nodded. Keeping to the shadow of the huge cab of the shovel, they planted the bomb on the side toward the Caterpillar. Even with the small amount of dynamite they'd had the cash to buy that day, they could damage both pieces. Vida checked the luminous dial of her old watch. Going in had taken them longer than anticipated, so they had only fifty minutes left on the alarm clock.

With Vida leading they retraced their steps, still moving cautiously until they were through the fence and into the woods and even then taking care they made as little noise as they could manage. Nevertheless, they went quickly, staying together. At last they came out on the access road and trotted side by side toward the highway, trying to listen hard for cars as they panted and ran. The bombing was in the nature of a tax they charged, she thought, for greedy and corrupt behavior; at the very least, it would make people talk about the power plant and why some people opposed it. The communiqués that Eva and Joel were mailing tried to touch all bases, but came down strongest on the possibility of cheap hydroelectric power in New England and the high cost of nuclear plants.

Vida had written a couple of sentences she remembered as she trotted slightly in advance of Kiley, turning now onto the main road. Here they slowed down and kept on the shoulder.

"Car," Kiley whispered.

They jumped into the snowy ditch and crouched behind some bushes. Vida checked her watch: eighteen minutes left—only eighteen! Vida had written, "Uranium and plutonium are the most costly substances known and among the most limited. To depend on them for our energy makes as much sense as burning gold." Then she talked about their short useful life and long, long afterlife. "It's like someone who hires a gunman who kills an enemy; then the gunman blackmails them for the rest of their lives, year after year, decade after decade. In this case the blackmail goes on for a hundred thousand years."

The car was past. They rose brushing snow. Vida's feet hurt with the cold. She trotted on more stiffly. Kiley was in advance now. Finally they saw the car. Tequila was on the far side of the road so that he could face them. Kiley got in front and Vida in back. "Turn on the heat," she said. "I'm frozen." Tequila started the car at once, heading for Eva and Joel.

As he drove, Kiley squatting awkwardly in front and Vida with more room in which to maneuver in the back seat, both changed out of the wet clothes and into sweaters and slacks. Vida's teeth were chattering. Why was she so nervous? Waiting to find out how things had gone with Joel and Eva. Her watch read blast in five minutes. They had shaved their safety margin too close tonight. Eva and Joel must be already calling in the bomb threat to clear out the watchman. He was too far from the blast to be injured, but it was well to get him off the premises. He would be told his office was about to blow up to get him out beyond the gate. However, Tequila should be making the pickup the moment they got off the phone, and they were just coming into the town. It would not do to leave Eva and Joel standing around outside the phone for any length of time. Where had Tequila left them? They drove past dark filling stations, a lumber mill, a funeral home, a school. It was past the time the bomb had gone off. She could hardly sit in the car. It seemed to her she could run faster than they were going. Main Street at last. Stores all shut. Skimpy-looking spruces were tied against the street lights, and red bunting with pasteboard bells dipped over the street.

"There's the phone," Tequila said. "But I don't see them." It was a freestanding pay phone in the middle of a block.

"Go slow along the block," Vida said, leaning against the back of the front seat trying to see past Kiley. "There. In the bakery doorway." She felt silly with relief. She slid over, opening the curbside door, and they hopped in, Eva first. "How did it go?"

"Fine, except where you were guys?" Eva said. "We called it in."

"Who talked?"

"I did," Eva said. "Joel mailed the communiqués and dropped the letter at the newspaper."

"I stuck it to the bottom of the outside door with masking tape. They'll see it when they go to open the door tomorrow." Joel craned around Eva. "What was with you all? We got scared."

"The terrain was harder than we expected," Kiley said briskly. "Such short delays are inadequate. As it was, we had to run back to the road. On ice that's risky. What if one of us had slipped and turned her ankle? We'd never have made it to the car by the time the bomb went. Roger's guilty of an error in judgment."

He was in a hurry, she thought, but would not say it aloud. They were all safe, anyhow. Back to Agnes' for cocoa in the kitchen. Agnes would be asleep and they would whisper, feeling like children staying up illicitly. Family troubles. Family. It was like a sore tooth, a broken tooth she could do nothing about but probe with her tongue. In New York she would manage to find out. If only she could reach Sam! Sam would tell her how Ruby was. He'd tell her straight, if only she could figure out how to get Sam on the telephone.

23

Joel and she were exhausted and fell asleep almost at once. In the morning she got up before him to chop wood with Eva. It was not until after the meeting at the A-frame to critique the night before's action, read the newspaper accounts—too brief for their liking—and discuss possibilities for the larger bombing at the utility's offices that finally, in the very late afternoon, Joel and she got time together to talk. Nonetheless she had noticed at the meeting that Eva and Joel seemed friendlier. They told their story together, prompting each other rather than interrupting or correcting.

Vida had done her hair and she was sitting in front of the Franklin stove in the parlor to dry it—there was no hair dryer in the house. One of the parlors was open and not exactly shabby but well used. The hardwood rockers and needlepoint chairs could take a lot of use, and had. The other parlor was kept closed up and unheated, making Vida imagine that it had forever been host only to weddings and funerals. Though most of Agnes' younger life had been spent in Boston, this house had belonged to her family for seventy years, and her mother and aunts had grown up in it.

Vida's hair was still damp and lank, but she could already tell it was going to work. She flirted with herself in the dusty mirror over the high kidney-shaped table. "Is it going to be good?"

Joel grinned. "Of course. Wasn't it my idea? Do I ever steer you wrong?"

"I'm glad it went well last night."

He mimicked her, repeating her mild statement and adding, "So pleased we didn't blow ourselves up and all get busted."

"Did you enjoy it at all?"

"I'd rather be with you and work on that end. That's the fun, I bet. I never did that. . . . But Eva's okay. She's funny sometimes. When we were waiting on the street, she said that if you left us there much longer we ought to get Santa Claus suits and buckets and bells to ring and we could finance the whole business and stand on the street without anybody paying attention."

"So you kind of like her, maybe, you monster?"

"Yeah. . . . If you want to spend the night with her tonight before we go off to the Big Apple, do it."

"Really? Are you testing me in some lousy way?"

"I'm trying to be generous and adult. I'm trying to give the ax to my own jealousy."

"Joel, it'd be good for me. It'd make things much easier between Eva and me. I don't want to hurt her. I know it's rotten for her to see I'm in love with you the way I never was with her."

She waited at supper, watching Eva across the table, able to smile in her calm oval face without guilt because she had something to offer, finally, that went a little way toward Eva. She loved the waiting, the sense of a present in store; but she felt impatient by flashes. Wary that if she waited too long Eva would have made other plans—agree to help Roger shop for toys for the children, agree to work on quilting all evening with Agnes.

She fretted while the meal seemed endless. Agnes ate slowly and asked a lot of questions. Roger and Agnes liked to argue their way through the evening news, offering opposing analyses and predictions. Joel was withdrawn, silent. Occasionally Eva took part when something caught her interest. Roger and Agnes were arguing heatedly about the changing political situation in China, a matter of equal ignorance to both of them. They had no special information. All they knew was filtered through the lenses of *The New York Times* and *The Guardian*, and they might as well have been arguing about life on Mars. Life on Marx, she thought, amused, and tried to catch Eva's eye.

Eva washed up afterward. Vida dried and put away, because she knew the kitchen a little better and because she wanted to catch a private word with Eva. Finally she managed. "Would you enjoy my company tonight, m'lady?" She played cavalier, taking Eva's hand to kiss it.

She followed Eva up the kitchen stairs. Just as Eva was opening the door to her room, Agnes came down the hall. Shit, Vida thought, she *would* happen along. What kind of lecture will we get? But Agnes beamed. "Have a good chat, girls. Now, I don't want a lot of tiptoeing around tonight. That young man you fancy is in the room next to mine, and I don't want to be kept up. You just behave yourself, Peregrine. Eva is always a lady when she stays with me."

Vida followed Eva into the room. Quietly Eva shut the door and tiptoed to the bed. "No tiptoeing," Vida said, shaking her finger.

Eva sat down, grasping the soles of her feet in her hands. "Is it really possible she doesn't know? Maybe she just doesn't like men."

"She likes men fine. She just doesn't approve of sex, except between consenting goats for the purpose of freshening." She sat down beside Eva and slid her arm around her.

Eva's back stayed stiff. "We can sleep in this bed, but no making love."

"Why not? Eva, I do love you. Let me hold you."

"Because you make it not matter. I don't want to make love with you again until it counts."

"Eva, it does count. Don't—"

"Don't say it."

Eva had known she was going to say, Don't withdraw from me. And meant she should not say it because she had done so herself. She was suddenly reminded of the flavor of intimacy between them—much in gestures, much unspoken and a lot that need not be spoken. In some ways they were suited. She had a pang of regret, while a fat tear oozed from her eye. In some ways Eva was infinitely more comfortable! They both leaned against the rickety headboard, side by side. "You look wonderful with your hair black like mine," Eva said. "What made you decide to do it?"

"Why not black like yours? It looks wonderful on you."

"And on you! You look even more beautiful now." Eva beamed.

"You never saw me with red hair. . . . Lark's the only person in the Network who remembers the way I was."

"And you, stupid. You remember. Don't you count?"

"Eva, I missed you. I missed you a lot. It's the truth. What I didn't miss was L.A."

"But I like it there." Eva's voice trailed off. "If only you were a sun person like me."

She could feel it growing between them, the myth, the body of explanations that would enable Eva to forgive her. Eva was a better person than she and longed to forgive. She was probably the most genuinely nice person in the whole Network, which was why Vida had got involved with her to begin with. And Vida, she was not so nice, offering up her hair dye as a sacrifice to each of her lovers in turn. But why not give a little pleasure?

Eva was saying, "I know now you won't come back to L.A. But I'm glad it's not over between us. That we haven't lost each other."

"Stay East then," Vida said impulsively. "We can all live together." She could make it work out, somehow. She loved them both. Eva didn't like to have sex that often. It would work out. Why not?

Eva smiled, squeezing Vida's chin between her hands. "I don't like living with men, you know that. Joel seems very nice, but . . . I really do love L.A. There's so much music, Perry. I got starved for music at Hardscrabble. It's cold here, you can't go outside. It bites you."

After every argument about L.A. for the rest of our lives, Vida thought, Eva will look at me to see if I haven't changed my mind. If Joel leaves me—he's so young and moody—would I go back? Wouldn't that be tacky? But who else would I go to? Better Eva than Lark; better Eva than anyone else she knew. Why couldn't she have both? Eva just thought she would not like living with Joel. "Joel isn't like Kevin—I mean Jesse—you know. He's not macho."

Eva hugged her, sharply. "Silly. We can compromise. We can live in a two-flat house in Kansas—that's halfway. I'll live downstairs and he can live upstairs and like Persephone you can go back and forth, half time with each of us. . . . Why not be Persephone rather than Peregrine?"

"No! I do not feel like a maiden carried off. And you're younger than me, and so is he. I think of myself more as a Ceres, if we're typecasting."

Eva only laughed at her. "Turn out the light. We'll be wakened at six, never fear, and it's ten. . . . Remember when we went backpacking near Mount Baldy and that butterfly sat on your wrist and dried its wings?"

"Did Alice really turn herself in just to have a baby?"

Eva sighed in the dark. "Perry, it's not a *just*. Don't you ever want a baby?"

"Actually, rather seldom. I want my family mostly." Ruby, Natalie, Sam and Peezie. "I want my life back."

"What I wish is I could play with other musicians more. Perform. . . . I used to have fantasies of appearing someplace suddenly in a mask and playing and then rushing off into the night. Or making records from underground."

"Why couldn't we do that?" She poked Eva's arm gently. "Why not?"

"I can't claim our little dribs and drabs of money for making a record of my music—come on. It doesn't make sense." But Eva turned onto her side to face her, rumpling Vida's hair gently. "Do you hate Alice now?"

"I'm kind of scared what she might say."

"She won't say anything. She's our friend. I trust her. I think she had a right to take her chances," Eva whispered.

"But she broke discipline, Eva. She should have come to the Board."

"We'd never have said yes, as a Board. We'd probably have separated Bill and Alice 'for their own good.' " Eva sounded a little bitter.

"*You* wouldn't ever do that. Would you? Turn yourself in? You wouldn't."

"Perry, don't you ever imagine it? I mean, then we'd have to face the problems of what to do politically now, with things all scattered. We'd have the same problems as other people."

"We'd be giving up, Eva. Letting them win."

"Maybe they win if we stay like this. What would we be giving up? We have to invent things to do now."

She felt frightened. Cold. "You wouldn't do that. Would you?"

Eva patted her shoulder tenderly. "Never. Don't sound so scared. I'm just talking. . . . You're my family. We're all so close I couldn't bear the thought of cutting myself off, the way Alice did. Only it makes me feel bad when they talk about her as a traitor. . . ."

In the dark Eva lay against her, silky and long and resilient and soft, but Vida could not bring herself to seduce her. She did not feel as if she had the right. Feeling the gentle rise and fall of Eva's breast against her side made her smell something sweet, the bush growing outside their old house that she had never identified. All trees and bushes were alien, as if she had found herself on another planet. She did not know the names of the trees along the sidewalk or the names of the weeds in the cracked earth of the yard. At the foot of the hill an old house was surrounded by a stucco fence covered with a vine bursting into huge purple flowers that rustled between her fingers when she touched the petals like the silk of a dress. Ruby, she always thought. Mama. In the rainy season the roof leaked in their bedroom, into a metal pan. Plunk, plonk. On warm nights the voices that floated like perfume from the next house were Spanish. For weeks at a time she would dream every night of Natalie or Ruby and wake up feeling entirely in exile. In the long hot dry days she imagined herself mummifying, like a dead mouse Eva had found once when all of them—Bill, Alice, Eva and herself—had been out in the desert rehearsing an action.

Eva thought living in the East was all Hardscrabble Hill. Vida fell asleep plotting how she would persuade Eva to love Vermont and persuade Joel to love Eva and Eva to love Joel and they would live together —yes, whether they liked it or not they would like it. She would make it all come out.

She got up before Eva, who like Joel was slow to rouse in the mornings. Eva woke in stages, the alarm set and ringing, the alarm reset, the alarm ringing again, the underwear half on and the body prone on the bed again with the long braids hanging off the edges swinging slowly like a pendulum. Joel was already at the table reading a morning paper that Roger, who had stood the night shift with Lark, had brought in. Lark was still with him—unusual, as they did not often hang together—and everybody seemed subdued. They had begun scouting the utility office.

"Good morning," she said heartily. "We're off to New York to bring back a barrel of money."

"In tens and twenties," Lark said automatically. "Make sure they're not sequential. Look at the newspaper."

"They've caught somebody?" she asked.

"Alice and Bill got sentenced."

She guessed, "Seven years? Ten?"

Joel handed her the paper and everyone watched her read. At first she could scarcely concentrate with those staring faces hanging there glum and watchful. The story was datelined from Los Angeles.

> Two anti-war activists who spent the last six years fleeing charges stemming from a draft board demonstration were sentenced in Federal Court here yesterday.
>
> Jean Diamond and Arthur Edward Baker, members of the self-styled Popcorn Conspiracy that attacked draft boards in Los Angeles in 1971 and 1972, turned themselves in at the office of the District Attorney on November 28. Diamond and Baker were arraigned yesterday in Federal District Court. They pleaded quilty to charges of creating a nuisance and obstructing governmental business and were given sentences of six and eight months to run concurrently.
>
> Miss Diamond, a 30-year-old blonde who has been living in Los Angeles under the name of Alice Cork, says that she and Baker plan to be married after they have served their sentences. She gave wanting a family as the major reason for their joint decision to end their six-year flight from justice.
>
> Baker, 29, is a native of Austin, Texas. He hopes to return to social work school.

"Six and eight months to run concurrently." She put the paper down quickly, as if it had grown weighty. "They'll be out by the summer. . . . I don't believe it. What does it mean?"

"Trying to drive a wedge in." Roger banged his pipe in the saucer that served him as ashtray. "Separate those of us who don't face heavy time. They're giving extra-light sentences to the smaller fish to isolate us."

Joel raised an eyebrow but said nothing. He was mostly not looking at her this morning, which worried her. Was he thinking of turning himself in? Or did he think she thought he was thinking that?

"It's bait, I agree. It makes me nervous," she said, clutching her forearms. What kind of sentence was hanging over Eva? She tried to remember.

"Of course, they'd send you and me up for life and throw away the key," Roger said. "They'd get us on so many heavy federal raps we'd never see daylight."

"Of course." She poured herself black coffee. "Well, on to social-work school for Bill. . . . I guess we should call him Arthur now. I never knew him as Arthur."

"Art, he was. I thought I knew him." Roger shook his head. "Who'd have expected him to lose his nerve?"

24

As they drove the old car to New York, she could feel Joel brooding. Was he envying Alice and Bill? She cast about for a way to bring up the subject without seeming to mistrust him. At last he muttered, "So you did spend the night with her?"

"Of course. We agreed."

"I only suggested it. I mean, if you really wanted to be with her instead of me. You didn't have to. You can't say I pushed you."

That was what he was troubled about. She felt a rush of relief capped with annoyance. "So it was a trap—a cunning trap!"

"What do you mean, a trap? You're too subtle for me—"

"Bullshit. You manipulate rings around me, Joel."

"You wanted to be with her and you were. Did you make love?"

She would not admit they hadn't. She had to keep the space with Eva she had won from him. "What do you think we did?"

"I wondered. . . . Did you enjoy it?"

"Stop it! Stop it or I'll jump out of the car! I mean it!"

"Sure, and go running back to her. Don't let me get in the way."

"How can you act this way? You said you were struggling to overcome your possessiveness. You think jealousy is real—you value it. It doesn't mean you love me. The me you're supposed to love has a longstanding relationship with Eva."

"You want me to pretend I don't feel what I feel!"

"If you feel in a stupid way, I want you to fight it. Jealousy is a cozy pain for you—just too damn comfortable!"

"It's not so comfortable! I was hurt." But his voice was by now more playing at self-pity than embodying it. "Why did you stay the night with her? Why didn't you do whatever you do and then come to me? I couldn't sleep."

"Sweetheart, we were talking. We had a lot of catching up."

"Did you sleep?"

"Some. I woke and missed you and lay awake a long time."

"But if you woke, you were sleeping. *I* didn't sleep at all. . . . What'll we do about lunch?"

"I packed it—hard-boiled eggs, cheese sandwiches on whole wheat, pickles, Winesaps and a jug of Agnes' cider, a little hard."

"And the thermos—did you fill it with coffee?"

"Oh, Joel, I'm sorry. I forgot. I left it there."

"Ha. Look in the back seat. I remembered. I made a whole pot and poured it in."

"Then let's have some. Want me to drive for a while?" They were at ease again.

They had their second flat tire on the Hutchinson River Parkway. While Joel was changing it, she called Oscar. He offered to call her back and two minutes later did, at the pay phone where she was huddled. She meant to talk him into calling Chicago for her under some pretext and getting word of Ruby. But Oscar had his own news. "Yes, deario, I'm off to the hustings to deliver blows for the good lavender cause," he said in his nonchalant way. "We're launching our annual assault on the piggy City Council. But Natalie is out of the can and drooling to behold you. I have a number you're supposed to call. . . . By the way, squirt, did Natalie have a big romance with a karate instructor, a Nisei woman, a few years ago?"

"Yeah. But it's been over for a few years too."

"Some gossip travels slowly. East Norwich is a long ways from the Lower East Side. Hmmm. Natalie, of all people. We're everywhere, as we keep telling the city fathers. Natalie, the original married lady—"

Natalie would have news of Ruby and Paul's trouble. She felt calmer, knowing she would find out everything about her family soon. "Natalie's home now? Back on the Steering Committee of dear old SAW, you guys used her being married and having kids as an excuse not to relate to her. Like that turned her into *your* mother."

"A very cold Touché. Your Leigh is a bore, by the way. He approaches me as if walking up to a large ravening dog, saying Nice, nice doggy and trying to move his feet without coming any nearer."

She glanced over her shoulder. Joel had the old tire off. "Just so he gives you the check every month. Do you have one for me?"

"I'm to get it from him at the council meeting. He's supposed to be covering us. I enjoy collecting from him. It makes him so twitchy. He walked into my office and I said, 'Behold the married man. You're gaining girth as well as descendants.' Frankly, he's getting a pot. He said, 'Come off it, Oscar. I've been married before and it never cramped my style.' 'Well,' I said, 'your first wife wasn't the crampy type.' 'It's an open marriage, Oscar,' he said. 'Oh,' I said, 'is it open for her as well?' Because how open can it be for her with a belly to wheel around? 'It's open for me,' he said. 'I'm not about to be boxed by anybody.' "

"That sounds familiar," she said with slow nasty relish. Joel was fitting on the spare. It was lucky Oscar had suggested calling her back, as she would have run out of quarters long ago. "I thought he'd discarded that rhetoric."

"My guess would be he finds the belly oppressive and he's passing time elsewhere."

"Already?" She could have bussed Oscar. He knew just the gossip to make her feel on top. "Oscar, I shouldn't be so tickled, but he hurt my pride."

"He did that before . . . years before. You came to me pretty sore, chicken—I remember that."

She was startled at his mentioning their romance, more than a decade in the past and in another life. She had vaguely assumed he must be ashamed of it. "You were very good to me." Joel was tightening the lugs.

"Leigh wants to see you, by the bye. He suggests a rendezvous."

"What does he want to see me for?"

"How do I know, squirt? He can't resist you."

"We can resist each other just fine. He can shove his little rendez-vousie. How's your lover? That good-looking young man I saw at the ferry."

"A shmendrick. He has fantasies he's a great chef, but of course he expects to cook by divine inspiration."

"It's all over, Oscar?"

"Except he comes by and complains. Let me describe an evening chez nous. I'd come home from school, worn out, exhausted by the good fight, wanting to roll over and play. He'd have every pan in the kitchen out and he'd tell me we're having a fish timbale, an intimate dinner at seven, then we'll go out to a movie and drop into our favorite bar for a Sambuca and coffee. At nine, the smell of burning crud. After ten, three dry fish croquettes emerge with runny spinach and some desiccated potatoes. I have to clean up. After all, he cooked. No! I had to get rid of him." Oscar laughed cheerfully. "Big blue eyes can't make up for ten burned pots to clean, and the food was giving me indigestion. . . . How's *your* pretty young man?"

"About five feet away, glaring at me. He's just changed a tire. I'm still crazy about him."

"You both have such big green eyes. I've never had another lover with green eyes."

"Are you going to flirt with him all day?" Joel rasped. His hands were covered with grease, and he was scowling. "You can walk."

"Oscar, I have to get off." She hung up and slid into the driver's side. "At your service. Actually, Oscar was flirting a little. It's the telephone. He'd never do so in person for fear I'd take him up." She glanced at her watch, pulling out into traffic. "I can't believe how long I talked to him!"

"Neither can I," Joel said sourly.

"I never gossip on the phone that way anymore. Feels wonderful! Oscar asked after you, as my handsome young man."

"What does Leigh want?"

"Who knows? Who cares?" She realized that she had fallen into a little trap, admitting she had a message from Leigh.

"When are you seeing him?"

"I'm not. He can communicate through channels. We better drive over toward the north end of the subway and look for a cheap motel."

The Board had decided to foot the bill for two nights in a motel rather than send them back to Park Slope. They took the Cross County west and found a modest old motel in Yonkers, where they checked in as Mr. and Mrs. Sam Walker. Joel took a shower to wash off the grease, while she went in search of another pay phone. She wanted desperately to see Natalie; she had to set up a meeting with the lawyer; she had nine prescriptions in her pocket to get renewed from Dr. Manolli, the M.D. who helped them. Joel knew she intended to see Natalie and the lawyer, but she could imagine no reason he had to find out about Dr. Manolli, who was a Board secret. All these activities had to be fitted into forty-eight hours to get them on their way back to Vermont by Tuesday afternoon at the outside, so it would be tight.

She got Natalie and said the few words in code that would establish where and when their real call would occur. "Hey, how's your weight? Did you lose ten pounds yet?"

"Nine! Off my hips." Natalie sounded choked with excitement.

"Off your hips, o-kay! And how are your first, second and third children?"

"My second is best. The first is okay. The third is . . . out."

Therefore she would call Natalie at 9 A.M. on one of the pay phones from their second list. The lawyer she set up an appointment with late in the afternoon of the next day. Again the lawyer insisted on meeting in Manhattan. She got Dr. Manolli's answering service. Useless. She had to talk to him. She would have to call later.

Joel stood at the window of their motel room, staring at the parking lot gray with snow. "This time *I'll* see the lawyer."

"How come?" She was startled. Simultaneously she felt how much easier seeing Natalie would be if she didn't have to run into Manhattan; and what a poor basis for decision that was.

"How come not? The contact was made when we met Mrs. Richter. That bitch lawyer knows me. In fact, she seemed a lot more comfortable with me than she did with you."

"She's a woman who relates to men more easily than to other women. We should encourage this?"

"We should try to reform her while collecting our money in tens and twenties?" Joel snorted, pinching his nose. "The truth is, you don't trust me not to botch it."

The truth was, she hardly did. She was used to doing things herself. Joel was impulsive, moody, easily distracted; and she had to trust him in the long run. "Why do you want to do it?"

"Because, nook, it's dangerous for *you* to go into Manhattan."

"You too."

"The Feds don't sit around with my photo. I'm a face among a hundred thousand. When they put the collar on one of *us*, it don't even make the evening news. . . . I never lived in this city. Nobody in New York cares who I am."

She hugged herself. "Why go alone? We could both go."

"That's just as dangerous for you as going alone. And yes, I want to go. You have to put it in my hands."

"All right." She had a dreadful sense of letting go. If anything went wrong, it would be her fault before the Network.

Natalie was thinner and her color was poor, her face broken out for the first time since she had tried the pill. Vida took Natalie's face between her hands, saying foolishly, "You went to prison for me."

"Well, aren't you worth forty days of idiocy and minor brutality?"

Startling herself, she giggled. "You're supposed to deny it was for me."

"I beg your pardon. Let me take that again, sweetie. Oh, no, dear sister, it was not for thee. I did it for Goddess and country. The movement. Herstory. The glorious revolution."

She held Natalie's hand as they walked a path among towering firs. A few inches of grimy snow lay over the hillside, but the sun glinted on the glassworks of tiny icicles on the dark branches. They were meeting, as so often, in the Botanical Garden in the Bronx, where Vida had come by train and Natalie by car. "But it does make me feel guilty."

"I did it for me too. After all, I have to live with myself. I'm liking myself better these days."

"Because you went inside? Because you took a stand?"

Natalie waved her arm. "Because of surviving it—the noise, the awful food, the lack of privacy. *Time!* I'll swear I'll never waste another day in my whole life dawdling around the house feeling depressed and unable to get out of my robe. Reading week-old newspapers and doing three tasks at once halfheartedly while the TV spills out talk shows."

"Don't be ridiculous! You waste less time than anyone I know."

"You don't know, sweetie. For years I've had down days. Days I just can't cope. Can't get on with anything. Can't get up and out or at it or whatever."

"Not enough to keep you from being invaluable politically." Then she remembered herself years before denying other confidences Natalie had offered about how she felt boxed in, ignored, walked over as a wife and mother. "Do you feel guilty about . . . down days?"

"Sure. But I'm beginning to think they had something to do with Daniel. For years and years I've treated him like the weather, the climate. Something given. My husband."

"Why didn't you ever leave him, Natty? Why?"

"Why didn't he ever leave me?"

"I can't understand. You weren't happy with him since, oh, maybe six months after Sam was born."

"Funny we both pinpoint it there. . . . I don't know why, it makes me feel good that you remember it the way I do."

She stopped. "I haven't given you enough. Ever. I moved into your home. I moved into your life. Same way in New York, I arrived raw and bleeding. I've never given you enough."

"Well, I'm the one always feeling guilty and having to be nice. That puts me at a disadvantage. But don't change the subject. I've been realizing things about how I acted with Daniel. I took responsibility for a lot of my life, but I always treated him as a given. I think I felt as long as I had him, I was all right—respectable, married, secure. You know, I think my mother dying scared me a whole lot."

Something. A cold finger touched her. "Natalie, what do you have to tell me? Natalie!" She grasped her by the arms.

Natalie looked away and then into her eyes, almost embarrassed. "A week ago, baby—six days. Last Tuesday. I flew out there for the funeral." She put her arms around Vida.

"Why didn't you . . ." But how could anyone reach her, tell her? "Mama's dead? Ruby's dead?"

Natalie nodded, holding her tight. She felt squashed. Angrily she thrust Natalie away and walked off the path into deeper snow, kicking it up with her boots. Boots Natalie had bought her in the fall at Filene's, she remembered aimlessly. Her head hurt. She ran into a fir as if it had suddenly leaped in front of her. The pain helped. She kicked the tree, kicked it again and again till her toes were bruised. She banged her head on the bark till Natalie seized her from behind. Then she turned, struck Natalie's shoulder and collapsed against her. She could scarcely tell what she felt. She was buffeted; she lurched and turned. It seemed to her she felt nothing but long shuddering tremors, the cracks in things.

They stumbled on, holding each other. Tears dripped down Natalie's round cheeks. When Vida hugged Natalie, Natalie's curly hair got in her eyes. They walked on through the firs till they emerged on one side of the conservatory. The sun striking the icy crust of a hedge hurt her eyes— broken glass it seemed. "How could she forgive me? I wasn't with her."

"It happened in the night. She had her third attack in the middle of the night." Natalie tugged at her arm. "It's cold. Let's go inside."

She let herself be towed. "Paul will say I killed her."

"He won't say anything of the sort." Natalie nudged her along toward the winter entrance of the conservatory, fumbling for her purse to pay for both of them. "She rallied after she saw you. They were talking about letting her go home in a week or two."

"Did Sharon catch on to what was happening that night?"

"You bet your boots. And the funeral was swarming with FBI and red squad. All those guys in suits standing at the back making notes, while the rabbi did one of those She was a real Yiddishe Mama routines."

"Ruby? That would have made her spitting mad."

"I felt like she was poking me in the ribs. I used to get mad when she did that. Sticking her sharp elbow in our ribs. . . . Did you ever feel embarrassed by her when we were kids?"

"By Ruby?" She was startled, following Natalie into the Orangery, where the scent of orange blossoms perfumed the air, lush after the outdoors. She did not want to breathe the perfumed air. "No. She was so vivid. I'd just get pissed with her for being hardheaded."

"I mean, we'd bring her to school for some event and she'd listen to the Principal and poke us in the ribs and hiss, Baloney! Other mothers didn't do that. In the hospital all the nurses and orderlies were telling her their love lives. She knew who was sleeping with who on every floor."

"Did she ever find out you were in the jug?"

Natalie blew her nose. "Come on, the john's just ahead. I can wash my face. Paul! After swearing everybody to secrecy, he let it out himself."

"But you never got to see her again?"

Natalie shook her head no. "I was going to fly this weekend with the kids. Sandy had sent me money for plane fare. I used it up for the funeral. I'm just glad I got out in time."

They were framed in the mirror side by side: Natalie's face red and moist; hers, dry and stiff. "It's dirty, how they get us! She dies and we can't be there. That's how they hurt us. I let her down. I saw her when I could, but I should have tried harder. It was risky. She couldn't learn to take care. She always thought I was just playing some kind of silly game."

"But sweetie, she had a good life."

"Not the first two thirds. . . . She was happy with Sandy, wasn't she?"

They drifted arm in arm through a room of monstrous topiary shapes. Puerto Rican men were playing cards, men in their fifties and sixties, while a row of women chatted under a tree that grew up to the high white metal–and–glass dome. "I think so." Natalie scratched her head. "They fought a lot. It used to startle me. He never fought with my mother that way, screaming in the kitchen. She got to him—that was it. She fascinated him the way my own mother never did. He was excited by her, she got under his skin, and he learned how to shout and rave. . . . I used to do that with Suki. We'd shout at each other."

"You and I have always been able to lose our tempers."

"When we're close. Not when we were fighting about politics all the time, remember? But I never could do it with Daniel."

"Oh, come on, you fought all the time. I remember."

"Not like you scream and hurt and kiss and make up. It's like a battle under the surface, where you're always fighting about the telephone bills and when will we get the furnace cleaned, but you're really fighting about how come you don't make love with me anymore and how can you make such a fuss about that little creep?"

Her legs buckled. She did not know how it happened, but she was sinking. Natalie pressed her back onto a park bench under an African tree with a punched metal label hung on it. They were in a long room shaped like a big quonset hut, all white metal and glass, with large aggressive plants around them like philodendron run amok. She felt drunk. Her eyes ran. She felt out of control, out of equilibrium, dizzy, attacked in all her senses, her head about to break open and spill. Silently she wept, while Natalie plied her with tissue after tissue.

"Hold on," Natalie was saying. "Poor baby."

"Natty, she never got to meet Joel! She wanted to so bad. She would have flirted with him. He likes being flirted with. It puts him at ease."

"Sometimes I used to wish I was Ruby's daughter." Natalie was daubing at Vida's face. "It seemed to me if I'd been born Ruby's daughter, I'd be beautiful like you and slender like you and know how to wrap men around my finger."

"Oh, Natty, I always get wrapped. I know how to attract, but I never keep my head. Once I'm involved, it's all the way—plunge, splash and drown. You only thought that because I wasn't real attracted to the boys we went to high school with. I think it was a class thing. They were too bland. I wanted a bit of electricity. A taint of danger."

Natalie smiled wryly. "Well, you got what you wanted, in aces."

As two young men entered the room, automatically she signaled to Natalie that they should move. They strolled onward. The air was cooler, moister in the next room. Ferns. "Inside, I got a funny message from Lohania. Then they told me I had a visitor one day and it was her. They let her see me. I was pretty suspicious," Natalie said.

"What did she want, Natty? Is she connected to Randy? How did she look?"

"She's maintained on methadone by him. It's all quite legal, and it binds her like a leash. . . . She looked not so good. She was nervous, tense."

"But she's working for Randy. You didn't say anything to her?"

"Now you think I'm stupid all of a sudden?" Natalie squeezed her arm. The next room was unpleasantly moist, so they kept moving. "Oh, look." Natty pointed ahead. "There's a bench in the desert."

"I like the desert," Vida said, since Eva wasn't around to draw hope from that statement. The sun was almost down in a blaze of red that seeped through the glass to fire the cactus, gnarled, knobby, menacing. "What did Lohania want?"

"She asked about you. I maintained I hadn't seen you in years. She didn't believe me. She said Kevin still feels ripped off by the Network and that they haven't done shit since he was booted out. Then she said to me, In the middle of all this mess, he's still real, you know that? He's got his politics still. She said I'd see I was wrong about him. Now, what does that mean?"

Vida shrugged angrily. "I don't suppose it means a thing except that Kevin's buying light time by shooting off his mouth. Randy and Kevin always did get along." Briefly her eyes began to run again. She took another paper handkerchief from Natalie. "I hope you have a lot of these?"

"All mothers do." Natalie stroked her hair. "I forgot to say I like your hair that way."

"I thought you hadn't noticed. I'd forgotten it myself."

"I noticed, but I was focused on how to tell you about Ruby."

"It's a funny place, this conservatory." She looked around. "A little seedy. . . . Randy was ambivalent about us. He wanted so bad to succeed he'd have killed for it. Maybe he did kill for it. But he loved the action, it let his fury out. He went to a second-rate Jesuit college 'cause he couldn't get into Fordham Law School. How he hated us!"

Natalie grimaced. "In the courthouse he came up to me. 'We're going to burn your buns this time,' he said in that self-consciously vulgar way of his, as if words turned to shit in his mouth. 'We'll send you up until the rest of your hair turns gray and your teeth fall out. The whole time you can know that that busy professor husband of yours is balling all the freshman girls. You're never going to see your kids again,' says Randy to me."

"I hate him. Finally I do."

"I said, 'It's nice to see a familiar face, Randy. Blown up anything lately? How you must miss the old days! Cheer up. It won't stay this quiet long and you can start some action again. Some plastic surgery and a new identity and you can trap some more kids and ruin their lives, right?' " Natalie made a sour face.

A man came through shaking a finger at them. "Time, ladies. Closing time. Got to move on out."

They rose and followed him reluctantly. Vida said, "I hate to think of Lohania as lost to us. That Randy got her after all."

"She was lost to us a long time ago." Natalie tightened her arm affectionately. "Oh, another lost country." She screwed up her forehead. "Tomorrow. The Rex Arms on West 55th near Eighth. Room 314 at 12:30 P.M. There! That's your message."

"Oh. Did Leigh go to the funeral?"

"No." Natalie looked surprised. "I told him, but I never expected him to go. You know Leigh—he doesn't like to put himself through that sort of thing. Besides, he feels guilty about divorcing you. Doesn't want to face us in a clump."

"So what does he want? What's this Rex Arms business?"

"To see you. He'll be waiting in that room tomorrow, says he."

"Let him wait." She smiled as they buttoned up, leaving the building. "It's getting dark. . . . Let him sit in room 314 in the Rex Arms till 12:30 A.M. In fact, I would enjoy immensely that he wait and wait and wait. It'd give me great pleasure."

"You don't want me to tell him you won't come? Or might you?"

"Don't tell him a thing. You shouldn't be having phone conversations about me."

"Oh, Vinnie, don't harrumph at me. We use a code."

"Well, use the code for maybe. Let him sweat it. Frankly, I'm not tempted. . . . How come he wants to see me?"

"The station just got bought by a conglomerate. He's afraid for his job. Making it as a free-lance journalist is a lot of sweat and he doesn't relish the idea."

"Does he still relish being a daddy?"

"In principle. That you can't cancel the baby if he gets fired is beginning to annoy him. You're his political insurance policy, you know. If he feels he's not doing anything with his life, if he gets worried about compromising his politics, if he misplaces his sense of direction, if he feels guilty, you're his ace in the hole. No matter what people think he's doing with his life, he has his connection with you. A link to the underground. He is helping fugitives. He's having clandestine meetings with a member of the notorious Network. Even though he looks like Clark Kent, he can duck into a phone booth and become Super-Leftie."

"Could I have another handkerchief? All I do is run off at the eyes, Natty. I thought it was love."

"Oh, shvesterlein, he does love you—or anyhow, he did for a long time. I just don't know what he meant by that."

"Something more than someone you say hello to on the street. Somewhat less than I mean." She shook her head. "It's late!" The gardens were dark, and nervously they hurried to Natalie's van. Natalie unlocked the door and stood by, reluctant to get in. Vida said passionately, clutching her by the shoulders, "I don't want to leave you today, I don't!"

"You're scared something will happen? I'm all right. I'm doing fine. Just take care of yourself."

"How are the kids?"

"Sam and Peezie are back with me. I'm in trouble for yanking them out and sending them off to Chicago. Their schoolwork is all confused. But it was good for Sandy and not so bad in the end for them. Fanon's with his father, and we're getting ready to take to the courts about him. I'm told I haven't a chance, but that's his lawyer tells me that. My lawyer says Phooey, we'll skin him alive. It's blood-and-guts infighting," she said cheerfully. "Let me give you a ride. It's dark and cold and windy."

"Just to the train." She climbed in.

"Joel's waiting for you. He'll help. Won't he?"

She nodded.

Natalie turned the key, pumped the gas, got the engine to turn over, wheezing. "This is so trivial on top of it all. But. I'm having a romance."

"A romance! From prison?"

"Sort of. She was on our defense committee."

"What's she like?"

"Actually, she's kind of like me. She's Jewish, she's thirty-seven, she's got two kids she's raising. She's been around the left for years and just started becoming a feminist in the past four or five."

"That isn't like you. That's more like me. What's her name?"

"Zelda. Everybody calls her Zee. When she was younger, everybody used to tease her that it was Z for Zaftig. . . . Sweetie, we only slept together once, in a great hurry. We have to be careful because of my lawsuit. My lawyer told me if I start having an obvious affair, especially with a woman, I'll blow it. So we hold hands and play with the kids together and take them to the circus and watch Peezie run and meet in strange restaurants. So sue me," she said glumly. "A romance at my age."

"But you're lovable, Natty, why shouldn't you be loved? Is she really like you?"

"Zee's wittier, a harder surface. She's been alone longer. She knows how to change a washer in the faucet and a tire on the car. More of a New Yorker than I am. She dresses better."

"What does she do?"

"She's a legal secretary. You sound like Ruby! Next you're going to ask me, 'Is your new friend, you know, *affectionate?*' Oh, Vida, don't cry."

"I'm not, I'm not. Drop me right there. Oh, good luck, Natty! Please have some good luck and some good loving for a change. She'd better be good to you or I'll blow her up."

"Sure." Natalie shook her head. "Big talker. You never even blew up Daniel."

"Do you want me to?"

"Sometimes!" Natalie laughed. "I'm not the grudge-holding type. I just want some money for the kids."

Vida walked off rapidly, and then Natalie passed her in the van and turned left out of sight. A romance! And she thought of Natalie as the practical one; except that Natalie would be practical. Natalie would manage her romance without endangering her court case or frightening the children. She would sacrifice her heart's desire to the children if she had to, but she would try to have a taste or two, a big bite.

The tears started as she strode along the platform. She bit her lip, bit her cheek hard until the tears seemed to withdraw back into her sinuses and her face cooled. No Ruby, no mama, no more. Was she an orphan? Or was Tom alive? She imagined him huddled drinking from a bag on Skid Row in Cheyenne, Wyoming.

As she pushed into the crowded train, she rejected the image. Surely he had moved in with another woman; a string of women. Her daddy would not rest alone. They were all that way—Tom, Paul too, Ruby and she herself; they did not often sleep alone. They were a family of sexual grabbers who hooked into people. They connected. Paul couldn't let go of Joy even after divorcing her. She wished she could see her big brother, just for one hour. Brief meetings were best; they could express their caring but not run out of things to say.

We made each other be sisters, Natalie and I, she thought, riding through the darkness. Yet the myth became flesh. We are sisters: one blood, one life, one work. No matter what's going on in my life, Natalie will be with me till death, and then there will be a hole in her or in me that nothing will soften—a black hole of pain, of absolute loss and entropy. It's by that possible loss I measure all others.

She could not think about Ruby—not yet. She could only watch the stations flash by and wait till she could be with Joel, who had gone into Manhattan and danger, who had been with the lawyer, who had been making the pickup of the advance money and learning the details of the Michigan job. She did not look forward to that, not at all. It would be risky. Oh, well, no one paid well for what wasn't. When there were no questions asked, it was because people who could afford to ask questions back wouldn't touch the job. She huddled, a motherless homeless child of—what? Was she thirty-six? Thirty-seven? She couldn't remember. So many false identities confused her. She had not celebrated a birthday in years. Would she, for once, with Joel? She felt paralyzed and cold.

25

When she got back to the motel, Joel was not there. True, he had farther to go, into Manhattan and back; but she had been with Natalie until four thirty. And the black Mariah was gone. Had he returned from the meeting with the lawyer and driven off someplace? But why? And where was the money? It was well after five, and full night outside.

Her impulse was to bolt the motel room. She felt impaled, fluttering there. She wanted to clear out and watch from someplace else—but where? It was cold outside, dark and windy. What was keeping him? She paced from bed to window. He must have driven to the train and left the car there. Flat tire? Battery low? Engine wouldn't start? He must be fixing it even now. Accident?

Turning out the room lamp, she stood at the crack in the draperies. Endless headlights and taillights slurred by on the road beyond the U-shaped court. In Yonkers it was rush hour. Cars, cars, cars, none of them Joel. Her stomach was hard and heavy as lead. She clutched herself with one hand lightly kneading as she grasped the draperies with the other. Although the room was stifling, she had her boots and coat on. If they had him, they would not know where to find her: he would never tell them. They could not call every motel in the surrounding area with the license number; or could they? But why would they think she was staying in a motel? Still, they would get to that. How long should she wait?

If they had him. No, she couldn't think. She willed him to appear. Please. Right now. Or the twenty-first car after that station wagon will be him. Nineteen, eighteen, seventeen. Where in hell? What had happened?

What kind of disaster, what flavor, what magnitude? She hallucinated his face. She kept seeing the black Mariah lumber in among the granite banks of hardened sludge. Please, please, please. Eleven, ten, nine, eight. Let me die instead. Him and Natalie, they're all I really have. Five, four. I'd be willing to catch the flu again. Let me get kicked off the Board. Kiley can win the next move. Three, two. Please, make it be him. I'll love him so well—better than I ever have. I'll give up the antinuke project. One, zero. No black Mariah.

It was time to try Dr. Manolli again. Slowly she zipped her jacket, checking that she had the room key. Past the line of rooms to the arcade she strolled, to the broken ice machine, the empty soda machine and the functioning pay phone. She was supposed to call between five and five thirty, and she was right on target. This time she got him.

"How about in the morning?" she suggested.

"Too risky. No, you come in at twelve fifteen. My receptionist's out to lunch and so is my nurse. If somebody's in the waiting room, you just walk right by as if you're delivering something. Go through the waiting room and take the door to the left. I'll be at my desk, eating a sandwich and doing paperwork. Twelve fifteen on the button."

Back she walked to the room, as slowly as she could. She didn't want to arrive. If he was safe, they wouldn't be able to clear out of town until tomorrow afternoon. They had to check out of the motel by eleven. She'd meet Joel at a Bronx subway station. Meet him—where was he? She was no longer conscious of her stomach hurting. Her chest ached. Fear soured her mouth. She wished she were lying unconscious at the bottom of a pit and felt nothing. One hand in the pocket of her jacket clutched the motel key. She was staring at the muddy ice so that she did not hear the car pass. When she lifted her head she saw it: the black Mariah nudging into their parking place. She stopped to make sure. Joel got out and banged on the door of their room. Stomped his feet and banged again. She hurried the last few feet.

"Where have you been?" she yelled. "Where were you?"

He pushed past her into the hot room. "Where were *you?* I finally get back and you can't even wait for me in the room."

"I waited for hours. I was making a phone call!"

"Who were you calling?"

"Never mind. Where the hell were you?"

"Never mind," he imitated. "I can guess."

"Joel, stop throwing up a smoke screen. What happened? Do you have the money?"

"Sure I got it." He held up a paper bag. "Shit, I thought we'd get an attaché case of money, like in the movies. But $750 in twenties isn't a big pile—just thirty-five twenties and five tens. You could stuff it in your pocket." He rubbed the back of his neck. "Uh, if you count it, you'll find eighty bucks missing."

"What have you been doing? Joel, this is no joke."

"I don't find it funny. Fucking bastards stole my car. I came from meeting her and my car was gone."

"You took our car into Manhattan? Why?"

"I get lost on that dirty stinking subway. Nobody ever gives you directions. It's noisy, and I can't tell one line from another. . . . So they towed my car."

"But you have it. . . . Joel, you went after it?"

"Damn right I did. We put six hundred dollars into that baby. Not to mention all my labor. What do you mean, I went after it? Do you think I'd throw it away?"

"But they could have our plates. I still don't know if they got them that time we were leaving the hospital."

"Sometimes you're a nut." He stomped around the room, flinging his coat at the bed. "Because of some half-assed might-have-been from Chicago, you want to throw away our car! Nobody cares about us, Vida! Nobody. It's ten years. You're living in a spy movie that's over."

Was she? She blinked hard. "Joel, why did you drive it into the city?"

"We have a car, why not use it? I hate that frigging subway. Every time the train hits a station, everybody shoves you. I won't run around the subway with a bag full of money. I'd have to be crazy."

"To take a car into Midtown, you have to be crazier."

"Fucking street didn't say No Parking. There were cars all along there and they didn't tow *them*. Just me, the bastards."

The anger faded back into her muscles. "I'm sorry I yelled at you."

"You're in some lousy mood."

"I was scared. And upset. I saw Natalie."

"Let's eat. That damn lawyer wouldn't buy me anything but peanuts and booze. I drank three bourbons and I got drunk as a skunk. But when I walked out in the street and my car was gone, did I sober up fast!" He snapped his fingers. "Still mad at me?"

"Joel, my mother's dead."

He swung around to face her. "Natalie just told you?"

She nodded. "I wasn't there. I couldn't even go to her funeral."

"She doesn't know that, Vida. And you did go see her. Remember that you went and saw her. It was dangerous, but you did it, and that made her feel good—right?"

She could only nod numbly.

"Take off your coat. Have you been crying?"

"I cried some, but we were in a public place." Even now the inner censorship of years made her say 'public place' rather than the name.

He sat on the bed and drew her down to sit beside him, her head lolling. "I got angry at you because I felt guilty. I thought I'd for real lost the car. And I know what those machers are going to say when we show up eighty bucks short."

"We have to make it up," she said without emotion. "It'll come out of our share."

"Want to go out to eat?"

"I'm not hungry."

"I am." He prodded her gently.

"It's the second time for Natalie—you know that? Imagine losing two mothers." Abruptly the tears rolled down her face again.

"That's better," he crooned, hugging her. "Cry it out."

"Better? No." Tears slid down, splashing on her bent arm, soaking into his raggedy rust-colored sweater. Her body was turning into salt water. She wept until her eyelids were too swollen to touch, until she could not breathe through her nose. Finally the tears slowed. "I still can't believe she's dead." She lay across him like a corpse. "Maybe that's why they have funerals. So you don't go on expecting love and a chance to explain or help or say something more."

He ran a bath and dumped her into it. That was a luxury. She lay spent, soaking, lapped about in water warmer than her last oozing tears. He took off his damp sweater and pulled a clean shirt from his rucksack. Their only luggage was a small backpack apiece. Then he went out to get sandwiches.

It took him longer than she expected. It was nine before he reappeared, as she lay curled on the bed in her robe. He carried in a pizza and a bottle of Italian red she viewed with suspicion. "I wanted to cheer you up," he said, waiting to see if she'd object.

"It's perfect," she pushed out. After all, he needed a treat. As she began to eat, she discovered her own hunger. The chianti was thin and dusty, but she drank it for the alcohol. They picknicked on the bed. This was not a fancy motel. The television set was black-and-white and the ice machine was broken; but they weren't about to watch television and they had nothing to put ice in.

After the last slice he licked his fingers. "Suppose I died? Would you mourn me? For a month? How long?"

"Look how long it's taken me to stop missing Leigh."

"You still miss him." He made a sour face. "Suppose I get shot? Like in Michigan. Suppose I'm wounded and you have to choose between leaving me there bleeding or staying with me and being caught."

"I'll shoot you myself. Quit this!"

"Did you get hold of Leigh?"

"I haven't tried to get hold of Leigh. I don't want to see him."

"You could. After all, you slept with Eva. You've seen him five or six times since we've been together."

"Once. Except for on the street that time. I don't feel good about him any longer, Joel. It's over, and I was a fool to hold tight on it so long. I wouldn't admit my old life is dead and I can't get those years back and I can't lead a life by remote control."

He relaxed against the headboard. "Now you get smart, woman. A little house. Even a trailer. Wouldn't it be cozy to live in a trailer?"

"But I like having a bathtub. A shower just isn't the same." She cuddled up beside him. "That A-frame would do us fine. Who owns it?"

He burrowed his face into her belly. "I only know it's somebody's ski chalet and they're off till mid-January in New Mexico. Wouldn't it be great to be snowed in together? Say, for a month?"

"You have to do one thing for me." She kneaded his shoulders. "You have to stop being touchy with Eva. I want the two of you to be friends."

"I like her okay." He stiffened his back. "How could we be friends?"

"Because you can't fuck her? Just because she's a woman. If she won't flirt with you, she's beyond the pale."

"That's not true." He sat up.

"Sure it is." She pulled him back down.

"Would you be with her if you weren't with me?"

"It wouldn't be *with* in that sense. We aren't a couple. And I can't go back to L.A. I don't belong in that desert-freeway landscape. I always feel as if I'm in a television series playing private eye. It undermines my sense of reality. I keep waiting for the music to tune up and the commercial to come on." She wanted to say right out, I want to be with you and Eva. But she felt the timing was bad. A. Persuade them to like each other. B. Persuade Joel he wanted to live with Eva and persuade Eva she wanted to live with Joel. C. Persuade Eva she wanted to live in Vermont. She had a month to work with, she figured. If only she could manage all the loose ends and sort of nudge it along without either of them figuring out too early what she wanted.

With her mother dead, she needed Eva more. She had to make everybody happy. When she let go of people they died. Bad things happened. She still felt guilty for Jimmy's dying, as if she had sacrificed him to Kevin and he had run off to prove his courage and burned for it. Too many losses. Joel was prodding her, repeating, "So who would you be with?"

"My own self. My history, my choices, my politics. Basically, that's how it's been for years. Alone, but without the fantasies emanating from my past. . . . And you? Who would you be with?"

"Agnes!" He rolled over onto her. "Goats and maple syrup. A great big house with sugar bush and a stream to fish in. That's contentment.

What more could a good old boy like me ask? A garage to tinker with my cars in and lots of broken-down old machinery to play games with.''

"She'd never sleep with you. Not once in forty years!''

"So she'd be just like Kiley. I'd make it with the goats.'' He took off his pants and shirt and was naked. Never in the coldest weather did he wear underwear. She was sure it was vanity.

"Let's make love slow this time. Make it last," she said.

"All right." He tugged at her robe.

She slid away from him and reached for her purse, getting out the diaphragm. "I don't ask miracles. Just a nice long cozy fuck."

As he lay over her, her skin took him in through every pore, his prick inside only the slightly more intense point of contact. Her breasts burned against him, the nipples rising into his chest. Her grief, her anxiety chafed her skin sensitive. She no longer felt solid but molten, liquefied. They were interpenetrated, his tongue in her mouth, his prick in her, arms and legs braided into confusion, sweat trickling mingled. She wondered if it would feel different if they were making a baby. Never would she have a child with him; debt to Ruby unpaid. Yet she lived for the children to come: children of her act rather than her body. That the world be different. For Alice that had not been enough.

She felt the breath swelling in her chest and throat, a desire to shout she bottled up in the motel, where they could hear the nasal drone of the TV in the room to either side. "I love you, I love you, I love you," she said over and over, churning under him, clutching. "I love you, I love you," he said into her neck, into her damp hair. "Oh, Vida, I love you!"

In the morning he went out for deli and coffee and brought back a bag to the room for a leisurely brunch, more baths, more lovemaking. "How come we aren't in a red-hot hurry this morning?" he asked. "Shouldn't we be making tracks?"

"I have one more errand to run."

"What kind?"

"For the Network. Just an errand. What you have to do is get my alimony from Oscar at Richmond. That'll cover some of the money lost yesterday. Then we can meet." She stopped to do mental arithmetic. She'd get him to drop her at the end of the IRT at Van Cortland and she'd take it down to 181st. Suppose Dr. Manolli ran half an hour slow and it took her half an hour to do business with him. At one thirty she'd be on her way. "Let's meet at the Cloisters at two and take off from there. You ever seen the Cloisters?"

"What is it, a bar?"

"No, it's a reconstructed monastery. A museum in Fort Tryon Park.

I'll show you on the map. At two I'll meet you there in the room with the unicorn tapestries.''

He made a sour face. "How will I ever find that?"

"Just ask anybody."

"Why can't we both go to Oscar? You don't care if I drive to Staten Island, right? I'm allowed to drive to Staten Island. It doesn't make me out to be a hick, right? So let's leave now, we both go to Oscar, and then we run your errand."

"I can't do it that way."

"Why?"

Because Dr. Manolli was worth platinum to them. Because only Board members were supposed to know the medical problems of everyone in the Network. Because Dr. Manolli could be contacted only by Board members. Because why did Joel always have to act so damned stubborn and curious when things did not concern him? "That's standard operating procedure. I have an errand for the Network. I'll see you at two. I'll probably be early, but I know I can make it by two. If you're there early, so much the better. By the way, you can park at the Cloisters."

He glared. "All right, let's get going."

"We don't have to leave for another twenty minutes."

"We don't want to be late for our little appointments and rendezvous, do we? You're not always right! You hand me these timetables like you're a goddamn social director. You run our lives like a fucking airport."

"Oh, let's be spontaneous, then. Like yesterday, when you impulsively decided to take the car into Manhattan because you were too lazy to ride the subway. Like taking a pet elephant along!"

"I knew you'd bring that up!"

In the car they sat rigidly side by side, each daring the other to speak. After a while she felt absurd, but did not try to make up because she simply could not take him along to the doctor's office. She would be in enough trouble with the Board because of the missing eighty. It would have to come out of their money, of course. She was more annoyed about the loss of the money than she had been the day before, when she had been frightened about him. If he got extra money from Oscar, that would help.

"See if you can touch Oscar for something," she said. "He ought to be good for a twenty."

"Why should I beg from your old boyfriend?"

"Oh, Joel, he's likelier to be interested in you than in me."

"So I should take advantage of that to try to get money from him?"

"Joel, stop it!"

"Stop asking you questions? Just take everything on faith. My girl-friend Moses."

"Stop twisting my intent like a corkscrew. Oscar likes us. He has a nice job and a comfortable life. He'll give you something. Tell him the car story."

"So he can feel superior too? You New York jerks. If you bombed into Sacramento and did something stupid, nobody in Sacramento would expect you to be born knowing the municipal ordinances. But every New Yorker thinks everybody with brains is born with the subway map of Manhattan imprinted on their circuits. If you ask some creep how much it costs to ride the subway, he laughs at you."

"Joel, at two we'll go home. And we'll have a home. Right after the Michigan job, we'll start looking."

"I don't know if I want to live with you," he grumbled. "You think I'm a moron."

"I love you. Let's just finish what we have to do and clear out. I'm on edge in the city. I'm always a little scared here."

"You don't wish you were living here? With the Mouth?"

"Not anymore. Truly!" As she started to get out of the car, she reached for the paper bag. "We split this here."

"What for? Are you planning to run out on me?"

"Sure. Or you'll elope with Oscar. For safety, love. It's an automatic precaution. If one of us is offed . . . you know."

"Spend it all on lingerie. See if I care."

"You'd love it if I did."

For the first time since they'd left the motel he grinned. "Frederick's forever! Purple satin! Black lace bikinis! Red see-through bras!"

"The Cloisters will put you in mind of the mortification of the flesh."

"Yeah? You don't care to have your flesh mortified. You like a good fuck and a hot bath and a crisp chewy bagel, the same as me." He gunned the engine and drove off, smiling, giving her a crooked little wave.

Riding the subway down, she picked up a *Times* off a seat to read and to screen her face. The headlines were all about the Middle East and a liquid-gas-tanker explosion. She read about the disaster with the sense of things getting entirely out of control. How can we win, she thought, when they're destroying so much so fast? A world gutted, disabled, the vision of a burning ship—but the ship was a planet. Still seeing people burn in the terrible wreckage, she skimmed the other headlines summarily; then her eye was caught.

ALLEGED I.R.A. GUNRUNNER
SHOT ATTEMPTING ESCAPE

A former anti-war activist allegedly turned gunrunner for the I.R.A. engaged in a running battle with the police yesterday on West 104th Street.

Kevin Droney, 33, was arrested in Manhattan on September 21 and charged with illegal possession of prohibited firearms. Assistant District Attorney Randolph Gibney described Droney as leader of a ring transporting automatic weapons to troubled Northern Ireland.

Come on—shot? Impatient, she skimmed

. . . released on $10,000 bail. . . . police guard as a cooperative witness in conjunction with a grand jury . . .

Gibney said Droney had agreed to cooperate with the office of the District Attorney in apprehending members of the Network, a revolutionary underground organization that has claimed credit for 51 bombings since 1970. . . .

At least, she thought vaguely, coldly, they don't say "so-called revolutionary" any longer; but we've done more bombings than that. They don't bother counting them accurately any longer. At least, no photographs were printed this time.

Officer George Gregarian said that Droney pulled a gun and threatened him yesterday at 9 A.M. in the hallway of an apartment building at 186 W. 104th Street where Droney had been living in the 3rd-floor apartment of Lohania Hernandez.

Gunfire was exchanged between the two men and Gregarian was wounded in the arm. Droney fled toward a car driven by Miss Hernandez, a naturalized citizen born in Havana, Cuba.

Gregarian called for help and a police cruiser responded in time to prevent Miss Hernandez from leaving the street. In the ensuing gun battle, Droney was shot three times. He was pronounced dead on arrival at Metropolitan Hospital.

Miss Hernandez, 35, a clerk in a travel agency, has been taken into custody on charges . . .

. . . fugitive for several years after Droney fled charges stemming from a 1970 bombing at Mobil Oil Corporation offices . . .

She looked up quickly, pierced with fright. She felt on display in the subway car. Kevin was dead. She did not feel like prancing on his grave. Poor Kevin. Poor Lohania. Lohania had spoken the truth to Natalie: he had not meant to cooperate for long. Had he been trying to contact the Network? He was stringing the authorities along. They had not bought him off. Randy was wrong about Kevin now as Kevin had been wrong about Randy then. She could not reread the article. Her eyes blurred, but she did not weep. She had cried herself out for Ruby till her tear ducts felt sore.

Kevin was bitter and hard, but he was true. Maybe he had sold them out, but nothing they couldn't survive. He had not sold himself. He had been biding his time. Ultimately, that mattered a lot to her; she was surprised how much. She would mourn his death in battle gravely and silently. Now she would at last forgive herself. She felt almost close to him. She was certain he believed passionately in what he was doing for Northern Ireland. That struggle would even heal him to his family and his past. She understood; she could not disapprove.

Why had they been unable to love each other? She did not know, but for the first time in years she regretted their failure; regretted they had not meshed as a couple rather than cursing herself for having become involved with him. They had needed Lohania to complete their family. They had not been sufficient as two. But why had they turned their anger and frustration so strongly on each other? How they had worked together the first years underground, twins, one machine, two arms of one swift body! For a moment she remembered his body, the lean fierce heft of his torso, the glint of lamplight on his yellow hair. The raw force of him. Lohania had been true to Kevin; all those years she had waited. She had thrown over whatever life she had built with bricks of pain in the intervening years to help him escape. She had been willing to cut herself off from her methadone source. Lohania too had proved ultimately incorruptible. Vida was impressed, and she was moved. Someday, she promised Lohania silently, she would see her again. The state would take revenge on Lohania for Kevin's act and once again she would have to do bad time, in a state prison under maximum security, Bedford Hills. No civilized time in places like Danvers for Lohania.

Numbly she moved toward the doors, got off. She breathed deeply, hyperventilating. She must make herself pay attention, break from the thick murk of depression. Look around, she ordered; be wary. Eyestalks waving. *Muerte en Sangre Fría* was playing at the movie house. Better a death chosen than a wasted life—right, Vida? She clutched her arms. A gaggle of empty buses half-blocked 181st Street as she walked toward Fort Washington. The neighborhood reminded her of where she had lived with Leigh—not physically, for the buildings were lower—because nobody in the lively street crowd seemed to own a majority: Blacks, Italians, Puerto Ricans, Jews. She made herself amble along past Thom McAn, a Daitch Dairy, a superdiscount cosmetics in the blare of "Silent Night." Most of the stores had Christmas decorations tacked up, aluminum trees turning to canned music, angels and shepherds and dusty white sheep under a pointy gold star. The liquor-store window was full of gift-wrapped whiskey. Christmas had crept up on her. She was not sure what date it was.

She had a desperate desire to give Joel something. If only they had not blown the eighty! A velour shirt or a bulky wool sweater. She could not spend the money. Instead, she ducked into a deli and bought him a dozen of mixed garlic and onion bagels, thinking of his last words to her. She considered putting them in the Bloomingdale's bag (from Natalie) she had folded up in her small rucksack, but actually the bagels fitted in with her change of clothes, toiletries and minimal disguise items. Striding on, she tugged at her green velour tunic that had once been a mini-dress, like Lohania's, like Natalie's. She had a strong urge to call Natalie, to hear her voice, to know her safe. Dangerous: Natalie's phone must be tapped. Just a bit of warmth. She noted every pay phone she passed, most of them broken, and kept walking. Identical apartment houses in a row with courts. Dr. Manolli's entrance was on the ground level to the side.

Even Dr. Manolli's office had a Christmas tree, this one red with crystal snowflakes. Muzak pumped into the waiting room, a thousand strings dreaming of a cooled-whip Christmas. Five women, two men and three children sweating there glared at her as she strode through to his door and knocked.

"What is it?" he called. Three years before, she had arrived with a badly swollen leg full of shards of metal. Would he remember? After digging out the metal, he had put her on antibiotics, which had given her a yeast infection. Four months had passed before she was healthy again.

"I have your mail they left next door," she said.

"Oh, yes, come on in."

The patients went back to gazing at the wall, leafing through *New Yorkers*, dozing, suppressing their children. Dr. Manolli was sitting behind his desk walled in by heaps of paper. "Can't trust anybody to do insurance forms," he said. "You got what you want renewed?" He was about five feet five, with a wreath of wavy gray hair around a bald dome that looked fashioned sensuously of marble. His complexion was clear and creamy. His eyes, a cool foresty brown, were magnified by his glasses. He was thin and elegant in his neat body and three-piece green-flecked gray suit, but his desk was unkempt as she remembered it, files all over the office, half-packed or unpacked boxes of yellowing paper.

He squinted at the first prescription. "How's her asthma? Just as bad?"

"She wrote it's a little better."

"Hmmm. Is he sticking to that diet I gave him for his ulcer?"

"As much as he can. When he isn't traveling."

"Medicine won't do a thing if he doesn't take care of his condition. And no aspirin. That's part of his problem."

They haggled their way through the prescriptions and notes on medical problems. At one point he shook his finger at her. "The septic leg. I remember you! What a mess."

"I *was* a mess." She glanced at her watch surreptitiously. She must not appear to be hurrying him, but she desperately wanted to be gone before his nurse and his receptionist came back.

"High blood pressure," he said, nodding. "Let's check you." She sat with the pumped-up device on her arm, trying not to fume lest she raise the pressure. He showed her the figures. "You're still running high. Cut out the salt. I'm going to put you on some medication. . . ."

"I'm feeling fine. Really. I don't want to go on anything if I can avoid it. I'll do without salt."

"I want to see you in a couple of months, then. Let's weigh you. . . ." He made her get onto his scale. "Weight's good. It's not weight that's your problem."

Finally he moved on to the next card. "Alice. She still hasn't had that operation for her deviated septum and poorly draining sinuses?"

"Never mind Alice." Vida took the card back. "She isn't with us any longer."

He raised his eyebrows, but made no comment. "For that migraine, I'll prescribe ergotamine tartrate, but Roger's not to use it often. Ask him to watch for nausea and feelings of numbness." He rummaged first in the drawers of his desk, a garbage heap of pill bottles. Then he poked around in a drawer of the filing cabinet. "Know I have it here. Might as well use it." At last he came up with a sample bottle. "Why waste these?"

She opened her backpack on his desk. Her palms were sweating. It was after one. She expected the patients outside to charge the door. Finally there was a knock and the door opened a crack. She shrank out of range, to the side. "I'm back, Doctor. Should I start sending them in?"

"Not yet. Hold the fort another few minutes." He went on going through the list, mumbling over each entry. "I'll give you some heavy B's." He threw some bottles of vitamin pills into her backpack. "Is Eva still on that vegetarian diet? You get her to take B-12 regularly, hear me?" He threw in some more bottles—randomly, it seemed to her, but they were probably vitamins. "I will not renew Kiley's barbiturates. I told her before she has to stop taking sleeping pills when she gets nervous."

"Kiley doesn't take them often."

"But she takes them in a dangerous pattern. It's basically a preaddictive pattern I can't encourage. I won't write her a prescription for barbiturates."

She felt a flash of full acidulous rage. Who was he to judge their levels of tension? He should try living on the run for years and years. Kiley wasn't about to be addicted to anything, but sometimes she simply forgot how to sleep. Vida dreaded walking out into the anteroom jammed with patients and now with his receptionist to look her over, but finally he glanced at his own watch. "My nurse'll be here any minute. Go out that way." He pointed to a door in the far wall she had assumed to be a closet. "It takes you into the corridor. The door will lock behind you automatically. Go left and through the service entrance. That's how I sneak in and out. Merry Christmas," he added as she was leaving. His calendar said today was December 23.

Hurrying toward the subway to take the IND, this time north to Fort Tryon, she worried over the date. There would be a lot of traffic for the holidays. Approaching the Cloisters, approaching the castle entrance, approaching then the room of the unicorn tapestries through mobs of schoolchildren herded from room to room to the drone of history on this, the last day of school, she observed all her usual cautions and went circuitously and warily, but her eye was perfunctory. It was more ritual than action; more prayer than surveillance. Her mind was on Ruby. She wanted to crawl back into the lap of her childhood and rest awhile. Come to Mama. She realized with a little queasiness that part of her passion for Joel was rooted in some subliminal identification of his warmth, his impulsiveness, his earthiness—even his testiness, his quickness of response —with Ruby. Well, why not? Why not seek in a lover the best traits of your first love?

Where the hell was he? She knew she had suggested as politely as she could that he get there ahead of her, but he was nowhere to be seen. Damn him. It was exactly two. She tried to concentrate on the tapestries, but irritation was nagging at her. Couldn't he do anything right? New York threw him. He had to do things his own way. Probably he'd got lost, thought he'd found some dandy new route and ended up going over the Triborough Bridge. All she wanted to do was clear out of the city. The later they waited, the heavier holiday traffic they would have to endure and the greater chance of something's going wrong.

At two fifteen, she did not know quite why, she went back to the lobby and called Oscar.

"Listen, Oscar, what time did my friend pick up from you?"

"He was here just before lunch. But I wish you'd called first, squirt. Leigh didn't give me that money."

"He didn't? What a jerk. How come?"

"Aren't you seeing him today?"

"No, I am not."

"Well, he thinks you are, and so does Joel."

"Joel thinks I'm seeing Leigh?"

"Yes, yes," Oscar sounded impatient. "So does Leigh."

"Well, I'm not. Oh, damn it, Oscar. Everything at sea." She hung up and ran back to the tapestries. No Joel. His damned stupid jealousy. He thought she was seeing Leigh while she was getting the prescriptions, so what had he done? Going out and getting drunk was not his style. What would he do? She had a moment of conviction and ran back to the phone. She had no choice; she had to call Natalie.

"Natalie? Me. Did my friend call you?"

"Yes."

"What did he want?"

"He said he had to reach you."

"Where did you say I was?"

"He seemed to think he knew. I thought you weren't going there, but he said you'd gone. He said he had to find you in a hurry. That it was desperate."

"So you told him that address?"

"I didn't know what else to do."

"Don't worry," she said automatically as she hung up. She started running before she decided, while she still swam in confusion. She acted first, running toward the subway, knowing she would have time to think on the way south. She ran, pushing herself, panting, her heart hurting, each breath serrated. If only Natalie had a worse memory or more suspicions of Joel's motives; but Natalie had never seen Joel as jealous lunatic. If only Leigh had been less arrogant in assuming she would meet him because he wanted to!

She sat on the train, clutched, quivering. Natalie's phone had to be tapped. The only question was how much Joel had said over the tapped phone and what they had been able to put together. Part of her demanded she clear out; part wanted to die on the spot with fear; part was determined she could still save the situation. Burst in, grab Joel, run for it. What had she failed to do? How had she failed Joel and herself?

She had told him she didn't plan to see Leigh, but he had not believed her, for in the past she had concealed meetings. His jealousy from Eva slopped over, contaminating this situation. What a stupid place for Leigh to suggest meeting! The train hurtled along. Her whole body thrummed with impatience. In normal times, whatever those might be, she would never have agreed to meet him in Midtown. What Leigh was doing was trying to fit her into his lunch hour. Then she realized she should have called at once, called the hotel room 314. But if she got off the train to do it now, she would have to wait till the next train. Too long. No. she was headed in the right direction, although the ride was interminable. What mess was she walking into? Leigh and Joel presumably were still there shouting at each other. How could Joel have assumed she would fit such a meeting in? He wouldn't think clearly; he wouldn't think; he would just bull in bleeding, expecting to catch her in bed with Leigh.

She wanted to bang her head on the filthy window. She was sitting at the far end of the car facing a corner decorated with glowing graffiti of names and streets. Faster, faster! Joel and she had lacked the leisure, the space away from hustling money, being on the run, to work out tensions between them. They must sit down and confront the ugly doubts and misgivings; they must face what they each most feared and mistrusted in the other. They çould come through: she knew it. She would not give up on him. No matter what danger his possessive impulses dragged them into, he was too powerfully entwined with her to relinquish; her love for him was too strong. She would not give him up. She would fight him to make it better, to make him better, but she would not give up.

She got off the train and ran three blocks and then stopped abruptly and stepped into a long steamy tunnel of a bar, back to the women's room. She went quickly past men drinking at the bar. A couple of men watched her all the way. In the women's room she opened her rucksack and with a spray can quickly streaked her hair gray, put pads in her face to round it, put on glasses with pink plastic frames. She wriggled into a dress and panty hose and crammed her tiny rucksack into the Blooming-dale's shopping bag from Natalie. The scent of the garlic and onion rose. How could he doubt her? She had a moment of anger: while he was stalking her presumed rendezvous, she was buying him bagels. Would he be embarrassed! As she hurried on, she tucked in the hood of her parka to make it a suitable coat for her new role. Middle-aged, slightly dowdy, respectable, that was the invisible woman she intended to be.

Still, the time was ten after three. Could they be waiting? If Joel had left, where would she ever find him? Nothing to do but charge back to the Cloisters. That idiot! Surely Leigh would not sit in the hotel bashing heads with Joel all afternoon. What would they talk about? Trouble, trouble, trouble. Yet what tugged at her as she picked out the hotel marquee across the street, on a building about ten stories tall and one hundred feet wide, was not an inkling of that kind of trouble. The hair rose on her arms. Slowly she ambled along the other side of the street, moving in the crowd, a shopper among shoppers. On the corner, a bun-dled-up nun huddled over a charity bucket. The first flakes settled like midafternoon ennui, little flat white yawns. She marched along the far sidewalk past the hotel, around the corner. She could not stop. She could not cross the street and enter. She could not.

Slowly she crept back around the block. As she came along the far side of the block, she stopped at the first functional pay phone to look up the number of the hotel. She called. "Room 314 please."

"I'll connect you," a woman said. There was a pause. "What room was that?"

"Room 314," she said, waiting.

"Just one moment, please."

"What room was that again, please?" the voice asked a moment later.

Vida hung up. She knew immediately they were putting a trace on the call. She kept walking around the block. She must be crazy, her Manhattan paranoia rampant. She must overcome her irrational fears, cross the street and go in and get Joel; yank him out of there and streak for safety. As she came round the corner to face the marquee again, that was her determination.

Again she strolled along the block across from the hotel. Why could she smell a stakeout? She could no more cross the street than a fish could climb out of its tank. She felt the surveillance. She cursed herself and kept walking. She could not cross.

The man sitting in a blue sedan on her side of the street, the guy reading a newspaper just inside the door of the lobby, they could be heat or just folks. The only way to find out was to go over. She could not cross; she could not enter. A strong magnetic wind blew against her. She could feel something wrong and she could not approach the hotel.

Why was she being so fearful? She stepped into a store, a women's boutique. The clothing was not suitable for the role she was playing, but she needed to watch the street. She felt crazed as she lilted to the salesgirl, "Something for my daughter. I'd like to bring her a present from New York City."

"Oh? Where're you from?"

"Erie, Pennsylvania." Abruptly her eyes stung, and she turned to finger a beige silk blouse. The car with the man sitting in it had left—ah, but the man holding the newspaper still stood just inside the lobby watching who came and went. Waiting for his wife? His mistress? Or her? She noticed a cab standing by the marquee, but it had its sign turned to Off Duty. When a couple tried to climb in, he waved them away. She felt a stab of certainty.

Slowly she walked in the direction from which she had come, back to the pay phone that was hers by use. This time she called Leigh's station. "Yes, I'm returning Leigh Pfeiffer's call. I had an urgent message to call him?"

"Oh, is this his wife?"

"Yes." A year ago, she would have denied that but meant it. Now she pretended it and had never felt less connected to him. "Is something wrong?"

"Don't be upset, Mrs. Pfeiffer. We had a phone call from Leigh's lawyer telling us the police are holding him for questioning. I'm sure it's some mistake. Apparently he was interviewing a deserter. We don't know anything more about it, but you should get right in touch with Leigh's lawyer. Do you have his number?"

"Yes, thank you. When was this?"

"We had a call just half an hour ago. The lawyer said that at first they wouldn't let Leigh make his call, but he was supposed to be downtown covering the gay-rights hearings so we had to be notified. That's where we thought he was."

"Thank you ever so much," she said mechanically, hung up and began to walk south toward the Port Authority bus terminal. She had to get moving; she had to keep moving; she had to walk and keep walking, although she did not know why. Leigh would be out by nightfall, for he had his journalist's cover. But the police had Joel. They had Joel and they had been waiting for her. Her they would not get.

She waded on as the flakes came down faster, beginning to wet the sidewalk, beginning to whiten the edges of buildings, the small squares of open ground around a tree or an excavation. They had Joel. She forced herself on, her life peeling off in strips. Part of her mind fixed on that loss, her heart ripped out of her; part of her mind worked rapidly, solving equations. Would they have Port Authority covered yet? Could they cover it with Christmas travelers in lines a block long? Should she head for the East Side instead, take the bus to LaGuardia, the shuttle to Boston, the bus north from there? She could go to ground in Boston if she had to. Contact Laura? No! She could not bear the thought of returning to the cabin on the pond without Joel. She would go crazy.

She felt as if she stood back there still paralyzed, gaping at the facade of the hotel where her lover had been taken while snow fell on her. Disguised as a hunched-over invisible woman of middle age, she trudged on through the snow falling with a slight hiss on the heated metal of cars waiting in stalled traffic. "O come, all ye faithful," "had a very shiny nose," hit her from loudspeakers. No more distractions. No humanity. No hostages. What can be taken from me now, except my life? I could piss that away and feel only relief.

Yet she could not walk into a trap. Joel and she would not be together in prison. Break him out? Some of those federal facilities did not employ tough security. He was still alive. Unlike Ruby, Joel was still alive. But tomorrow, the next day, the next day, stretching away toward a gray horizon, she woke up and he was not with her. Shaking her head in exasperation, she must have mumbled because a young man glanced at her and veered away as if startled. Crazy, he judged. She could not afford to seem crazy and tried hard to compose her face. He was so inept as a fugitive! Perhaps because he had been underground all his adult life, it was too normal to him and he did not take the precautions she lived by. Nevertheless, he was alive, even though she could not see him, hear him, touch him. Only she felt dead, the ghost of a life broken off a second time midway. Another great wound through the center of her life. She did not know if she wanted to survive it.

But she still had Natalie. Herself. Eva. Work. Her history, her political intent, her ability to cause trouble. What she had was what she had had in September, except for Ruby, except for the false promise of Leigh. Natalie must keep an eye on Joel for her. She shook her head heavily to and fro as the snow settled on her hair. How could she go on? She could not cry yet. She had to survive, even if she could not remember now just why—a life in the service of something that had once felt far more pressing. She stopped abruptly and pulled the bag of bagels out of her rucksack and threw them into a trash can. She could not bear the smell; she could not bear the hope they leaked in fragrance. I am at the mercy of history, she thought, feeling its force concretely as a steel press closing on her chest, but I can push it too a bit. One thing I know is that nothing remains the same. No great problems in this society have been solved, no wounds healed, no promises kept except that the rich shall inherit. What swept through us and cast us forward is a force that will gather and rise again. Two steps forward and a step and a half back. I will waste none of my life.

She hurried faster toward the Port Authority terminal and Vermont.

MARGE PIERCY
Woman on the Edge of Time

'The most serious and fully imagined Utopia since Ursula K. Le
Guin's *The Dispossessed*'   *Kirkus Review*

'This novel is perhaps the most important in the Piercy canon'
                                              Time Out

'Utopian novels like *Woman on the Edge of Time* are important
for visualising a better future . . . they may inspire people to think
about changing the world as much as a library full of books on
political science and economy'   *Socialist Standard*

Fiction   £2.95

The High Cost of Living

'She speaks for all outsiders, all those not comfortably basking in
society's approval'   *The Glasgow Herald*

'The novel is unusual in that it describes a complex relationship
between a gay man and woman; it is unusual too in that it neither
plays down the significance of being homosexual in a hostile
society nor presents homosexuality as being the only important
feature of the characters. It is a powerful novel which presents a
sombre but fully realized world; and it has flashes of anarchic
humour'   *Gay News*

Fiction   £2.95

Also by Kristen Britain from Gollancz:

Green Rider

First Rider's Call

The High King's Tomb

Blackveil